Blackfeather

First Paperback Edition
ISBN 978-1-939275-66-0

Blackfeather

An Erotic Paranormal Romance Western Adventure

Devon Layne

ELDER ROAD BOOKS
BELLEVUE WA

Contents

Cast List

Twenty-first Century

Laramie 'Ramie' Wyoming Bell: Narrator. Teen girl on a cattle ranch in Wyoming.

Kyle Redtail Bell: Ramie's six-month younger half-brother.

Phile Bell: Ramie's three-years younger brother.

Caitlin Bell: Ramie's three-years younger half-sister.

Cole 'Pa' Bell: Laramie and Kyle's father.

Mary Beth 'Mom Mar' Bell: Cole's cousin/wife. Ramie and Phile's mother.

Ashley 'Mom Ash' Bell: Cole's wife. Kyle and Caitlin's mother.

Aubrey Diaz: Ramie's best friend in high school.

Annie Wilcox: Neighbor girl thought to be fast and easy.

Forrest Knight: High school friend of Ramie and Kyle.

Shelby Morris: High school friend of ramie and Kyle.

Merv Longsteer: Cheyenne medicine man who owns a trading post.

Kurt: Gun shop owner.

Nineteenth Century

Miranda Lewis: Teen girl who becomes Ramie's host in 1865.

Dorothy 'Dolly' Lewis: Miranda's mother.

Theresa Bell: Miranda's stepsister.

Jonathon Bell: Miranda's stepfather.

Harriet: Kidnapped girl.

Katie Forster: Kidnapped girl who goes with Miranda.

Beulah: Kidnapped girl who stays at trading post.

John: Owner of trading post.

Kyle Wardlaw: Young soldier. Kyle's host.

John 'White Horse' Hamm: Cheyenne brave educated at Harvard working as Kyle's translator.

Blackfeather

1
Just Kidding

KYLE AND I couldn't wait to get on our horses after school let out for the summer. We started out easy, but horses like to kick it a little going uphill. Before long, we were whooping and hollering and cantering up the trail to Centennial Ridge. I was thirteen-and-a-half and my best friend—my brother—had just turned thirteen. Seventh grade was behind us. *YeeHah!*

Kyle's my half-brother really, but who cares? Mom Mar had me in November and Mom Ash had him in May. We do everything together—riding, roping, hunting, fishing. Even fighting with the brats. Everything. Kyle's got my back and I got his.

By the time we'd made it up to the ridge, though, I was feeling a little punky.

"Kyle, I gotta pee."

"Yeah?"

"You're a lotta help. I need to head for the bushes."

"Ah, just do it here. I gotta go, too. I'll point this way and you point that way."

Well, I usually find a bush to pee behind, but we hadn't made it to the woods yet and the nearest human being to us had to be close to a mile away. So we just jumped off the horses and I faced uphill a few feet from where he faced downhill. An old raven was sitting on a rock about twenty feet away just watching me.

"Shoo, bird. I gotta piss. Don't need an audience." He didn't go anyplace, but something caught his interest behind him and he turned that direction. I pulled my pants down and squatted.

I got hit with such a bad cramp I almost fell over.

"Ow! Ow, ow! Oh, shit!"

"You okay, Ramie? What's wrong?"

1

"Don't look!"

"I ain't lookin'. What's wrong?"

"Just stay put." I stuffed some toilet paper in my drawers and pulled them up. My first time and I'm up at the top of a freakin' ridge with my brother. "Kyle, get my light poncho out of my pack and toss it over my saddle, would ya?"

"What's wrong, Ramie? What do you want to sit on your poncho for?"

"'Cause I don't want to get my saddle bloody," I said in a huff. *Damn it! My gut hurts.*

"You're bleeding? Ramie, what do we need to do? I gotta get you down to a doctor. We need to tie off the flow. I got a bungee cord in my saddle bag. We can use that for a tourniquet," my idiot brother said. He was panicking. *Why do I have to explain this to him?*

"You can't tie it off with a tourniquet. I ain't gonna die. Just… I got cramps. Help me up on Pooky. I want to go home." All right, I was getting whiny. I've got to hand it to Kyle, though. He didn't hesitate to do what I told him to. I could depend on him.

It was a long trip back down to the ranch. It was never as fast going downhill as going uphill. We rode along quiet-like and I tried not to be bitchy. Mom Ash warned me that when it hit, the hardest thing was not to make enemies of everyone around me. It wasn't their fault. There was a howl off someplace south of us.

"You think that's them damn wild dogs?" Kyle asked.

"I don't know. Sure didn't sound like a coyote."

"We should take a summer hunting trip and just go shoot 'em. They're scaring all the game away." Well, we agreed about that, but Pa was firm that we didn't shoot animals for sport. Oh, we hunt and fish, but animals are food. If you ain't gonna eat it, you don't shoot it.

"Did you peek, Kyle?"

"No!" That was a little too fast.

"Ya did, too."

"How can you say a thing like that?"

"I know you peeked."

"How would you know that?"

"I peeked."

"Ramie! You…" he looked over at me. I held his eye as he tried to get his upset on. Then we both started laughing. *Oh, god!* That just started the cramps up again and I doubled up over my saddle horn. I felt Kyle's hand on my shoulder.

"Is there anything I can do, Ramie?" he asked. I knew I could ask him anything.

"You got my back?"

"You know I do." I looked up and smiled at him. It was a little weak, I suppose, but at least it didn't come off like a grimace.

"Would you rub down Pooky so I can go on in? I'll make it up next time. Promise."

"Let's just tie 'em at the post while I get you inside to Mom Mar. I'll come out and take care of him when I get Dado. Come on. You can lean on me when you get down." I slid off my horse and was thankful Kyle was waiting for me. He supported me on the way in and when Mom Mar saw me come into the kitchen she knew immediately what was going on.

"Kyle, I'll take care of Ramie. You take care of the horses. Your Pa will be out to talk to you in a few minutes and explain everything. Get going." Kyle left me with Mom Mar and headed back for the horses. It embarrassed me to think that Pa was going to go explain to him what a period was and that I'd just started mine. I was pretty sure he'd figured it out by now anyway. He wasn't stupid—just clueless.

WE HAD TO work on the ranch that summer, but we got plenty of time to just ride. I love horses. A lot better than cows. *Someday I'll have a horse ranch.*

Only thing was, we got new orders from Pa that no one could go off alone out of sight of the house. One of the hired hands radioed down that he was sure he saw a pack moving down in the valley southeast of where the herd was grazing. He wasn't sure if it was wild dogs, coyotes, or wolves. Either way, Pa didn't want the young ones riding out even together unless Kyle and I were with them. With our rifles.

So we mostly spent the summer wrangling Caitlin and Phile. Why Moms ever decided to add them to the litter is beyond me. They had two perfectly good kids already. I swear those two were raised by coyotes. We managed to have a pretty good time of it anyway. When the cattle came down from the upper range at the end of August, I was pretty sad that summer was almost over. School would start Tuesday after Labor Day.

"WE GOTTA TALK to them," Mom Ash said. It was still hot and all the doors and windows were open for air. The brats were sent to bed. Kyle and I were watching TV but we could both hear our parents in the kitchen. "We can't know for sure and they need to be prepared."

"But she's still my baby," Mom Mar said.

"Honey, she's still my baby, too," Mom Ash said. "Both of them are. You know it's for the best. When they get back to school anything could happen."

"Kyle. Ramie," Pa called from the kitchen. "Come to the office, would you please?" Pa always asked stuff like that so nicely. You didn't make the mistake of thinking it wasn't an order, though. When Pa *asked* you to do something, you did it. He never hit me. I know he laced Kyle's hind end with his belt the day my brother almost burned the barn down, though. The brats, now, that was something else. If they weren't getting a spanking, it was just because somebody gave up.

"What is it, Pa?" I asked. I was going to go hug him but he pulled up his chair behind his desk and motioned us to the couch where Moms were sitting. Moms were together in the middle of the couch so Kyle and I had to sit on opposite ends. *This can't be good.*

"First of all, we've done our best to talk to you about the facts of life and you've lived on the ranch all your lives, so you've seen cattle and horses breeding. But people are more complicated than cattle. You've got emotions and a brain that will let you control your behavior. School's coming up and it will be different with kids' hormones kicking in. We just want you both to know that if you have any questions, we're always available to talk with you. You can come to any one of us, or all of us. We'll answer you truthfully and fully if we are able to. And if anyone approaches you sexually, just say no," Pa said.

Mom Mar groaned. Kyle and I nodded. *Say no? Some dude makes a pass at me and he'll go home in a sack. If they find the pieces.*

"Get on with it, Cole," Mom Ash said. Apparently that wasn't the conversation she was waiting for.

"All right, Ashley," Pa said. He sighed. "Now that you are both more grown up, we have to tell you some things that might be hard to believe at first. Kids, you might be time travelers."

I leaned forward and looked at Kyle. He leaned forward at the same time and Moms leaned back with a shake of their heads. Kyle and I started laughing. We were waiting for Pa to say "Just kidding."

"We thought we'd done something wrong or something," I laughed.

"For Pete's sake, Cole," Mom Mar said, still shaking her head. "You say it like that and I don't even believe it anymore. Kyle. Ramie. Stop laughing. Your father is serious and I want you to pay attention. It might sound crazy, but it's real—and embarrassing, too."

Kyle and I stopped laughing. I looked at Mom Mar and could see her face turning red. *Dang! What's that about?* Mom Ash was sitting there with her arms folded waiting on Pa. Pa had his elbows on the desk and was running both hands through his hair.

"All right. Settle down and I'll tell you. We don't know if this stuff gets passed down from generation to generation or if it was a one-time thing. We just want you to be prepared so you recognize what's happening and don't get yourselves or your hosts killed like I almost did. Well, did. I did get my host killed eventually."

What followed from the mouth of our father was a science fiction story about him being sucked out of his body whenever a redtail hawk called and getting plunked down in the body of a 19th century kid. He did his best to explain how it worked, but he didn't have much of an idea, really. The hawk called and he left his body. He said Kyle was named after Kyle Redtail, the man he inhabited in the 1880s, and I was named after Laramie Wyoming Bell, the girl he fell in love with. He even pulled his antique Smith and Wessons off the hat rack where they'd hung ever since I could remember and said they were his in 1889. And then he said Kyle and Laramie had become our great-great-great-grandparents. He even showed us the family Bible.

Then he dropped another bomb and Mom Mar turned beet red.

"The reason we're telling you about this now is that… well, kids develop faster these days than they did in ours and we thought we were pretty fast. The first time I traveled was right in the middle of when Mary Beth and I were losing our virginity together. I never asked Grandpa

Philemon how he got started. I don't suppose you even remember him. The only other person I talked to who had traveled, though, started in the middle of her first sex experience, too. She was younger than me when she started and I was sixteen. Geneive was about your age. Her story isn't a very happy one," Pa said. He looked sad. "She's gone now. None of us knew *exactly* why we were selected to travel. It helped us save a lot of ranches here in the county. But it seems like it created the problem, too. Maybe there won't be any more time travel. We just want you kids to be prepared. And not to have sex too soon."

I opened my mouth, but nothing came out. *Holy fuck! Pa's gone batshit crazy!*

"Kids, go to bed now. Don't ask questions," Mom Ash said. "Tomorrow morning, you'll start to think up some really good ones. Tonight, just sleep on it."

Kyle and I kissed and hugged our parents and then headed upstairs to bed. As the oldest, I had a room all to myself. I was sorry Kyle had to share with Phile, but there were only three bedrooms plus our parents' room. Maybe we could send Phile and Caitlin back in time. Permanently.

WE WERE ON that dang bus headed to school on Tuesday morning early. At least we didn't have to *walk* to Centennial to catch it. We drove two four-wheelers a couple miles to the elementary school where we caught the bus. There were only eight of us who rode the bus from Centennial down to Laramie for junior and senior high school. Of course, it had to stop at half a dozen places along Snowy Range Road to pick up kids from the outlying ranches.

Kyle sat next to me and we started talking about what Moms and Pa told us Friday night. We didn't ask any questions the next day or any of Labor Day weekend. I didn't want to encourage my parents. I didn't believe it at all. Kyle, though... he sort of loves science fiction and I think he watches too much TV.

"You going to do it?" he whispered.

"What do you mean *do it*? The way Pa described it he didn't have any choice. That hawk screamed and he was gone. You can't just decide to do it."

"Yeah, but you know what he was doing. And that Geneive girl he talked about, too. It happened when they... *did it*, you know?" He was turning red. You'd think he was Mary Beth's biological son instead of Ashley's. Mom Ash never blushed at anything.

"Sex?" I said a little too loudly. A couple kids turned and looked at us. "If that's what it takes to time travel, you can tell me about it when you get back. Have a boy stick his dick in me down there? No way. It's disgusting!"

"I'm going to do it. Right on my sixteenth birthday like Pa." He shifted in his seat and moved his hips around a little. My brother was becoming a pervert right in front of me. He was looking up front toward Annie Wilcox.

"If you're supposed to be with another virgin, you'll have to look further than *her*," I whispered. "She ain't going to wait till you're sixteen." *I wouldn't be surprised to find out Annie was already giving it out.* Kyle folded his arms over his chest and dropped his chin to pretend he was sleeping. *Guess that conversation is over.* I took the same position. We looked quite the pair, I'm sure.

WE GOT THROUGH eighth grade without learning anything useful. Well, I liked history the way Mr. Carlson taught it. He said history books don't always tell the truth. He took two classes at a time for a walking tour of Laramie and showed us an official plaque right in the middle of town that had it all wrong. It made me wonder how much other stuff we get taught that isn't true. If I could get a first-hand look at the Civil War, for example, would I think Abraham Lincoln was as much a hero as we make him out to be? Pa said there were still unanswered questions about both Lincoln's assassination and Kennedy's and Mr. Carlson agreed. I had to open my big mouth and Mr. Carlson 'suggested' I should write a paper on Lincoln's assassination. Kyle helped me look it up on the Internet, but I suppose unless you were there you wouldn't really know. *Maybe it wouldn't be bad to time travel.*

PA AND MOM Ash took us hunting on my fourteenth birthday. Kyle and I knew our guns pretty well by then. We'd been taught how to shoot from the time we were kids and had to practice every week. Some things Pa and Moms were all in agreement about. We were ranch kids and we needed to know how to live on our own.

Mom Mar handled the base camp and the kids while we rode up into the mountains. There were only a few inches of snow on the ground in the high areas and the elk were still pretty high up. Later we might see some come down to the river, but they just don't get along well with ranches. We found a good place and hunkered down with a thermos of soup to watch for a prize. It was a fruitless day. We were cold and wet and hungry by the time we got back to Mom Mar at the base camp. Most I saw were a couple squirrels and an old one-eyed raven that sat in a tree and just sort of watched us all day.

"Pa, why don't we raise more cattle?" I asked as we rode home. "We've got plenty of pasture and range land. You said there were 5,000 head when we were born and we don't have a tenth that now. Better yet, we could raise horses."

"Well, little girl, we did have a season or two with a pretty big herd. But it wasn't because we could justify supporting it. Even with 6,000 grazeable acres, that isn't enough to support a herd that size and we had to dry feed even in the summer," Pa said. "We were in the middle of a range war and it was all economics. The price went down and we couldn't sell them. Dry feed alone ran us well over five million dollars. MB, that about right?"

"Yes," Mom Mar said. "Don't forget we had to hire close to thirty people and not all of them were cowhands. That was another million. Then when we finally got the market back, we had to fatten them on the feedlot. Rack up another couple million."

"Don't forget that for close to a year, none of us slept," Mom Ash added. "I don't mind working hard, but don't get between me and my bed. Our bed." She stretched. After sleeping on the hard cold ground last night, all of us were thinking about how nice our beds were. I was doing some fast calculating. Kyle looked over at me. He knew I was adding it up.

"Eight million," I mouthed at him. His mouth fell open.

"Um... Pa? I guess I never thought about it. Are we rich?"

"Well, we don't lack for anything. It's part of the legacy from when I was… uh… traveling," he said. "We created Gold Watch Cattle Company and pretty much subsidized the entire cattle operation of the county that year—well over fifty million."

"Wow!" Kyle breathed. I could see his eyes light up. I was pretty sure he was going to go treasure hunting if he ever went time traveling. He didn't have a practical bone in his body.

2
No Way

HIGH SCHOOL was… different. I don't know why. It was mostly the same kids we'd been in school with since fifth grade, but last year we were the oldest kids in school and this year we were the youngest. And some senior dude I didn't even know asked me out on a date. *Oh no way, José. Troll.*

On the other hand, we did hang out a lot with our friends at school. Aubrey Diaz, Forrest Knight, and Shelby Morris ate lunch with us in the cafeteria. We studied. We did chores. We rode when we could, but as winter set in that was pretty limited. We fought with the brats over who got to watch what on TV. And gave up. Kyle and I spent more time on our computers and sometimes late at night we even messaged each other across the hall.

My birthday came with the annual hunting trip. Kyle got a nice white-tail buck. I kinda gave him the shot. If he'd have missed, I'd have had my first big boy. But Kyle's just as good a shot as I am. Sitting around the campfire, Pa gave me the birthday lecture on what a great man Kennedy was and that I was born on the anniversary of his death. Even Mom Mar rolled her eyes at hearing the story again.

"Let me tell you that when Cole and Ashley came into the house that afternoon and found me straining away upstairs, there wasn't a thought about any dead presidents," she said. "They were all business getting me into the tub. You came sliding out before the midwife even got there."

"I've never forgiven Mary Beth for such an easy birth when Kyle took twenty-three hours of moaning and pushing before he deigned to enter the world," Mom Ash said. "Don't you forget, boy. Twenty-three hours of pain I endured to give you your start."

"Yes, Mom Ash," Kyle said contritely. We all giggled.

"Oh yuck!" Phile chimed in.

"You hush, boy," Mom Mar said. "You balanced the scale when they had to use a can opener to get your big butt out of me. For a month after the C-section, I couldn't even pick you up because you were too heavy."

"Was I a hard delivery, Mom Ash?" Caitlin asked innocently.

"No honey. You didn't start being a pain until you were about eight."

KYLE TURNED FIFTEEN in May of our freshman year and my world fell apart. Moms and Pa told him he could move out of Phile's room and stay in the bunkhouse.

Back when we had a bunch of summer cowboys, the bunkhouse was just a couple big rooms with bunks, a locker room, shower, and toilet. But needs change over time and our two full-timers had wives and one had a kid. Pa had the bunkhouse remodeled into apartments. They weren't big, but there were two little efficiencies, a two-bedroom, and a one-bedroom apartment. And Kyle was getting his own.

"Mom Mar, it's not fair. I'm older than him. Why don't I have my own apartment? I'd even keep it clean. You know what his apartment's going to look like in a couple weeks? You'll have to tear down the bunkhouse and decontaminate the place. Mo-om!"

"Ramie, you hush. Have some consideration for your brother. How would you feel if you had to room with Phile?"

"Why not send Phile out there?"

"You know he's too little. Besides," Mom Mar dropped her voice, "who would trust that little monster on his own?" We both giggled about that, but I still wasn't happy.

I didn't begrudge Kyle his own space. I had a room of my own and it wasn't his fault there were only three kids' rooms. When it came down to it, though, I missed him. He only came into the house for breakfast and dinner. I ended up studying alone and picking at the brats. I got pretty pissy with Kyle, too. Half the time he didn't even answer my messages.

The last day of school, he headed for his apartment and I headed for the barn. I threw my backpack in a corner, saddled Pooky, and in ten minutes I was riding down toward the river. We weren't supposed to go out alone, but I didn't care. I didn't have any friends and Kyle probably wouldn't poke his head out until a Mom called us for dinner. Maybe I'd be in Albany by then. Who'd even care?

I just barely got to the river and started to skirt the watering hole when I ran out of steam. I was feeling so damned sorry for myself.

"You're lucky, Pooky. Life is just one big long buffet table for you. You get brushed and fed. And I love you." I hugged his neck and let the tears come. *Must be getting to my time of month.*

I wandered down by the water and looked up the hill. An old raven was pecking at something dead in the grass. When I looked his way he eyed me, but never moved from his meal. He had to turn his head to look at me because one eye was all cloudy.

"What do you want, old Blackfeather?" I demanded. "You're always sneaking around and never saying nothing. Go away." I plopped myself down and looked at the sky through my tears. Guess I was tired, 'cause I drifted off to sleep.

I CAME AROUND slow-like. The sun was just starting down behind the mountain. It wouldn't be dark for a while yet, but the mountains kind of cut the amount of sunshine in the afternoon. I glanced over to where Pooky was still ground-tied with Dado.

Dado?

I looked around and right behind me, Kyle was sitting, whittling a stick with his pocketknife. He grinned at me.

"Must be easier places to nap than out here," he said.

"What are you doing out here?" I snapped.

"Ramie, I know we ain't been gettin' along all that good lately, but I still got your back. I saw you take off like a bat outa hell and I just figured I'd better get saddled and ride."

"You really got my back, Kyle? Still?"

"Like always. I'm sorry I ain't been friendly since I got throwed out of the house. I thought maybe you were mad at me, too," he said.

"Kyle! Nobody's mad at you! What do you mean throwed out?"

"I'm just like a hired hand now. Bet Pa sends me to the upper pasture with the cows all summer. I don't know what I did. Did I hurt you, Ramie?"

"Kyle! No! I miss you. I thought you hated us all. I was so jealous of you." I scrambled up on my knees and threw myself at my brother to hug him. I missed his pocketknife, thankfully. "I'm sorry, Kyle. How could you think you were thrown out?"

"Well, shit. Ramie, I got sent to the bunkhouse, didn't I?"

"This is so screwed up. You wouldn't believe the hissy-fit I threw over you getting to move to the bunkhouse while I had to stay in the house like a baby. Kyle, we used to study together and sometimes watch TV at night and then you weren't there any longer," I said. I hugged my brother, getting madder and madder at Moms and Pa. "Let's go watch TV like we used to."

We stood up and he put away his pocketknife after wiping it off on his jeans. We mounted and rode up to the ranch road then turned toward home.

"Ramie, you sure it's okay to hang out in the house?"

"I tell you what I think," I said. I was getting more and more pissed. "I think Moms and Pa got some explaining to do."

"PA, WHY DID you send Kyle to live in the bunkhouse?" I demanded at dinner.

"You know, Ramie. Now…"

"Don't tell me what I know. Tell me why," I said. There was silence at the table. Even the brats dropped their silverware and watched to see the explosion.

"Young lady, you mind your manners," Mom Mar said. Pa was frowning at me. I didn't like it when he frowned at me. Maybe I'd really gone too far.

"Fine," Pa said. "Your question. We *gave* Kyle an apartment in the bunkhouse because he's a young man now and shouldn't have to share a bedroom with his little brother. *You* have a room of your own and always have had. When we took Caitlin and Phile out of the nursery, Kyle had to share his bedroom with Phile. Now you need to drop this jealousy thing and learn to live with the fact that your brother deserves his own space, too."

"Kyle thought he was being punished—thrown out of the house," I said flatly.

"What? Kyle!" Mom Ash was out of her seat and around the table so fast the little ones ducked. She grabbed Kyle into a hug. "Why didn't you tell us? That was your birthday present!" Kyle's lip was quivering and he reached over to grab my hand. I squeezed it.

"Really? You didn't just want to get me out of the house?"

"Why on earth would we want to do that?" Mom Mar asked. "Do you want to move back with Phile?"

"No!" Phile yelled. Mom Mar pointed a finger at him and he hushed. You could tell he was building up a head of steam, though. After all, the conversation wasn't about him.

"I like having a room of my own," Kyle said, "but it's so damned lonely out there alone."

"Language," Pa said simply.

"Sorry, Pa. But it is. I don't have a TV and half the time the Internet don't even work." I didn't know that. I squeezed his hand.

"Well, that didn't work out the way we intended. Why didn't either of you just come out and tell us this right away?" Pa asked. "You've always been able to talk to us about anything."

"Yeah," I said, "but that was before you guys… uh…" I glanced at the brats, "…went crazy." There was a moment of dawning understanding on the part of our parents. You could almost see them turn on the lights. Pa nodded a little and Mom Ash gave Kyle one more squeeze before she returned to her seat.

"When'd they go crazy?" Caitlin asked. She was digging into her mashed potatoes and peas as if nothing else that had been said this evening meant a thing. She was so oblivious to everything in the real world except Phile that it was a wonder she even heard that.

"About the day you were born," I sniped.

"Never mind," Mom Ash said. "It was just a misunderstanding. You'll figure it out when you get a little older."

"Oh," Caitlin said, disgustedly. "Sex stuff." That eleven-year-old could really get on my nerves.

After Kyle and I cleaned up the dinner dishes, Pa called us into his office. This time Mom Ash and Mom Mar were sitting together so there was room for us to sit beside each other. I sure hoped I wasn't in trouble. Pa settled into his big leather chair next to the cold fireplace and pulled the ottoman under his feet.

"So, we're crazy," Pa sighed.

"Sorry, Pa," I said. "It's just so…"

"No. I understand. I just didn't want you to end up like Geneive," Pa said. "So here's the deal. First, Kyle, you are not exiled. If you don't like living in the bunkhouse, get your butt back into the house. Or Ramie, you can move into the other efficiency so you can see what it's like to be on your own like Kyle is. But we expect both of you to be in the house for meals and there still won't be a TV in your apartments. That's why we have a family room. And you shoulda told me the WiFi doesn't work."

"We expect you to respect each other's privacy, as well as that of the folks living in the other two apartments." Mom Mar reminded us. *I'm getting my own apartment!*

"Second, just forget about time travel, treasure-hunting, and being our own ancestors. They're just legends. Learn from them if you can. Otherwise forget it," Pa said. He looked sad. I felt bad, but give me a break, okay?

"Uh… Pa?" Kyle said. Uh oh. I just knew what was coming next. "What happened in the uh… legends to a person's body in the present when he went time traveling? Did he just disappear?" I rolled my eyes. I love my brother but how can he take this stuff seriously?

"Oh. No. It uh… As I understand… They say he walked around in a sort of dream-state. He kept functioning or passed out or got sick. It's only the mind that travels to the past and arrives in a host," Pa said.

"And the host doesn't know someone has taken over his body?"

"I think… Experience… He is in a similar state. But you… or he… the legendary ancestor could just sit back to watch or take control. That's what got my… his host killed. According to the legend," Pa said.

"What about traveling to the future?" You get Kyle talking about science fiction and he's likely to go all Dr. Who on you. And Pa was all over it.

"Only the past." Kyle was likely to keep asking questions and we'd be there all night. I pinched him and he jumped.

"Okay. Thanks, Pa."

Now can we go move my stuff into my new apartment?

3
Virgin Voyage

KYLE AND I got to ride herd for two weeks during the summer. Phile and Caitlin weren't happy about it because they had to stay close to home without us to watch them. We had a little responsibility on the range but it was all where we loved to be—on our horses. The guys taught us what we were supposed to watch for during the long days in the saddle.

"I'm glad you're up here for a couple weeks," Rafe said. He was our ranch foreman and we rode up with him to where the two summer hands and Jess, our other full-timer, were. Jess and Rafe traded a week on the upper range and a week at the ranch. "Mostly we just want you to circle the herd like we do. You don't have to even keep an eye on them that much. Pay attention to what's outside the herd. Birds suddenly scattering. Things getting quiet. We're more concerned about predators this year than we've been in the past."

"What are we looking for?" Kyle asked. "Mountain lions?"

"I'm not saying there aren't any out there," Rafe answered. "But folks are talking more about wolves than ever. And we can hear them sometimes. Mostly at night, but wolves will track in the daylight, too." We nodded our heads and were hoping we'd get to see one.

Cattle scatter all over everywhere to graze, unlike what is usually in a movie where they're all bunched up. A cowboy can ride five miles to circle a herd of three hundred head. Half the time they are lying down chewing their cud. We rode the perimeter letting our horses graze and watching like Rafe said. A couple times we heard them way off in the distance. Guess we hadn't been hearing wild dogs after all. We kept our rifles with us all the time, but unfortunately, we never saw a wolf.

WHEN KYLE AND I rode down from the upper pasture, we spent one night camped out, not wanting to go back to the ranch yet. We made a fire and just stared up at the night sky while we lay back on our bedrolls. I loved being out there with just the two of us.

"You gonna do it, Ramie?" Kyle asked softly.

"Do what?" I asked. Sometimes he starts off a sentence in the middle of a conversation he's been having with himself all day.

"You gonna, you know. Try to time travel on your birthday?"

"That old story," I sighed. "Look up there. There's a million stars out there. Why travel in time instead of traveling out there to a different world? It makes just as much sense."

"You know they believe it, no matter what they say." We saw a shooting star and pointed as we made a wish. "I sorta believe it, too."

"I know you do. But, hell, Kyle, it's just too weird. It would be easier if he said he dreamed it all. I'd believe that." My eyes were getting heavy.

"Still," Kyle whispered. "I'm going to try."

MOMS AND PA agreed! I get to stay in the bunkhouse.

I was freakin' pumped. It wasn't like Kyle and I spent *all* our time together, but we were near each other and somehow that made me feel better about the whole school year.

Kyle didn't let up on me trying to time travel. Of course, in Kyle's book, that meant finding somebody to have sex with on my 16th birthday.

"Look around you, Kyle. There isn't a boy here I'd let anywhere near my coochie. Yuck!"

"Oh, come on. There's 350 kids in our class, give or take. Statistically, half of them are guys. That's 175 eligible guys."

"174," I said, looking at him. I wasn't going to sleep with my brother. *If he wasn't my brother… Damn!*

"Picky, picky. You could go with an older guy. There's 350 of them. Another 175 if you take a freshman. Pure. Innocent. Gullible."

"Kyle! I am not laying down my virginity in order to chase after some fantasy. Besides, we always go hunting on my birthday. What do you think I'm going to do? 'Hi Moms and Pa. This is John Doe. He doesn't need any other name. He's just here for the sex.' That is *so* not going to happen!"

My sixteenth birthday came and went. The wolves got my elk. I kept my virginity.

We finally saw the elk herd just below us and moving up. There were about twenty of them and we discussed which one was the best for me to take my shot at. There was only one elk tag available in this region and I got it. The herd never got close enough to take a shot.

One minute they were moving toward us, the next there were half a dozen wolves between them and us and another half dozen streaking in from the sides. Two of the herd were down before any of us could react. I pulled my rifle up but Pa put his hand on me and told us to get out our cell phones and start recording what we saw.

"Pa, we gotta do something. They're killing them!" The big bull hooked one of the wolves with his antlers and threw him clear across the meadow. But two more were on him and in seconds, he was down. I figured they had their kill and the rest would escape, but the wolves kept attacking.

"They're killing them all!" Kyle shouted.

"God damned killing machines!" Mom Ash shouted. She fired her rifle in the air.

"Why aren't we shooting the wolves?" I begged. A young bull was surrounded and staggering. A cow had her belly ripped open.

"It's against the law," Pa said. "Touching one of those wolves is worth a quarter million dollar fine and five years in prison. This is what the fucking conservationists want."

Only three of the herd were untouched and as soon as one bolted, a wolf was on her. The whole thing took about fifteen minutes. Pa had us switch back and forth with our cell phones so someone was always recording but we weren't running out of battery or storage space.

I was crying. Every single elk in the herd was down. And they weren't eating them. Not all of them. You could still hear the cows bellowing as their calves were ripped out of their stomachs. In an hour, the gorged wolves slunk off leaving fresh carcasses scattered over the field.

"Let's go down before the scavengers get there," Pa said. "We can't interfere, but we can sure plaster this video all over the Internet." We recorded the whole scene. They killed three or four for every one they ate.

Buzzards were already circling overhead. We could hear coyotes moving in. Pa had us move back. My phone was dead. I looked at Kyle and he shoved his in his pocket.

I couldn't eat anything Mom Mar cooked at camp that night. Caitlin and Phile had juvenile tags for pronghorns and hadn't seen what we saw. It was a good thing. Even Mom Ash was crying when we got to camp.

"Why, Pa?" I asked again. "Why couldn't we save them?"

"When a predator kills prey, it's called natural selection. Unless the predator is a human. Someplace along the line we lost the idea that humans are part of the equation. Conservationists wanted to re-introduce wolves into our ecology. Except these wolves were never part of our ecology," Pa said. "When we met with the FWS, we were told what we could expect if we touched one of their wolves. We weren't asked for input. We weren't listened to. We were simply warned."

I didn't get much sleep that night and we were all pretty tired the next day. I kinda figured that was my last birthday hunting trip.

Then Kyle started in.

"I'm gonna do it. Ramie, I just know that I'll go time traveling and I'll find treasure and be rich and everything."

"Kyle, we're already rich if any of what Pa told us is true. What do we need? Why do you want some old treasure? And who are you going to get to do the deed?" It was a little bit of a dig. Neither Kyle nor I had dated anyone. I didn't know who he thought he'd get to sleep with him on his sixteenth birthday. Pa had to sleep with his cousin.

"Um… Annie Wilcox said she would."

"Kyle! No! No, no, no. You can't just go buy it."

"She said she'd do it for free."

"Yeah. Like a drug dealer gives away the first hit. Aren't you *interested* in somebody? Someone who's interested in *you* instead of one who gives head for twenty bucks a pop?"

"Who am I going to find like that, Ramie? Look around you. They're all way out of my league."

"Kyle, there's 350 people in our class. Statistically, that means that 175 are eligible girls," I mocked.

"174." We looked at each other and busted out laughing.

"Let me handle it, Kyle. You'll have to go on some dates and romance her," I said.

"How am I going to go on a date? I can't drive yet."

"I can." Kyle looked at me blankly. "Ain't you glad you got a big sister who got her drivers' license when she turned sixteen?" I said sweetly.

"You'd drive me on a date?" he asked.

"We'd have to double. I'll tell Moms that I want to go out but I don't want to get stranded with some boy thirty miles away so I want to drive and I want you to double date so I have a chaperone. They'll think it's really cute."

"But Ramie. I don't mean to sound like a pig, but I'm a pig. She's got to be cute."

"Oh Kyle, what girl in our entire school wouldn't be cute if you got her naked?"

"Um… Millie maybe."

"All right. I'll give you that one. Don't worry. I've seen this one naked."

"When? I mean you know someone already? Who?"

"One, in the locker room. Two, yes. Three, Aubrey Diaz." That shut him up.

"Aubrey is…"

"Don't you dare say she's fat. She isn't. Maybe she's not skinny, but believe me, what's there is all girl."

"You gotta be kidding. Aubrey's hot. But she's our friend. What if I'm no good at it and she doesn't want to still be friends?"

"It will be fine as long as you promise that you'll love her, Kyle. It doesn't have to be forever, but it has to be for real. I'm not making a virgin sacrifice of my best friend just so you can time travel. She likes you and if you don't like her, the deal's off."

"Yeah, but wow! Aubrey."

Sometimes guys short-circuit. Even my beloved brother.

"So, Aubrey, you still interested in banging my brother?" I asked casually at lunch.

"Oh, my God, Ramie. You are so gross." She paused and looked around the cafeteria to see if anyone was in earshot and lowered her voice. "I would bend over backward for that boy!" she said. "Or forward, or on my knees, or any way he wanted me. He is so hot!" I blushed, hearing her talk about my brother that way.

"Please don't give me a description of all the things you want to do to him," I complained. "Talk about gross. It's my brother. Yuck!"

"It makes no difference. He looks at me and still sees a sixth grader with a skinned knee. No interest at all."

"I wouldn't bet on that. Look, I shouldn't even say this, but you know how guys are. My brother wants to get laid on his sixteenth birthday."

"Good luck with that!" Aubrey snorted. "What's he going to do? Hire Annie Wilcox?"

"Actually, I think he's got his eye on you."

"Fuck off! You're jerking me around."

"I didn't think you'd be interested. I probably scared him off anyway when I told him if he hurt my friend I'd geld him."

"Don't do that! I mean, don't scare him off. I mean, don't geld him either, but I might… be interested," she said. Aubrey turned red in the face. "He'd actually consider me? I'm part Mexican and he's so… blond."

"Tell me about it. All those blond jokes? They're about my brother."

"What should I do?"

"If he asks you for a date, say yes. And just let nature take its course."

"Be honest, Ramie. Have you done it? What's it like?" she panted.

"No way. I'm not opposed to sex. God knows, I've got blisters on my clit from rubbing it so much." We laughed. I didn't want to admit how true it was. "But look around at what we have to choose from. Who would I even *think* about having sex with?"

"Adam Long."

"Come on. I mean a real boy, not a movie star. He's good for a putting myself to sleep after a long day, but he's not going to come walking through the door of Laramie High and ask me out. Besides, *Entertainment Tonight* says he's with Lori Monroe."

"Yuck. What a slut. Who hasn't she been with?"

We kept talking about movie stars and who was hot but the seed was planted. Now I just had to get Kyle to ask her out.

I GOT FORREST to go with us when Aubrey and Kyle went out. We all had fun. I felt bad for Shelby. She was my friend, too. After three sort of dates, all of a sudden it was like we were two couples and Shelby. I kept trying to not be a couple with Forrest but I had to have *someone* to go out with. Shelby was sulking a lot when we were together. By the first of April she was pissed.

"You guys just cut me out and left me on my own. Some friends. I can't believe Kyle chose Aubrey over me. Am I not cute enough for him? I'd have put out for him. I've seen him stare at my tits. I know he likes them. And you! You immediately snatch Forrest up. What am I supposed to do? He was my last hope."

"Shelby, I didn't know you felt that way! I'm sorry. I'll ditch Forrest. It was just so I could drive my brother on his stupid dates and not feel left out. I never meant to leave you out in the process," I said. *Dang! Shelby would have done Kyle, too? What's my brother got?*

IT ALL FELL apart anyway. Trust a boy to screw things up. Aubrey and Kyle were making progress. Definitely. There was a lot of kissy-face going on in the backseat. Forrest tried to catch me with one or two, but I managed to turn my cheek to him. I was no more interested in getting sexy with him than with my brother.

Forrest drove that night. He was pretty proud to be a newly minted driver with his Mom's car. I left my car at Aubrey's and we all went to the Arcade. We had a good time and I was giving Kyle and Aubrey a little time to say goodnight before I got out and headed for my car to take Kyle home. I started to reach for the door and Forrest caught my hand.

"Forrest?"

"Ramie, I gotta say this this." He drew a long stuttering breath. *Oh no.* "I think I love you, Ramie. That's it. I do. I love you." He started leaning toward me and I could see a kiss forming on his lips.

"Forrest! No! Don't do that. We're friends. We're helping Kyle and Aubrey. You know that. Don't go spoil it all with that lovey-dovey shit. Oh God! Yuck!"

"You don't like me?"

"Of course I like you. We have fun when we're out. But we're not in love."

"Are you breaking up with me?"

"We were never going together, Forrest!" He sat there looking bewildered. I couldn't quite get my hand out of his.

"Oh. Okay. Um. Can we just fuck, then?"

I just looked at him with my mouth open and jerked my hand out of his. I opened the door and got out, slamming it behind me.

"Kyle! We're going home. Now!" I shouted, breaking up what looked like a pretty intense kiss.

I asked Shelby to join us the next week. Should have done that in the first place. Stupid me.

"I can't, Ramie. I'm going out with Forrest. You broke his heart and *I'm* gonna put it together again. I hope we can still be friends, Ramie, but… You know… Your loss."

I went to the library while Kyle and Aubrey did whatever they were going to do and then just walked around town for a while. That's when I got another idea. *Oh man. I'm just full of them.*

"Aubrey, why don't you come out to the ranch next weekend? You can stay with me and we'll come back into town Sunday afternoon."

"Really?" Kyle asked. The closer it was getting to his birthday the antsier he was getting. "That would be cool. We could go for a ride."

"I never rode a horse," Aubrey said.

"Don't worry," I plugged on. "We'll teach you."

Talk about a disaster. Aubrey was so afraid of the horses that the gentle mare we chose for her wouldn't even stand still while we got her mounted. Aubrey was near tears by the time we got her back to the corral. As soon as we got the saddle off, the horse ran for the back pasture and rolled in the mud. I thought for a minute that Aubrey might join her. Now that would be a bonding experience!

I was trying to establish Aubrey coming out to the ranch to spend the night with me so she and Kyle could get together on his birthday, but horses weren't going to do the trick.

Two weeks later, we found something that worked. She loved the four-wheelers! We do a lot of work over a lot of acres. Driving a truck sometimes isn't practical on really rough terrain and riding a horse can take too much time. So we use three- or four-wheel ATVs to move around the ranch in a hurry. They're no good for herding the cattle, but getting you up the mountain is no problem.

Aubrey loved it. We raced from the ranch up to the lower ridge. I let Kyle and Aubrey beat me by about ten minutes so they'd have time for some serious making out before I got there. Then I pretended I was having problems with some dirt in my gas-line and told them to go on ahead and meet me back where they left me. I figured I had a good hour or so.

I tossed my poncho down on the ground to keep from getting wet and just lay down to daydream. I looked up and saw that old raven sitting in a lower limb of a Douglas fir. He was always hanging around. Never said anything but just sat and stared at me out of one eye like I was an idiot. Well, maybe I was.

KYLE'S BIRTHDAY FINALLY came around and our pattern was so well set there was no question about Aubrey being welcome to come and help celebrate. We made sure we stayed in our rooms well past midnight when everybody was asleep before Aubrey slipped out of my apartment and went next door to Kyle's.

I don't know why *I* was so nervous. Maybe Kyle would get to go time traveling. Hell, maybe he'd take Aubrey with him. Maybe I should have let Forrest fuck me. *Maybe. Maybe. Maybe.*

Maybe I should have noticed sooner that the walls were so thin. And my apartment was so hot. I could hear giggles and moans coming through the wall. I sat in my bed sweating and realized I had one hand in my panties and the other pinching my nipples while I listened to them.

Oh damn! Hurry up and do it so I can go to sleep.

I staggered to the window and opened it to let a little night air in. The chill breeze didn't seem to cool off my room and before I knew it I was back in my bed with my ear pressed against the wall.

"Yes, Kyle. Do it," I heard Aubrey gasp.

There was a flutter at my window and that damned old raven sat right there looking at me—watching me as I rubbed my nub and listened to my brother and his girlfriend make love.

"Oh!" Aubrey and Kyle cried out together.

"Yesss," I hissed as my orgasm claimed me.

Awkawkawkawk!

I'd never heard the raven screech before.

And then I was gone.

4
Who are you?

I WAS STARING into a mirror. No, a darkened window that showed my startled reflection. Only it wasn't me. The girl that looked back at me was... just not me. She was pretty. I couldn't tell the color of her eyes but they looked startled like something had just slapped her. She was wearing a shawl and a dark dress that was buttoned up all the way under her chin.

Oh my god! It happened. I'm in a different person. I'm so sorry, Kyle. What do I do now?

"Who are you?" My host was panicking. How did she even know I was here? I didn't try to do anything. *I* was panicking. She should just go to sleep or something.

I tried to pull back, but she hung onto me like I was a bad dog. I tried to take control, but she tightened my leash and held me down. It wasn't supposed to be like this! Pa said.

"Who are you and why are you here? Go away!"

She was talking to me! She knew I was here! I could feel my heart in my throat. I could see the wrinkles in my forehead. There were tears leaking out of my... her... our eyes.

Don't be scared. I don't know if I was thinking it to myself or to her, but she heard me.

"Scared? You just jumped into my head. I can feel you. I can hear you. Who are you?"

Ramie. I felt compelled to answer.

"I have been possessed. I will not let you have my soul, demon!" She was beginning to hyperventilate. I couldn't get enough air in my lungs. Her lungs. What was happening? "Demon Ramie, by the power of our Lord and Savior Jesus Christ, I command you out of this sacred temple of the divine and consign you eternally to the flames of hell from whence

26

you came," she screeched at me. The words screamed in my head. To my ears she barely whispered—could hardly speak.

I don't actually think it works that way. Stony silence. *I want to go home. I don't believe any of this.* Maybe she couldn't hear me anymore. But I could feel tears still dripping from my… our eyes. I jerked her head back toward the dark window. *Bitch.* I gave her the finger. She jumped back and snatched her hand down in her lap. *Hah! You can't deny I'm here and still fight me for control. Where am I?*

She refused to answer. I reached up and tweaked her left nipple. *Oooh. Sensitive.*

"Stop it! All right, you are still here. I will go to a priest. I will not be possessed by Satan's damned minion."

Stop cussing me. I'm not damned. I'm not a minion. I'm not evil. I'm just scared. Just like you are.

"Why? Why are you here in me?"

I don't know. Honest, I don't.

"Miranda, you're talking in your sleep again," the woman next to us spoke. "Wake up, dear. Now you can start over."

"Yes, Mother," the girl said.

So you're Miranda. Nice to meet you, too. You don't have to speak out loud. I can hear your thoughts.

"You can't!" she thought. At least it wasn't out loud.

I can. Please talk to me. Please tell me who you are and where I am.

"I am a poor sinner and you have come to torment me for my sins."

No. I don't give a damn about your sins.

"You are a foul being."

I'm not. Really I'm not. I'm sorry I'm here. I don't want to torment you.

"Why are you here?"

My Pa told us he was a time traveler and we didn't believe him. But it's nothing like he said.

"That is impossible."

That's what I said. But here I am. When am I? What date is it?

"Good Friday, the fourteenth day of April in the year of our Lord 1865."

Oh god! No!

"Do not take the name of our Lord in vain, Demon Ramie."

No. It can't be. I'm dreaming. You aren't real.

"I'm real. It is you…"

Miranda, it's the day they shot President Lincoln!

"What? No! They can't. Who?"

An actor. John Wilkes Booth.

"But we've just won the war. Lee surrendered. That's why we are traveling."

I was afraid to say anything. I tried not to think. When I held my breath I realized Miranda was struggling.

"Let me breathe!"

I'm sorry. I forget that when I do something it affects you, too. I wish I was in my own body. I don't mean to make your life miserable.

I tried to relax and just be a rider, watching the world through Miranda's eyes. Pa said he could give control to his host and just watch. But Miranda's thoughts were flashing all over.

"Are you still there?"

Yes.

"How do you know the president will be killed?"

It's history for me. A long time ago. Pa's a fanatic about Lincoln and Kennedy. He lectures me every birthday. I had to write a paper about it for school.

"What can we do?"

What? What do you mean?

"I cannot sit idly by while my president is assassinated. You said you did not know why you were here. I do not know why you are here. Has this murder been committed already?"

What time of day is it?

"Nearly dawn."

It happens tonight. Ford's Theater around ten o'clock.

"We must tell someone."

And end up in a loony bin? How could you tell someone that a person from the future invaded your head and told you that the president would be shot while attending a play? They would lock you up.

"Loony bin? Ah. An asylum." Miranda was silent but thoughts continued to rage about saving the president. I couldn't tell which were hers and which were mine. They seemed to get jumbled up together. Could that be it? Was I sent back in time to save the president?

"Are you a Confederate rebel?"

No.

"Then you must help save the president."

I tried again to be silent and calm. Pa had done this. I could do it. He traveled in time, inhabited the mind of a young man, had his adventures, and returned.

"Demon Ramie, I command you by all the powers of heaven to save the president," Miranda intoned in her self-righteous voice. Where did she get this stuff?

Miranda, you can't just order me to do stuff. First, I'm in you. For all I know I AM you. I can't do anything unless you do. Second, I have no idea what to do. You don't even have a phone so we could call someone. And finally, I AM NOT A DEMON!

She shut up. I tried to ignore what she was thinking, but surface thoughts are hard to ignore and I was finding that Miranda was a spitfire. She was also still convinced that I was a demon who had possessed her. She was the one controlling everything. I don't know why she thought I was possessing her. I let it slip that maybe it was my mind that she had possessed. That gave her a start.

"How do you know these things about our president?" she asked.

It's history to me. I live a century and a half from now.

"So you know where it will occur and when and by whom."

In general terms. I know it will be tonight at Ford's Theater. Whenever they take pictures of clocks, they are set at 10:10 to commemorate the time. Unfortunately, I don't have any idea where in Washington Ford's Theater is. I don't know what John Wilkes Booth looks like. I've never been to Washington. I looked it all up on the Internet.

"What is that?" How was I going to explain the Internet without sounding like a demon?

It's like a big book that pretty much everyone can use. You just have to be careful because not everything in it is true. Like all books.

"The Bible is true."

Right. Not going there.

"If I were to… let you have control… would you then be able to stop the assassination?"

Why don't you do it yourself?

"How? I'm just a girl."

So am I. I don't want to control you, Miranda. I'll help you if I can, but you know much more about this time and place than I do. It's not like I've lived here all my life. I don't really even know who you are or why we are on this train.

"My mother is to be married. We are to meet my new stepfather and stepsister in Washington, District of Columbia, on Saturday. There will be a wedding with some of his friends present. He is known in Washington. Then we will board the train again for Baltimore."

You'll be staying at a hotel tonight? In Washington?

"Mother mentioned Willard's Hotel."

I began to get an idea.

IT WAS AFTER nine-thirty when we were able to slip out of the hotel. There was quite a festive party going on in the hotel and Miranda's mother, Dorothy Lewis, left for the party at nine after bidding Miranda 'goodnight.' When we were sure she was gone, we slipped out.

Of course, we went the wrong direction and didn't realize it until we'd practically walked into the White House. Security here was nothing like it was in my day. No iron fence. No armed guards. A couple soldiers on duty at each door. We actually had to stop and ask directions from one of them. It turned out that the theater was only a block from our hotel in the other direction. I was certain Booth wouldn't just walk through the front doors of the theater. There were two Union soldiers lounging there.

There must be a stage door. That's the way he'll go.

We crept around the building staying to the shadows. *If only we make it in time.*

I saw the horse first. A man was holding the reins and another man in dark clothes came striding toward the door.

That's him!

Miranda bolted toward the figure screaming. He paused and looked toward us as we barreled down on him. He didn't have time to reach for a weapon. We hit him just as he reached for the door. The impact hurt. He was a solidly built man and taller than I expected. Nonetheless, Miranda was a dynamo and he tumbled backward off the steps.

"Not tonight you won't, you rebel cur!" Miranda screamed. She began immediately to pummel him.

"Get off of me!" he cried. "I must get inside. You don't understand." She continued to rain blows on his head. He gave a mighty shove and we rolled to the ground. Miranda took a deep breath to scream, but it was cut off before it gained sound.

A shot echoed from inside the theater.

"You three-penny whore!" he screamed at us. "I could have stopped it. I could have..."

His voice cut off as we locked eyes.

Kyle!

I could not gain control of her voice. Miranda turned and fled. There was a flapping of wings swooping down toward us.

Awkawkawkawk!

I was gone again.

5
Caught

"**I**'D JOIN you but I'm a little sore down there," Aubrey giggled. She was staring at me from just inside the door. *What?*

I got my bearings. I was sitting on my bed leaning against the wall with my hand in my pussy. *Oh, fuck!*

"Sore?" I said.

"Don't give me that. Sitting where you are, I know you were listening. Was it as good for you as it was for me?"

"Aubrey, I'm sorry. I didn't mean to." I was breaking up into tears. We failed. I got sucked into another time where I could have done something and we failed. President Lincoln was assassinated. And not only that, Kyle was there. And Miranda made *him* fail.

"Hey. It's all right. I think I owe you that much. Oh god! Ramie, it was so beautiful. I came a dozen times. How many times did you come listening to us?" Aubrey asked.

"Aubrey! I wasn't… I didn't mean to… Once. I think I passed out."

"That good? Wow! I was near passing out a couple times, but he just kept going and going. And I kept coming and coming. Your brother is an Energizer Bunny!" she laughed. "Can we get a little sleep before we have to get up? I'm exhausted."

We turned down the covers and crawled in. She had no idea what really happened. And Kyle just kept fucking the whole time? *Crap! What's he made of?*

IN THE MORNING, I woke up with Aubrey snuggled against my back. She had an arm across me. It wasn't uncomfortable or anything sexy. In fact, I imagined that after having her cherry busted last night, she just wanted to be close. I rolled back a little and put my arm around her. It was after seven and Moms would be calling us for breakfast if we didn't get up pretty soon. Aubrey sighed.

"Thank you for last night," she whispered.

"I didn't actually do anything," I laughed. "I think it's Kyle you want to thank."

"Oh, yeah. I plan to. A lot." She giggled and I couldn't help but join in and be happy for her and Kyle. "But you made it happen, Ramie. And afterward, when I had to leave his room or risk getting caught, you let me cuddle with you so I wouldn't be alone. I know how much Kyle means to you and I'm just so thankful that you trust me with him."

"Hey, Kyle is his own man. But I'll tell you the same thing I told him. If you hurt my best friend I'll geld you."

"I don't have balls, Ramie!"

"Fine. Then I'll spay you!"

We both broke up giggling.

AFTER LUNCH, I drove them into town. I think I was more eager to get her home than Kyle was. I was bursting to talk to Kyle about time traveling. They took so long hugging and kissing at the door I fell asleep in the car. Kyle nudged me awake and we headed back toward Snowy Range Road.

"Well?"

"Well, what?"

"Ky-yle. Tell me about it."

"That's kind of personal, Ramie. Besides, I bet Aubrey told you all about it already."

"You're going to make this hard on both of us."

"Drop it, Ramie." His voice was cold. I started getting angry. *Damn it! I saw him there.*

I pulled into the ranch and followed Kyle straight to the barn. He saddled Dado without hardly brushing him down. I grabbed Pooky and got my saddle cinched.

"You don't have to come," he said flatly.

"Yes, I do," I said as emotionlessly as I could. It wasn't easy.

"Why?"

"'Cause I got your back, brother." He looked at me and grabbed me in a fierce hug. I swear I felt tears splash on my cheek from him. Then he swung up into his saddle and was off at a fast jog. I pulled myself up onto Pooky and followed.

When we'd been out about an hour and were on the other side of the watering hole, he finally pulled up, jumped down out of the saddle, and dropped his reins. He walked to the water's edge and splashed some of the icy water on his face. I put a hand on his shoulder.

"I know what happened. Talk to me." I said softly. He just looked down like he couldn't look at me.

"I don't know how to share this with you Ramie. She's really beautiful. It was like being lost in a dream. I didn't plan on really falling in love with her. I don't know for sure, but I might be. What if she doesn't feel that way?" he said.

"Or it might be that you just got laid for the first time and she's always going to have that special place in your heart. If you didn't have feelings for her, I'd be pretty pissed at you."

"We talked a lot, too. You know, all the time we've been dating, we were just working up to last night. We never really talked about things. She's really different than us."

"I guess there's worse things. Tell me about the time travel."

"You don't believe in any of that. I guess I don't either now."

"But Kyle…"

"If any of that stuff is real, I guess you can't just plan it and say 'I've had sex, now take me away!' The thing is, I couldn't even get disappointed about it, even after she went back to your room. I just kept thinking how wonderful she was and how it all felt. Time travel? Well, it either happens or doesn't. I don't much care right now."

"I went," I whispered. "I know you did, too."

"Yeah. Right. You don't have to play those silly games with me, Ramie. I'm a big boy now."

What the goddam fuck? He thinks he can just push this off? I saw him in the eyes of that young man we tackled. I saw him!

"Kyle…"

"I really don't want to talk about it for a while, sister. I just kinda want to think about it."

"Sure."

We mounted up and rode for an hour before we got back and brushed down our horses. We really didn't say much else. Was having sex really that much better than time traveling?

Well, if he's going to be that way about it, fuck him.

I HAD PLENTY of time to think about it that last two weeks of school. I covered for Kyle and Aubrey so they could get it on after school a couple times. I drove him into town one last time before he got his license and parked the truck near the old train station where there weren't many people. I went to the Arcade and drank sweet coffee at Coal Creek Coffee Company. Kyle and Aubrey stayed in the truck. I had to pound on the window and wait for them to finish when I got back two hours later. The truck really smelled sexy.

I guess I understood a bit about why Kyle didn't want to talk. It was weird. I had a hard time believing it wasn't just a dream, myself. I guess if I had a lover to occupy me all the time, I'd probably not want to think about it. I had to do something, though. Especially after Kyle got his license and drove himself to Aubrey's for their dates.

I started planning my horse ranch.

IT WAS SUNDAY and I was sitting in Kyle's room waiting for him to finish in the bathroom so we could go in for dinner. I was fooling around with his computer, checking some of my favorite sites like HorseClick and EquineNow. I had some money saved and was clicking through just to see what was available when this one pair caught my eye.

"Oh no!" I screamed. "Kyle, we gotta do something."

He came out of the bathroom in his jeans and bare feet with no shirt on. At least his pants were fastened, though the belt wasn't buckled. He bolted to me like I was on fire.

"What's wrong, Ramie? Are you okay?"

"Yeah, yeah. I'm fine. Quit hugging me. Look at this." I showed him the ad.

"Pair of cart horses. Might be lame. Take both for $200."

"The slaughterhouse will get them," I moaned. "We've got to go get them."

"Pa would kill us. How are we going to get them?" I liked the way Kyle jumped straight from the objection to the solution.

"Let's go talk to Pa. Hurry! They could be gone already." Bless him, Kyle shoved his feet into his boots without any socks and grabbed a shirt. I carried his laptop to the house while he snapped up his shirt. Moms stared at us as we ran through the kitchen to Pa's office. "Pa! Pa, we gotta talk to you."

"Whoa, kids. What is it?" Pa asked. He was in his big chair with the newspaper propped open and a mug of coffee.

"Pa, we gotta save these horses. Please. Look at them. They're beautiful."

"Part draft and part pinto cart horses? What do we need them for?"

"It's not what we need, Pa. It's what they need. Look. $200. The slaughterhouse will get them," I complained. All right, I'm usually pretty tough, but there were tears in my eyes.

"Ramie, it says they might be lame. That's no way to start a horse ranch. Are you sure? If they are in pain, they might have to be put down anyway."

"I'll pay for them," Kyle said. *He'd what?*

"Kyle, I didn't mean for you to have to pay," I said, hanging onto my brother for support. "I just think that we could take care of them and give them a home."

Pa had already reached for the phone and was dialing. I know he hates to see horses go to slaughter almost as much as I do. In ten minutes, he'd closed the deal. He told them we'd be there by three o'clock and not to let anyone else have them. He hung up and I jumped in his lap.

"Thank you, Daddy. Thank you!" I said. *I almost never call him Daddy. I'm sixteen years old and I feel like his little baby girl again.*

"Come on and let's eat dinner. We need to tell your mothers what's going on and, if you don't mind, I'll stand behind the two of you so they don't throw anything at me," he laughed.

By three o'clock, we were ten miles east of Fort Collins and the owner had led two tender-footed matched pintos out of the corral.

"I picked them up when I bought out a stable in Denver," he said. "These two have just been worked so hard they can barely walk. I really expected the slaughterhouse to call. In fact, they did just after you called this morning."

"People should be shot for treating animals like this," Pa said angrily. "Look. There's hardly an inch of hoof on them."

"We'll do our best for them, Mister," I said. "We'll put them in the deep pasture and check on them every day. Maybe they'll just need a rest."

"Well, good luck to you, kids. Send me a picture when they're all healed up."

It took us a few tries to get them up the ramp into the trailer. I climbed in the middle seat of the truck between Pa and Kyle. I wrapped my hands around Kyle's arm and buried my head against his shoulder so nobody could see my tears.

WE STABLED THE horses until we could get the vet to come out and look at them. He got here Monday afternoon and his assessment wasn't great. The hooves had been worn down right through the sensitive laminate and into the coffin bone. He shook his head.

"They're standing," he said. "Keep them on a soft surface if you can. When everything dries out this summer, you might need to put them on straw or sawdust. Mostly it's going to be wait and see."

Kyle and I brushed them and combed out their manes and tails. We left them in the barn on a fresh bed of straw. In the morning, we carefully led them out into the near pasture. We'd moved the other horses to the south pasture. I didn't want the other horses getting feisty with them. The pasture was lush with late spring grass and the horses loved it. Kyle and I rubbed them down again. Caitlin and Phile were standing at the edge of the pasture holding hands. If you just happened to see them, they were cute kids. It was when they were doing something or saying something that they turned into monsters.

"Ramie," Phile said when we got closer, "can we help?" *What? What did you do with my little brother?*

"I suppose so," I said cautiously. "Mostly they just need rest. You know you can't go chasing them around like you do the other horses."

"We don't…" Caitlin started automatically. Then she hung her head. I'd seen them. "We won't," she amended.

"The vet says they need to stay off hard and uneven ground while they heal. We're just trying to make them comfortable as we can and let them know they're safe now," Kyle added. "Can you do that?"

The kids weren't paying attention. I looked around behind me where they were staring. Both horses were standing right behind Kyle and me. We stepped aside. The two horses hesitantly stepped forward and nodded their heads to Caitlin and Phile. The kids let them snuffle them and breathed softly near their nostrils. Just because they'd never shown affection to the horses before didn't mean they hadn't been taught how to act around them. But this was way beyond anything I'd ever seen them do. Kyle and I stepped around the kids as they started petting the horses. We left them out in the pasture.

"BELLS AND BOWS love being here at the ranch," Caitlin bubbled at the dinner table. She and Phile were shoveling food in as fast as they could between words.

"They hated the city," Phile said. "They want to be ridden. They don't want to pull carts."

"Uh, you've been talking to them?" Kyle asked.

"Not really," Caitlin said. *Okay it was just a game, I guess.* "They've been talking to us. It's like I can hear what they're saying."

"Ramie, Bells said I should tell you I love you. I do, you know. Thank you for bringing Bells and Bows to the ranch," Phile said.

Moms and Pa were sitting at their end of the table with mouths open and food or drink forgotten as they stared at us. I'm sure they were wondering who the aliens had left in place of the brats.

KYLE AND I got sent to the upper pasture for two weeks. It was kind of an emergency. One of the hands fell and broke his leg. We had to send a helicopter in to pick him up. It took both Kyle and me to replace one good cowpoke. I mean that seriously. Things were tense up on the range. We'd lost two calves to wolves. But still, no one had seen the damned things.

38

We were on twenty-four-hour alert. That meant Kyle and I rode together right after breakfast until about six. We had a walkie-talkie so we could check in with the base camp every half hour. Somebody was always on the horn while two others slept. When we got off, they started rotations all night long. I was sound asleep before sundown.

It still wasn't clear what we could do if we saw a wolf. The Forest Service was being kept busy verifying kills and writing checks. Of course, they only paid us for a calf, not for what we could sell it for when it matured. We had to leave dead animals where they lay until an officer could come up and register the complaint. At least we had some compensation for killed animals. They still warned us that we could chase the wolves off, but we couldn't touch them. I wondered what would happen if I accidentally shot one. *Oops.*

Pa sent two more hands up by the time Kyle and I got to come home. At this rate, it was going to be as costly as Pa's range war. We only had 500 head.

KYLE WAS PRETTY damned happy to get back to the ranch. I figured he'd call Aubrey as soon as we set foot in the house. When we got close enough, we saw Caitlin and Phile out in the pasture with our two rescued paints. The horses were just grazing. The kids were…

"KYLE? ARE THEY picking up rocks out of the pasture?"

"Damned if they aren't, Ramie." We rode over and watched Caitlin and Phile as they walked back and forth over the pasture pushing a wheelbarrow. Every few feet they'd pry a rock out of the ground and put it in the wheelbarrow. At the barn corner of the pasture there was a pile of rocks four feet high.

"Whatcha doin', squirts?" I called.

"Bells and Bows don't like the stones in the field. They hurt their feet. We're just clearing it out for them," Caitlin said. I glanced at the pile over in the corner and shrugged. I looked at Kyle and he nodded.

"Want some help?" I asked.

KYLE TOOK OFF Friday night and a plume of dust followed him all the way to Centennial. Aubrey sure had him pussy-whipped. *Wish I had somebody.*

I actually spent some time with Phile and Caitlin watching TV. *I swear, something's come over those two. Ever since I brought home those horses.*

I finally got tired and headed out to bed.

AROUND MIDNIGHT, I heard the truck pull in and Kyle's door close. I was almost back asleep when I heard Aubrey giggling in his room. *What? Kyle you stupid…* If Aubrey was out here, they'd either get caught in the morning or she'd need to be in my room. *Damnation.* I went to make sure my door was unlocked. Then I went back to bed.

Only I couldn't sleep. I could hear them right through that thin wall, giggling and moaning. I couldn't help myself. It was like getting addicted to porn or something. I leaned up against the wall. It's not like I had my ear *plastered* against the wall, but I was close enough to hear. I pushed my panties down and pulled my t-shirt off. *How could I possibly sleep with them having sex next to my head? Just a few inches away.*

A flicker of movement caught my eye and that old one-eyed raven landed on my windowsill. It was almost like he was a pet these days. He was always hanging around. There was something about letting him watch me masturbate, though. His one good eye turned toward me. I stared at him as my fingers flicked against my clit. Next door, I could hear Aubrey moaning, saying, "Yes, yes, yes. Give it to me, baby."

I threw my head back and squeezed my eyes closed as my climax rushed in on me.

Awkawkawkawk!

6
Fight

"**D**EMON RAMIE, come to me. Help me in my time of need!"
What the fuck? Where am I?
"You came!"
Miranda?
"Help me, Ramie. They're after me."
Who?
"I don't know. He grabbed me and I ran. There he is!" She was panicked and backing into a corner. This wasn't good.

"Aye, little miss. You'll make a fine toffer," a voice growled. A grizzled man came down the narrow alley toward us. Miranda turned to run again and tripped over her dropped basket. He grabbed her arm in one hand and her waist in the other. The war was fought to end black slavery but no one did much to stop the kidnapping of young women to press them into service in western brothels.

Let me drive.
"What does . . .?"
Don't fight me! I took control of her body so suddenly that Miranda was as startled at her loss of control as at our aggressor's actions. I slammed an elbow back into our attacker. I lifted my right foot and stomped with Miranda's sturdy-heeled shoe on the man's instep. He howled. I spun to face him as he hopped on one foot and saw the knife at his belt. Instead of running, I stepped toward him and grabbed the blade, jabbing it into his stomach. I wrenched it free and jumped back, nearly falling over the stupid basket again.

"If you get that tended to at once, you might not die," I said with Miranda's voice. The man looked up at me in horror as he saw his own blood dripping from his knife. He fell. I guessed it was too late for a doctor. If anyone found us, we'd be the ones hung. I scooped up our

41

basket, wiped the blade on his back, and rushed away. I dropped the knife into the basket so it wasn't visible and walked hurriedly toward the noise of a market.

Miranda! Where are we? The poor girl was in shock.

"Baltimore," she answered weakly.

I don't care what city. Do you have a home here? Can we get to it?

"Yes." She hesitated as we looked around. "That way." She didn't move. *Fuck!* I started walking.

You'd better keep telling me which way to go if you ever want to get home again.

I was a little snappish, but fuck! I'd just killed a man! I wasn't feeling all that charitable.

What happened back there? Why were you out alone?

"I went to the market to get fish for dinner. A trawler had just come in. I got turned around when I left the market and then that man started chasing me. Then I summoned you and you saved me. Thank you, Demon Ramie."

Damn it, Miranda. I'm not a demon. You can't summon me.

"But you came!"

Well, I was coming when I got here but you kinda spoiled that.

"Ramie, I will call you by whatever name you wish. I will hide your presence. You have saved my life and I will ever be your obedient servant."

I don't want any obedient servants. Is this the place?

"Yes. We will enter by the kitchen door to give the fish to Charlotte. But… she'll see the knife."

I pulled it out of the basket. Just looking at it made me sick. I tried to give her body back to Miranda but she was as repulsed as I was. We threw up in the alley. And then threw up again.

"Heavens, girl!" a woman said from the kitchen door. "You are ill!"

"Yes, Charlotte," Miranda said. "I don't feel well all of a sudden." She stood and I snatched the knife behind her back. Miranda handed the basket to Charlotte. "Here is the fish."

"You'll not be eating this fish tonight. I'll bring you broth in your room. Go at once and get in bed!"

Miranda and I were only too happy to comply with the cook's command.

IT WAS OVER. The adrenalin ebbed from Miranda's body as we fell onto the bed and fevered shakes replaced it.

I killed a man.

I didn't feel grown up enough to kill anyone. Why did I have to come back here? Tears ran from our eyes. Miranda felt the same things I had. It might have been my mind driving it, but I'd used her body. Not only was I a murderer, I'd made her one as well. The exhaustion and terror caught up with me and we slept where we landed on the bed.

I HEARD THE latch on the door and quickly shoved the knife under Miranda's pillow.

"Miranda? I brought you some broth. Charlotte said I should stay here until you drank it all." Miranda rolled to her back and sat up. I saw the girl for the first time.

Caitlin!

"Thank you, Theresa." Miranda accepted the cup of broth and brought it to her lips. I looked over the rim into the girl's eyes.

No, it wasn't Caitlin. There was no recognition there as I had experienced when I saw Kyle in Washington. It was just the girl's striking blonde hair and beauty that made me think of my little sister. I thought they were about the same age.

"Charlotte said you were ill on the way back from the market. They would not let me come see you until now." I rummaged around in Miranda's head, demanding to know who this girl was. Miranda stayed focused and drank the almost tasteless broth. Might as well have just boiled water out of the bay.

"I do not know what came over me, dear," Miranda said. "I am sure I will be better soon. I may be asleep when you come to bed."

"I will be quiet. Father and Miss Dolly want me to sit at dinner with them. I will come to bed afterward. Do you need help getting dressed for bed?"

"No, Theresa. Here. Take the cup and tell Mother and Mr. Jonathon that I am improving. Thank you." The girl took the cup and leaned in to give Miranda a peck on the cheek. When she was gone, Miranda let out a breath as if she'd been holding it the whole time the girl was in the room.

Who was she?

"Theresa. My stepsister. Please do not possess her! My mother and her father were married in Washington after you possessed me. Where did you go?"

I went home. And I have no desire to possess anyone.

"Did you suffer when you returned? I was upset with you, but I do not wish you to be tormented in hell."

Miranda, home is the 21ˢᵗ century. If I'm suffering, it is when I am here.

"I am sorry. Demon Ramie, I release you from my summons to return from whence you came." She sounded so contrite. I couldn't help feel a fondness for her. I'd just saved her life, I guess.

Please, Miranda. Stop calling me a demon. I already told you that you can't summon and dismiss me. It just doesn't work that way.

"Yet you were… That was… He was…"

I killed him. I'm so sorry. I didn't mean to kill him. I just wanted to protect you. Maybe I am a demon.

I was weeping again and the tears flowed down Miranda's cheeks as she undressed and prepared for bed. My emotions were so out of control. If I'd had my own body I'm sure I would have passed out from overload. I didn't know how Miranda could handle it. She pulled on a nightgown and then pulled her chemise out from under it. At least she didn't have a bra to contend with. Her bloomers followed and she slipped beneath the covers of her bed.

"You are right," Miranda said gently. She spoke aloud. "I know not what kind of spirit you are, but you saved my life. Please accept my apology."

It's nothing. I didn't believe any of it, either. How could I expect you to? Maybe it's easier to accept a spirit riding in your head than an actual person from a different time.

"Am I a murderer, De… Ramie? My hand. I took this knife," she pulled the blade from under her pillow. "I can still feel what it was like to plunge it into him. I will go to hell."

You had no alternative and no choice. When it was done, it was my hand. If anyone is going to hell it is me. He would have raped and killed us, or even worse have sold us to a brothel.

"Us."

I'm sorry. It was your body that would have suffered, but what you feel, I feel.

Miranda was still trying to grasp having another person in her head. I'd at least been prepared a little. I knew what to expect, even though I didn't believe it. Did I believe it now? Or was it all a dream? If only Kyle had confirmed my first trip when I saw him. But he didn't admit to traveling at all. Damn him!

"Is that called driving?" she asked. She was still working on me being in her body and taking control.

Driving means... well, in my time we drive cars. I suppose here we have carriage drivers. It's the one who takes the reins and controls things.

"Tell me when you wish to drive. How did you learn... to kill?"

I never learned that. I've been rassling with my brother for years. It's a different world where I come from and we live on a ranch. You learn to throw a calf, cut a line, skin a deer.

"Will this protect me? Must I learn to fight with it?" She turned the knife over in her hands.

I don't know. I hope not. We need to hide it for now. If Theresa sleeps with you it would be too easy for her to find it. As soon as possible, we need to make a sheath for it so you can fasten it to your ankle where we can get to it in an emergency.

Miranda began to put it under her pillow again but instead lifted the edge of the mattress and placed it there.

"It will give me nightmares."

It might save your life.

Miranda slept fitfully. I drifted. Her dreams and mine relived the day in disjointed jumps. The dreams were interspersed with my own recent experiences. Riding. Tending the horses. Hearing Kyle and Aubrey. Putting my hands in my pants. Feeling the swell of my orgasm.

We awoke with a start and quickly glanced at Theresa sleeping beside her. Miranda's heart was beating rapidly—her breathing shallow. She quickly pulled her hand from beneath her nightgown.

"What was that?" she gasped.

That was a really nice come.

I was still letting the feeling wash over me. It made me so peaceful and calm. I was sure I could sleep easy now.

"You put my hands in my… privities."

I didn't! I was kind of dreaming about it, but I didn't make you do it.

"You dream of… sexual congress?"

Doesn't everyone?

"It's not right. The priest…"

Has no business with your privities, as you call it. Just don't disturb sweet Theresa. Other than that, come as often and as hard as you like. It was really nice. Now let's go to sleep.

I COULDN'T FIGURE out why I was still with Miranda. It had been two very busy days spent packing. I figured my job here was done. Why wasn't I back home in my own body? Pa had said he never knew how long he'd be gone. It could be a couple hours or a few months. Either way, only a little time would pass back home. I just wasn't sure I wanted Aubrey to come into my room and find me with my fingers in my pussy again. It was a little embarrassing.

Why are we packing?

"We're moving west."

Where west? When?

"Mr. Jonathon says we'll spend the winter in St. Louis and then on to Omaha in the spring. He has contracted to set up supply depots along the route of the transcontinental railroad."

Omaha to Promontory, Utah where they drove the golden spike.

"What is that?"

I just remember the golden spike at Promontory, Utah. It was in American History. I can't remember the date.

"We are moving everything and more will arrive from Chicago."

I don't know why I'm still here.

"Perhaps if I… I mean you said that when you were transported, you were… You had your hands…"

I was diddling my clit.

"I am not certain of the exact meaning of the words but I know what you were doing. Perhaps if you did it again you would return home." I started laughing and some of it escaped from Miranda's mouth.

"Miranda, there are fifty bolts of whole cloth to be stacked and labeled. If you have time to waste on frivolities, you can use it to help Theresa."

"Yes, Mister Jonathon." Miranda sighed and went to work on stacking the fabric for shipment. Tomorrow morning, everything would be moved to the train station and loaded into Mister Jonathon's personal boxcar.

I don't know if it will work. I've done it many times and did not go time traveling. But if you will loan me your fingers and your 'privities' tonight, we'll give it a try.

"I am very warm just now."

Well, don't worry. If it doesn't work at least we'll get a good night's sleep.

IT DIDN'T WORK. We did get a good night's sleep. Miranda refused to do anything herself and insisted that I 'drive'. She considered it roughly the equivalent of killing that bugger who tried to kidnap us. It wasn't she who did it. She just happened to reap the benefits. I nearly suffocated her, though, to keep her from squealing. I was sure I wasn't that noisy. God, I hoped not! Kyle…

I wished he was sharing this with me. Not the orgasm but the time travel. I couldn't figure out why he wouldn't talk about it.

IT WAS NOT yet light when we left the house and the carriage took us toward the railway station. We all bade a tearful goodbye to the housekeeper/cook. Mister Jonathon gave her assurances that the new tenants were good people and would treat her fairly. Our personal baggage amounted to a suitcase not much bigger than a roll-aboard. Without wheels. Maybe I could give Miranda that idea and she could become wealthy. My luck with changing Lincoln's assassination, however, indicated that the idea would not fly—so to speak.

Of course, because Mister Jonathon had to supervise the loading of his boxcar, we were at the train station hours early. Theresa, Mother, and I sat at a café across from the train station and sipped a cup of tea. Whenever I was around Theresa, I just marveled at how much the younger girl reminded me of Caitlin. Both girls were thirteen years old. Both had beautiful long blonde hair. Theresa's, of course, was tightly braided and wrapped on her head—a style that Miranda also employed. We had spent an hour last night before bed just brushing our hair side-by-side and then braiding it for each other. Miranda's stepsister was a doll.

As we sat, I saw a large dark shape appear out the corner of my eye. I grabbed control of Miranda and my hand was on the knife concealed in her high-topped shoe before I hesitated. A wolf. How could there be a wolf in the middle of Baltimore? I registered the collar and leash before I pulled the knife to slash and stayed my hand. A large man strode beside the wolf with a sandwich-board placard that read 'Exotic Animals, Mysteries of the West, Wild Indians. Laughman's Circus Maximus.'

The wolf hesitated beside our table and looked directly at me. His golden eyes seemed to bore through Miranda to look straight into my soul. The wolf shook from nose to tail and then plodded along after his master. A shiver passed through my body. I relaxed my hand on my knife, made sure my skirts were concealing it, and surrendered Miranda's body back to her. She immediately caught her breath, choked slightly and was patted on the back by her mother.

"Poor girl," Mother said. "That wolf gave you quite a start."

"I think he liked you, Miranda," Theresa laughed. We went on drinking our tea.

"What was that about?" she asked me silently.

Wolf. I hate them. They are killing machines. They have no other purpose.

I shared my memory of the pack attacking the elk nearly a year ago. It had given me nightmares for weeks afterward. I should have been more careful. Miranda nearly threw up and her mother was once again patting her.

"There, there now, Miranda. There is no reason to be so nervous about traveling. We had a wonderful train ride out here from Pittsburgh even though the events in Washington rather spoiled our plans. Your stepfather has taken care to make sure our accommodations on the train are almost luxurious. You girls will have a compartment of your own with an attendant to turn down your bed." It sounded lovely.

It was nearly two in the afternoon before we were ready to board. We'd eaten a light supper at the café when Mister Jonathon returned. And then waited because a horse platoon being sent to Omaha to protect railroad workers was on its way.

"Ah, there they are. We shall be underway soon now," Mister Jonathon said. Miranda looked up and watched as about three dozen men on horses rode toward us. People all up and down the street were standing to cheer the fine-looking recruits. It seemed they were all from the surrounding region.

There was a flash of golden hair under the cap of a soldier on a coal black horse. I looked up just as he rode past and straight into his eyes.

Kyle!

My voice was cut off by the squawk of a raven sweeping between us.

Awkawkawkawk!

7
Lovers

"KYLE!" I called out.

"Oh, shit!" Aubrey was standing in the doorway. I was sitting on my bed propped up against our common wall with my hands in my panties and I'd just yelled out my brother's name. Correct that. I wasn't wearing panties. They dangled from my ankle and my t-shirt was bunched up beside me.

"Aubrey! You startled me. I was asleep."

"Asleep and dreaming about your brother while you jill off. Ramie, that's so sick."

"It's not like that. Honest. Aubrey, please don't think that of me." I started crying. "It's not. It's not."

"Shit," she said again.

She came over to the bed, pulled her clothes off and crawled in. I was still crying and she reached out to hug me. It wasn't the first time I'd been in bed with Aubrey. We'd had lots of sleep-overs. Sometimes she even stayed in my room all night. We'd hugged and cuddled with each other. We'd seen each other naked plenty of times and I was plenty envious of her beautiful body. But we'd never hugged each other… naked. This could be even more embarrassing.

"I guess it wouldn't be that bad if it *was* like that. I read that lots of brothers and sisters have a sexual attraction to each other. Tell me about what's going through your head," Aubrey whispered. "What are you thinking?"

"Just right now, I'm thinking what a total fox you are and how lucky my brother is," I sniffed. "Honest, Aubrey. I wasn't masturbating about my brother. When you guys go at it in his apartment, it's like I can hear everything. I don't mean to eavesdrop, but you sound so sexy I just get carried away."

"So why'd you call out Kyle's name when I walked in?"

50

"Oh." *I have to come up with something quick.* "How long ago did you guys come in? Midnight?" She nodded. "It didn't take you long to get started." She giggled.

"We weren't planning to come here, but we got so revved up I couldn't stand it. I shouldn't have barged in on you without letting you know," she said.

"When you guys get going, it's like having a porn video turned on. I thought I'd rub one off and then I'd be able to sleep, but it was really intense and I sort of wiped out. I was asleep and dreaming. You know we've had some wolf problems. I dreamed we were riding and a wolf was chasing us. It was really scary. There was a wolf coming at us from the side and I screamed at Kyle because he was going to get eaten." There. That had enough elements of what had happened that I could live with it but there was absolutely no sexual connotation.

"So I'm a big bad wolf about to devour your brother," Aubrey laughed.

"Aubrey! No!" I moaned. *Shit! I can't get anything right—even when I make it up.*

"You know I'm going to get one of those dream books and find out what wolves and getting eaten by them means," she said. "You did look kinda like you were having a nightmare. Or an orgasm. It's hard to tell." Aubrey cuddled down into the bed and pulled the covers over us.

"I know you're my brother's girlfriend, but the two of you are my best friends in the world. I love you." I whispered as we nodded off to sleep.

I woke up so completely at peace it was amazing. I couldn't remember a single dream. I was all warm and cozy spooned in front of Aubrey with her cheek on my neck and her hand softly petting my...

I sat up straight and Aubrey flopped onto her back, her breasts jiggling around and flattening slightly against her chest. She opened her eyes and smiled at me.

"Do we have to get up?" she moaned. "I was having such a nice *dream.*"

"Aubrey!" I hissed. "Just what were you dreaming?" She grinned.

"I've never done that before," she said. "I mean wake up naked with someone. You know, Kyle and I have never slept together. We have sex until we're exhausted and then either he goes home or I slip in here. Holding you and waking up touching you with my bare skin was so nice."

"You were petting my boobs," I whisper-shouted. She was really shocked. I could tell she didn't realize she was playing with me. I agreed that waking up naked with her was a nice feeling, but maybe we shouldn't do that anymore.

"Oh my god! I'm sorry, Ramie. I didn't know I was doing that. I didn't mean to violate you. You must think I'm some kind of horrid lesbian!"

"Aubrey! What's horrid about lesbians? Criminy! You don't think Mom Mar and Mom Ash are horrid, do you? I'm not saying you are or aren't a lesbian, or bi like they are, but it wouldn't be horrid. That's a terrible thing to say."

"I'm sorry. That's not what I meant. I don't know what the hell I meant. I never even think about them, you know, being together. That doesn't bother me. I mean, I was just upset that I was doing something without your permission and that was horrid of me. Not that if we were *interested* it would be a bad thing."

That gave me pause. I looked at Aubrey. Her black hair and tan face with sleepy eyes. Her full round breasts. Her flat tummy. While I was looking her over, she flipped the sheet back and uncovered herself all the way down.

"I'm sorry."

"Go ahead and look. I was feeling you up. Least I can do is give you an eyeful," she said. She had a tuft of dark hair that concealed her pussy lips. She had wide hips and shapely legs. I breathed a huge sigh.

"I guess I was just curious. I didn't mean to make a big issue out of looking at you, but damn, you are pretty," I said. "I mean, I told Kyle that when I suggested you get together, but it's been a while since eighth grade gym class. You are *really* pretty." I was being a little too effusive. I shut up. We both got out of bed and started getting dressed. I was pretty sure Aubrey was looking at me as much as I'd looked at her, so I didn't rush getting my panties on.

"Do you ever think about it, Ramie?" she asked quietly. "I mean about other women?"

"You mean like sex?" I said. She nodded. "You know, except when you and Kyle are pounding each other in the next room, about the only time I think about sex is when I'm rubbing one off so I can go to sleep.

I mean, I fantasize about different guys. Maybe even double-teaming a guy, but not like actually going to bed with them."

"Like who?" she giggled. I blushed.

"Well, maybe like Stan Armitage."

"No! He's so geeky!"

"Yeah, but if you put a bag over his head his body is pretty hot."

"And gag him so you can't hear his voice," she laughed. "You're right, though. From the neck down he's not bad. Who gets to double-team him with you?"

"Well… you." I was really blushing and realized that we were just standing there in our panties. "I used to think about Shelby sometimes, but she got so snotty after she and Forrest got together that we haven't spent any time together for months."

"That didn't go anyplace anyway. They fucked each other, got mad, and won't speak to each other anymore. I'm so glad it wasn't that way for Kyle and me. What do we do when we're together with a guy?" We were sitting on the bed and I watched as she tucked her tits into her bra. I didn't bother with one and just pulled on a t-shirt. "I wish I could do that. Sometimes I hate having big jugs."

"I bet Kyle likes them." I grinned as Aubrey smiled.

"Come on. What do you think about?"

"Um… I don't know. I guess we just do stuff to him. I don't have a very good imagination. It's usually enough to just imagine we're there together and are going to have sex. It's not like I write up whole stories about it. I think about us getting together and then I come and fall asleep."

"Why bother to have me there?"

"It's like… normal." Aubrey looked at me with one of her coal black eyebrows raised. "It's the whole thing with Pa and Mom Mar and Mom Ash," I plunged on. "They all three share a bed. They love each other in any combination. It just seems normal to me."

"Wow. Do you suppose Kyle thinks that way, too? I mean that normal is two women and a man? Like, who is he thinking he wants me go down on?" I laughed out loud and shoved my feet into my boots.

"Kyle doesn't have any better imagination than I do," I said. "You could probably bring a blow-up doll to bed with the two of you and he'd be fine with it."

53

"Well, that's encouraging."

AUBREY HUNG AROUND and had lunch with us Sunday morning. I think Kyle took too big a risk last night and the parents suspect she's not really spending the night in my apartment. He took Aubrey home and was gone a long time before he finally got back. I couldn't wait to talk to him. I still had to wait my turn. Pa told him to saddle up because they were going for a ride. I started to get Pooky and Pa waved me off.

"Men-talk," he said. "Moms want to see you."

I headed for the house. *I can't be in too much trouble. I'm not having sex with anyone.*

"HOW ARE YOU doing, honey?" Mom Mar asked. She and Mom Ash were cuddled together in Pa's big chair in the office. I had my feet tucked under me on the couch.

"Pretty good. It was fun being up on the range. We gotta do something about those wolves, though. They're spooking the cattle."

"Yes," Mom Ash said. "About your brother and Aubrey. How are you doing?" I just knew Mom Ash wouldn't let me slide.

"Um… okay," I whispered. "You know they're both my best friends. I'm happy for them."

"Are you sexually active?" Mom Mar asked. I turned about fifty shades of red.

"No!"

"You know I don't just mean with a boy," Mom Mar said. "You and Aubrey have been close and she stays overnight with… with you a lot. We just want to tell you that's okay. You don't have to hide a relationship with her from us if you develop one."

"But be careful," Mom Ash said. "Boys—even Kyle—have fragile egos. Try not to hurt your brother. He's seen Mary Beth and me for enough years that he can deal with the concept, but he might not be ready for the reality in his own life."

Wait! What? Moms thought I was having sex with Aubrey??? Or might? You gotta be kidding! I think.

54

"Moms, it's not like that! She just comes to spend the night with me so she and Ky…" *Shit! Did they just trick me into admitting Aubrey was spending time in Kyle's room?*

"Yes? So she and Kyle what?" Mom Ash smirked.

"Mo-om," I moaned.

"Oh, quit complaining," Mom Mar laughed. "We could see what you were doing for Kyle from the beginning. That's why he's out riding with Pa. And just for safety's sake, it's high time you went to see Doctor Martin. She's very kind and you should probably be prepared for dating and the possibility of sex—male or female. The thing is, you've got to be more careful around the kids. On one hand, they're thirteen and know everything there is to know about life. On the other hand, for all that they are hellions, they're children."

"But we are serious about the other, too, Ramie," Mom Ash said. "It was obvious to see how close you and Aubrey are when you walked up to the house for breakfast this morning. If the two of you get involved, just try not to hurt your brother. Whether Aubrey is in the equation or not, he's still going to be your brother. You've always been best friends as well as siblings. Don't mess that up when it's more important than ever."

"What were you doing in Baltimore?" I demanded when I finally got Kyle alone after supper. We were walking out to the bunkhouse to get ready for bed.

"Huh? What are you talking about? I figured you were all antsy to find out what Pa and I talked about."

"I am. But in Baltimore. In the cavalry. Who is your host?"

"Ramie, I don't have any idea what you are talking about. You know as well as I do, I've never been farther from home than Colorado. And don't particularly want to."

"But…"

"Pa wanted to make sure I was using condoms when I was with Aubrey. He didn't say they were okay with us making love, but he didn't forbid it. What did Moms tell you?" The abrupt change of subject left me speechless.

What the fuck? I goddamn saw him in Baltimore in 1865. And he still won't talk about it. Fine!

"They wanted to make sure I wasn't hurting you when Aubrey and I have sex," I said. *There. Chew on that a while.*

"Oh." He hesitated in his step. I turned to tell him I wasn't. I didn't really want to hurt him. I didn't get a chance to speak. "It's okay," he said. "I mean, Aubrey and I love each other, but we're not like we own each other. I know you've been close to her for as long as I have. Longer. You saw her naked before I did, remember? I can deal with that. Yeah. It's kinda hot."

"I'm not, Kyle. I was teasing. Really. And if you don't want to talk about the other, I won't ask again. I just get kinda lonely sometimes." I could feel how red in the face I was getting. This was so embarrassing. I was not trying to get into Aubrey's panties. *Was I?*

"Hey, sister. I still got your back," he said as he put his arm around my shoulders and gave me a squeeze.

"Let's go up to Casper next Saturday," I said. I could change subjects pretty fast, too. "Can you take a day off from seeing your lover?"

"Hell, yes. We ain't joined at the hip, you know. I'll go see her on Sunday."

On Monday, I went down to the trading post in Laramie. It was run by an old Indian I knew named Merv Longsteer. He nodded to me when I went in.

"You just prowling around today or you want something special?" he asked.

"Knife," I answered briefly. "Good one I can learn to defend myself with." Miranda had a knife in her boot thanks to our encounter in Baltimore. But I was willing to bet she wasn't getting any opportunity to practice with it. If I got dropped back into her in an emergency again, one of us had to know how to use that knife.

Merv motioned me around the counter and into the back yard. He turned and tossed me a knife. I jerked aside and let it land on the ground before I realized it was a plastic thing. I bent to pick it up and Merv flashed toward me with an identical blade faster than an old man should be able to move.

He snatched the practice blade out of my hand and retreated to the other side.

"Let's try that again," he said. That started my training. Merv had taught hand-to-hand combat for the Marines in Viet Nam and the Philippines. He tossed the knife to me again and I managed to grab it mostly by the handle. He slowed down and showed me different grips and why they were useful. I went down to Laramie for a couple hours every day that week to work with Merv. At the end of the week, he showed me the knife I should buy. He said that buying the knife paid for my training.

8
Paying the Price

"**R**AMIE! GET your skinny ass into my office right now!" Pa yelled at me as he pounded on my door. "Kyle! Same orders. Now!"

Kyle and I stumbled out of our apartments, pulling on our boots with shirttails flying. Pa was already back to the house and we rushed to catch up. One thing you did not want to do was cross Pa when he was mad.

And I knew why. I glanced toward the near pasture and saw the four new horses grazing peacefully with Bells and Bows. Kyle and I got back from the auction with them about midnight. We clattered into Pa's office and stood at attention in front of his desk. Moms were sitting on the couch. I caught a glimpse of the kids just outside the door where they couldn't be seen but could hear every word. I couldn't blame them. This was going to be good.

"You two asked permission to go up to the Casper trail ride this weekend. Is that where you went?" Pa demanded. It was all on me.

"Um… yessir," Kyle said.

"For a while," I added.

"And?"

"All the riders on the trail were new, it seemed like. It wasn't much fun, so we left," I said. Pa looked at me waiting. I plunged on. "Well, there was an auction at the stockyards. We just stopped to have a look around. We were just looking. But then these four were led into the ring and they were kind of skinny and looking poorly. We just thought they needed a good home and no one was bidding on them."

"Except that guy from the slaughterhouse. He offered a penny a pound on the hoof for them," Kyle added.

"Thirteen dollars a horse, Pa!" I said. My eyes were stinging when I thought of it. "We bought the four of them for a hundred. They needed us."

"And you just happened to trailer Shadow and Spooky up to the ride that day in the big trailer instead of the two-horse trailer. Laramie Wyoming Bell, are you deceiving your parents?" *Oh shit! I blew that.* Pa would tolerate about anything but lying. That's what he was mad about. Not the horses.

"Yes, Pa. I'm sorry. But they were gonna go to slaughter." Pa sighed. He looked at Kyle and shook his head. He knew darned good and well that if I wanted something, Kyle was pretty helpless to stop me.

"Ramie, we can't rescue every horse that's headed to the slaughter-house. We already picked up two in the spring. And they can't *do* anything. They can't even be saddled. This is a working ranch. Everybody has to pull their weight. Animals included," Pa said.

"But . . ."

"Pa, please don't be mad at Ramie." That was a new voice. Caitlin and Phile were standing in the door. "We know we're not supposed to lie, and that was wrong of Ramie. But please don't send the horses away. We gotta help them."

Way to go, Phile! I had a sudden and unexpected burst of love and pride for my younger sibs. Over the past summer, since I begged Pa to let us go get the two Pinto draft horses, the brats had changed into... well, almost into human beings. At thirteen they were tolerable most of the time, and they'd really taken a lot of the responsibility for tending to our orphan horses. But thinking back to the way they were headed before we brought the first two home... Pa had to see the difference.

"They need us," Caitlin jumped in before anyone could answer. "Nobody ever needed us before."

That derailed the conversation. Phile and Caitlin got a lot of hugs. Even from me. I realized Phile was almost as tall as me now.

"Phile. Caitlin," Pa said. "Come stand by your brother and sister since you are in on this, too."

"Pa, it's all my fault," I said. "I knew it was wrong and I convinced my brothers and sister to go along with me. When I read the auction announce-ment, I knew those four would go to slaughter and there was something about them that just overrode my good sense. I apologize and I'll take what-ever punishment you say, but please don't blame my brothers and sister for my lack of good judgment. And please don't send those poor horses away."

"It's not the horses," Mom Ash said as she came up beside me. "It's the lying." She smacked me hard on the butt, careful to hit the side that didn't have my cell phone in the pocket. I flinched. It wasn't that it hurt that much, but Mom Ash never hit us kids. At almost seventeen, I figured she was the only one who dared to. I hung my head.

"I'm sorry, Mom Ash," I said contritely. "We shoulda talked to you and been honest about what we were doing."

She went back to the couch, curled up, and laid her head on Mom Mar's shoulder. I loved seeing my moms together. It always made me feel warm inside.

"All right you four," Pa said. "Ramie, I don't ever want to hear another lie escape from your lips. And that includes arranging to deceive your parents even when you do it without talking. You're the oldest and you should know better than to lead your siblings into that kind of behavior. And don't think you're off the hook, Kyle. You're supposed to have your sister's back. Don't you think you could have stopped her from making such a foolish decision?"

"Yessir. I guess."

"School starts in two weeks," Pa continued. "There will be no dates and no visits for the girlfriend for the rest of the month. You two will have to explain the situation to Aubrey and hope she doesn't get interested in someone else while you're grounded."

"Pa, that's not fair to Kyle when it's my fault. He was gonna see her this afternoon."

"Call and explain. You want a partnership. All partners share the blame. This is a ranch. It's been a ranch in our family for five generations. You are the sixth. You don't like cattle. Too bad. I raise beef. Mary Beth and Ashley are active members of the Wyoming Cattlewomen's Association. We do not intend to stop raising cattle. It's a profitable business. You might think we don't need money, but it's important to have a good business out here. It ain't a hobby."

"Yessir," I answered.

"For the next two weeks, you four will be responsible for the cattle. Rafe and Jess are due vacations. They worked hard this summer. You can meet them on the cattle drive from the upper range tomorrow. You four know the operation. There's inspections and vaccinations to be done in the next two weeks. That should keep all four of you busy enough you don't have time to worry about dating anyway."

I guess we all moaned at that. We knew what had to be done when the cattle came down from the upper pasture. They were coming down early because of the wolves. But Pa wasn't done yet.

"You whelps want to raise horses. Well, there's nothing wrong with that, but you're not just going to keep rescuing horses without some way to keep a ranch running. You need a profitable business. *Our* cattle ain't going to pay for *your* horses. It's a big ranch. There's room for both if you show how you can at least *start* getting some revenue from your venture even if it isn't profitable right away. Now go get breakfast ready. We've got cattle pens to prepare."

That was it. We were dismissed. It was obvious that since Moms had been in our meeting, they weren't cooking breakfast. We kids headed for the kitchen and started working. Pa wanted us to start working, today.

I fried bacon and Caitlin made up biscuits. Kyle shredded potatoes while Phile got the breakfast table set. With all seven of us sitting down at the same time, I scrambled a dozen eggs and added cheese to them. In half an hour we paused for a moment of silence to 'consider the land' as Pa always said. Then we tucked in.

Having Phile and Caitlin come to our defense got me thinking about the two kids. I wondered if Pa told them about time travel. Well, the way we treated him after he told us and then how Kyle reacted to me, I sure wasn't going to say anything.

Kyle called Aubrey and after they had some 'I'm sorry. And I love you,' he handed the phone to me.

"You're so bad, Ramie," Aubrey giggled.

"I'm sorry, Aubrey. And stupid. We'll make it up to you."

"You sure will," she said. "If they'll let you use the phone, call me, or chat with me on your computer at night. Otherwise, I'll see you at school."

"It does suck to not get to play on Labor Day," I said. "I promise, I'll do something really nice for the two of you."

"I'll hold you to that."

PA WASN'T KIDDING about sending Rafe and Jess on vacation. Either he or Mom Ash was always around to supervise but they worked us from sunup to sundown. Mom Mar brought sandwiches out to the feedlot at noon for us and there was a big meal when we got back to the house. By the time we got showers and headed for bed, we were too tired to stay up chatting with Aubrey. We got a little break on the weekend. The herd still had to be cared for, but we didn't do extra stuff like sorting, marking, tagging calves, castrating bulls, and vaccinating on the weekend.

Even Pooky and Dado were glad to just wander the fields for a while without working all the time. And working the cattle didn't excuse us from our duties with the six rescues we had. Kyle and I spent a lot of Sunday afternoon trying to figure out how we could make a business out of rescuing horses.

We had a big picnic on Labor Day and our parents relented and let us invite Aubrey out for the day. And night. We'd all be headed to school together in the morning. With Caitlin and Phile in junior high now, there'd be five of us headed into Laramie on Tuesday morning.

We loaded the three- and four-wheelers up with all the picnic supplies and rode them up to the family plot. It was always a special place. I think it meant something different to Pa than to the rest of us. It was an odd arrangement of flat stones with no markings on them. The rows had just two or three stones each.

Pa always had a private memorial when he went up there and this year he decided to share it with the rest of us. He pulled the family Bible out of an oilcloth he brought along.

"This first stone is where Theresa Ranae Bell is buried. Her husband was killed years before she died and we don't know where he lies," Pa said. He had the Bible open but he wasn't really reading. He was just holding the pages open. He looked at each of the stones and just recited the story or the part of it that touched him. "Here lies Kyle Redtail, my ho… our ancestor. Next to him for all eternity lies Laramie Wyoming Bell. They had two children. This stone is a memorial to the son they lost as an infant. Kyle's other wife is buried next to her husband in the Alexander plot at Green Hill Cemetery in Laramie. Arthur Senior did not wish to start a burial plot on his ranch, next door to us."

Pa stopped and slowly caressed the stones that lay there. There were no markings on the stones themselves. Just flat, smooth granite, cut from the mountains around Centennial Ridge and the Medicine Bow. Kyle and I went over to him and touched the two stones, too. We knew that what Pa cut off was that Kyle Redtail was his host. That didn't matter so much to us. What mattered was that these were our namesakes. Laramie Wyoming Bell and Kyle Redtail.

"Here lies our… their daughter, Kaylene Redtail Bell. And her lover, Robert Hood. They were never married, but lived together as husband and wife. Their daughter, Mildred Arlene Bell, was my grandmother. She loved a soldier before he went to war. He did not come back alive to marry her, but beside her stone lies his. This last stone is my father, Earl Thomas Bell, killed in the range war twenty years ago. Sometime in the future, your Grandma Bell will lie here beside him. Grandma and Grandpa Alexander have asked if they can lie next to her. That is good. It shows how we made the two ranches back into one. And God willing, one day long in the future, there will be three stones in the next row. Me. Mary Beth. Ashley. Before you kids came along, there has only ever been one child per generation on the Bell side. There were several others on the Alexander side, but of course they aren't in the Bell family Bible. There are pages for eight generations in this old book. On the page that records my birth is my marriage to Mary Beth and Ashley, we've also written in the births of our four children. But you will all have to decide what gets recorded on the last page. For all those who lie here, God rest their souls."

I KNEW IT was coming. I prepared a little better this time. I went to bed naked like I knew Kyle and Aubrey would, but I pulled a sheet up over me as I leaned back against the wall. I dreaded Kyle and Aubrey making love, but it excited me, too. I never had such strong comes as when they were making love next door. The downside was that when I came, it knocked me out and I went time traveling into the mind of Miranda Lewis. Or I dreamed I did. At least twice. I wish I could get the come without the confusion of the time travel.

I started stroking and diddling myself long before I started hearing their passionate moaning next door. When it started, though, it lit a fire in my pussy. I could just imagine how wet she was when she begged him to put it in. I could feel it as my juices flooded my fingers. I plunged my fingers in and out of my hole and was panting hard before Aubrey reached her crescendo.

Then there was a fluttering of wings next to my window. I heard Aubrey's voice mounting higher and higher as the bed squeaked on the other side of the wall. I could feel my orgasm approaching but the raven cut it short.

Awkawkawkawk!

I was gone.

9
Sold

"THERESA, RUN to the hotel!" Miranda commanded. I felt rather than saw her stepsister as her footsteps retreated rapidly. "Leave her," Miranda continued. "She's too young." I looked through her eyes at the three young soldiers who had her trapped against the wall. Blue trousers with a gold stripe. Dark blue double buttoned shirts. Tan hats. These looked like the same soldiers we saw in Baltimore. Where was Kyle?

"We only want you anyway," one said. Six feet tall. Pocky complexion. I corrected myself. Five-eight tops. Miranda was a lot shorter than me. A boy who didn't look more than 15 looked after Theresa but didn't move.

"And what do you want with me?" Miranda asked. One of the things Pa warned us about was to look first and not try to just jump in and take over our host. He'd got his killed that way. I wasn't sure Miranda knew I was there yet and I didn't want to distract her. I did make a subtle suggestion, though and her right foot crept up the wall as she leaned back against it. Before long, I could reach the knife she still carried in her boot.

"Just a little tupping," scar-face said. "Probably won't have a clean white girl again for months."

"Probably never had a clean white girl, have you?" Miranda prodded back. I could feel her awareness seep into mine as she surrendered control of her body while she kept them talking. I got hold of the haft of the knife.

"Soldiers, attention!" a voice shouted from the walk behind them. The pock-marked private looked up and sneered.

"We're off duty until we board tomorrow morning, Corporal," he snapped.

"You are never off duty when you are wearing that uniform," the voice snapped. He stepped around the privates to position himself next to Miranda. "I said, attention!" The soldiers pulled themselves upright into a pretty sloppy attention. "Private Randolph, you took an oath to protect the citizens of the United States from the savages of the plains and mountains. This is a citizen of the United States. Do not become the savages you are supposed to protect her from. Dismissed." The three soldiers growled a little but turned and shambled away. Miranda breathed a sigh of relief.

"Thank you, uh…" she started.

"Corporal Jason Wardlaw at your service, miss," our rescuer came to attention beside us and bowed. *Kyle!* No. There was no Kyle there. But I was sure this was the same soldier. *What's going on? Where's Kyle?*

"Thank you, Corporal," Miranda continued. Then she gasped. Just over Corporal Wardlaw's shoulder there was an Indian dressed in buckskins. "There is a…"

"My companion," the Corporal said. "John Hamm is my translator and friend."

"I am pleased to meet you, Corporal. Mr. Hamm. I am Miss Miranda Lewis. Again, thank you for your intervention. It would be a shame to have bloodied his uniform before he had blooded his weapon." I know the Indian saw me slip the knife back into her boot sheath and the hint of a smile crossed his face. Miranda firmly took control of her body from me and I rode quietly in her mind as we turned toward the station. The Indian walked silently behind us.

"He may wear the uniform but he has no respect for it," the Corporal said. "May I escort you back to the hotel and your chaperones?"

Way to go, Miranda!

She blushed. A raven looked up at us from the street where he was tearing at a bit of garbage.

Awkawkawkawk!

I was gone again.

WHAT THE FUCK?

I was sitting in my bed and still rubbing myself. I was building up to a good one and could hear Kyle and Aubrey still going at it next door. I heard them yelp and moan and I tipped over the edge. *I went time traveling without having come?*

I lay there in bed with the light off for another twenty minutes before I heard Aubrey come into the room. She went to her accustomed side of the bed and slipped in next to me. I rolled toward her and spooned behind her. She was naked. I smashed my bare boobs into her back. It surprised me, but I didn't want to just jump away. I acted like it was just natural.

"Not good enough to pass out tonight?" she whispered as she caught my hand and pulled it around her.

"Girlfriend, I have no idea what you are talking about," I giggled. "Did you knock him out?"

"Yeah, but that's not so difficult."

Now that our little hug and joke were through, I felt I could roll back away from her and my embarrassment. She held my hand against her stomach.

"I do like cuddling at night. Thank you for being here like a sister for me," she whispered. I gave up and just lay there next to her. She hugged my arm around her and before long we were asleep.

WHEN I WOKE up in the morning, Aubrey still held my hand around her but she'd moved it—or we'd moved it—so it was held against her breast. I thought I'd better gently extract it, remembering our joint embarrassment when she'd woken up holding my breast. At the same time, it was incredibly pleasant to cuddle and hold her like this. My fingers reflexively squeezed against the supple flesh and I felt the nub of her nipple harden against the palm of my hand.

It was nice.

I was raised with women who were lovers and who loved my father. But somehow, I'd never thought about whether I could ever feel that way about a woman—not only loving her as my friend, but loving her sexually. I still wasn't sure but there was no question that holding Aubrey like this was pleasurable, apparently for both of us. She moaned softly in her sleep.

"Kyle," she whispered. That was my cue. I pulled my hand gently away from her and rolled the other direction. This was my brother's girlfriend. I wasn't going to get between them.

OUR JUNIOR YEAR in high school seemed to be when we actually started to learn things. Freshman and sophomore years still seemed like elementary

school. Classes our junior year were way more intense and we were working our tails off to keep up. Pa had made it clear to us that if we didn't go
to college, we weren't going to have a horse ranch. That was motivation
enough to keep us on top of our studies.

Having ten horses to care for in 'our herd' plus the rest of the ranch
horses, kept us working. We had six rescues, Pooky, Dado, and the kids'
horses. I'm not sure they'd ever even named their horses. They did saddle
them and ride with the rest of us, but these days they spent every available moment with Bells, Bows, and the other rescues.

In addition, there were a dozen working ranch horses and mules.
When we finished our servitude with the cattle before school, Pa assigned
all horse care to the four of us. He was still waiting for our business plan.
When does he think we'll have time to do that?

By the end of September, I'd pretty much put it out of my mind
as I struggled to keep up with school and the horses. After dinner
Saturday night, I planned to study my Algebra. Kyle would want to
see my worksheets the next day. Saturday night, of course, he was
headed into town to take Aubrey out. They hadn't come back out to
the ranch since Labor Day.

I studied until my eyes started to droop. It was about ten o'clock
when I went outside and just looked up into the clear night sky. I leaned
against the porch post and let my mind wander. My eye was caught by a
flicker and I turned to see the old raven sitting on the rail nearby. It was
almost like he was becoming a pet.

"I don't know what you're staring at, old Blackfeather," I mumbled.
"I don't think I'll be rubbing one off tonight. I'm almost asleep as it is."
He bobbed his head up and down, looking at me out of his one good eye.
Awkawkawkawk!

"Demon Ramie, save us!" she was chanting over and over.
What the fuck, Miranda!

"I know you aren't a demon, Ramie." At least she wasn't saying *that*
out loud. "I've been chanting for days, praying that you would come and
help us."

Who is 'us' and why can't I see anything?

68

"There are four girls in addition to me, and we are under a canvas in the back of a wagon. Ramie, they grabbed me in Vincennes, Indiana. I don't know where we are now. My hands are tied behind my back. I tried to talk my way out by telling them I could summon a demon and when she came they would die."

Great. Damn it, Miranda. How did you get into this pickle?

"I take it you mean how did they capture me? Mister Jonathon sent me to get sweets for Theresa and me when the train stopped in Vincennes. He was being uncommonly generous. Gave me a small purse. I didn't even make it to the drugstore. Two men pulled me into an alley and threw a bag over my head before I could even see them. The others were already here when they tied my hands and threw me under the canvas. We have been traveling hard for two weeks."

What's with the chanting 'Demon Ramie, save us?'

"I thought it would scare them into letting me go."

So we're both tied up in the back of a wagon. And it stinks in here!

"They have not let us stop to make a toilet for the past three days. And we have had no food."

I'm sorry, Miranda. Truly. I suppose they took your purse and your knife.

"As soon as they grabbed me they broke the string of the purse. They seemed pleased. The knife is still in my boot."

Thank God for small favors. Let me see if I can reach it. Miranda, if you want me to help you'll have to let me take control.

"Yes. Of course." She was still slow at relinquishing control. It must feel really weird to consciously let go and let someone else take control of your body. Once I was fully in command, I could also fully feel the biting ropes and the gross pile of shit in my drawers.

I pulled my legs up and managed to touch my boot with my hands. A girl next to me moaned and pushed against me.

"Hush," I whispered. "The demon is setting us free." It was a struggle to get to the knife and get it out of the sheath without dropping it. My hands were nearly numb from lack of circulation. Once the knife was in my hand, though, I managed to reverse it so it was against the rope that bound my wrists. It took dozens of little sawing movements to bite through the cord. At last, the tension eased.

The first order of business, once I had hands free, was to push off my drawers and wipe as much shit off my ass as I could before I shoved the mess down by my feet. The second task was to tear the bag from over my head. I still couldn't see anything.

"Are you really…?"

"Unless you wish to die by my hand, close your mouth and say nothing," I whispered to the girl next to me. She gasped and I think she passed out. I had to think fast or the girls would revolt. "Demon Ramie, by the powers of the Dumbledore, endowed upon me by Gandalf the Grey, smite these villainous scoundrels who have captured your faithful servant," I shouted out.

"That's enough out of you, cunt!" one of the men in front of us yelled. "One more word and I'll put an end to your maidenhead through the shit and all."

"Pray for your soul, foul cur. The demon shows no mercy to those who offend her minions!" I changed my voice as much as possible from Miranda's. Now I was truly the demon. And the canvas cover was thrown back.

"I warned you, whore!" a man who might have been shaved and clean a few days ago growled at me. They were his last words. I rammed the knife into his throat. He gurgled as I pulled it free and jumped onto the back of the one driving the horses. I wrapped my arm around the startled driver's neck and pressed the knife against his throat.

"It wan't me! Silas did it all. He said we 'ud have it easy. All I had to do was drive a wagon full of whores to Texas. That old man din't say you 'as a witch!"

"What old man?"

"Yer pappy. Silas beat him at cards and he paid with you. We wanted the blonde, but he 'ud only part with you."

"Where are we?"

"Just crossed into Tennessee on the way to Memphis!" he squealed.

"Fuck."

The knife in my hand moved without my volition and the driver slumped forward.

"What the hell?"

He was lying. He was as much a part of it as the other one.

70

"You can't blame that one on me." I was pissed. I was going to let him live.

Then I'll rot in hell.

I KEPT CONTROL as best I could. Miranda was constantly complaining about being dirty and the girls in the back had started caterwauling. We approached a stream and I pulled the horses to a stop. We pulled the canvas off the girls and then the canvas bags from over their heads. One of the girls didn't move and when I checked I discovered she was dead.

I no longer felt so bad about Miranda killing the bastard.

"Listen up," I commanded the other three. "I'm going to free you. Before I do, you should know that we're leaving the bodies here. If you run away, you'll get caught. And then you'll get hung for the murder of these three. Your only hope is to stay together until we are safe. I am Demon Ramie and I have spoken."

Miranda was going to owe me big time for this. Demon, my ass. Nonetheless, the girls obediently got out of the wagon and went straight to the stream to clean themselves up. I did the same and washed my chapped butt and petticoats. The girls all discarded their bloomers. I searched the bodies and relieved them of several fat purses and their guns before we dragged them into the bushes. The girls all dumped their soiled drawers on top of the bodies and laid the unknown dead girl next to them.

"What are we going to do now, Demon Ramie?" one girl asked. She'd been pushed forward by the other two.

"We will leave this cursed place and find a decent campsite," I commanded. "There is a fair amount of money in these purses. We'll divide it equally. When we get to Memphis, we can all go our separate ways." They nodded their assent and we crossed the stream, still headed southwest with the road. I strapped the two guns around my waist to make sure no one else could get to them. I'd have to instruct Miranda on how to use them.

I was exhausted. I'd been tired when I got summoned out of my body and even though Miranda's body was a little more rested than mine, my mind was done for. One of the girls had experience driving and took the reins. After I was reasonably comfortable that Miranda could handle the girls, I rendered control back to her. I tried to meditate as I rode along in her conscious mind, just spacing out. The girls were all pretty quiet until we'd made camp. They found saddlebags with vittles in them and all ate for the first time in two days. I was just nodding off when a flicker of movement caught my eye.

Awkawkawkawk!

10
Kissing a Girl

"**R**AMIE? RAMIE?" Kyle was standing right in front of me. I started out of my reverie.

"What?"

"You're asleep on your feet. You didn't even look up when I pulled in."

"Kyle, I was…" I couldn't tell him. He claimed to not be time traveling, even though I'd seen him twice. Still, the last time I'd seen that corporal, Kyle certainly was not there. And how did I go off time-traveling if I wasn't listening to him and Aubrey making love? I looked over and the raven had his head tucked under his wing, sitting on the porch railing. "I was talking to my buddy, Blackfeather," I said, nodding toward the bird. "We were discussing how jealous we were that *somebody* was getting laid." Kyle laughed at me.

"Not tonight, we weren't. Wasn't the right time."

"Aw. Too bad. So sad."

"Go to bed, Ramie. You look like you've been up for days. I'll call you for breakfast." Kyle headed for his door and I turned to go into my room.

Up for days? Yeah, I have been. And I'm worried about Miranda.

SEEMED LIKE NOTHING happened for weeks except we went to school and worked our asses off on the ranch. And Kyle and I worked up a rudimentary business plan. It was nice that Aubrey was over and helped us. She still didn't much care for horses, but she thought it was pretty cool that we might be able to make a business out of them. I still had to sell Pa on the idea.

"So, I figure we can board up to a dozen horses. There's good riding trails. It's minimal cost, even in winter. The south pasture could support another couple dozen rescues," I said. "I've been reading a bunch about them and most just need a safe place and dependable food and water. Rescues won't be for riding or working. They've earned their retirement. Though we'd be watching for a stud and some brood mares among them. And for the future, we'd like to acquire the thousand acres south of us just to let rescues run wild. When we get to that point, we could have a herd of over a hundred horses with no problem."

"What's the real business, Ramie?" Mom Ash said as she looked at my spreadsheet. "Mostly, this just looks like a trade-off of boarding horses for rescuing horses. That doesn't turn a profit."

"Horse-breeding," Kyle responded. He was right with me. "We want to breed top quality ranch horses."

"Not show horses," I added. "We know a lot about bringing up a foal and gentling him. But it's long term. That's why there's no line item for it in the revenue yet. It will take until we're nearly out of college to get our first batch ready to sell. We looked at Bows' and Bells' pedigree. They were abused horses, but they come from good stock. Their hooves are recovering pretty well and we think this spring we could have Bolt cover them. That is, if you don't object, Pa."

"Am I getting a stud fee?"

"Um… well…"

"I'm kidding, Ramie. That's one of the better ideas you've got for this ranch. I was afraid you were going to try to throw show horses or racers. What's this?" he asked, pointing to the top of the sheet.

"We had to come up with a name for the operation. We chose LK Stables. Laramie and Kyle," I said. Pa nodded.

"What about the kids?" Mom Mar asked. "They seem to be as much a part as you are."

"Those wild Indians don't want any part of the business, Ma," I said. "They say they just want to be ranch hands and spend time out with the horses. They really do have a nice touch with the rescues. I still think they should have an interest in the business, though, even if they take no part in managing it."

"I wonder," Pa said. He went to his fireproof file cabinet and started rummaging around. He pulled out an account book that went back years.

"When the ranch was started back in the 1800s, your great-great-great-grandmother was raising horses. It wasn't until about 1920 that they started raising cattle to any large degree. That's when we acquired the Bell Bar-B brand. Then, when your Ma and I took over, we changed the name and brand to the Alexander Bell Cattle Company mark. The first horse ranch here, though, was known as the LK Ranch and this was the mark," he said showing us the LK brand.

"That's so cool. We could resurrect the brand!" I said.

"It's still registered to us. We've kept all ranch brands renewed every year. They are part of the property of the ranch. You'll need to verify with the Wyoming Livestock Board where you intend the brand to be used and on what kind of animals," Pa said. "You can do all that when you register your business."

"There's so much to be done we didn't know about!" Kyle moaned.

"That's why you are in school and are going to college. This is a good first cut," Pa said. "We'll look at it a little more closely and make some suggestions. You still have to come up with a good case to invest in your business. So far, all I'd be willing to invest is hobby money."

Investment? Damn. I hadn't even thought of that.

I LISTENED TO Aubrey and Kyle make love in the next apartment. I saw the raven dancing on the windowsill. I rubbed off a pretty satisfying climax. And nothing happened. I was really worried about Miranda. I wanted to go help her. She was cut off from everyone she knew with three kidnapped girls and a team of horses. There was no telling what was happening to her. I sat with my laptop and looked at maps and checked Wikipedia for the stats on every small town we might encounter between Memphis and St. Louis. And from St. Louis to Omaha. I had no idea how quickly the traveling girls could make the trip.

By modern roads and Interstate Highways, it was less than 300 miles if you crossed the Mississippi at Memphis and went north on the west side of the river. It was close to 350 miles if you stayed east of the river and approached through Kentucky and Illinois. I got caught up in the Adventure of Huck Finn—a condensed version—and was trying to figure out why they chose to drift on the river most of the length of Missouri to Cairo, to get to Illinois, when they could have just floated to the other side of the river and been in Illinois. What should Miranda do? There was no bridge across the Mississippi south of St. Louis. We'd have to barge across the river and that meant being dependent on other people. I didn't like that. We should turn north.

I still had the laptop open when Aubrey came in.

"Were we so uninteresting you had to look up porn on the internet tonight?"

"Really, Aubrey! I was doing research on… the ranch, you know." She tried to sneak around to see what was on my screen, but I closed the laptop. Then I realized I was sitting in bed naked because I'd started on my research before I thought about getting dressed. Aubrey stripped off her pajamas and got under the covers with me.

"I like sleeping with you, Ramie. Can we live together when we go to college?"

"You mean share a dorm room? That would be cool."

"It would be better if we all three lived together." I turned and looked at her. Her face was close to mine. *What's she getting at? Besides my lips.* Her lips were right there and she just moved in a little and sort of kissed me.

"What are you doing, Aubrey?"

"Kissing you. Haven't you ever been kissed before?" she giggled and pushed her lips against mine again.

"Um…"

"No! Really?"

"Who would I kiss?" I asked. I almost regretted not kissing Forrest back last spring.

"Kiss me. I'll teach you everything I know."

Her kisses were nice. Really nice. It was also nice to have her rubbing her soft breasts against mine. I knew the mechanics of kissing. I've read romances that I snuck out of Mom Mar's room. I wasn't expecting it to make my nipples kind of ache.

Aubrey pulled me down in bed.

"Do you like me, Ramie?"

"Don't be silly. I love you! You're my best friend besides Kyle." I moved toward her to convince her and then jerked back when she touched my lips with her tongue.

"It's okay, love. It's the way to do it. You'll like it." I nodded.

"It just took me by surprise. Aubrey, I don't know what to do. Are you sure it's all right to do this? You're my brother's girlfriend."

"We talked. You should talk to him more. After all, he's your best friend, too. He said he told you it was okay."

"Yeah, but I was just joking with him."

"He wasn't. And neither am I. Ramie, I don't just come out here to be with Kyle. I like being with you. Sleeping with you. Holding you. Right now, I'd like to kiss you some more."

I HAD SOME serious thinking to do. I woke up in the morning cuddled against Aubrey's back and holding her boob in my hand. We didn't, like, make love or anything, but she did teach me a lot about kissing. And I liked it. I liked it when she touched my nipples while she had her tongue in my mouth, too. And I liked waking up with that soft cushy tit in my hand and her hard little nipple under my thumb. I wondered what it would be like to make love to her. *How do you even do that?*

Mary Beth and Ashley were as demonstrative with each other as they were with Pa. There was always kissing and giggling going on around the house. But once they closed the bedroom door, I had no idea what went on. I understood how men and women had sex. I'd been around enough breeding cattle and horses to understand the mechanics of that. But when two cows got interested they just humped at each other.

The internet was seriously no help. If I was going to have a relationship with Aubrey, I was going to ask her where she got information. I might even have to talk to Mom Mar. *Now I'm blushing.*

But that was the real question. Was I going to have a relationship with Aubrey? That included sex? Even though she was my brother's girlfriend? Even though he said it was okay?

I was sprinkling little kisses on Aubrey's shoulder, shifting her dark hair as I breathed on her neck. She rocked her head back and forth as I kissed her and rubbed my hand against her breast.

"Mmm. What a nice way to wake up," she murmured. She twisted herself around so she could give me a kiss. It wasn't like last night when every kiss was getting us warmed up. This was just so soft and sweet and gentle that it made me all content inside. "You suppose there's some way to arrange it so I could go to sleep with Kyle every night and wake up to you every morning?"

"You do want the best of both worlds, don't you, honey."

"I think I've got the best of both worlds. We don't have to rush, Ramie, but someday soon we're going to get there."

"Pa, would you teach me how to shoot your Smith and Wessons?" I asked. He looked up from his desk and cocked his head. I don't think I ever surprised my pa before.

"That's a heavy gun for a woman," Pa said. "It wouldn't hurt for you to feel what it's like."

"Sometimes, a woman doesn't have a choice," I said. Pa looked me in the eye and I couldn't look away. He nodded slightly.

"This is a Model 3, single action. That means you have to pull the hammer back with one hand and pull the trigger with the other." He went on explaining the mechanics of the gun as we walked to our shooting range. He handed me one of them and held out his hand with six bullets. When I'd loaded, he took the second gun and loaded it. "Once you lock the hammer back, it only takes about five pounds of pressure on the trigger to release it. Don't get your finger on the trigger until you are ready to fire."

We worked on the range for an hour and then Pa took me back to his office and made me break the guns down and clean them. It wasn't that unusual to go out to the shooting range because we'd all been required to practice with our rifles at least once a month since we were twelve. This was the first time I'd ever asked to practice with a handgun. My arm was sore from lifting it.

"Pa, can we go into town and buy me a handgun?" I asked.

"All right, little girl. Tell me about it."

"It's all the history stuff we've been studying," I said. "Like John Wilkes Booth used a single shot Deringer to kill President Lincoln. The only back-up he had was a big knife. All the soldiers outside were carrying revolvers but nobody else got a single shot off. I dream about this stuff now." I hoped he bought it. With Kyle denying he was time traveling, I wasn't confident that I was. Maybe I was just hallucinating. It's not like I could point to Kyle having sex as a trigger. He and Aubrey weren't even around. *I* wasn't even having an orgasm. I had to be dreaming it all.

"And in your 'dream', what kind of handgun do you see?" Pa asked. Even if he didn't believe me, he was willing to play along. I just couldn't admit he was right about time travel. It was too impossible. *So why am I so worried about a girl in my dreams?*

"I think it's older than your Smith and Wessons. Something Civil War era." Kyle's door slammed and we saw him headed for the truck. He was taking Aubrey back into town.

"Kyle!" Pa shouted. "We'll take the Explorer. Let's all go." Kyle was real surprised, but he and Aubrey came over to where we were getting in the big SUV. Mom Ash came out of the house and had a quick conversation with Pa before she ran in the house and came back out with Mom Mar.

"You kids be careful and mind your manners," Mom Mar yelled at us as Mom Ash got in the front next to Pa. The three of us kids slid into the back seat with Aubrey sandwiched between Kyle and me. "I got roast chicken for dinner tonight. Don't let it get all dried out on us."

Pa pulled out to head to Laramie and Aubrey held hands with both Kyle and me.

11
Guns and Ammo

PA SURPRISED us by stopping at the gun shop on Second Avenue *before* we took Aubrey home.

"You're hanging around these ranch kids more and more, Aubrey," Mom Ash said. "You ought to get a look at what they're looking at."

"Are we getting guns?" Kyle asked.

"Ramie's interested in some reproductions, but it's a good idea for you to have good side-arms when you are out running around the ranch. We've been hearing more reports of wolves in the lower hills lately and you might not have time to reach your rifles," Pa said.

Kurt at the gun shop showed us a bunch of good handguns and Pa made Kyle and me pick out a good sidearm. He told Aubrey to pick one out, too, and he'd keep it up at the ranch for when she visited. She was a little shy of them but once Kurt took us out to his shooting range and she fired off a few rounds, she got a little more enthusiastic. We all walked off with Remington Model 1911s.

But I really wanted to look at Kurt's classic revolvers. I pointed out the one I wanted to look at. I was sure it was almost like the ones I took off the dead kidnappers and strapped to Miranda's hips.

"That's an 1851 Colt Navy reproduction," Kurt said. "Most everything about it is like the originals. It's a single action, six-shot revolver. The only difference is that this one takes cartridges and the original was a percussion gun. You had to stuff the cap, powder, and ball into it with this tamping rod built onto the barrel."

"How do you do that?"

"Well, it's a simple process but it takes a little getting used to. Let me see what I've got here." He turned and opened a gun safe behind the counter. I was sure he knew exactly what he had. Kurt was like that. He laid a gun almost identical to the reproduction on the felt cloth. "This is a restoration. A few years ago—well, back in the 70s—they tore out the interior of the last brothel in Laramie. That's where Lovejoy's is now. It's on the historic register and I was on the crew that was assessing the reconstruction. We came across this gun jammed into the paneling and I bought it. Wasn't much. Took me ten years to restore it."

"Pa, I want this gun," I said. There wasn't any question in my mind. I'm sure every Colt Navy felt exactly the same, but damn it! I'd held this one in my hands before. I knew it.

"Whoa! Nobody said it was for sale," Kurt said. "Course, I'd trade it for your Pa's Smith and Wessons. That would be even."

"No!" I answered before Pa could say anything. "Those guns belong at the ranch. If you won't sell it to me, at least teach me how it loads and fires. Will you do that, Kurt?" He chewed on the inside of his lip.

"How many times a week are you meeting with Merv Longsteer?" Kurt asked me. I looked at Pa quickly and saw his mouth twitch.

"Two… Twice a week. Lunch on Monday and Wednesday," I said. Apparently, Pa already knew I was leaving school in the middle of the day to go visit Merv. I was coming along with my knife skills and I was damned glad of it.

"I've got an after-school job for you if you want it. Tuesday and Thursday afternoon. Still get you home in time for dinner. If your brother and his girlfriend want to work, there's enough for the three of you."

I DREAMED ABOUT the gun that night. Kurt showed me the rudiments of loading the Colt Navy. I kept going over every step in my mind. I was asleep long before Kyle and Aubrey were finished. I had visions of Miranda in my brain and cool air from my open window whipped me away. There was that old raven sitting there and calling me.

Awkawkawkawk!

I COULDN'T BREATHE. It was dark and skinny hard fingers gripped my throat. The bony hand of death had me in his grip. I could see a deeper darkness settling in. I swung my arm with all my force at the monster killing me.

I hit her with the barrel of the Colt in my hand. Hit her hard. She fell off of me and I rolled away coughing and trying to stand up to breathe. I swung the Colt around frantically, looking for a target. There were stars in my eyes but I was beginning to see shapes. Two of them were huddled by the wagon. The other lay sprawled on the ground at my feet. I kicked her in the shoulder and she rolled over moaning.

Well, at least I didn't kill the little bitch.

"Demon Ramie, you saved me. I thought you'd abandoned me."

Miranda, I'm not...

"I know. I'm sorry. What should I call you? You are so powerful and you can take over my body."

I'm not trying to take over your body, Miranda. She was killing us.

"Yes. Thank you. I..."

Could you just call me Ramie? Or if you have to, friend?

"Friend Ramie. You are my friend, aren't you?"

I've been worried sick about you. Are you okay? How long have I been gone?

"You have been gone only a day, but I feel so empty when you are not with me. We are all... frightened. Harriet has been frantic. She sometimes strikes the other girls without provocation. And now this."

You're going to be bruised.

"It is painful, but I am alive, thanks to you."

The girl, Harriet moaned and one of the other girls silently brought water to her. She looked cautiously at me the whole time but carefully helped Harriet drink. I realized I was still holding the Colt in my hand. I didn't really want to let go of it but resolutely shoved it in the holster. I left my hand there, but relinquished control of Miranda's body to her.

I'm sorry I took control without your permission.

"Must I forgive you for saving my life? It shocks me, but I cannot object. It is such a strange feeling to not have control over my own body."

Let's see if we can get some answers from this bitch.

Harriet was staring at us. Snarling like a wolf.

"Why did you try to kill me," Miranda demanded. "I have been only kind to you."

"Witch! You summon demons to do your bidding. Unholy abomination." I guess that summed up her feelings pretty well.

Bet she's from Massachusetts. Don't say that!

"You cannot travel with us if I cannot trust you," Miranda's voice rasped. It hurt to speak. "That goes for you two, as well. I am going to St. Louis. I am taking that wagon and horses. If that is not where you wish to go, leave with her in the morning."

We sat the rest of the night against a tree near the horses. She slept, but I stayed awake. It was odd. I couldn't see anything because Miranda's eyes were closed. But I could hear the girls settle down and their breathing even out. I could feel the cold brass of the Colt beneath my fingers. Extending just those senses, I could tell exactly where everyone in the camp was.

It was a long night.

I HEARD HARRIET get up before dawn. Miranda was asleep but I could still manipulate her body—still hear clearly where the girl was. I drew the Colt and held it in my lap following the movement of her steps. Soon, after a quick whisper to one of the other girls—Katie?—she slipped away and I heard her ill-concealed steps as she crashed away from camp and faded into the woods. I opened one eye and Miranda began to stir in the back of my consciousness.

My throat hurt. I lifted my chin to swallow and groaned. Katie was up out of her blanket and scampering to me with a canteen. Beulah rolled over and continued to sleep. The girl held the canteen to my lips.

"Poisoned?" I croaked. She looked truly horrified as she shook her head. *Lighten up, kid. It was a joke.* I gulped at the water. Every swallow hurt. I hoped the bitch hadn't done any long term damage to Miranda's windpipe or vocal cords. I could live without ever feeling that again.

"Must we get up? I am so tired," Miranda moaned in our minds.

I don't feel comfortable with that girl wandering around in the woods. We are nowhere near far enough away yet.

"Where are we going?"

Where do you want to go, Miranda? Your stepfather sold you for his gambling debt. Do you really want to chase after him?

"He owes me. He could do the same thing to Theresa. I can't let that happen. I have to get to her."

I've been studying maps. There are no bridges across the Mississippi south of St. Louis. We'll have to head straight north as much as possible and sort of follow the flood plains through Kentucky. We still have to get across either the Mississippi west or the Ohio north. It's 300 miles as the crow flies, so we can count on twice that with horses and a wagon. Let's move.

KATIE WAS GOOD with the horses. She'd been raised as a servant in Philadelphia. Her father was the coachman for a rich family. The war, however, had ruined her life. Her father had left to fight and the rest of the family was deemed too expensive to keep by the rich folks. The long story made short was that her own mother had sold her to kidnappers with her knowledge. She knew she was going to become a prostitute and was responsible for her own life.

Beulah was a sullen girl who made no secret of her desire to return to her life in Athens, Ohio. She was convinced that she'd simply been in the wrong place at the wrong time. She planned to go home.

I let Katie drive the wagon, giving her the general direction to find a path north while she chattered away. I carefully examined the two Colts as we rode. They were in reasonably good condition. I wanted to get them cleaned as soon as it was possible and to teach Miranda all about how to use them. We were cooperating on the use of her body. I merely gave her instructions on what to do to examine the guns and check the firing mechanism. In the typical fashion, there was one empty chamber in each revolver with the hammer locked over it. I expected Miranda to be skittish over having the six-shooters strapped to her but I was in for another surprise.

"My hands have killed three men with a knife," she informed me silently. "How much harder can it be to kill a man with a gun?"

I'm so sorry, Miranda. I used you to kill those men.

"You might be able to claim that for two of them. I was the one that sliced the third's throat to your protests. I may as well burn in hell for three as for one."

Don't lose yourself, Miranda. You were not born to be a killer. God willing, there will never be another.

"I take a strange comfort in you, Demon Ramie. Even you pray to God."

Well, I ain't very religious but I won't deny He exists.

WE TRAVELED FOR four days west sticking to wagon tracks that showed minimal traffic. I figured eventually we'd hit the Mississippi and turn north to the Ohio. There was sure to be a ferry there. What we encountered was a small village. It couldn't really even be called that. There was a building with a buckboard at a hitching post and a couple shacks that didn't look lived in. As we approached, two men came out of the building, one with a sack over his shoulder that he dumped in the buckboard. The two men stopped and waited for us to approach.

"We need supplies," Miranda said to Katie. "Let me talk to them. Be ready to get away."

Katie assented and Beulah stayed mostly hidden in the back of the wagon.

"G'moro. And what have we here?" the taller of the men asked in a thick Irish accent. He wore an apron so it was safe to assume he was the shopkeeper. I let Miranda handle the negotiation while I kept a hand near the guns.

"Refugees from the ravages," Miranda said. "Our farm was burnt. My sisters and I have little and have decided to take it northward. We need supplies."

"It's a bad time to head north," the other man said. "God's vengeance on the Yanks is snow."

"I reckon we have little choice in the matter," Miranda said.

"Well, come in, young miss. Ye might be wha' we're needin' here. Let's do some bartering. Sam'el, you be gone now," the shopkeeper said. The other man chuckled and mounted his buckboard.

"Whichever one you choose, bring 'er out fer dinner with the missus and me," he called.

Miranda, be careful with this man. You'll be bedded before the night is over.

We went into the shop. It was pretty modest by the standard of what Mister Jonathon had in his shop, but it was clean. Katie stayed on the buckboard, but I was surprised that Beulah jumped down and followed me.

"Now, you are not from Mississippi and you are not sisters," the man said. He introduced himself simply as John. "Why are three frightened girls alone on this road? I could see into your wagon and you haven't even enough supplies to be refugees. What happened to you?"

"We were kidnapped and were being transported to Texas to become whores," Beulah blurted out. "We got the best of our kidnappers and are trying to get back home."

"Got the best of them, did you? Where are the bodies?"

"A week east of here," Miranda said. "Off the road with one of the girls who had already died. Hidden, but if anyone looks they'll be found."

"And that's where you got the guns you are toting," he nodded.

"My 'sister' is formidable," Beulah said with a touch of admiration in her voice. "I, on the other hand, need a man by my side."

What the fuck?

"Well, now, you see, I knew we could do some bartering," John laughed.

BEULAH TOOK ME completely by surprise. Until this time, she'd struck me as a sullen girl who just wanted to get home. She'd opened up a bit over the past four days and finally confessed that she didn't like her home all that much but had no alternatives. Apparently, she found one.

John had been widowed the past year and was definitely looking. Willingness was more important than either beauty or brains so he had no difficulty in courting Beulah instead of Katie or Miranda. The deal we all struck was to live in the store—little more than a trading post—while John courted Beulah over the winter. His own farmhouse was located a mile away but there was a room in the store where we could stay and we would handle customers and trading if he was not there. Once Miranda revealed that she had been a shopkeeper in Baltimore and was intending to set up shop in Omaha, John almost changed his attentions to her. Miranda did not have to repel his advances. Beulah stepped between them at every opportunity. The girl was determined.

As we huddled together on a straw bed that night, Beulah turned on Miranda.

"I will keep your secrets, witch," she said. "I bear you no ill will and thank you for your rescue of us. But if you step between John and me, I will kill you."

"Beulah, I do not plan to be here longer than it takes the snow to melt in the spring. By that time, I hope you are wedded, bedded, and pregnant. That is a blessing on you, by the way, not a curse," Miranda said.

"How about you, Katie?" Beulah demanded.

"I expect I will part my legs for some man—or many men. But for now, I cast my lot with Miranda. If you will have me, demon mistress, I will serve you," the young girl said.

"Let us not talk of servitude," Miranda said. "Nor of parting your legs for many men. I will rejoice in your company when we move onward."

In the darkness of midnight with both girls sleeping, I arose and stepped outside. It was a still crisp night. Winter seemed far away but there were mountains between me and our destination. I knew that staying put was wise.

"Are you leaving me, Demon Ramie?"

I'm not a… Never mind.

"Friend Ramie?"

Friend Miranda. I can almost feel it. I've only an inkling of what draws me out of my body and into yours. I thought it was sex but the raven calls at any time.

"The raven."

I believe so. My pa said a redtail hawk would call him out of his body. Somehow it never occurred to me that a raven might call me from mine.

"'Once upon a midnight dreary, while I pondered, weak and weary, Over many a quaint and curious volume of forgotten lore—'" Miranda recited.

'While I nodded, nearly napping, suddenly there came a tapping, As of someone gently rapping,' I added in her mind. Everyone had to memorize "The Raven" in eighth grade.

"'Rapping at my chamber door.'" We saw a shadow cross the moon above us. "Hurry back to me, Friend Ramie."

Awkawkawkawk!

12
Aubrey

I WAS SURE Moms and Pa knew Aubrey was sleeping with Kyle. I don't know why she kept sneaking back into my room after they were done. It was Halloween and had been two weeks since I'd last traveled to visit Miranda. I wasn't as frantic this time as I'd been the last time I left her. She was safe for a while; I was sure.

Aubrey and Kyle were especially long and noisy that night. I couldn't help myself. I stripped and found I was already pretty juicy. It was damned near too cold to keep my window cracked open, but I saw the old raven out there. I was sure that when I came he'd call me. Seemed he liked watching me, the avian pervert. When Aubrey went off for the third time and I heard Kyle moaning like he was in agony, my orgasm ripped through me with such force I lay there in bed shaking for ten minutes. I'd kicked all the covers onto the floor and was still sweating.

The old raven nodded his head in appreciation but never said anything. I was still spread-eagle on my bed showing myself to God and everybody an hour later when Aubrey slipped in.

"Oh my God!" she said when she caught sight of me. "You look like an open invitation."

"You knocked me out," I complained without moving. "How do you stand it when you come like that? Aub, you're Superwoman." I didn't care if she looked at my body or even if she saw my dripping pussy. I was still sweating and reliving that incredible come. Aubrey dropped her robe and crawled across the bed toward me. I could feel my nipples tightening, looking at the feral expression on her face. She lowered her lips to mine and then our tongues met. The whole time she was dragging one of her big titties across mine and making my nipples ache. *Why did I never think of this when I suggested Kyle date her?*

"You taste funny," I said when we broke our kiss.

"Oh. Oops." She dropped her face and in the dim light, I was sure she was blushing. "Sorry."

"What?" I asked.

"Um... I gave Kyle a blowjob to send him off to sleep."

"A blowjob?" The horror dawned on me. "Aubrey! You fed me my own brother's sperm? Yuck!"

"No! I swallowed all of that. I just didn't think of rinsing the taste out of my mouth."

"Ew! Gross."

"Aw, it's not that bad."

"Well, if you want to kiss me afterward, rinse your mouth out first." She jumped up and ran to the refrigerator as I watched her cute ass bouncing in rhythm with her tits. She grabbed a bottle of water and rinsed her mouth out thoroughly. I still hadn't moved. She stalked back toward the bed.

"Now can I kiss you some more?"

"Oh hell, yes," I moaned. I really liked this kissin' stuff.

Somewhere in the middle of it, Aubrey threw her left leg over mine and pushed it up against my wet pussy. My hips sort of lunged forward when she made contact and I caught my breath. I felt her short hairs sliding up my thigh in the same rhythm. We'd woken up a few times holding each other, usually with one of us grabbing the other's breast. But this was the first time I looked straight into her eyes as I lifted my hand and felt the smooth soft skin of her tit yield to it.

"Is it okay, Rames?" she whispered.

"Your tit is perfect," I breathed back at her and caressed her lips with my tongue again.

"I mean... everything." There were tears in her eyes and I knew mine were running, too. I kissed her cheek as one escaped and ran toward her nose.

"As long as 'everything' means you're gonna make love to me. Yes, honey. It's so okay."

Saying that sent a shiver down my spine. I'd just asked my best friend—my brother's lover—to fuck me. I was almost seventeen years old and no one else had ever touched me down there. I could feel how slick my juices were making her thigh as she continued to slide it up and down my pussy. And I could feel the gentle scrape of her pubes

89

as she slicked up my side with her wetness. I caressed her breast and flicked her nipple a little as she whined into my mouth. Her fingers pinched at my nipples and I felt like a thousand volts of electricity connected my tit with my puss. We were no longer pretending to accidentally brush against each other, waking up in the morning holding a tit. We'd agreed to make love.

My heart was racing a few hundred beats a minute. I pressed my lips against Aubrey's and begged for her tongue in my mouth. I could feel her shaking against me—feel the pressure of her body lying on, moving against, mine. While her left hand played with my nipples, her right hand caressed my face and my hair. I squeezed her bottom and pulled her more tightly against me.

"Ramie?" Aubrey pulled back enough to look into my eyes, her brow furrowed and her lips quivering as she gasped for breath.

"Oh, Aubrey!" I screamed. I crushed her to me as my whole body convulsed. She cried out pushing hard against me.

Off in the distance I heard the call.

Awkawkawkawk. Knockknockknock.

Oh, go away, old crow.

IT WAS OUR first time that night, but not our last time. Aubrey rolled off me far enough that I could breathe. She kept her leg across me, though.

"God, Ramie, that was as good as getting my cherry popped. I love you!"

"I love you, too, sweetheart. You came on my hipbone. Didn't that hurt?"

"No. It was just right. Just enough pressure." I slipped my hand down between us and ran it through the slippery fluid. I brought my hand to my nose and sniffed. I put my tongue out and licked my fingers.

"You always use a condom with Kyle, don't you?" I asked.

"Yeah. We ain't stupid. Why?"

"I just wanted to make sure that I wasn't going to get a mouthful of his come when I lick your pussy," I giggled.

Aubrey moaned.

IT WAS JUST dawn and I cuddled against my new lover. We were exhausted. I held her close. I was so afraid she'd disappear and I'd find out it was all a dream or that I'd get tugged out of my body again and end up in 1865. I'd begun to love Miranda, but I was in love with Aubrey. We kissed again and almost far off I heard that raven call again.

Awkawkawkawk. Knockknockknock.

Well, there went that theory. I thought every time he called I got sucked out of my body, but that was the second time tonight. There was something different about it, though. Maybe it was a different raven. They have a lot of different caws but I'd never heard Blackfeather use the knocking noise before. I could feel a little tug but it was like overhearing a conversation and knowing it wasn't me he was talking to. I snuggled back against Aubrey and we finally went to sleep.

KYLE WAS ANTSY as a wild mustang when we finally dragged ourselves in to breakfast. Make that lunch. Moms were looking at the three of us with their eyebrows in their hairlines. The brats were snickering. Pa grabbed his sandwich and told Kyle he needed help on a stretch of fence Jess had reported was damaged. I was still eating when I heard the tractor start up and saw Kyle and Pa through the kitchen window. Kyle was looking back toward the house as he and Pa headed out.

"Kids," Mom Mar said to Phile and Caitlin, "they're going to be working on that stretch of fence on the north side of the rescue pasture. Get out there and make sure the horses stay away from where they're working. They'll come right to you instead of investigating that downed fence." We all pushed our chairs back and started clearing the table.

"You. Sit," Mom Ash said, pointing at Aubrey and me with both index fingers like six guns. *Oh shit.* Caitlin and Phile hustled up and left the kitchen without clearing their plates. Mom Mar never said anything to them.

"Moms?" I said.

"You have a little brother and sister," Mom Ash lectured me. I nodded. "Close your damned window at night!" Aubrey looked at me and started giggling.

"Um… sorry," I said.

"Girls, I guarantee you that there is nothing you did last night that the two of us haven't done," Mom Mar said blushing. "But you've got to have some consideration for others. Caitlin and Phile don't need that education. They're thirteen years old. And how is Kyle going to take this?"

"We were going to talk to him right after lunch but Pa hustled him off," I complained.

"Are you breaking up with Kyle?" Mom Ash asked Aubrey.

"No ma'am. We um…"

"I know you've been lovers for months," Mom Ash said. "Even with windows closed, you can't hide things like that from parents. But this opens a whole new can of worms when it comes to relationships. We didn't just fall into our relationship by accident. I knew what was between your pa and Mary Beth before I joined in. I talked to both of them, separately and together."

"And we aren't brother and sister," Mom Mar continued. "How are you going to handle that? You're not planning to sleep with your brother, are you, Laramie?"

"No! Gross!"

"Mary Beth? Ashley?" Aubrey said weakly. "You want me to go away? I don't want to hurt anybody." There were tears in her eyes and I put an arm around her and hugged her.

"Don't be ridiculous, girl. We're not upset about your relationship with either Kyle or Ramie. It's the relationship with both of them that has us concerned," Mom Ash said. "We should have talked to all of you sooner but…" Mom Mar and Mom Ash spent a long time looking at each other. I wondered if, when I'd been intimate with somebody for as long as they had, I'd be able to communicate silently with my partner like they seemed to do. "Well," Mom Ash continued, "last time we tried to communicate with you like that you told us we'd gone crazy."

"We're pretty stupid kids, aren't we," I sighed.

"No you're not stupid," Mom Ash said. "You just don't have the life experience you need to make good choices all the time. And you don't get the life experience except by making bad choices. Kyle will be back later this afternoon and the three of you have to talk together. Now you've got chores to do and you slept the entire morning away."

"And you, young lady," Mom Mar turned on Aubrey and the girl shrank into my arms.

"Yes, ma'am?"

"You'd better start calling us Mom Mar and Mom Ash like our other kids do," Mom Mar finished. Both moms wrapped their arms around us and held us tight.

"You ain't invited to watch us," I said firmly. We didn't manage to get together until after dinner. Turned out that stretch of fence all had to be replaced for close to a hundred yards and there were rotted posts, too. Kyle and I would have to ride all the fences on a regular basis if we were going to board horses this winter.

"Hell, just listening to the two of you last night was enough to give me a come so powerful it knocked me out. I don't know if I could take watching you."

"Well, it serves you right," I laughed. "God knows I came often enough listening to you two."

"I reckon you could *try* to sneak a peek," Aubrey said with a bit of devil in her eyes. "You could learn a few things from your sister."

"Aubrey! You teach him. I am not doing demos!" I kissed her and then she turned to Kyle and he kissed her. I sighed. It was sweet.

"Aubs, honey, could you give me and Ramie a couple minutes? I need to talk to her about something else. Ranch business," Kyle said.

"Sure. I'm going to go take a shower. Probably the only time I'll be touching my own body all night!" She giggled, gave each of us a quick peck, and scurried off to my apartment to take a shower.

"What is it, Kyle? I already put down that we need to ride those fences at least once a week."

"You were there!" he hissed. Oh. Not really ranch business.

"Of course I was there. I was screaming as loud as Aubrey."

"Not there. You were in D.C. the night we tried to stop the assassination." *What? Why would he want to talk about that now? After denying it for so long.*

"That was months ago, Kyle. You wouldn't even talk to me about it. Why are you bringing it up now?"

"Months? What the hell are you talking about? It was just last night. I don't know how you could keep caterwauling like that all night while you were time traveling just like me."

"Kyle? Last night?"

"Right in the middle of all of us coming, I got sucked out of my body into a young guy in Washington, D.C. It was Good Friday Morning, 1865. After all your projects on President Lincoln and Pa's lectures, you think I wouldn't recognize that date? Took me forever to get the bastard under control so I could get to Ford's Theater in time. Then you come and attack me right at the door and rassle me to the ground while John Wilkes Booth killed the president. Why'd you do that?"

"Fuck!" I sat there just thinking about what he'd said. For me that happened six months ago. All that time I thought he'd been denying being a time traveler and now, if what he's saying is true, he travels to find me in a place I was a long time ago. "Fuck, fuck, fuck. Kyle, this don't make any sense. I was there trying to save Lincoln. I thought you were Booth. But brother, I wasn't time traveling last night. I was losing my cherry to our girlfriend. For me, that all happened back on your birthday last spring." I shook my head. Hell, this was going to be so damned hard. Kyle was lost in his own world. I knew how much I hurt when he wouldn't talk to me about it. *But what should I do now?*

"Right when I was losing my cherry to our girlfriend," Kyle whispered.

"Yeah. That's what I said."

"No. It's what I said. You started traveling right when I was coming in Aubrey the first time. I started traveling right when you were—however you were doing it."

"Oh, damn. We're all out of sync." *What will happen if we keep going to the same places at different times?*

"I got an idea," Kyle said with a big grin. "Let's go make love to our girlfriend and see if anybody goes on an adventure tonight." I grinned at him. *Why not?*

13
Wolf

NEITHER OF us traveled. But what an adventure. We obeyed Moms and Pa and closed the windows, even though I had to turn off the heat. Seemed like it was either all on or all off. In a month or so, when it was snowing and cold, 'on' would be fine, but right now I wished for just a little fresh air.

Cold or not, that wall between our apartments was like paper. I swear I could almost smell Aubrey getting turned on. Then I pulled the covers up over my head and I really *could* smell her. *Oh yes.* That was way too warm, though, and I pushed the covers off me and sprawled out on the bed with my fingers flying over my clit. *Oh god, oh god, oh god. I want that girl.* By the time Aubrey left Kyle and came to me, I was lying in a pool of my own sweat and come. She walked through the door stark naked.

"Aubrey!"

"Why should I put my clothes on five feet away just to take them off again when I walk in here?" she asked. She came to the foot of the bed and looked up my body before she just fell forward with her face in my pussy and started licking.

"Yes!" I screamed. It hadn't been that long since my last orgasm and I was primed and ready to go when she started tickling my button with her tongue. She didn't let up and I just kept coming. I couldn't breathe. I pushed at her head and she kept on. And when I thought I was going to pass out, she clamped her lips over my clit and lashed it with her tongue again.

Then I did pass out.

IT WAS THE first time Kyle and I walked Aubrey to her door together and both gave her a kiss that let her know we were serious.

"I think I am the luckiest girl in the world," she sighed. If she hadn't opened the door and gone in, we'd probably still be there kissing her.

Kyle started up as soon as we were in the car.

"Did you travel? Nothing happened last night. Well, nothing except me coming a quart listening to you two. But I didn't go anywhere! You been doing this so much longer than me. Did you go off last night? How does it work?"

"Kyle. Kyle! Stop! I didn't travel last night either. I haven't been off since Halloween night. We're way out of sync on this. The first two or three times I went, you two were having sex and I thought that was what was triggering it. And don't be embarrassed about listening to us. If you are, then I got to be embarrassed about all the times I rubbed one off listening to you. But then it happened and you weren't even home. I was just… masturbating. And one night I was just standing on the front porch and poof! I was gone. That's where you found me that night. I started thinking it was the raven that was calling me. But then, when I was with Aubrey, I heard the raven calling but nothing happened."

"God, Ramie! How many times have you been off time traveling without telling me?"

"Around once a month or so. But I tried to tell you. I saw you at Ford's Theater and tried to talk to you the next day. But you kept insisting that you weren't traveling so I quit talking about it."

"But how is that possible? You went back there six months ago and I went back to the same moment just two nights ago. Do we go back and forth?"

"I don't know, but I'll tell you this. You are going to get on a train in Baltimore headed for St. Louis. I'm getting on the same train—or my host is. You've got to follow that girl anytime she gets off the train and protect her, Kyle. You've got to."

"I'll do it if I can get him to. He doesn't just fade away and let me drive. I had a hell of a time convincing him to try to save the president."

"Kyle, I don't like this, but we gotta talk to Pa."

WE STOOD IN front of Pa's big chair in his office. He had Moms on his lap and they were all looking at us.

"Well? Did you talk?" Mom Ash demanded.

"Yes, Mom Ash. We're good," I said.

"Don't stop talking," Mom Mar said. "You've got to think of what will happen if she breaks up with one of you. You're still brother and sister, don't forget. You can't divorce each other."

"We'll talk about it all, Mom Mar. But it's going to take a long time to cover everything. We all agreed that we're just playing it by ear right now but we'd keep talking." I almost snorted when Kyle said, 'playing it by ear,' since we were listening to each other through the wall. "But Pa, we need to talk to you."

"About time travel," I added. Pa jumped so suddenly I thought he'd dump Moms on the floor. He grabbed hold of them and settled back down.

"Sit down," he said. "Can I assume that you don't think we're crazy any more?"

"Sorry, Pa. But it still feels like it could all just be a dream. Like one of those lucid dreams we read about," I said. I touched my throat where Harriet had tried to strangle me. It sort of felt sore even now.

"So. How long?"

"I started back in May. Kyle just started a couple nights ago."

"The gun?"

"Yeah. And the knife." I started crying. He was going to find out. I was so ashamed. Kyle put his arm around me but he'd hate me, too. There was nothing to do but get it over with. "I killed three men, Pa."

I was wailing. Moms were closing in on us hugging from both sides. Pa was on his knees in front of me holding my hands.

"It's okay, baby girl. It's not you. It's not you." Kyle squeezed me so hard I thought he'd break my shoulders. "I remember the first time my host killed a man while I was in his body. I retreated and stayed silent for days. You just got to remember, it's not you."

"But it was, Pa. My host wasn't in control. They were gonna rape her."

"And you took on three at a time?" I shook my head.

"Two different occasions. First time it was just one guy who was going to grab her and put her on a trawler to ship to a brothel. It was his knife I grabbed and sliced him open." I gasped as I remembered his blood and guts spilling over my hand. "The second time, two men had kidnapped a bunch of girls and were hauling them west to Texas to be whores. I got loose because they never checked her boot for the knife. I raised a ruckus and one of them lifted the tarp to beat me and I cut his throat. The third one was sort of her. I had the knife at his throat questioning him and she moved the hand and cut him." I looked up into Pa's eyes could see his tears. "I don't *want* to believe it's real, Pa. If it is, I'm a killer."

"Ramie, you were saving your host's life. That doesn't make you a killer, it makes you a hero. Now let's try to set things straight and see what kind of help you really need."

We talked most of the night. Kyle didn't know about me killing men. Mostly, we talked about the mechanics of how time travel worked.

"I thought it was Kyle and Aubrey making love that triggered me to go," I said. "Then I thought it was just me masturbating. Then it seemed like I had a connection with that old one-eyed raven that hangs around and he was making me travel."

"That sounds like the most likely," Pa interrupted. "For me it was a redtail hawk that kept showing up at the most inopportune times. When he called, I left."

"Yeah, but then the other night I heard him calling and I didn't go," I said.

"Is that the night Kyle went?" Mom Ash asked. I creased my brow and nodded. "Cole?"

"Anything is possible," Pa answered. "We've got half the known time-travelers ever sitting in this room. The other three are dead. For me, it was always very specific. I'd see him or his shadow, he'd screech, and I'd jump between times. All I can say is to try to be aware of when it happens next and keep building your data. And watch each other's back."

"Thanks," I said. I might have sounded a little grumpy. "Any other advice?"

"Yes. Don't try to change anything. You can't do it."

"What do you mean, Pa?" Kyle asked.

"History is history. We already know what happened. You can't change it. I don't mean it's against the rules. I mean it can't be done." I looked at Kyle. Pa caught it. "You already tried, didn't you?" We nodded. "What?"

"We tried to stop President Lincoln's assassination," I said.

"You could have got yourselves killed!" Pa said. "What happened?"

"Neither of us knew the other was there. We stopped each other," Kyle said.

"You're damned lucky. If it's already happened and we know about it, don't bother to try to change it. You can only hurt yourselves."

"What's the use of time traveling?" I asked.

"It's all the things that are still in the box," Pa said. "Look up Schrödinger's cat. You've got computers. History is an open box. We know what happened, or at least what the result was. But there are lots of questions that are still unknown. They are still in the box. Until you open it, you don't know if the cat is alive or dead. Those are the things you can affect. You can affect the kind of people your hosts are, too. I know Kyle Redtail was a lot mellower after I started visiting. You can influence what kind of people your hosts are or become."

THE ONE THING definite was that whatever happened, we weren't in control of it. It was hard to accept that, especially not knowing who *was* in control. It didn't make a difference. With or without Aubrey, we weren't traveling.

I studied up as much as I could on the routes from Tennessee to St. Louis. I'd ordered a bunch of USGS topographical maps online and plastered them all over my walls. Nobody much came into my room and when Aubrey looked at them, she just assumed they were Wyoming maps. I practiced with Merv Longsteer twice a week on my knife work. While Kurt had some legitimate work for the three of us, he spent a good bit of time working with me on how to quickly load and safety the old Colt Navy. Kyle liked what he saw and chose a Colt Army .44 caliber repro to start practicing with. Aubrey rolled her eyes and minded the store while we were at the practice range.

She practiced with her gun, though, especially on Saturday morning when we all had practice out at the ranch now. We'd hit a rhythm and she came out to the ranch almost every Friday night and went home on Sunday. I wasn't traveling, but I was really liking this sex thing.

THIS SATURDAY WAS going to be special. It was my seventeenth birthday. Thanksgiving was as late as it ever gets this year, which meant my birthday was the weekend before. We had a family meeting when the hunting lottery rules came out and all went down to pay our fee and enter the drawing, but we'd decided that we wouldn't be taking any deer or elk this year regardless. There just weren't enough with the rate the wolves were killing them.

Since there wouldn't be a hunting trip this year, Aubrey and I were pretty lazy getting started Saturday morning. She made me lie back and do nothing while she gave me her 'birthday special.' After that, I didn't want to move. I was like a wet noodle. We finally called Kyle and all went in for breakfast. We weren't really doing anything but sitting at the kitchen table and laughing about me being so old.

Phile and Caitlin came bustin' into the kitchen at a dead run.

"Ma, Pa! We hear wolves down in the bottomland. It's got all the horses spooked!" Caitlin yelled. "They were galloping toward the river." That was all we had to hear. Kyle and I were running one direction and Pa and Mom Ash were headed the other. Mom Mar grabbed Aubrey and held her in her seat.

"Sit. Caitlin and Phile, you stay out of this," Mom Mar commanded. "Stay in the upper pasture with the work horses and keep them calm. Take your rifles, but do not head down to the lower pasture. Cole, Ashley, Kyle, and Ramie will coordinate their search and don't need the distraction of you kids. Protect the stock up here." With that, Mom Mar was on the phone to the cattle hands to alert them.

Kyle and I grabbed our parkas and rifles. I saw Pa come out the back door fastening on his Smith and Wessons. Mom Ash held two rifles. Kyle and I hopped two three-wheelers and the parents loaded in the four-wheeler. Pa motioned that we should head straight for the pasture and they'd circle around above the ridge.

The horses were nervous and gathered in a circle at the water's edge when we reached the pasture. There was no question they sensed something. It takes a strange kind of wolf to attack a herd of horses. Cows are more to their liking. You can cut a cow out of a herd, or more likely a calf, and run it down pretty quickly. Horses don't respond the same way. They know those tricks. They don't run away as easily or break the herd. Still, there was something wrong. You could sense it.

I looked around, standing up on the three wheeler. The only thing I saw was that old raven with one cloudy eye, sitting up on top of the shelter looking south. I motioned Kyle to follow the river and I headed out below the lower ridge toward the pond.

At the west end of the watering hole, as I rounded an outcropping, my heart jumped into my throat. One of the four horses Kyle and I brought back this summer was stranded with his back feet slipping on the frozen mud. He was still pretty skinny and the big wolf that faced him was pacing back and forth waiting for the horse to make a bad move. Just one wolf?

"Oh, no, you don't," I growled to myself. I grabbed my rifle and steadied it against the handlebars of the three-wheeler. I had to kill the engine to keep it from vibrating. I was a good hundred yards away, but I didn't dare try to get closer. I didn't have time. I drew down on the wolf and squeezed the trigger.

I saw the impact and the wolf roll in the air as it leapt toward the old horse. Then everything happened at once. I heard a snarl above me and saw a second wolf at the top of the ridge about ten feet above me. I swung my rifle around as the bitch sprang at me. I knew I was going to be too late. That old raven swooped in between us screaming *Awkawkawkawk*. I heard the rifle go off and felt the weight of the wolf as her teeth hit my throat.

Then I wasn't where I was any more.

14
Husband and Wife

"I WILL NOT wear breeches," Miranda croaked. I could still feel the wolf's teeth at my throat and realized Miranda's voice had truly been damaged by Harriet when she attempted to strangle us. It had been beautiful and lyrical but now was harsh and raspy.

"I am just telling you that it ain't safe for two girls to go alone through this country. You should pretend to be boys. These buckskins could be cut to fit you and you would look like a couple country boys out to seek your fortune," John said.

"It is uncouth."

What's going on, Miranda?

"You've chosen a fine time to return. I thought you'd left us."

Well, I did just leave, but I can't control when I come and go.

"Why now?"

Why? I... Oh God!

"Take not the name of..."

I know, I know. Miranda. No. No.

I couldn't put it into words but I knew. I knew that it had to be. Miranda's continuing pain would be a constant reminder to me of the wolf's teeth on my throat. I couldn't have survived.

I think I'm dead.

"Lord have mercy," Miranda said aloud. "Excuse me. I must walk alone for a few minutes." She left the little store and headed for the barn, passing Katie on her way. She simply waved the girl away. When we were behind the barn she stopped and we wept.

The wolf. There is no way I could have survived with her teeth on my throat. I heard the raven cry as I felt her hit me and I was gone. My poor brother. My poor Aubrey. My poor parents. I'm dead.

"You cannot be dead. You *must* not be dead."

I don't think there is anything I can do about it.

"But if you are dead and you are in me... Then it is... Forever. I must share my body with you and my mind. I will never be me again. I will go insane."

No, Miranda. Even if I have to silence myself and ride without ever thinking a thought, I will not force you to bear me like that. Just please give me a little time before... before...

"It is May and we are preparing for our departure to the north. I can always use your help, it seems, when we are traveling. Truly, Friend Ramie, I wish you no harm. I have been angry with you for leaving me and now I am angry that you have returned. It makes no sense, but my heart has thrown these thoughts at me. Let us try to help each other for a while."

Miranda, please be my friend. I don't have anyone now.

I WAS SO self-absorbed that I scarcely noticed the activity going on around me. I could see no way that I could have survived the wolf attack. I couldn't have moved my rifle far enough to hit her. I'd felt her teeth on my throat and Miranda's sore throat was a constant reminder. Why didn't anyone prepare people for the truth about dying? You just get ripped out of your body and planted in someone who doesn't want you there, with no friends and no family.

As we worked putting bundles in the wagon, tears kept flowing down Miranda's cheeks and I couldn't tell if they were hers or mine. I'd heard how, when people lost a loved one, they regretted harsh words and unsaid feelings. But that was supposed to be the regrets of the living. I was dead. I didn't tell my family how much I loved them. Didn't tell them often enough. Now it was too late.

John was a good man and was happy with his new wife. Beulah was already rounding in pregnancy and did her best to emphasize it by the way she stood and walked. And as far as I could tell, she was happy. John stopped frequently in the day to pat her tummy. He had also decided that he would help us on our way as much as possible. We were not equipping to homestead as we intended to catch up with Miranda's family. But we needed to travel and to camp. Victuals, blankets, and tarps for shelter were among the things he stocked for us. He also gave us a wooden box with firing caps for the pistols and a horn of powder. I found a shot pouch filled with lead balls lying on my bedroll.

That got me thinking, though. The pistols would be handy for protection if we were close. I had no confidence in my own ability to hit a target more than twenty feet away and was reasonably certain Miranda had not been target practicing. If we needed to hunt for food, the Colt Navies would be useless.

We need a rifle.

"Really? I can't even shoot these sidearms you insist I carry. Why must we have a rifle?"

A rifle is easier to shoot and more accurate than a revolver. We might need to shoot a deer in order to survive.

"I hate this. Demon Ramie, you must talk about this with John. I simply cannot."

We went to see John and I told him what I thought. He nodded.

"I see the point. I would like to help you but rifles do not fall from the sky like raindrops." He stopped and thought a minute, looking at my slight frame and shaking his head. "Well, there is one." He dug around behind a barrel and came out with a long gun. It would reach from the floor to my armpit. "I don't want to say where I got this damn Yankee rifle. And do not tell anyone where you got it. In fact, you should carry it out of sight. It is a cartridge rifle. You load it on Sunday and shoot it all week. That should be suitable for your needs. It takes a .44 cartridge but I believe the sighting is catawampus."

"I cannot simply accept this as a gift," I said. "It is a fine rifle." I'd seen a reproduction in Kurt's store, though I'd never fired it.

"Indeed. I have coveted your Colt Navies. I will trade you one for one. With one condition," he said. I contemplated the benefit of giving up one of the Navies in trade for the Henry. It seemed like a good trade.

"The condition?"

"Wear the buckskins I gave you and travel as a boy. I do not fancy sending you into the wilderness to be raped and enslaved." Miranda struggled to regain her voice, but she'd given me control to negotiate the trade and I wasn't giving it back.

"It is acceptable," I said. He slapped a box of .44 Henry rimfire cartridges on the counter and I removed one of the gun belts. I took the rifle and cartridges to the back room where Katie and I had slept for the past eight months and began stripping off Miranda's dress.

Stop! Demon Ramie, I will not wear trousers! No lady would ever wear them.

"Miranda, hush. The rules have all changed. Hell, just look in the mirror." It was a small glass and I moved it up and down to show her naked body to her. I blushed in spite of myself. "Damn it, Miranda, *I'd* do my best to get between your legs. These buckskins will hide some of your womanly charms so that one day perhaps your husband will have the pristine joy of you. Now put the damned pants on." She stopped fighting me and I slid the buckskins up over my legs. They were soft and felt good going up our thighs. The shirt dropped over my breasts and we felt our nipples rub against the sensuous material for the first time. At least the shirt hid a bit of her shape.

What about Katie? She is a woman and just as pretty.

"She can travel as our sister or wife. Whatever."

As soon as I was dressed, I took the rifle to the wagon. Like many wagons, it had gun clamps under the seat. I had trouble getting the rife to fit correctly and ended up lying on my back on the floor looking up at the bottom of the seat. I could see the problem right away. Sliding the rifle in knocked the hammer up against a metal box strapped beneath the seat. I worked the box free of the straps that held it and nearly killed myself as it fell on my shoulder.

"Ow! What have you done to me?"

You're back in control again, I see. Are we cooperating?

"Yes. What is this? It is heavy." We pried the latch open on the box and opened it to reveal a small fortune in gold coins.

That is our passage to your new life, Miranda. You are no longer dependent on finding your family in order to survive.

"They are twenty dollar gold coins."

Double eagles. I estimate about a hundred of them. Remove two and let us put the rest back where we found them. Now that I see what was obstructing things, we can reverse the position of the rifle and it will fit in the brackets.

"What are these two coins for?"

I don't like taking charity and the rifle John just gave us is worth twice the Colt Navy we traded. Not to mention the fact that he has supplied our journey. We'll just leave them on the counter for him.

THERE WERE MANY tearful goodbyes in the morning when we left. Beulah came in from the ranch and hugged Katie and Miranda, thanking them for understanding what she wanted and not getting in the way of her claiming John as her man. From my limited dealings with him, I felt confident that he was a good man and would treat her well, so I felt no qualms about leaving her behind. I sadly noted that it was the eighteenth day of May when we departed the little Tennessee trading center. My brother's birthday, only a century and a half before he was born. My only hope was that since he was time traveling, I would someday meet him in the body of his host, the corporal.

A rutted wagon road was the best route to where John said there was river traffic. He had been helpful planning our journey. There was a sometimes ferry almost due west of the trading post, but John was of the opinion the river was too high this early in the spring for that ferry to run. At Dyersburg, though, there was steamboat traffic and a ferry that could accommodate our two horses and wagon would be more likely. He tried to give us money for the ferry, but we gently refused and said we'd make our way. He'd be surprised to find the gold coins on his counter.

Miranda was sullen as we left. Katie took the reins and competently guided our wagon. I understood. Miranda's throat hurt, as did mine. Okay. It was the same throat, but hers was partially crushed by the madwoman we rescued over six months ago. Mine bore the emotional scars of wolf's teeth. What is more, I caught a flash of movement through the trees east of our wagon road. She did not fight me as my fingers closed on the grip of the revolver but the wolf that haunted me did not materialize.

In spite of the fact that John considered this the "main road" north, it was little more than two ruts that did not quite match the width of our wagon wheels, so we constantly slid out of one and into the other. We could have walked much faster than the horses pulled the wagon, but the horses and wagon would be valuable as we made our way west. Miranda was convinced that we would not find her family in St. Louis as it was only to be a winter stop-over before they started for Omaha. That just added to her foul mood.

Eventually, Katie pulled the horses off the road into a copse of trees where we could make camp for the night. Our travel days would be short. The horses needed to be rested and we needed time to make and break camp each day. We were not just traveling, we were living on the road.

"Miranda," Katie said as we heated jerky and potato soup over the fire, "you still look like a girl."

"So I have teats," she answered with a touch of venom. Miranda was still not happy about dressing in the buckskin trousers. Not to mention the fact that the large shirt had been rubbing against her nipples all day and she didn't know what to do with the feeling.

"It's not your teats that is the problem," Katie continued calmly. "It is your hair." Miranda looked at her in horror. "I believe that to maintain our charade we must cut your hair."

"You vile girl! You think that you will make a man of me. No woman cuts her hair until married. I have tied it in a knot and put it under this ghastly canvas hat. That is adequate."

"That is part of the problem," Katie persisted. "Miranda, you are a beautiful woman and nothing done to your hair will stop that. With it all pulled up under your hat, you show your elegant neck. No one would mistake that for a man. Many of the mountain men we saw at the trading post had hair cut at their shoulders. With such a cut, you would hide your neck without showing the long tresses of a maiden. Miranda, I am frightened that anything we might do would give us away before you have reached your family."

You should listen to her. She makes sense.

"My hair? You have taken away my shape, my voice, and now my hair? I am no woman."

You are all woman. Miranda, it is for our safety and will make travel easier.

Miranda lifted her pants leg and pulled the knife from it. For a moment, I feared she would do harm to herself. She was angry and hurt. Instead, she handed the knife to Katie and pulled off her hat. Her long auburn tresses fell from their pins and tumbled to her waist.

"Consider killing me instead of my hair, Katie Forster. I would prefer it," she said. Katie pulled the brush they shared from their bag of personals and began brushing Miranda's hair. Miranda sat silently with tears running down her cheeks. At last, Katie began cutting the locks just above the line of Miranda's shoulders. When she finished, she laid the knife in Miranda's lap and gathered the hair. It was better that she take it away before Miranda could see the long locks lying on the ground. Miranda continued to sit staring into the fire. I could not read her thoughts.

She ate mechanically from the plate Katie gave her and Katie cleaned the dishes and banked the fire. Darkness fell and still Miranda sat while Katie did the camp work. I was getting a little impatient with her. Katie spread our bedrolls and lay down.

"Come, husband. Lie down and sleep."

"I am not your husband!" Miranda screeched. Her voice hurt me to hear it. "I am not a man! I am not!"

"I cannot call you Miranda. What if someone heard?"

"Then call me by my Demon name," Miranda continued. She was completely out of control. "Henceforth I will be Ramie Lewis."

Miranda!

"Drive, Demon!"

I saw a flicker across the firelight and reached for the revolver at my side.

Awkawkawkawk!

Miranda's body went limp and I barely caught her before she plunged forward into the fire.

15
Alone

I WAS STILL here. I suddenly felt alone in Miranda's body. It was as if she'd taken a vacation and left me to housesit. I could feel her in all her memories—the furnishings of her mind—but I could not hear her. It was disorienting. Even at times when I'd taken or been given control of Miranda's body, she was always there. Sometimes she fought me for control. Sometimes she was just standing by to take it back. Now, it felt like I was in my own body.

My own body. My own dead body.

What if Miranda had been sent to die in my stead? *No!* I begged old Blackfeather not to sacrifice her for me. *Please, no!* But there was still silence. I saw no sign of the black bird.

I SLEPT THE night beneath the blanket Katie offered to share with me. I awoke with her hugging my back. I tested Miranda's memories and found this had not been uncommon over the past few months. Miranda often awoke with the younger girl tight against her.

I gently pulled away from Katie and went to the bushes to relieve myself of my morning dew. *Oh my!* Miranda certainly had creative expressions that suddenly were mine to access. She had giggled with Theresa one morning about having to use a privy for their morning toilet and I realized that Miranda had often awakened in the few short weeks they had been together with Theresa hugging her back. It was not only a comfort to the two younger girls, but to Miranda as well.

I wanted that comfort. I was trapped in a foreign world and feared for the life of my host. My own, I was sure, was gone.

When I returned to camp, I stirred the coals and managed to get the fire restarted. I threw a rasher of bacon into the frying pan and hoped there was something in our packs to serve with it. Katie rose and slipped away. When she returned she poured a ladle of water into a pan and measured some cut oats into it. I was instantly grateful that there would be bacon grease to season the tasteless mash.

"Katie," I whispered through my painful voice, "I will walk beside the wagon for a while this morning. There is no sense in the horses having to pull us both through this muck."

"We can take turns, Mi... Ramie Lewis."

"We will see," I said. I tried my best to mimic Miranda's way of talking. I would have to remind myself often not to use contractions or twenty-first century slang. I didn't want to leave Miranda with questions to answer when she came back.

She had to come back. She had to.

When I started walking in the morning, I pulled off my shoes and went barefoot. Shoes were precious and we would travel 300 miles before we could reasonably expect to replace them. Miranda's shoes with their high-top laces were also likely to give away the fact that I was not really a man. I thought about what it would take to make moccasins. Once we were across the river, I would have to hunt and kill a deer. Then we would have to tan the hide and smoke the meat. That meant we would need to be camped for a week or more. It would not be a fast trip.

The next section of the road was the worst we'd encountered. For perhaps a mile, Katie removed her shoes and walked ahead, pulling the horses through the mud as I leant my support in pushing the wagon until we forded a stream and the land began to rise. It was a drier stretch of road, but we were so exhausted that we camped. We used the opportunity to wash the horses' legs and check their hooves before tethering them for the night.

As I made a fire and gathered wood for the night, Katie took the kitchen knife and disappeared for half an hour. She returned with a basket of bark. I smiled at her.

"What have you there, Katie girl?"

"Slippery elm," she said. "If you can start a kettle of beans, I will work on making something that will soothe your throat."

Katie was quite the pioneer woman. I knew she had experience with animals and she watched critically as I checked the horses' hooves earlier. Miranda had known nothing about animals. But Katie was showing her skill in other ways now. Knowledge of herbs was something I didn't know about her. Well, I certainly would not complain if she could relieve my throat. And if she poisoned me... so much the better.

She didn't. In fact, the tea she made was soothing and relaxing. After we had finished our meal and cleaned our utensils, we crawled into the bedroll together, weary as we could be.

"Will you hold me tonight, husband?" she whispered. I started to protest about not being her husband and realized it was Miranda's left-over sensibilities that I was expressing. In fact, I looked forward to holding the girl through the night and did just that.

As hard as Katie worked and as domestic as she seemed to be, she did not like rising in the morning. And so, when I awoke with her little breast snuggly in the palm of my hand, I did not rush to release it.

Is this what Aubrey feels when she holds my little tits in the morning when we wake up? They are so small—so different from her bosom. My own—or Miranda's—breasts were much bigger than Katie's, though I guessed that Katie was still growing and if I got her settled someplace where she had adequate food, she would fill out.

Those thoughts disturbed me and I crawled out of the bedding and made my way to our toilet. *My poor Aubrey.* If I ever returned to her I would show her how much I loved her. And I would hug my brother until he couldn't breathe. I needed them so much. My only hope was that he would find me in this life and at least tell our parents and Aubrey that I loved them. And in this life, if I could find and love that corporal, I would hold him whether my brother were present or not.

That thought startled me until I realized that I was reflecting Miranda's own memories of her time on the train talking to Corporal Jason Wardlaw. She was already smitten. I wondered why he had not escorted her on that fateful afternoon when she was kidnapped.

AND SO, MY new life in Miranda's body progressed. Each day I woke either wrapped in Katie's arms or with her wrapped in mine. We worked well together and broke our fast and then our camp. We walked alongside the horses in companionable silence or with Katie chattering about the various plants and herbs she spotted along the way. She often ran to collect some as I led the horses on.

In another week, we crested a rise and saw the town of Dyersburg a mile away. We decided to camp early and make our way into town the next day. We would try to find passage across the river.

"You have changed, Husband Ramie," Katie whispered in my ear that night. "Miranda is gone, is she not? You are the Demon Ramie that has taken her body." Katie shivered against me but did not move away. I wanted to deny and tell her she was foolish, but there was a yearning in my heart to let her know the whole story. I settled for a compromise.

"You must never say things like that, Katie dear. And you must accept that there may come a time when you wake up and realize that it is just Miranda sleeping beside you. You are a good girl. Please protect us the way you have always done."

"I have told you before, Mistress Demon, if you will have me, I will serve you. However you wish, I am yours."

"Katie… Katie, do not take service to me too seriously. But I will take you in my care and treat you well. Do you the same for me."

It was the first night that Katie and I slept facing each other in our embrace.

I PREFERRED NOT to pull out twenty dollar gold pieces to pay for our passage across the river. For one thing, I had not told Katie of our treasure. For another, I feared it would draw suspicion toward us. Katie and I pooled the coins in our purses and after some considerable searching, found a man who poled his barge across the river about once a week to ferry people and goods to the other side. He asked two dollars for each person and horse and another dollar for the wagon. We would leave on Monday.

That left us the weekend and we chose to camp at the edge of town rather than take a room at the hostelry. Late that night, I slipped out of the bedroll and pulled the strongbox from its straps under the seat. I would not offer the ferryman a double eagle, but shopping at the local mercantile was a different matter. We needed some serious supplies before we headed across Missouri.

I SPENT SOME time in the morning smudging my face with loam and then brushing it off. When Katie realized what I was doing, she helped and it was she who thought of brushing it with our soft hairbrush. When we were finished, she inspected me thoroughly.

"It looks like just a dark shadow across your cheeks and chin," she said. "From a distance you simply look to have a dark beard that has been carefully shaved. Near, it is difficult to tell if it is whiskers or dirt. Either way, you look more manly."

"You are a sweetheart," I said and gave her a quick kiss on the cheek. She stood there looking at me and blushed. I wiped a bit of dust from her cheek and smiled at her. "I am going to barter for some things at the mercantile. We need more supplies. Stay here with the wagon and the camp. I'll collect you later and we'll take the wagon to pick up the supplies."

"Where will you get money to buy supplies?" she asked. I simply furrowed my brow and scowled at her. "Forgive my impertinence, Husband Ramie," she whispered. "Just please be careful and come back for me." I nodded and set off for town.

When we first set off, I expected that we would go straight north to St. Louis, or as straight as possible. But we could not reach the city before late summer at the rate we were traveling. Miranda's family would be long gone toward Omaha. I hatched a new plan to cut across the state and try to intersect with them in Kansas City. It would be a long haul, but if we were diligent I was sure we could cross Missouri northwesterly to catch them. I'd promised Miranda in effect that I would do my best to find and protect Theresa. I would do so.

To make that trip, however, we needed more extensive supplies than what we'd acquired from John. I was determined that we would travel hard for five days and camp for five days in order to rest, hunt, and take care of domestic needs like baking bread. Miranda knew as much about the practical side of a kitchen and household as Katie knew about horses and herb lore. Together, we could do this.

"My wife and I leave across the river on Monday morning. We will have a rigorous journey and I require supplies," I said to the shopkeeper. My croaking voice, though it hurt, was a benefit to my disguise as a man.

"And how would you be paying for these supplies," asked the clerk.

"I sold my father's farm in Mississippi to a carpetbagger for a double eagle," I said. "Surely that will supply a wagon for such a journey." He nodded. He was apparently experienced in supplying wagons because he had a list on the counter of what he thought we would need. I checked it and said no to a couple of items and added a bit extra on a few others including a sturdy pair of boots for myself. I cut quite a picture in the store in buckskins and barefoot. I was sure to add a few peppermint sticks to the order to give my wife a treat. He tallied a total of sixteen dollars and twenty-five cents and looked at me questioningly. I dug in my pouch and produced the gold piece. He reached for it and I withdrew my hand. "Gather the supplies together. My wife and I will be by with our wagon shortly to load it and settle our bill."

When we had loaded the wagon and received the proper change for our coin, we stopped at the local butcher. There we bought a cured ham, a side of bacon, and one large, freshly cut steak. Then we went back to our encampment to wait out the weekend. We packed two potatoes in wet clay and then put them in the coals of the fire. After an hour, I charred the steak over the fire. Katie and I ate well that night and snuggled together beneath our blankets.

I'd been as circumspect as I could in town and Katie kept a shawl over her head the entire time we were there, but I was still watchful all weekend as we sorted and prepared our wagon for the coming trip. I'd acquired an axe and a saw, several yards of hemp rope, another knife, and a new flint and steel as well as flour, oats, honey, dried fruits and vegetables, and salt. The wagon was a good bit heavier when we had it loaded on Monday morning than it had been when we arrived on Friday.

Our crossing was uneventful and I gave the ferryman an extra two bits in thanks for his work. I felt generous.

JUNE SECOND FOUND us camped just southwest of the growing town of Campbell. We found a space near the St. Francis River Ferry where we could have privacy and be away from the raucous town of Campbell. I had no desire to take my wife into the town and we decided that when we had recouped from our week's travel, we would cross the river and then follow it north until we found a good passage west again.

It was here that I unstrapped the rifle from under the seat and set about to find us some meat. I needed a quick kill so we could cure the meat and hide and be on our way. Luck was with me that evening as I saw three white-tails come down to the river about a quarter mile from where we camped. I stilled my breathing and drew a bead on the buck. Just before I pulled the trigger, a gray streak came out of the brush, pinning the herd against the water. There was a flick of white tails and they took off. The wolf lunged at a small doe and brought her down with a piece missing from her neck.

God damned wolves! I shifted my aim and fired. The wolf turned and gave me a withering look. *Damn it!* John warned me the sights were catawampus on this gun. I levered another round into the chamber and before I could figure out how to adjust my sights, the wolf sprinted off into the woods. I heard a crashing through the brush behind me and in a minute Katie was approaching.

"Did you get it?" she asked breathlessly.

"Well, I ain't gonna leave it lie," I said. Katie looked at the fresh kill and the chunk out of its throat.

"No rifle did that."

"A wolf accidentally helped me. Keep an eye out in case he returns." I pulled out my knife and field dressed the doe, dumping the guts on the ground. I used a length of rope to tie the legs together so we could drag it to camp. I was surprised when Katie drew the kitchen knife and began hacking at the intestines. Once she had them free, she squeezed the crap out of them. She wrapped them in a ball and we dragged our prize back to camp.

We were up most of the night skinning and butchering the deer. We set up a drying rack under a canvas tipi and kept green wood on the fire all night. In the morning I cracked the skull and mashed the brains in a bucket in which Katie and I took turns pissing. I knew the theory of tanning a hide and had seen Pa do it to an antelope hide once, but I'd stayed pretty far away because it was so gross. I found the process had not improved as we scraped the skin and applied the brain and urine mixture, rubbing it in.

Katie scrubbed the guts, turned them inside out and scraped them, then scrubbed them some more. I finally realized she was making sausage casings. We didn't have a grinder, but she minced up all the meat we couldn't preserve in dryable strips, mixed it with salt and cornmeal, and packed it in the guts to make sausage. She was a good girl.

We slept in shifts for the next two days so that one of us was always tending the fire and watching for scavengers. Our camp smelled great for a while as the meat smoked. Then the stink of tanning took over. We would have to adjust our travel schedule for longer breaks if we were to tan hides at each stop.

The smell drew a different kind of scavenger. The ferryman showed up about the time we were finished drying the meat and packing the sausage.

"Reckon you'll want to cross the river with all this," he said gesturing vaguely at the wagon and horses. I nodded. "Haven't had fresh venison in a while. Been living off fish most of the spring. Reckon you got plenty, though."

I settled in to start bartering, drawing on Miranda's experience at the trading post last winter. Cash seldom crossed hands there. It was pricey in my mind, but in the end he settled for a third of the dried meat and sausage to get us to the other side. Wednesday we loaded the wagon and ferried it across, leaving Katie with the horses. I rode back with the ferry and we loaded the horses for the second trip across. It was less than a quarter the width of the Mississippi, even adding the two trips together. I didn't tip him. He had enough meat to eat for at least two weeks.

16
Pioneers

I WAS NO more equipped for the life of a pioneer than Miranda was—either mentally or physically. I didn't know half what was needed, even though I'd researched the USGS maps and the Internet non-stop while I was waiting to travel again. *I could use an Internet connection right now.* I wanted to talk to Kyle and thought about the number of nights we'd spent Skyping each other from our rooms. I missed Aubrey. I missed sex.

We met few people as we traveled. The region had been 'settled' for almost fifty years, but the population was sparse. Most people kept to themselves and when possible we camped near, or even in, the few small towns we passed. Most had no difficulty with us setting up our lean-to at the edge of town and getting water from the common well.

When people chatted with us, we kept to the story of being displaced from Mississippi and traveling to Kansas City to join my aunt, Dolly Lewis. I figured that no one would know Miranda's mother and if someone happened to know her, we'd be able to speak intelligently about what her plans were.

I underestimated the number of winding detours we had to take getting through the Ozark Mountains and around or across the many rivers and streams. I scouted during our pauses but still had to backtrack a couple of times. Through it all, I kept seeing the shadow of a wolf pacing us. Twice, I'd aimed the rifle at it and then found nothing there. I felt I was being stalked. Perhaps my spirit was not meant to escape the attack that killed me.

It took us two months to reach Springfield and we spent three glorious nights in a hotel. We even ordered a bath in our room. It was unheard of luxury for us. Katie insisted that I bathe first as the 'man of the house.' I laughed at her and before she'd finished scrubbing my back, I got her naked and in the tub with me.

We were both lean. My tits poked out more than hers. It was nice to set the girls free. I'd kept them from being obvious in my buckskins by binding them and padding the shoulders. That had the added advantage of protecting my shoulder a little when I used the rifle. The first time I'd used it, I was bruised for a week.

I was afraid that when Miranda came back to her body, she would like it even less than when she left. I refused to accept that she would not come back. The hardships of the road, pushing and pulling at the wagon, carrying water, and practicing with the Colt had hardened my muscles. Katie had hardened as well, but she was still a lithe girl. I guess that was why I got a little carried away when I was scrubbing her and spent more than enough time washing her breasts. Her hard little nipples poked into the palm of my hand and she leaned back against me.

"Do you wish to take your pleasure, husband?" she whispered. *Oh shit!* Over the months, we'd often hugged each other, given little kisses, and slept cuddled together on the hard ground. This wasn't the first time I'd caressed her breasts and I'd woken up in the night on more than one occasion to find her hand on mine. But that was just the companionship of the road. Wasn't it?

"Katie, sweetheart, as you can well feel, I am not really a man. I cannot give you that kind of pleasure. And I am not truly your husband."

"Yet, I know we have both found pleasurable sensations holding each other," she said kissing my cheek. "And I have found a way to enjoy my own company, though it embarrasses me to say it."

"Don't be embarrassed," I chuckled. "It is the world's oldest pastime. I am glad you have found pleasure in yourself on our long lonely journey." She turned her face and her lips met mine. In a few moments, our kiss had exceeded the fond pecks we had become accustomed to. She was inexperienced, but a quick learner when I touched her lips with my tongue. The caress of her hand on my breast sent shivers up my spine.

We got out of the tepid water and used the sheets provided for us to dry each other carefully. Then Katie led me to the bed and pulled back the blankets. She lay on her back with her legs slightly parted and beckoned to me.

"Come to me, husband. I am yours, Demon Ramie." *Miranda will kill me.* I lay with Katie and began kissing her with rising passion as our hands explored each other. I knew what turned Aubrey on but didn't depend on that. I sought out each of the places that caused a flush to deepen on Katie's chest and her breath to quicken. And at last I dipped into her thick bush and slid through her wet folds as she gasped into my mouth. Her prominent clit wasn't difficult to find and once I started to rub it she rose rapidly, moaning into my mouth as she stiffened and shook in her first orgasm administered by another's hand.

"Are you all right, Katie?"

"I love you, husband. I know one day we may take men to us, but you are my first love. Let me return to you what you have given to me." She covered my body with kisses, finding new ways to suckle my teats. The thinness and hardness of my body seemed to leave my nerves much closer to the surface. Everything tingled. I'd found the things that turned Miranda on by rubbing off an orgasm when I thought I was unobserved. I'd become pretty good at keeping quiet and not moving while I came with Katie holding my breast early in the morning.

When her fingers started exploring my pubes, she found me every bit as wet as I'd found her. I moved my hand over hers and guided her fingers to exactly the spot I liked best and lifted her lips from my nipple to my mouth. I held her tightly as she found ways to touch me that I had not tried and I kissed her passionately. *Oh yes!* My orgasm was building as I gripped her bare ass and pulled her to me. I screamed out, ignoring the way it ripped through my throat. My eyes were closed but I sensed the flicker at our open window.

Awkawkawkawk.

I'm sorry. I'm sorry. Please don't send me away again, Demon Ramie. I am so sorry. Please let me come home.

"Miranda?"

Demon Ramie. Dear sweet Friend Ramie. I am sorry I was angry. Please let me stay with you forever.

"You're back! Oh Miranda, I am so glad you have come back."

Katie, completely unaware of what was going on in my head, had redoubled her efforts on my pussy and my body was rapidly reaching its climax.

You have used my fingers in my privities to call me back. Oh, thank you, Friend Ramie. I feel the pressure and I feel... I am... Oh!

"Oh my god!" I gasped. I clasped Katie's head against my bosom where she was clamped down on my nipple as I shuddered through the orgasm. "That was so wonderful!"

Miranda had nearly passed out inside my head with the intensity of the climax. She was about to get another surprise.

"Don't freak out, honey, but those aren't my fingers in our privities."

What? But they are so... Who else...?

"Little Katie and I have been making love."

A woman? How? How did you even have time?

"Miranda, how long have you been gone?"

Just a few minutes. Maybe two hours at the most.

"Welcome to the world of time travel. It has been over two months here."

Two months? Two months of my life gone?

"Shh. Gentle, love. Look into your memories. You will discover all that has happened. All that I have done is in your memory now that you are back." I could feel her going back through the days as if she had been here living them. In turn, I felt her opening so I could see what she had been through in the past two hours of her consciousness.

I sat straight up in bed.

"Kyle!" I shouted as the image hit me from Miranda's memories. "Aubrey. Moms. Pa!" I felt Katie's grip tighten around me.

It was horrid. I awoke and opened my eyes. Pain bit into my throat and I was surrounded by strange beings. Some were only as big as my hand. And the boy with yellow hair. The black-haired girl lying next to me. A squawking noise and wild people breaking into the room. I was so frightened I passed out again. And then you... or Katie... you were calling me back into my body.

"My brother. My lover. You saw my family, Miranda. You woke up and saw my family. Do you know what that means? I'm not dead. I'm not dead!"

IT TOOK A bit to get our memories back into sync, all the time being held and crooned to by Katie.

"So you are back, Miranda," Katie sighed. Miranda was silent.

Answer her.

"Yes. Yes, Katie, dear. I have returned. I promise I am not the harridan that left you. I have been to the demon's lair and have seen the horrors that await me. Yet, I remember how kind you have been the past two months," Miranda said.

Horrors of my lair? Please!

"Then you know that I love your Demon Ramie. But I will not presume upon you. I am sorry that you found me in such a state," Katie said.

"Do not apologize, Katie," Miranda said. "As long as she is here, Friend Ramie will make the decisions. She will decide where we go, what we do, how I think, and how I feel. I surrender all."

Miranda, don't you want to drive?

"No, Friend Ramie. I could not have done what you have done the past two months. I will learn from you so that if you are forced to part from me again I can take care of your Katie."

It is still hard. But don't you see, Miranda? If I'm truly alive then I might be called back to my own body at any time. You might not be forced to share with me.

"But I will gladly share with you. The feeling of waking up and not knowing anyone or anything. I truly did not understand what it was like for you. I know your life is not a horror to you, but still, there was pain in your throat and captured souls dancing in a small box. I am so glad you are alive. Those who looked upon you love you. I could see it in their eyes but I was so overwhelmed. I am glad that you will one day go home as I have come home. If you take me, please treat me kindly. If you do not, I will miss you more than life itself."

Happy to be home or not, Miranda was still uncomfortable as Katie bound my bosom with a strip of cloth to flatten me as much as possible. "It keeps our titties from being rubbed erect all the time," I told Miranda. I dressed in the newly washed buckskins and strapped on my gun. More than any other thing, taking the gun off made me feel naked. We collected our wagon, checked through our belongings and turned north out of Springfield.

I explained my rationale for not going to St. Louis to Miranda as I engaged in a project to comfort my mind. Using the point of my knife, I carefully engraved my initials in the brass of the grip on my gun. I knew this gun in my heart. Kurt had let me handle it. The next time I did, I would know if this was all real or a dream.

We determined to push on as far toward Omaha as possible. As much as I wanted Miranda to take over her body again, she was mostly content to ride and watch. This road was more populated than those we had traveled across the southern part of the state. We passed or were passed by travelers in both directions. Most were local but some, like us, were headed to Kansas City to begin a trek westward.

I continued to practice with the revolver and occasionally made Miranda take over to draw and shoot. She was impressed with the fact that her body was strong enough to handle the gun, though we held it with both hands. Her accuracy was as good as mine. She saw the sense in the heavy padding I'd built into the chest and shoulders of the buckskins the first time the Henry bucked against us when we hunted.

Our hunting, too, had improved and we were now more experienced in treating and tanning the hides. We had two dozen good buckskin hides in the wagon that we could use for trade when we came into town. Katie was working on sewing moccasins for both of us. Though the boots I bought were sturdy, I wanted to save them for cold weather so I walked barefoot most of the time. Miranda's feet were hard and calloused.

Miranda took over control of her body to do the menial tasks at the campfire and to work on the hides. It was hard and back-breaking. She wanted to give me a rest. It took a while before she realized that even if my mind rested, we shared the same pain and exhaustion of the body.

We camped during our bleeding time of month, hiding well off the traveled roads so that we did not accidentally expose our predicament. That was when we hunted, smoked meat, and tanned hides. I tended to spend most of three days under a blanket sleeping before I felt like moving. I blamed Miranda. It was her body and there wasn't a tampon to be had.

EVERYTHING'S UP TO date in Kansas City. It was less than 200 miles from Springfield and the roads were better. Our gentle draft horses plodded along at a reasonable rate and we increased to about ten miles per day when we traveled. It was early September when we reached the city.

I took five gold coins to a local bank and had them changed to silver dollars. We divided these between Katie and me, and stashed some in our bedroll. We made our purchases, including passage across the Missouri River, without calling attention to our money. The next time we could make a similar transaction with reasonable anonymity would be in Omaha. We pushed on over ever-more-improved roads until we arrived in St. Joseph. It was mid-October and we needed to hunker down for the winter.

I found a room to let for the winter at a reasonable rate and went about looking for a job. Miranda stepped in.

"We are traders," she said. "We have skins and we can build up a stock of other goods. This is something I can do." I relaxed and went along for the ride as she drove.

"HUSBAND RAMIE, ARE you here?" Katie whispered in my ear as we cuddled in bed after we had bathed that night. Relieved from traveling, we had stripped off everything and washed our clothes, as well. Miranda receded at bedtime rather than embrace Katie of her own volition. I knew, though, that she was almost as fond of the girl as I was.

"I am here, Katie dear. What do you wish to say?" I felt her squirm against me and try to melt her small breasts into mine.

"Husband, you have not taken your pleasure since… Springfield. And my cunny aches for your fingers."

"Katie, I won't use you, but I will love you as you love me."

"Will it be all right? With Miranda?" I could feel Miranda raise an eyebrow in her mind. She was a little horrified but also fascinated. She'd had no relief since that first night, either. She knew it would be her body, but as long as I was driving she could acquiesce.

"I think it will be fine. Kiss me and hold me, darling. Let me love you."

Miranda had no trouble at all as our kisses heated up and Katie's talented fingers brought us off to two spectacular comes. I loved it when Katie fastened her lips around my nipple and began flicking it with her tongue as her fingers pressed against my clit. It was nearly enough to knock me out. But as soon as I'd caught my breath, I determined to give the girl even better than she'd given.

We kissed and she squirmed as I tickled her and licked her teats. She thrust her center up at me, begging me to touch her. Instead, I worked my way down her freshly bathed body and pushed her legs apart. When I dove between her thighs and licked through the hair that matted round her opening, she squealed and grabbed a pillow to muffle her delight. She had a strong, earthy scent and flavor and much to Miranda's fascinated horror, I licked it thoroughly. Katie went rigid, screaming into her pillow.

I don't know where that damned raven called from, but he jerked my soul right out of my body.

17
Alive

I COUGHED AND choked, gasping for breath. Strong arms went around me and held me. I was disoriented as I felt the soft mattress. Kyle was holding me. I grabbed hold of him and squeezed with all my strength.

"You're back!" he said. He rocked me back and forth.

"Well, I guess that worked," Pa said as he came into the room. Moms were right behind him.

"What worked?" I asked. Kyle reached toward me and lifted a necklace and a black feather off my chest. I looked down noticing my tits were barely covered by the sheet. "Teeth?"

"Canines from the one you shot and the one Kyle shot," Pa confirmed.

"You shot it? I thought I was dead. I thought I was never coming back. What day is it?"

"Wednesday," Mom Mar said, pushing Kyle out of the way and hugging me. "You had a bit of a concussion, but mostly you've been fighting the fever from infection. Doc Hawkins shot you full of antibiotics and said you'd come around soon."

"I feel… My throat hurts." I complained. Same feeling I'd had for the past four months as I worked to get Miranda's throat unbent. *Won't it ever go away?* Pa got to me and kissed me on the head and Mom Ash gave me a hug and touched my neck. I flinched. Mom Mar grabbed the mirror off my dressing table. She held it up to me and pulled away a gauze bandage. I saw a pair of angry red rips along my throat. They were closed but swollen.

"She was already dead when she hit you," Pa said. "Fortunately, her teeth just gouged you but she wasn't biting. They tested the body for rabies Monday and it was clean, so we just need to get you past the infection."

"Those teeth had your blood on them, Ramie," Kyle said. "Merv Longsteer came out and gave you a purifying ritual. That's the feather.

He made the necklace and said there was a spirit in you that needed to go home." I got dizzy. I wasn't dead. She could have ripped my throat open just from her momentum.

"Aubrey?" I asked.

"She went to school this morning to get our assignments and explain where we'd all been this week," Kyle said. "She hasn't left your side since we brought you home from the doctor."

"Neither have you," Mom Ash said. "Ramie, your pa and I were way too far away and at a bad angle to get a shot. Luckily your brother was in better position. We got you to the doctor and he told us to just keep ladling broth into you and make sure you woke up every couple hours. Your little brother made rabbit stew that he shared with you, even though I know he made it for Caitlin. That fever really knocked you out."

I WAS HUNGRY as the dickens but too weak and shaky to do anything but eat in bed and lie back exhausted. I wanted to see my horses but when the kids came in to hug me they assured me the horses were fine. They'd been out on the four-wheeler 'patrolling.' They were both hoping for a chance to shoot a wolf. Mom Ash tossed me a t-shirt so I could sit up in bed without exposing myself. That was the least of my problems.

Kyle sat with me while we waited for Aubrey to get back from school. "She'll probably be a little late. She hasn't been home all week and I'm sure her folks will want an explanation as to why she thinks she's spending Thanksgiving weekend here. I heard Pa on the phone, though, inviting her parents out for Thanksgiving with us all. One of us was always here with you, Ramie. Always."

"You still got my back, brother." He held my hand as I gathered my thoughts. "Kyle, you said I woke up every couple of hours. Did you notice… was there anything different about me?" I asked.

"Yeah, you were kind of delirious. Once though… It's why Pa called Merv. It was pretty late last night. Aubrey was on the bed with you and I was sitting here in the chair. We had a movie playing on the laptop. All of a sudden we realized you were watching it. I hit the panic button on the 2-way and Moms and Pa were out here in less than a minute. All that time you were staring at the laptop and then at me and then at Aubrey.

When Moms and Pa came rushing in you looked like you were in a flat-out panic. You started to hyperventilate and then passed out."

"You wouldn't believe what happened. I was traveling," I whispered. At least my voice hadn't suffered as much as Miranda's. "I was gone for months, Kyle. Right at the beginning, Miranda threw a fit and all of a sudden I was alone in her body. She wasn't there. She was gone for over two months. When she suddenly snapped back into her body, she was frightened out of her wits. I managed to see the memory and saw you and Aubrey. That was the first I knew I was alive."

Tears were leaking out of my eyes. My precious little brother kept holding me in his arms.

"Pa pulled me aside and said that he'd once been sick in a fever and had been traveling for several months. He guessed you might be, too. He hoped your host hadn't died. But last night, after we saw the panic attack, he decided to call Merv."

"Bet that freaked Aubrey out," I snorted.

"She was gone when he got here this morning. He strung the teeth and beads and when he put them around your neck, your sheet slipped and I think he saw your boobs."

"Whatever," I laughed. "He's a doctor-like."

"Yeah, but… I sorta saw 'em, too. It was an accident and I'm sorry, but they were there and I saw, and I had to tell you so you wouldn't think I was sneaking…" I laughed and pulled the sheet down to my waist. Of course, I had a t-shirt on now. Still, you could see the points of my nipples pretty clearly through it.

"Kyle, there ain't much there to see so don't worry about it. Not compared to Aubrey, for god's sake. Speaking of which, you can go back and sleep in your own room tonight. You don't have to sit up with me."

"I'm not just going to go sneak off and make love to Aubrey," he said indignantly.

"I said *you* could go. I didn't say *she* could. I think she still owes me part of my birthday present." We laughed. I heard a car pull up and figured that might be her. "Kyle, one thing. When you travel next, Miranda and Katie are renting a room in St. Joseph, Missouri. I'm disguised as a man traveling with his cute young wife. We're traders. If there's any way you can do it, come and get us. Okay? It's been really hard."

AUBREY ENTERED THE room with a squeal and dropped books on the floor as she rushed to me. I hugged that girl so hard the air swooshed out of her lungs. We were both laughing and crying and kissing each other. Kyle pushed his chair back away from us but I reached out and grabbed his hand before he could get away. In a second, I felt Aubrey's hand with mine.

"I was so worried about you, Ramie!" Aubrey cried. "Are you really going to be okay now?"

"I'm back in the land of the living," I said. "And I have my two favorite people in the world by my side. I know you were both here while I was fevered. Thank you both for loving me. Right now, before dinner, I'm going to go take a shower." Aubrey started to protest. "I'm fine, honey, but I feel like I've got a couple months of stink on me." I reached for my cell phone and flicked to the alarm clock. "I'm going to shower for 25 minutes," I said, showing them the time I'd set on the phone. "If you rush now, that gives you thirty minutes to fuck like bunnies before I'm ready to go up for dinner. But you better get started now!"

"But Ramie, I should shower with you and make sure you're okay," Aubrey said.

"Later. I'm giving you two half an hour. I expect to have *you* all night, sweetie!"

MAKING LOVE WITH Aubrey was sweet and gentle. We lay in bed for a long time just holding and kissing—saying how much we loved each other. She found my special places with her fingers and with her tongue. I loved her and when I went down on her I couldn't help but compare her neatly trimmed hair to Katie's wild bush. Aubrey was fresh and clean and smelled a little of Ivory soap. When she came, she flooded my mouth with her juices and I lapped her up like I was starving.

But when we'd made love, we just lay there and held each other. We whispered as she caught me up more on what had gone on for the past five days. I petted her bottom and held her close against me. And finally, Aubrey got around to telling me what was really on her mind—the sudden waking and panic of the night before. I tried to pass it off as just being my fever playing tricks, but Aubrey wasn't buying it.

"Ramie, honey, you looked like you'd just been caught at something. You kept looking at Kyle and then at me and then back," she said. "Ramie, are you sleeping with Kyle?" *What? Oh shit!*

"No! God, Aubrey! He's my brother. I love him like I love myself, but not to fuck him."

"You don't need to act like he'd be terrible. I mean he's a pretty damn good fuck."

"But he's my brother. I admit that sometimes... remember when I told you I sometimes fantasized that you and me were both doing Stan Armitage?"

"Don't tell me you think about both of us doing Kyle!" Aubrey giggled.

"Not exactly," I moaned. "Mostly I think about him and me doing you together."

"Oh. Oh!" She grabbed my hand and pulled it down to her pussy where I felt a hot flood of new juices.

"That's a lot different than me ever doing him."

"But why, Ramie? I think I could take knowing you were intimate with each other as long as you didn't leave me out or lie to me about it. I mean, I know the laws and social stigma and all. But... I mean, look at Mary Beth and Cole. Technically, they are too closely related to be lovers, too."

"There's a huge difference, Aubrey. Mary Beth and Cole lived half a mile away from each other and were two years different in age. She never had any school classes with him. She wasn't raised living across the hall from him like Kyle and me. I don't think she'd ever smelled one of Pa's farts until after they were lovers. If she had they'd probably never got together!" We started laughing so hard we couldn't breathe. That evolved into tickling each other and those tickling fingers found some places that really liked to be tickled and neither one of us could hold back our scream when we came. I reflexively glanced toward the window to make sure it was closed. I was positive I'd heard the raven in the back of my mind.

"Okay," Aubrey said as we finally settled down. "Just, if it ever happens to come to that, please be honest with me. I don't want to lose either one of you. But I know there is something between the two of you that you share and I don't. Maybe I can't. But I hope you'll love me enough and trust me enough to tell me what it is."

Will that day ever come? Will Kyle and I be able to tell her we are time travelers?

MOM MAR PRONOUNCED me healthy after all the turkey I put away at Thanksgiving dinner. Kyle and I went out to saddle Pooky and Dado. Aubrey went home with her parents with the promise that she would be back on Friday 'to study.' Kyle left me with the horses for a few minutes and when he got back, he handed me my rifle.

"I cleaned it while I was sitting with you. Should be all set. That was a hell of a shot you made," he said.

"I can hardly remember it; things happened so fast. How's the horse? That was Lucky, wasn't it?" I asked as we started toward the pasture. The horses were all down toward the river.

"Yeah. He had a couple bites. There was no question he was fighting for his life. Arlen Logan from Fish and Game came out to verify it was a predator kill. When he heard we had wolves, he left immediately and ran out. He wasn't happy about Pa pulling the canines, but when he saw the bite on your neck, he just nodded and let it go. He took the carcasses with him, first to test for rabies and then to give to the University for study." Kyle seemed to run down while we went to check on the herd. I got up beside Lucky and looked at the bite on his rump.

"You sure earned your name, didn't you old boy? I hope you kicked him a good one before I got there." I remounted and we rode over toward where the action had been. I could see where I'd been and where Lucky had been when I shot the male that was attacking him. I could see the ridge right above me where the female jumped at me.

"Arlen says that the male weighed over 180 and the female nearly 170," Kyle said as we rode. "They want to check them to see if there's a species mutation. Don't much see a Canadian wolf over 150."

"Kyle, where were you when you bagged that she-wolf?" I asked.

"Oh. Back over there, I guess." He waved vaguely behind us.

"Wait. Take me to exactly where you took the shot," I demanded. He looked at me and we rode back a ways.

"I was coming up from the river. I guess I was right about here," he said. I dismounted and grabbed my rifle from the scabbard. I sighted up along the ridge where I'd made a pretty damned good hundred-yard shot.

"Kyle. It's gotta be 200 yards up there. If you'd missed you coulda killed me!" I heard him sniff and turned to see tears in his eyes. He reached out and touched my neck softly.

"Ramie, if I'da missed, you'd have been dead anyway."

It was all-out tears then. Kyle grabbed hold of me and just cried on my shoulder and I wept because through it all, my brother had my back.

"Don't... Don't get so far away again, Ramie. I was so scared. If that old raven hadn't made the wolf look up just then, I might have missed. I hit her right under the chin. I swear that old bird was trying to protect you. Ramie, I'd die if something happened to you. Please don't ever do that again."

I looked back up toward where I'd been just in time to see a raven swoop in and settle on the ridge.

18
Business

I NEVER TOOK that wolf-tooth necklace off. It wasn't like it was on a chain with a clasp. Merv knotted the cord around my neck and it was just too short to pull over my head. Oh, I didn't wear it outside my clothes or anything. But I always felt those teeth against my skin. I did, however, take to wearing a bandana around my neck. I had two ugly red scars that I didn't want people staring at.

On Saturday the next weekend, Kyle, Aubrey, and I went up to the Bearclaw cafe to get a burger. I saw Harold Watson from the Bar-Double-D with a bunch of other ranchers having coffee. That name always got us laughing as kids because we'd switch the 'r' and the 'a' around. The three of us were chowing down on the world's best burgers when I looked up and the guys were standing around our table.

"Can we see it, Ramie?" he asked. "The teeth?" *Whoa. News travels fast.*

They were respectful, though, and it didn't seem right to withhold something that was as important as killing wolves on rangeland. We'd all had problems and lost cattle to them. A hunting pair was unusual. We suspected there were more up on the mountain. I pulled the thong out from under my shirt and the guys all nodded their heads when they saw the size of those teeth.

"You two done good," Harold said. "You're good people. Thank you." There was a moment of almost reverence as he looked at my bandana. Well, in for a penny… I pulled the bandana down and away from my neck and they all let out various curses and blessings when they saw the welts.

"My niece is looking for a place to board her trail horse for the winter," Al Robertson said. "I saw a poster you put up about taking horses in. You still got room?"

"Yes," I said. "We're ready for boarders. Have her give me a call."

By the end of the next week, L&K Stables had its first paying customer.

I'd put up little half-page notices that L&K Stables was open for boarding and would be offering stud services in the spring. Each one had half a dozen little tear-off strips with our phone number on them.

I guess advertising pays. Of course, a little notoriety about the kids who protected their stock and survived a wolf attack didn't hurt either. Both Kurt and Merv told the story when they saw someone glancing at the flyers in their stores. I think Merv embellished the story somewhat with a tale about spirit walkers or some such. Whatever, it didn't hurt our reputation.

The first of January, I read on EquineNews about an accident in Colorado where a driver lost control of his truck on ice and jackknifed his rig. He was pulling a horse trailer and while the driver wasn't hurt, the horse had fallen and was pretty banged up. I called them right away and found out that the horse was going to live but had a lot of bruises and cuts. The owner had decided hauling horses wasn't anything he was going to do again and I offered to buy the horse. Kyle and I drove down and, for a mere fifteen hundred dollars, came back with a registered American Saddlebred stud that stood close to sixteen hands. He needed rest and recovery, but he was a proud boy.

I hadn't traveled back to Miranda since my birthday, but I wasn't too worried about her. I'd left her in a pretty safe place as long as she didn't blow her cover. She was doing what she knew how to do best. She was trading goods and building her stock. When that girl got her own store she was going to be a terror. And I also knew now, that time had no relevance. I could wait five years of *my* life and return to the next day in her timeline.

Boarding horses and picking up a couple more rescues kept Kyle and me pretty busy after school. Aubrey continued to spend about every other weekend out at the ranch and on the off weekends one or both of us would go into town and take her on a date. We didn't want her thinking that the only thing either of us wanted was sex. We even had a couple of weekends at the ranch when we didn't have sex. One night we had an old-fashioned slumber party and the three of us sat up in the family room all night watching movies.

I wouldn't say there was no kissy-face and touchy-feely going on, but we didn't actually have sex.

"I'VE GOT SOME bad news," Kyle said as we drove into school one Wednesday morning. It was an unusual day as the junior high had a day off, so we didn't have the kids with us on the drive. I looked at him.

"What?"

"I went traveling last night," he said. "I plunked into Jason's body just in time to almost get him killed. He was having a tussle with a private in his troop. I hate those fuckers. They were ganging up on his friend, John—did you ever see the Indian he travels with?" I nodded. I remembered how startled I was the first time I saw the Indian shadowing him. "Well, Jason stepped in between them just as I showed up and almost got killed when he realized I was there. Private Randolph was coming at John with a knife. I barely knocked it aside in time to keep from being skewered."

"Well, that doesn't sound like bad news. Thank god you knocked it aside."

"Yeah. The private is cooling his heels for thirty days in the brig at Fort Number 3. But in the meantime, the troop was sent on to Omaha. Riding across Missouri is no vacation."

"Yeah, tell me about it."

"Anyway, I remembered what you said about camping out in St. Joseph. When we got there I looked high and low. There was no sign of Miss Miranda or any couple who were spending the winter trading. We were only there two nights and then pushed on toward Omaha. I got snatched back before we reached the city."

"We weren't there? Maybe we'll meet in Omaha, then. We must have already left."

"I'm so pissed that Jason lost you in Indiana. It was that same damned private that got the entire troop confined to quarters for that section of the trip."

"Wait. Kyle, when were you in St. Joseph?" I asked.

"Near the end of October. They were pushing us to get on to Omaha before we were hit with bad weather."

"What year?"

"Right after the train ride from Baltimore in '65."

"Damn it! It's the damned time sequence being out of sync. You got there a year before we did, but here it was months afterward. How are we ever going to get together? We should be having this adventure with each other."

WE WERE GETTING through school. The end was in sight. Just another month. And our horse-ranch was beginning to take shape, too. We'd rescued three more horses, but it wasn't just a rescue operation. Harley, our Saddlebred stallion, was gentle as a lamb. He had a good pedigree, and we already had three people come out to look at him for standing stud to their mares. He was strutting around the secondary paddock like he owned the place. We were keeping him and Pa's Bolt way separate.

He was a big boy and Kyle and I were walking out to the pasture when we saw him covering Bows. We hadn't intended to breed the two pinto mares yet, but they were healthy and their hooves were regrown so that they could enjoy life. It sure looked like Bows was enjoying it. And so was Harley. Kyle and I leaned against the fence to watch.

We're ranch-raised, so it's not like we've never seen animals breed. We've seen the bulls down in the pasture cover half a dozen cows in a couple hours. We'd had to get out there and separate out the rest of the estrous cows or the damned bull would just keep fucking till he keeled over. It looked like we'd have to bring Harley in, too. As soon as he was done with Bows, he started in on Bells. Kyle shifted back and forth a little and moved some closer to me. I knew what was going through his mind. Well, maybe it wasn't his mind. I think those kinds of things just bypass the brain.

"Is Aubrey coming out this weekend?" I asked. We looked at each other and started to giggle. He edged away and blushed. I punched him in the shoulder and blushed myself. Poor Aubrey was going to have a sore pussy by the end of the weekend.

We started getting calls booking our studs. One buckskin AQHA stud and one dun American Saddlebred stud. We had modest stud fees for our first time out and over a dozen mares showed up in May and early June. Our boys were having a good time.

Between the time we spent taking care of horses, doing school work, and dating Aubrey, I was still busy looking at maps and plotting out where Miranda was. Our journey had taken us far away from the USGS maps that I had on the wall. I'd planned to go from Tennessee to St. Louis when I bought those maps and instead I cut west. All that planning for nothing. But I got some map software for my laptop and did my best to plot what our route had been.

Getting from St. Joseph to Omaha was a pretty direct and main route. I estimated that we'd make that trip fully loaded in less than three weeks if the roads weren't too muddy. What would happen then?

Miranda's stated goal was to rescue her stepsister and make sure her mother was cared for. But what if they'd already left Omaha by the time we got there? Kyle was there by the fall of '65. The earliest Miranda could arrive was the spring of '67. Where would they go next? Mister Jonathon was supposedly there to establish a supply line for building the railroad. I thought Omaha would be the base of operations while he ran up and down the railroad as it was built.

I started doing searches on the Union Pacific and found they began construction the first of January, 1866 and by that fall were already as far as Cozad, Nebraska, following the Platte River. If Kyle's unit was moving with the railroad, he was probably wintering at Fort McPherson. I managed to project a huge map of Nebraska and Wyoming on my wall and draw out the route of the railroad and the stops. I even went down to the Railroad Museum in Laramie and looked at their maps and the schedule. Laramie would be founded overnight in April of 1868. The railroad would get there in May.

Kyle studied the map, too. He nodded and pointed out various forts along the way and where known Indian problems came from. There was nothing safe about the West. I gave him a blue Sharpie so he could mark his travels on the same map.

Kyle's birthday was coming up, but it was on Monday. Aubrey visited the weekend before his birthday and spent Friday and Saturday with me.

We teased Kyle something fierce but she didn't ever go to his room until she woke him up with a blowjob on Sunday morning. The next twenty-four hours were his.

I, on the other hand, was fucked within an inch of my life.

I'm not a sexy girl or even particularly pretty. In my opinion, at least. Aubrey tells me different, but she's as horny as I am. She's also beautiful. I'm nearly six feet tall, skinny, and ruddy complected. I guess I should use more lotions on my skin or something. My tits not only aren't a handful, they're barely a mouthful. And the only mouth that's ever been full of them is Aubrey's.

She, on the other hand, has dark tan skin that is so clear you can almost see through it. She's a perfect five-four and has an hourglass figure that singes eyebrows when she walks by. She's got a real bikini butt and I could bury my face between her breasts and stay there all day. My idea of heaven is making love to Aubrey.

I spent a lot of time in heaven Friday and Saturday nights.

Aubrey had never watched horses breed. We had a mare each for Harley and Bolt on Saturday. She watched in fascination. Every time either Kyle or I walked by her, we petted her and kissed her. I'd keep whispering in her ear when I touched her—dumb little things like 'Bet you want Kyle to mount you just like that, don't you.' Her first little gasp told me I was right.

"By midnight tonight, when Kyle finally gets into your pussy, you'll already have come so many times you'll pass out before he fills the first condom," I told her as I scrubbed her in the shower before dinner. I pinched at her nipples, never quite squeezing them, but letting my soapy hands grip and slide off them. They kept sticking out farther and farther. "Kyle's not going to be able to eat his dinner tonight. He's going to be staring at your teats, drooling to get his lips on them."

"Ramie, it's Kyle we're supposed to be teasing. Why are you teasing me like this? I want you!"

"Aubs, don't you think he's standing on the other side of this wall in his shower? I bet he's got his ear plastered against the wall and his cock soaped up in his hand just waiting to hear you squeal." I moved my fingers down and shampooed her pussy. I got everything very clean and she squealed twice in the process. If Kyle really was in the other shower, I hoped he was fast at his recovery.

We stepped out of the shower and I dried Aubrey off, taking time to suck on her nipples some more. I never got a chance to dry myself.

She pushed me out of the bathroom and I landed sprawled on the bed. Her mouth was glued to my pussy, pushing aside my sparse hair with her tongue. Watching the horses and teasing her had me on a hair-trigger, too. When she did that thing where she runs her tongue up one side of my hole, around my clit, and down the other side, it was me that was screaming.

We were late getting up to the house for dinner and both of us blushed all through dinner.

WHEN AUBREY SLIPPED out of my room at midnight and went to Kyle, I was exhausted but sexually energized. I knew what I'd be hearing soon and figured I wasn't done for the night, but I had to give my pussy a rest for a little while.

I opened my window to get some of the fresh night air in and some of the sex smell out. I hadn't seen the raven since November, so I was surprised when he flitted down immediately and landed on my sill.

"Well, if it ain't old Blackfeather," I drawled. "You came too late to see the sex and I'm too sore to rub one off for your entertainment, you pervert." Of course, I was standing there in all my glory but I pretty much ignored him and went about studying the map, tracing the line from St. Joseph to Omaha and then along the railroad to Laramie. I wasn't expecting the old bird to land on my shoulder. His claws were sharp but I froze so he didn't get scared and gouge me with them.

He turned his good eye toward me and leaned down to look at my wolf's teeth.

Awkawkawkawk!

19
Warehouse

A SOLITARY BRASS bell rang when we entered the shop. I had no idea where we were but it seemed like a city, so I assumed Omaha. I should have studied maps of that.

"We gon' have some good fun with you now that your Ma and Pap are gone," a young man said to the woman at the counter. *Theresa!* "You just relax and let me get my hands into this tight little bosom of yours." He was behind the counter with her and had a hand on her blouse, working to open it.

"Let me go, you spurious cur!" Theresa cried.

I feel you, Demon Ramie. You are here. Please help me.

"We're closed! Get out of the shop," the fellow yelled at me. "This don't concern you."

I reached for the Colt Navy to find nothing at Miranda's hip.

They can't be worn in the city.

I lifted her foot and pulled the knife from her boot. Miranda quickly resigned complete control to me.

"The young woman said to let her go. Do so at once," I growled. I'd almost forgotten how gravelly Miranda's voice was. It no longer hurt as badly, but the beautiful musicality of her voice was gone forever.

"None o' yer affair! This tart been teasin' the help ever since she got here. Now she's gonna pay." Theresa squirmed and bit his hand. He reached across and slapped her face. That was all. I took two steps and leapt the counter. He pushed Theresa away and turned to swing at me. He hadn't noticed I had a knife until I blocked his punch with it. One of his fingers fell to the floor with the impact as he drove the back of the blade into my forearm. He screamed and fell back holding his hand.

"A man who hits a lady deserves to have no hands," I said as I advanced on him with the knife.

"I'll kill you!" he yelled. But he was backing up and ran around the counter and out the door. At the last possible instant, Katie stuck out her foot and tripped him on the way out, slamming the door behind him and locking it as he sprawled on the dirty street. I picked up the finger. Two knuckles of his pinky.

"Katie," I said, "pack this in salt until we can strip the meat from the bone. I'll wear it as a necklace."

"Yes... Husband Ramie," the girl said. I guess I was recognizable when I arrived, even to Katie. I cleaned my blade and sheathed it, releasing Miranda's body back to her control. Miranda rushed to Theresa to embrace her, but the frightened girl scooted away as quickly as she could.

"I suppose you want what he would take as well," Theresa said. She grabbed the broom and swung at Miranda.

"No. No, sister."

"I have no brothers."

"No you don't," Miranda agreed. "You have a stepsister to whom life has been unkind."

"My stepsister died in Indiana," Theresa said.

"Is that what they told you?" Katie said coming to the counter. She was a hard woman in the body of a still-pretty girl. "Your stepsister was sold by your father to become a Texas whore. She saved the lives of three other girls, including me, by killing our kidnappers. And to thank her for her kindness, one of those stupid girls attempted to strangle her and thus ruined her sweet voice. For over a year, her only thought has been to find her stepsister and make sure she did not suffer the same fate."

"Miranda?" Theresa said, still holding the broom in front of her.

"I am so sorry, Theresa," she said. "What Katie says is true. Mister Jonathon lost in a card game and used me to settle his debt."

"You killed them?"

"My hands have killed three men, stepsister. They all deserved to die. Please do not think ill of me," Miranda said. I could feel the tear run down her cheek. "Where is your father and my mother, Theresa? Why are you here alone where ruffians like this can attack you?"

"I am fifteen, Miranda. I should be able to run a mercantile," Theresa said. Then she began crying, dropping the broom. "Miranda, I'm so frightened. My father is following the railroad. He sends orders to me and I fill them on the next car out. Your mother… Miss Dolly is ill. This was the first time I've come to the warehouse alone."

"Can you take us to her, Theresa?"

"The next train is in two days. No one else has come to work today. I think they all knew I would be here alone. I can take you to your mother. It is… really you, is it not, Miranda?"

"For good or ill, it is really me. And this is my most faithful companion, Katie Forster. Please take me to my mother."

IT WAS A tearful reunion. Dolly did not believe it was her daughter until Miranda had removed her shirt and shown a birthmark beneath her left breast. Miranda had aged with the hardship of the trail and, at seventeen, was a somewhat gaunt and wiry woman whose breasts were still firm, probably thanks to the bindings that Katie kept wrapped around them. *About as good as a sports bra, I suppose.*

When she had heard the story fully, it was all we could do to keep Dolly in her bed. She swore she would hunt Jonathon down and kill him herself. She had not known Miranda was missing until the train was nearly a day away from Vincennes. They sent telegrams back to every station where they had stopped. They were in St. Louis when a message was returned from New Albany that said a body that matched the description had been found and buried. She wanted to go back, but Jonathon was intent on moving on to Omaha as quickly as possible.

"He had all our stock loaded on a barge that took us three weeks to get to Kansas City. In the face of winter storms, he left us in Kansas City and hired men to move the barge on to Omaha. He arrived here in December, in time to be on hand for the laying of the first rails west. We went by stage coach in the spring and already this warehouse was nearly full. Shipments were arriving by rail from Chicago and Jonathon was shipping them out to Columbus, Nebraska by the time we got here." Mother stopped and coughed until she spit blood-caked phlegm from her mouth.

"What ails you, Mother?" Miranda asked as gently as her harsh voice could muster.

"I have consumption. Imagine. I, who have not a poetic bone in my body."

"You have arrived to see my suffering once more," Miranda moaned to me.

I am so sorry about your mother, Miranda. But I am glad I arrived when I did. We got here in time to save Theresa. That was your goal.

"She thinks I am hideous. And I am. Will I ever wear women's weeds again?"

Have faith and give her time. I believe it would be a good idea to get a dress as soon as possible and start putting on a little weight if you can.

"It is still going to be hard work. But it feels so good to have my breasts unbound. I swear, Katie has wrapped them more tightly each time."

She's a good girl.

"You left me with… with my face… in her privities. What was I to do?"

Oh dear. You didn't leave her hanging did you?

"Hanging? If anyone finds out what I did, I'll hang. I… finished what you started."

It wasn't that bad, was it?

"It was… pleasant when she returned the action."

Did you repeat it?

"Once. Just before we left St. Joseph. It was most embarrassing but she can be insistent."

Well, we girls must all stick together.

"Husband ramie? Are you still here?" Katie whispered in my ear after Theresa was asleep.

"I'm here, Katie."

"Will you lie with me, husband?" I felt Miranda cringe a little but she kept silent.

"Katie, honey, let us have consideration for the others in our bed tonight. Theresa has her back tight against mine and I would not disturb her."

"But…"

"Shh, Katie, dear. Let me hold you and kiss you."

Our kiss deepened and was accompanied by gentle caresses, but I did not let it get beneath the new nightgowns that we wore. While Theresa

142

had been in a desperate place yesterday, the fact was that she was privileged and pampered. In all likelihood, she had been teasing the workers at the warehouse. She wasn't unkind or spiteful, but I don't think she thought about how her actions could be interpreted.

After Katie had drifted off to sleep, I lay awake a long time pondering the present situation. I was back in 1867. Miranda and Katie had done well as traders and arrived in Omaha with a larger wagon than that with which we had arrived in St. Joseph. With the gold that was left in our strongbox, we could set up business here in Omaha—go into competition with Theresa if we desired. I knew, however, that Miranda did not want that. We could combine what we had with the Mercantile, but I cringed at making Jonathon wealthier.

You were kind and considerate when Katie called.

"She has her needs as well."

I am not... opposed. But thank you for considering how it might affect Theresa.

"You can always speak up, you know."

It was such a relief to render you control when we faced that man. I would have done it, but I might not have been as effective.

"You've come a long way, Miranda. I'm proud of you."

Will you be with me long?

"I don't know. I never know how long."

I miss you when you are not with me.

"I miss you, too, love. We will be too tired to work in the morning if we don't sleep."

Sleep, Friend Ramie. I will watch over your dreams.

THE MERCANTILE WAS more of a warehouse than a store. Theresa and Mother were responsible for receiving shipments ordered from Chicago and St. Louis. They shipped the weekly supplies needed for the traveling mercantile at the railroad worksite. Two sullen men arrived at work in the morning and found three women in charge. One was armed. They did their work. The one with a missing finger did not show up.

There was very little walk-in business. That was where Miranda spotted our opportunity.

"Theresa, we need more space for our expansion." We had unloaded our wagon and the front of the shop was filled with skins and crafted goods from St. Joseph.

You've turned into quite a hunter.

"I had a very good teacher," Miranda answered silently.

"We would have to get father's permission to move to a larger space," Theresa said. "What are we expanding to?"

"It is a new world, Theresa. We no longer need your father's permission for anything. If he ever returns here, he will discover a business that no longer is his. People are moving west. When we approached Omaha, there were so many wagons that we waited two days to get across the river. None of them had the basic essentials needed for a successful journey. We will become outfitters for the pioneers."

I could see the vision taking shape in Miranda's head. It was a good idea. Some people would go by train to the places already settled, but many more would push into the open lands to homestead. They needed supplies for their journey—everything from picks and shovels to kitchen stoves and pans.

Homestead in a box. Exactly what is needed to start in the wilderness, all contained in a Conestoga wagon. Brilliant, Miranda.

"Thank you, Friend Ramie. We have work to do."

AND WORK WE did. While Mother was no longer well enough to come to the warehouse, she was able to write orders that we sent to Chicago. We expanded into additional space next to the warehouse. We sold several top grade hides and received enough money to pay the rent until our first customers arrived. Katie proved brilliant at packing a wagon, keeping things needed on a daily basis near the top while things needed at the homestead were secured at the bottom of the wagon.

By mid-July, the first wagon packed by Ramie Lewis Outfitters rolled out of Omaha to join a wagon train to Colorado.

"Who is Ramie Lewis?" Theresa asked, as she watched Katie paint the name on our window.

"My husband," Katie sighed. Theresa looked at her curiously and then turned to Miranda. Miranda, in turn, handed the conversation to me.

"When I arrived here, you thought I was a man," I explained gently. "Our journey was not like we were used to in Baltimore or even what you found here in Omaha. There were only the two of us with no law or protection. It was safer to travel as husband and wife than it would have been as two women. Ramie is the name I chose as a man."

"It is unusual," Theresa said.

"It is short for Laramie," Katie explained. When had I told her that?

"How lovely." Theresa turned her attention back to Katie. "Sister Katie, you must tell me all about your travels… with your husband," she whispered. The little imp grinned at me.

MOTHER'S HEALTH FAILED entirely in September and we laid her to rest just before Miranda's eighteenth birthday. We debated long over telling Jonathon. Without a wife, we decided he would likely send a man to run the business or remarry. Neither were good options for us, so we simply did not tell him. The tracks had reached the border of the Dakota Territory and Jonathon wrote that they were in severe weather and he would not return to Omaha this winter. He wanted to move west as quickly as possible in the spring, to purchase a store in the farthest outpost before the mountains. That suited us fine. We used the winter months, when no wagons were leaving, to build our stock and continue supplying the needs of the railroad.

Omaha not only functioned to supply the West, but also to supply Chicago. The cattle yards were full and trains filled with beef on the hoof left for Chicago daily. We were expecting a shipment from Chicago on the day that fate took a new turn.

Miranda walked near the railroad toward the station. Every place in Omaha was near the railroad and chaos was the norm. There were the usual loading and unloading of cars and at the cattle pens, half a dozen cowboys were mounted and trying to drive herd up into a cattle car. One recalcitrant steer kept cutting out of line at the ramp and charging off in a different direction. This inevitably led to half a dozen others following and the loading stopped while order in the herd was restored. I loved watching and held Miranda in place as one more time the steer broke loose. This time, he spotted a gap between two cowboys and charged through it, leading half the herd with him. He hit the fence. It swayed a bit but held and would have been fine if the poke, who was after him, hadn't thrown a rope and missed. The shadow flickered through the air and then the rope hit the leading steer. This caused the herd to surge after him and the fence gave way.

We had thirty head of cattle headed our way. Miranda was so shocked by the stampede that she froze. I could not rend control from her. I heard hooves and felt a strong arm around my waist that swept me up, out of the path of the stampede, and into the lap of a young cavalryman on his horse. The horse danced around a bit, but the cattle divided as a second man in buckskins drove them off the boardwalk.

The soldier gently lifted me down. I looked up into his face and Miranda's heart did a double-flip.

"Corporal Jason Wardlaw at your assistance, Miss. I do hope you are unharmed. Please forgive my ungentlemanly handling of your person," he said.

"You are timely in arriving. We have met before. Miranda Lewis, kind sir."

"He told me," the corporal whispered. He dismounted and bowed over Miranda's hand. "I am so glad to see you here and safe. I have looked for you constantly as I journeyed."

"Thank you," Miranda squeaked. She started to turn away.

Oh no you don't! You've been waiting for him since you were kidnapped from the train. I wrenched control away from Miranda and turned back toward the tall hero.

"Please forgive my hesitance. I have not yet caught my breath. I would be pleased to have you call this evening at Four Montgomery Street so I may properly thank you."

"Miss Lewis, I would be delighted. This evening." He tipped his hat slightly and turned to his horse. I saw Jason's Indian friend still brushing the dust from his buckskins.

"Please, bring your friend as well. My sisters and I will make dinner for the two of you." I relinquished control of Miranda and she sat on a bench. The corporal saluted her and rode to where the Indian was mounting his horse.

"What did you do that for? What am I supposed to do now?" Miranda was panicked.

Go home and prepare to receive a gentleman caller.

"But I have no idea what to do with a gentleman caller! I have no chaperone."

You're eighteen, Miranda. We've dreamed of that young man since he first rescued you in Maryland. You at least owe him dinner and a smile. If nothing else comes to mind, I'm sure he'll have some ideas.

"But I…" Miranda was full of objections but our attention was drawn down the platform where a large black bird was hopping his way toward us pecking scraps out of the cracks between the boards. About ten feet away he looked up at us and I saw his one milky eye.

I think it's time for me to go home. My ride is here.

"You can't leave me now! Not with a *man* coming to visit me!"

The raven cried and I was gone.

20
Massacre

MY FEET were cold, which didn't seemed strange; I was stark naked and drawing marks on my wall map with a Sharpie. Somehow, I'd filled in a line from Springfield, Missouri all the way to Omaha, Nebraska with marks and dates for campsites. I might not know where I was going, but I guess I knew where I'd been. I looked at my shoulder and could see the six indentations of the raven's talons on the front of my shoulder. I could feel the two behind. At least he hadn't broken the skin.

I was exhausted and flopped down on my bed. I knew Aubrey wouldn't leave Kyle tonight. And I was too tired to do anything more if she did. I closed my eyes and slept.

OUR JUNIOR YEAR came to an end with the usual fanfare plus the delivery of our class rings. We wore our own rings for exactly one day. Aubrey came out to the ranch after the last day of school and dragged us to the barn. What she wanted, she said, couldn't be done in either of our rooms. When we got to the barn, she sat both Kyle and me down on a hay bale and got down on her knees in front of us.

"This isn't the same as a proposal, but it's the only place I can be where I can see both of you. I want you both to be able to see me when I tell you I love you. I love you. And I want to go steady with you." It was a bit of a surprise, but I figured that one day Aubrey would want to declare that she was with Kyle in a public way. Exchanging class rings was the usual way for high school seniors. I nudged Kyle.

"Give her your class ring, Kyle," I said. "Unless you don't want to go steady with her." Kyle fumbled around with his ring.

"But what about…?"

"You, too, Ramie," Aubrey broke in.

"Me too, what?" I asked.

"I want your class ring. I'm gonna wear them both."

"You want to tell the world that?" I asked. *Was I ready to tell the world? Well, hell yeah.* I pulled my new ring off my finger.

"I'm such a slut," Aubrey giggled. She dug in her pocket and then pulled her ring off her hand. She held out both hands to us. "I bought two class rings. If you didn't want to go steady with me I'd have thrown one away."

We laughed as we organized who got what ring and how we were going to wear them. Aubrey's fingers were a little smaller than mine and her ring wouldn't go all the way on. Kyle barely got it over the tip of his pinky.

"We gotta get chains," I said. "We can't wear them like this."

"I think we should all get chains. I can wear your ring, Ramie, but then no one would know it wasn't my own. Kyle's is too big for my thumb," Aubrey laughed.

"We've got to go show Moms," I said. "I can't believe we're going steady!"

"Can we make out first?" Aubrey asked. "I'm going steady with the two people I love most and neither one of them has kissed me yet." We had a little tussle over who got to her first, but we both managed to get kissed. In the heat of the matter, I put my hand on her breast right over Kyle's hand. We just giggled some more. Hell, she's got two breasts. We'd alternated kissing Aubrey before, but it was the first time we'd really made out together. I didn't care.

It would have been nice if we'd had more than the weekend to celebrate the end of school. The Moms weren't impressed when they saw us all wearing each other's rings.

"So what's new?" Mom Ash asked. "She's been going steady with both of you for months. The question is whether she's riding the herd with you next week."

"Huh?" Kyle and I both asked. Intelligent. I knew we'd have to spend a couple weeks up there this summer but I didn't realize it would be next week.

"There's just too much pressure on the guys up there," Mom Mar said. "Cole and Ashley are going up, too. You won't all have to stay all summer, but we need all the help we can get."

"But what about our horses?" I asked. *Let's get to the important part.* We had six pregnant mares and four boarders now.

"Well, you've got two hired hands. How do you figure I planned to keep control of those two this summer? And you know they handle the horses as well as you do. Aubrey, you are welcome to be here as much this summer as you can be. I could use an extra hand, and we'll take regular trips up the mountain on four-wheelers," Mom Mar said.

"I feel like part of the family," Aubrey grinned. I kissed her. As soon as I was done, Kyle laid one on her.

"I don't think there's any question about that," Mom Ash laughed.

Between our chores and working with the kids on what needed to be done with the horses for the next few weeks, we didn't have a whole lot of time to fool around that weekend. We just didn't sleep much at night. And something else seemed to change. Until that weekend, we'd been pretty divided in our loving. Kissing, sure, but sex was private—except for the sounds coming through the thin wall.

We watched a late movie in the family room Saturday night. Everybody else had gone to bed but we just wanted to all cuddle up together. Aubrey was kind of smashed between Kyle and me on the sofa and we were all making out like crazy. If Kyle was kissing her, I was nibbling on her neck or ears, and I had one hand up under her shirt pinching her big nipples. Aubrey was breathing pretty hard when Kyle's hand nudged mine aside on her tit. She had a hand between my legs and I was pretty sure she was stroking Kyle, too. I drifted down and she sucked in her tummy so my hand slid right down beneath her waistband and into her panties. She was so wet and slippery that I nearly came just from touching her. She moaned into Kyle's mouth and I sprinkled kisses on the back of her neck as I found her little clit and started rubbing it.

Aubrey came. It would have been loud if Kyle hadn't kept her mouth sealed to his.

"Oh god! I love going steady with you two!" she gasped. "Having both of you making love to me was just so damned hot! I thought I'd never stop coming."

"You should take your boyfriend back to his room and fuck him silly," I whispered in her ear. "Then come to my room and let me lick you to another one."

"We could… We could all do it together," she whispered.

I looked up at Kyle and could see my blush reflected in his face.

"I don't know, Aubrey. That's like… a little weird."

"Like me going between the two of you isn't?" she giggled.

"But I'm never in the room with my sister while you're… you know."

"I'm not quite ready to watch my brother banging you," I laughed nervously. "Not tonight anyway. You two go ahead. If I'm asleep when you come in, Aubs, wake me up!"

It had always been exciting to think about what Kyle was doing to Aubrey in the next room. Sometimes, I'd tease her about it when she was lying with me and I was feeling around up inside her for that spot that always seemed to make her go crazy. I'd ask her if her boyfriend ever rubbed her there with his prick just to watch her butt bounce off the bed while she came. But I was willing to wait my turn. I didn't need to actually watch it.

Monday morning we headed out for the upper pasture where the hired hands already had our herd. There wasn't much time to just sit and mope about Aubrey. We rode all day and after dinner, we slept under the stars. Kyle and I had tents. Pa and Ashley commandeered the little camp trailer we had on the upper range. Rafe, Jess, and the other two guys all had their own tents, too. And don't think it was cruel for them and that Pa got the best. Our campsite was pretty well developed and the tents were all on platforms off the ground with cots in them and air mattresses. For me, I just liked the idea of sleeping under the stars as long as it didn't rain.

Aubrey and Mom Mar and the kids all came up on the weekend and brought a picnic with them. Camp food wasn't bad and we all took turns tending the camp stove, but Mom Mar's fried chicken and the strawberry-rhubarb pie Aubrey made were like a little taste of heaven. We slipped off with Aubrey for a while before we had to mount up and circle the herd on the night shift. We kept our privates in our pants, but we all had a good come.

WE'D BEEN UP there three weeks and Kyle and I were settling down for the night. Pa and Mom Ash were in the camper. Jess and Arlen were riding the first shift tonight and Kyle and I would be going out at midnight. Nighttime was usually pretty quiet. The cattle clustered together at night and mostly lay down so they weren't attractive to wolves. A bobcat might try something, but since they are individual hunters and not pack animals, they tended to go for smaller game. Mostly, we rode around slowly so we didn't disturb anything and listened for any restlessness that might indicate a predator was near.

We were on our horses when Jess and Arlen got to camp and they said it was all quiet, so we rode out to take up our stations. We were talking quietly when a black shadow came across us and that raven landed on my shoulder again. At least I had a shirt on.

"Uh-oh," I whispered. "Kyle, I don't know what I'll be like when he takes me. You got my back?"

"I got you, Ramie," he said. Old Blackfeather turned his head so his one good eye could see Kyle.

Awkawkawkawk. Knockknockknock.

NOTHING HAPPENED. I was still sitting there looking out over the moonlit herd. Kyle was sitting beside me on Dado. The horse shifted a little.

"That was strange," I said. The raven lifted up and flitted away in the darkness. "You ever see anything like that?"

"See what?" Kyle mumbled.

"Kyle?" He didn't answer. His head kept turning like normal, listening to the night. *Shit! Kyle is traveling.* So that was what it looked like. I asked him a question or two and he mumbled a response. We continued our ride around the herd, watching and listening. I looked at him to make sure he was stable in the saddle. The lights were on, but nobody was home.

We got back to camp at four in the morning, and after we got our horses unsaddled we just lay down.

"You okay, Kyle?" I asked.

"Okay. Love you, sister," he mumbled as he fell asleep.

"Love you, too, Kyle." I sat on my bedroll. Rafe and Jim had ridden out as we arrived. Nobody else would stir for a couple hours. If I was still awake, I figured I'd get coffee and bacon started.

I saw the shadow in the pre-dawn light and heard a faraway call of the raven. Kyle jerked in his sleep and started to whimper. I reached over and touched his shoulder.

"You okay, brother?" His eyes came open and he looked at me through his tears. He didn't say anything but just started shaking his head back and forth. Then he started sobbing. I did the only thing I could and caught him up in a hug and just rocked him, sort of crooning softly like I'd comfort a baby. He was back but he wasn't happy. *God! I hope nothing happened to his host.*

He finally cried himself to sleep and I kept holding him while I nodded off. That's where Mom Ash found us.

"I DON'T KNOW, Pa," I said. I switched to Ashley's next shift so I could ride with him. "I know he went traveling last night. I saw him go and I saw him return. It's weird. He kept functioning but it's like he just wasn't there."

"I scared Mary Beth half to death once when I went while I was driving on the Interstate."

"Oh shit."

"I don't know what to tell you, little girl. You kids seem to be doing things I never did. I recognized Joe Teini and Philemon as travelers when I looked in their eyes, but it wasn't like I knew who they were. And you and Kyle can recognize each other. But you are all out of sync."

"It's hard, Pa. It's like I already lived through things that he hasn't gotten to yet. So when he gets to it, the box is already open. But if he's still behind me, I know his host is okay. I saw his host the last time I traveled. Only Kyle wasn't in him at the time," I said.

"All I can say is do your best to help each other. Once Laramie died, I never went back again, even in spirit. I don't know what will happen to you."

"Thanks for talking, Pa. I can't imagine what it was like for you with no one to talk to."

"It was a lot better when I finally let Mary Beth and Ashley in on it. You know you're eventually going to have to tell Aubrey if you plan to stay together."

"WE JUST KILLED them," Kyle whispered. We didn't have to ride for another couple hours and this was the first time he'd been willing to talk. "The whole company was gathered together and Captain told us there was a raiding party lying in ambush. All our Indian scouts were locked up. He didn't trust any of them in an actual encounter. We were given our orders to engage and destroy the enemy." I reached over and took his hand and he squeezed it.

"I was so scared, Ramie. We'd never been in an actual fight. All I could think was that we had to kill them before they could kill us. We rode over the ridge at a full charge and into the camp. We could see them scrambling and fired our carbines first. Some fell. Then we pulled our revolvers. You can't aim worth a damn when you are riding at a full charge. You just point in the direction of the most people and shoot from about twenty-five yards away. More fell.

"We were pulling our second guns and were right on top of them when I saw two children looking up at my gun. There was no ambush waiting for us. It was just women and children and old men. We were cutting them down. They weren't even armed. They were standing around a flagpole with an American flag flying. They thought they had a treaty and we just killed them."

Kyle was weeping. So was I. How could I ever look at that fucking Jason again?

"I pulled up and screamed to cease fire but it was too late. Those little kids ran past me and into the woods. You just don't know what it's like to be scared for your life and not understand what you're doing. More of them escaped. About fifty fell. I tell you, if I get that damned Private Randolph in my sights I'll kill him," he said with venom.

"He was just like all the others, right?" I asked. "Why him?"

"He's a filthy man. He jumped off his horse and started slicing scalps off their heads. He didn't even look to see if they were dead. He was howling and laughing and holding up fistfuls of hair and blood. That started the others."

"Did you…?"

"No! I was sick. Jason was sick. Don't think he was any worse than me. We were together on what we were doing and what we saw. I hope he deserts. I hope he takes John Hamm and that they go back to Omaha and we can find you and Miranda. I just wanted to kill myself."

21
Courting

OF COURSE, we did get breaks, but not at the same time. I came down for an absolutely luscious week in the arms of Aubrey. My sweet, sweet girlfriend. I thought about how my attitude had changed about that. Yes, she was also my brother's girlfriend, but now I thought of her as *my* girlfriend. It was fine that she was his, too, but my relationship with her wasn't defined by that.

While I was down on my 'vacation', Phile and Caitlin pounded on my door. I opened it and they held out their laptop to me. *Damn! Another batch.* I checked with Mom Mar and loaded the kids in the truck with me. We dragged the horse trailer to Valentine, Nebraska where there'd just been a rodeo. On the heels of the rodeo was a notice that the stock contractor was selling off four of their broncs. We got there in time to load them into our trailer before the company left town. The horses weren't performing well and the contractor decided he needed better stock. They weren't as cheap at $200 each, but they were never going to be pleasure horses the way they'd been trained. I wrote a check on our business account and they laughed all the way to the bank.

I cautioned the kids about how to treat these animals. I didn't want them out there playing rodeo. The horses seemed gentle enough when we were loading and unloading them. Of course, we isolated the four of them in the paddock until the vet could come and check them out. I checked their papers, vaccinations, and Coggins test and figured they'd be okay with the herd. Unlike racing horses, bucking horses are all geldings but they can vie for dominance in a herd. Our Saddlebred stallion, Harley, pretty much ruled the rescues. We didn't let him and Pa's Bolt in the same field.

The night before I went back up to the range, I made slow, sweet love with Aubrey. I wasn't satisfied with just having sex with her. We were both willing enough for that. But I wanted to show her how much I loved her. I could see the three of us being together for a long time—maybe forever.

It was important to me to explore everything about her, to let her know there wasn't any part of her body I was afraid of or ashamed of. And I had to show her I was willing to share my body at the same level.

"Are you really satisfied with just me?" she asked as I was coming down from the massive orgasm she'd just delivered. She'd had most of her hand up inside me and it had been pretty intense. My hands are so big I didn't try to get more than two fingers in her but that had been quite enough.

"What do you mean, honey? Of course I'm satisfied with you."

"But are you really a lesbian then? You don't want to have a guy?"

"Shit. I can't say that for sure, you know. I've never been with a guy. I'm not repulsed by the idea of fucking a cock, so I don't think I'm a lesbian. I'm just in love with you, sweetheart. You're all I want," I assured her.

"If there ever comes a time… You know, if you ever decide you need a man… I mean, I love Kyle and I love fucking him, so I know how good that is, and if you find a guy you want to go all the way with, I'll understand, okay?" she was looking at me so intently that all I could do was kiss her again and try to assure her that all I wanted was her.

"I traveled again," Kyle told me when we finally got some time alone together. "It was kind of vindication."

"How do you mean?"

"I was sent to Omaha with dispatches and got called into the Colonel's office. I was questioned about the massacre and he was livid. My Captain got recalled and a new order has been received to engage only when attacked."

"That's good to hear, Kyle," I said.

"It is, but after what we did, we're going to get attacked. I get so scared when I'm out there. I just know I'm going to die."

"Well, you know what Pa says about opening a box? I guess one of the benefits of us not traveling at the same time is that I can tell you that you aren't dead. I know you are all right."

Kyle hugged me. He squeezed me so tight I lost my breath.

"Thank you," he whispered. "By the way, I saw your stepsister—the little blonde? She was at the train station. She seemed to be doing all right."

"Jason isn't interested in her, is he?"

"No. He's almost obsessed over finding you—I mean Miranda. I guess that little nudge I gave him got him started thinking of you. The girl—heck, she could be my sister."

"First thing I thought when I saw her was that she looked like Caitlin."

BEFORE KYLE TOOK his break to be with Aubrey, we found two calves that had their throats ripped out and had been gutted. The carcasses were about half consumed and our raven was sitting pecking at one with a bunch of other scavenger birds. We took pictures with our cell phones and cut the ear tags off to bring to Pa. If I ever saw one of those wolves… I touched my necklace. The teeth seemed hot against my skin.

"RAVENS ARE CALLED wolf-birds for a reason," Pa said.

"They are?"

"They lead wolves to prey and feast on the kill. Well, that's the Cheyenne legend, anyway."

It was a week before I'd been able to ask Pa about my raven seeming to taunt me. He said it was outside his experience since he'd been called only by the redtail hawk and to his recollection had never heard one scream except when he called him. We were out on our patrol that morning. Mom Ash was in charge of breakfast and we'd risen before four to take the dawn watch. The cattle had begun to move.

"There's your totem now," Pa said, as the raven did acrobatics in the early morning light. I sat astride Pooky and just stared at the old bird. Suddenly, he swooped down and landed on my shoulder. He looked over at Pa and then hopped to the other shoulder.

Awkawkawkawk!

MIRANDA PAUSED AT the door.

"Demon Ramie! What do you want?"

What? I'm a demon again? What did I do?

"I apologize, Friend Ramie. You come at a most inopportune time."

Why? What's hap…

I was flooded with Miranda's memories.

Jason is here? That's wonderful.

"Behave. He is a gentleman and I am a lady and we are attended by our chaperones."

Sure. No problem. This is great!

Maybe I'd get to see my brother in this other timeline we flitted in and out of. Miranda opened the door and there stood the handsome young corporal. I couldn't see Kyle in his eyes, though. Behind him was his Indian friend.

"Won't you come in, gentlemen," Miranda said softly. Her voice was scarcely above a whisper. I supposed at this register it did not sound as harsh. Jason and John Hamm stepped into the room and Miranda led them to seats near the fire where Theresa and Katie sat on cushions. Jason immediately took a seat while John stood. There was another chair.

Tell John to take the other seat.

"He is a savage!"

He'd like to sit down.

"But where will I…?"

Grab a cushion. It will endear you to your suitor.

"John Hamm. You are a guest in our home," Miranda said graciously. "Please take the chair next to the corporal."

"Thank you, Miss Lewis." His voice was also soft and cultured. Where had this man learned English? "I would not take your seat, though your offer is kind. I assure you that if I may sit, I will be more comfortable on the floor."

"As you wish, sir." Miranda handed him a cushion. "You sound… unlike what we are taught the…"

Native Americans, I supplied.

"…the Native Americans sound like."

"Would you prefer that I speak only in sign language or grunts?" he asked. There was a note of humor in his voice.

"No. Of course not. You were schooled in the East?"

"Indeed. I received my education at The Brick School in Boston."

"However, did you come to be at Harvard?" Theresa asked as Miranda settled in the chair and faced Jason.

"I was adopted as a child by a trader who took me to the East. It was quite a shock. I rather prefer life on The Plains." Theresa continued to engage John as we turned our attention on Jason.

"I am pleased that you were able to entertain us on such short notice, Miss Lewis," Jason said. "Sadly, I am not told when I will be called upon to deliver dispatches back to Regimental Headquarters."

"This is your third visit, Jason. Please call me Miranda."

"I do not wish to presume upon your favor."

Ha! I barked so loud in her mind that it came out her mouth. Miranda was so taken aback that she did not stop me when I took over her voice.

"That is indeed kind for a man whose first words to me were to call me a three-penny whore," I laughed.

"I… Madam, I would never do such a…" He paused and looked intently at Miranda. "Ford's Theater," he whispered. "You spoiled my attempt to save the President."

"And you spoiled mine," I added. Theresa, Katie and John laughed at some private joke. They were paying no attention to our whispered conversation.

"Why were you there?" he asked.

"Like you, a friend told me of the plot and I thought I could stop it by tackling the assassin outside the theater. Unfortunately, he was already inside and you strode up to the door with murder in your eyes," I said. Miranda was appalled but too shocked to attempt to say anything.

"A friend," he continued to whisper as if they were words of endearment. "Does your friend visit you often?"

"I never know when or for how long. We have so much in common, Jason."

"Yes, Miranda. And it is such a relief to know that we do. I will make no secret of the fact that I have grown fond of you. Perhaps even before our chance meeting at the cattle yard."

"That is something else that we find in common," I faded back and Miranda stuttered a bit as she found her voice.

I found myself completely enamored of Jason. What a kind and gentle soul. So like Kyle in many ways, yet so different. I don't know if it was all Miranda or if I helped to light the fires that were definitely kindled in them this night. When the night was over, we stood staring into each other's eyes.

"Please call again whenever you are in town, Jason. Do not be concerned that you have not given notice. I receive no other gentlemen callers," Miranda said.

"No army or renegade party could keep me from you if your words call me hither," he said. I swooned.

"And where are you off to next?"

"The rails have just reached Laramie City, in the Wyoming Territory, and we have been assigned to Fort Sanders. We will be scouting over the mountains this summer."

"My stepfather has already established a presence there. I am certain he will move westward with the rails."

"I don't know that," Jason said. "The way westward over the mountains has almost no population other than that we bring. The train runs daily now to our supply houses bringing ties, gravel, and merchant's wares. No one returns to the city at night once the rails are ten miles beyond. He may stay there until we near the Mormons at Salt Lake."

"I pray daily for your safety, Jason. Hurry to return to me."

"Why did you tell him of our first encounter?" Miranda demanded.

He'd have found out soon. Now he knows.

"But why?"

Miranda, Jason has a friend, just like you do. A friend like me.

Miranda was silent as she tried to comprehend what I'd said. I'm sure she thought she was the only person in the world with a time traveler in her head.

"And you know this friend?"

Yes. We are very close.

"Are you manipulating Jason and me together so that you and your friend can be together?"

Whoa! Miranda! I haven't really tried to manipulate either you or him. I have encouraged him to find you when we were lost, but our timing was off—just like at Ford's Theater. I think it is partly because when I asked him to follow you from the train, it had already happened for us. He couldn't get there to change you getting kidnapped. When he looked for you at St. Joseph, he was there nearly a year before you got there. But I have not manipulated his emotions, or yours, to get you together. And you have met him enough times without my presence to form your own opinion about him.

"I *do* have a favorable opinion."

I can tell.

"What?"

Your privities are damp.

"Ramie, you are my friend, but sometimes you act the very demon I thought you were!"

The problem is that if I blush, she blushes. As a result, we both were embarrassed and then burst out in a fit of giggles. Miranda had a stray thought and quickly clamped down on it.

Wait a minute there, girlfriend. What was that about?

"Nothing!"

You know I'm going to find out.

"But… Very well. You will find out in a few minutes. Katie can be quite demanding. Especially after Jason has visited."

Oh dear. I should have known. Is she jealous?

"I do not believe so. She seems… quite amorous."

And you? Do you mind? I can tell her not to disturb you.

"No. I find her attentions quite… enjoyable. And now that Theresa has moved into Mother's room—most of the time—I do not object to Katie's advances. But what will happen if… if I should get married?"

Let's play it by ear. For now, if you don't mind, I'd love to have my little Katie.

"Drive."

Almost on cue, Katie entered the bedroom. She wore her flannel gown and moved to sit on the bed, looking at me as I stared back at her.

"Wife, why have you bothered with clothing when it is time for bed?" I demanded. Completely taken aback, Katie jumped back to her feet.

"Husband Ramie. You have returned!"

"I have come to ravish your body, maiden. Remove your nightgown and then help me off with this. Are your privities as moist as mine?"

"They are, Ramie. They always are when…"

"Ah, you like our young corporal, I see." I was playing with her breasts and she loosened the ties of my nightgown. I let it fall to the floor. Miranda had gained a few pounds since our long journeys and it felt good on her. *God! I love her body. So lush. It reminds me of Aubrey.* As soon as I was naked, I turned and took Katie in my arms, kissing her deeply.

"Oh!" Katie moaned. "Miranda kisses me, and she is very loving, but I always know when you are here my demon husband."

"I have craved your kisses and your touch since I last held you in my arms, Katie. Sweet Katie, let me love you," I said. I did just that. I'd learned a lot in nearly a year as Aubrey's lover. She had taught me how to find places on her body that I never imagined were erogenous. I licked from the hollow of her throat up across her chin and kissed her lips a dozen times without letting her capture mine. I suckled her breasts and drew spirals around her nipples with my tongue. Katie rose rapidly. By the time I parted her bush and began licking at her clit, she was too far gone to care how much noise she was making. Poor Theresa. If she did not know before what was going on in this room she would know tonight.

Katie was desperate to return the favor and before long I felt her talented tongue parting my nether lips and drinking from my unending fount. She teased, licking all the way from my pucker to my clit and back again, as anxious to find and explore my body as I was hers. I rolled her onto her back and dove between her legs again, settling my pussy down on her mouth. To feel her tongue while I tasted her juices was too much and we both tipped over again.

"I love you, Husband Ramie. I love you," Katie whimpered as I held her.

"Katie, dear," I said softly. "Are you jealous of Jason?"

"Oh! Ramie. Miranda. Please do not think that. I find myself drawn to him like a moth to a candle. I revel in his presence, though I would do nothing to interfere in your love," Katie sobbed.

"What would you wish, child?" I asked softly. "In the best of all possible worlds, what would happen?"

"Ramie, you always talk to me as if I were important. I love you. I love Miranda when she is alone, as well, but I fear she does not think well of me."

"Not true! Not true!" Miranda broke in on my control. "Oh, dear Katie, I am so sorry I make you feel that way. Ramie is strong and confident and knows what to do about everything. I am lost and do not know how to tell you I love you, too."

"Miranda, is it true? Are you fond of me as I am of you?"

"I am, dear girl. God help me, I am."

"Then Husband Ramie," Katie said, switching to me. I still wasn't sure how she could tell when it was me and when it was Miranda. "You ask what the best of all possible worlds would be. My dear Miranda would marry the man she loves. She would be happy and bear him many children."

"And you?" I asked.

"And I… I would be your mistress."

A woman as a woman's mistress? Miranda was confused.

"And his," Katie finished in a whisper.

Can that be?

I let Miranda take over the conversation. She did so with a kiss.

As we drowsed in post-coital bliss, I continued to hold Katie's nearly flat breasts—so much like mine in my other life. Her thumb casually stroked my left nipple, keeping me aroused all night. Perhaps in this life, we could have something similar to what we had in my own life. One man and two women, or one woman with a man and woman. Only in this life, *I* would have a man. That Jason really got my engines running.

That thought was washing over me when I heard the raven call.

22
Opened Box

"I ALWAYS WONDERED what that looked like," Pa said. Black-feather was still sitting on my shoulder. The sun was just coming up. "Sometimes Mary Beth and Ashley didn't even realize I'd been gone until I was back. Your spirit bird is a lot friendlier than mine was. If that redtail hawk had lit on my shoulder, I'da shit my pants."

I glanced at the raven on my shoulder. You don't realize how big a raven's beak is until you see it six inches from your eye. I reached in my saddle pouch and pulled out a piece of jerky. The bird took it from my fingers and then flew off. I breathed again.

"Does he always come to you like that?"

"No. Once he flew into my room and sat on my bare shoulder. I had marks from his talons for a week. Pa, I just never know when he's coming for me or what he'll do. It was like I just knew he wanted some jerky and was waiting for it. But I don't go off traveling every time I hear him, either. I've come to believe that he calls both Kyle and me with different calls."

"Ravens have a number of different calls. I suppose it's possible."

"Pa… I'm not like, crazy am I? It's all so real when I'm there. Then I get back here and life just goes on the way life always does. But I remember everything so clearly and I… Pa, I think I'm falling in love."

"You ain't crazy, Ramie. There's a reason for you being here and a reason for you being there."

"But I love Aubrey. How can I go and fall in love with Katie? And Jason?"

"Hmm. That must be interesting. But don't let it worry you, honey. I fell in love with Laramie Wyoming Bell to the depth of my soul but it never once affected how deeply in love I was with your mother and Ashley. Remember, you are also dealing with the mind and heart of another person. In that time, it is not only you that is falling in love."

By the time we got the cattle all driven back down the range, we'd lost two more calves. I was exhausted and ready for school to start so I could get some rest. We barely got the cattle down before the first day of school. We had two full weeks of school before Labor Day this year. And that whole time, Aubrey wasn't able to come out to the ranch. Kyle and I both went into town to take her out on Saturday night. We fell easily into our patterns, just kind of flowing from one to the other, so that Aubrey got attention from both of us.

She spent Labor Day weekend with us at the ranch and we had our year-end picnic up at the gravestones.

"Your family stories mean a lot to you, don't they?" Aubrey asked as we cuddled together late that night. Pa had recited the names of our ancestors as we touched each stone that afternoon.

"More and more. Honey, we are tied to this land with bonds of family that go back generations. Every year, it seems like the bonds grow tighter."

"Is that what the map on your wall is all about?" she asked. It would have been hard to hide all that from her.

"Sort of. It's like charting the journey to Laramie. Learning where we all came from."

"I know where my family came from. Great-grandpa swam across the Rio and joined the U.S. Army the day after Pearl Harbor. While he was in the army, he studied for citizenship and came out a free member of this society. He fell in love with a cute gringa and moved north so they wouldn't be tempted to go back to Mexico."

"And now your parents own a restaurant in Laramie," I sighed. "Aubrey, you don't much like horses. And you are a city girl. Do you think… Would you ever be happy living on a horse ranch?"

"Ramie," she giggled, "we're only seventeen." *Shit! That sounded like I was proposing to her!*

"I didn't mean…"

"Shh. I know. That doesn't mean we aren't all thinking about it. Ramie, I've been making love to Kyle for a year-and-a-half now. And with you for a year. It's getting so that it's hard to imagine any other kind of life. I might not be tied to the land like you and Kyle are, but dearest Ramie, I am tied to you."

LONGTIME RESIDENTS OF Laramie will sometimes tell newcomers, "Laramie was founded by some pioneers who came over the mountain and got down here by the river seeking shelter from the wind. They planned to move on as soon as the wind died down. They are still down there by the river."

Of course, we all know that the railroad got here on May 10, 1868 and that night there was a town. The U.P. had a government grant of a big tract of land and divided it into lots. The lots went on sale in April and the day the train got here there were already whorehouses waiting for it. A lot of the town was just tents but there was a fair number of wooden buildings. Some just for sleeping, but most for commerce.

Commerce included JB Mercantile where Jonathon sold boots, gloves, trousers, shirts, hats, and sundries. It also included several tents and hastily erected buildings that had a bar with liquor in front and a row of cots in the back with available, if not willing, ladies lying on them waiting. Commerce meant relieving the railroad workers of as much of their pay as possible in as little time as possible. Commerce could also mean relieving the Union Pacific of as much money as possible. A saw mill and treatment factory was set up and logs came down from the mountains to be cut and treated for railroad ties. A gravel pit opened for the ballast. A blacksmith kept the horses shod.

And if commerce couldn't supply your needs, then a simple gunshot would. Laramie was lawless and had no government. Half the population were criminals.

Of course, we're a lot more civilized today, but the wind is still here, and when winter comes whipping through, sometimes it brings commerce of any sort to a standstill. Laramie is at an elevation of 7,100 feet. Centennial is 8,100 feet. Six miles up the road, Snowy Range Pass is 11,000 feet and the road is closed five months of the year.

This winter was brutal.

About the first of November, snow started flying. We had nearly two feet by my birthday. We'd already missed three days of school when the weather up our direction was a white-out. Our teachers were all considerate of the situation and we could get our assignments online. Mr. Hammersmith even posted his geology lectures as podcasts so we didn't miss any of his classes. *Damned technology!*

Friday after school, Aubrey piled into the Explorer with us and came home for the weekend. Even our dating had been limited by the weather, and we were looking forward to a fun weekend. Sunday was my birthday.

"…Happy birthday to you," the family sang before I blew out all eighteen candles on my cake. We had ice cream and I started getting presents. Phile and Caitlin presented me with a replica LK branding iron. We don't actually brand horses with a hot iron, but it was really cool.

"You wouldn't believe how many places we had to call," Phile said. "They thought we wanted something to brand steaks on the grill with!" We all got a kick out of that. Aubrey gave me a new belt for my jeans and, when I looked closely, I saw that it had a Colt belt buckle.

"Kurt has all those belt buckles in the store and it was between this and the Remington buckle, but Kurt said he thought you'd prefer the Colt for some reason. I guess between the two, it's the prettier one." She held up both hands in a kind of girlie way and looked like the only reason to have a belt buckle was because of how pretty it was. I kissed her.

"Children," Mom Ash reprimanded us as she shoved another box at me. Inside this package was a pair of short Lasso cowboy boots. They were hand-tooled and had crystals embedded in them.

"Mom Ash! These are beautiful! Where am I ever going to wear them?"

"Oh I figured you'd probably want to go to prom or something this year, and need nice shoes." We all started laughing and I thought, 'hell, why not?' Kyle handed me his package. I opened it up and found a new pair of chaps and spurs. I'd been complaining that I'd really outgrown my chaps but I sure never expected a new pair for my birthday. Those damned things are expensive. They were the same color as my new boots and even had some crystals down the side. He'd obviously coordinated his gift with his mother.

Aubrey stood up and held the chaps up to me. She held the spurs in her hand and then looked at Kyle. I saw the devil in her eyes as she caught a corner of her lower lip in her teeth.

"Kinky," she whispered. *Oh god! Come to think of it, maybe I'll wear them to bed tonight!*

Mom Mar and Pa held out a good-sized package to me. It was heavy.

"Eighteen is a pretty important birthday," Pa said. "Seems you need something special to remember it by."

I was a little nervous opening the package. When I finally got the plain corrugated cardboard box open, I saw something I never expected to see outside of Kurt's gun shop. There was a sleek black holster holding an 1851 Colt Navy .36 caliber. I just dropped it and rushed to Mom Mar and Pa.

"You didn't…" I panted as I crushed myself to my parents. "You didn't give him the Smith and Wessons, did you?" I was so afraid of what he'd say. Those guns belonged in our family. Pa shook his head.

"Even for you, I wouldn't part with those irons," Pa laughed. "Kurt and I reached… an agreement. Your Ma had the holster-belt made by your old friend Merv."

"Thank you. Thank you. You don't know what it means to have it."

"I think we do, honey," Mom Mar whispered. "We ain't *really* crazy."

MAKING LOVE WITH Aubrey Sunday night was heaven. Kyle begged off having her come visit him.

"I sorta got a headache tonight," he sighed as we walked toward the bunkhouse. "I don't feel much like company. Do you mind just spending the night with your girlfriend, Aubs? I just don't think I'd be fit company." He was so full of sighs and drama that we all busted out laughing.

"You are going to have your ear plastered against the wall and your cock in your hand the whole time," I laughed.

"And all the time, he's going to be thinking of my girlfriend in nothing but her new chaps and spurs as I lie helplessly naked in the middle of the bed, waiting for her to put her brand on me," Aubrey laughed at him. Kyle groaned.

"Why'd you have to go paint that kind of a picture," he said. "I gotta get back to my room so I can tune into the regularly scheduled broadcast." We laughed at him. I gave him a big hug and a kiss on the cheek. Aubrey kissed him considerably more intently and I saw her rub his crotch a little at the same time. Then we went in.

"Now get outa your clothes and into them chaps, miss," Aubrey commanded me. Hell, what could I do?

THERE WAS NO school Monday morning. It wasn't canceled. Kids in Laramie had to go to school. But buses weren't running up to Centennial. Wouldn'ta made a bit of difference if they did because we'd be at least until noon plowing the ranch road into town. Moms sat all five of us kids at the dining table and commanded us to get started studying. Kyle, Aubrey, and I listened together to Mr. Hammersmith's lecture and wouldn't you know that he called us out in class as having celebrated my birthday too enthusiastically to get to school. I called his office right after the podcast and he laughed at me.

"Just wanted to make sure you were listening," he said. "I expect you'll just stay out of town tomorrow, too, so if you have any questions on the assignment, just let me know." He was a nice guy.

We spent the day in the house and even baked cookies. Even with studying, we had fun.

Later that night, I listened to Kyle and Aubrey making love in the next room. It was sweet. It made me happy to hear them and I didn't even rub myself. I didn't expect Aubrey to come in tonight. Didn't see any sense in her running through the snow from one door to the other to pretend something that everyone knew was different. I sat in my sweats and pulled the gun to me. Mom Mar and Pa were generous, but they really didn't know what this meant. I just looked at it for a long time. I hadn't taken it out of the holster, even when they'd given it to me. I needed this to be private time.

It slid smoothly out and I checked the six chambers. They were clean as a whistle. I strapped the belt around my waist and pulled the gun. It was smooth. Not a bit of drag. I brought it up and cocked it with my left thumb while my right finger hovered over the trigger. I returned it to safety, positioning the cylinder between two chambers. Then I did it.

I rotated the gun to look at the brass butt.

"PA! PA! PA!" I screamed as I ran through the house toward his office. I hadn't bothered to even put on my boots. I ran through the snow in my bare feet, slipping and sliding on the linoleum in the kitchen. I was crying and carrying my six-shooter. I ran into the office without pausing. Moms and Pa were all cuddled in his big chair with a fire going. Mom Mar didn't have a shirt on and Mom Ash had hers pushed off her shoulder. I should have been embarrassed but I was crying too hard.

They opened their arms and I collapsed on top of all three of them.

"I opened the box," I gasped. "I opened the box."

"What did you find, honey?" Pa asked.

"It's all real. I'm not crazy. You're not crazy. It's real and I'm scared."

"I thought you knew it was real," Pa said.

"I wanted it to be a dream. If it was just all a dream, then I could wake up and maybe, when I went to sleep, I could dream better. But it's not a dream and I'm a murderer."

"Shh, baby, what you told me was self-defense," Pa whispered.

"But I still killed them. I took this gun from the second man I killed. I marked it with my initials. I marked it with the knife I used to kill all three of them." I held the butt of the gun up to Pa and he traced my initials engraved in the brass. They were faint, almost polished away when Kurt restored it. But they were there—LWB.

"You poor baby," Mom Mar said. "With a knife? How horrible for you."

"Tell us, honey," Mom Ash said. "It will be better when you tell us and it isn't all held inside."

I told them. I told them about the man in Baltimore whose knife I took and used it to gut him. I told them about the kidnapper who had no idea he was about to die when he pulled the tarp off of me. And I told them about holding the knife to the third man's throat while I questioned him.

"Then Miranda twitched my hand and I cut his throat," I moaned. "Sometimes, I go to sleep and see all that blood covering me. And I know Miranda does, too."

Pa rocked me and Mom Mar petted my hair. Mom Ash went to fix us some tea. I whimpered as I held the gun and slid it into its holster.

When I'd settled down, Pa stood us all up.

"Strap that on, baby girl," he said as he reached for his Smith and Wessons. He settled the left belt around his hips and then the right. It looked like they used to fasten tighter.

"You've gained weight, Cole," Mom Ash chuckled. "What are you up to now?"

"Just come with me, sweetheart," he said, taking my hand. "Put some boots on." We went to the front door and shoved our feet into a couple pair of Sorrels. We stepped out onto the front porch. Moms stopped at the door.

The bunkhouse was off toward the barn and we most always used the kitchen door. Out the front, the snow was deep and clean looking out toward the river. The full moon was almost directly overhead and everything was bright white with black shadows. Pa pulled his Smith and Wessons from their holsters.

"I killed five men right out there where you are looking," he said softly. I heard Moms gasp behind me as I stared up at my father. He pointed the guns to one point and then another as he spoke his tale. "There isn't a day I walk out this door that I don't see exactly where their bodies landed. It wasn't even a time as primitive as when you are visiting. The hawk called and all of a sudden it was 1906."

"But I thought Kyle Redtail died in '92," I said.

"He did. I was long dead. Arthur Alexander came into the office and went straight to my guns, hanging right where I still keep them. 'I know you're still here, Kyle,' he said. 'I know you watch over them—us—all. I love Kat. I'll die to save her and Artie and Bonnie. And Laramie and Kaylene, too. We're all family and I'll fight for them now.' He had to be near seventy-five and broke down, wheezing and coughing, as he reached for my gunbelts. 'You got to help me, Kyle. I don't know how to do this. Help me save them.' As soon as he touched my guns, I flowed up into him and wrapped myself around his old body.

"Six riders had taken it upon themselves to claim the spread by raping our women. I stood in this very spot and killed five of them. The sixth cried for mercy and ran for his life."

I was crying again. Pa holstered his guns and turned toward me. He put both hands on my shoulders and I looked into his eyes. I'd never seen my father cry.

"Every day, Ramie. Winter, summer, spring, and fall. Every day I see their bodies hit the ground right out there. And every day I know that I would do the same thing again. Kaylene was just your age. Artie and Bonnie were a little younger. Laramie and Kat were standing in the doorway behind me, right where your moms are now. I would kill those men again to keep them safe. And so would you."

I went up to my room in the big house that night instead of going back to my apartment. Mom Mar came and cuddled me all night long.

23
Hard Winter

WE MADE believe we were snowed in all Thanksgiving week. There was only one day of school left anyway. Kyle and Aubrey came in surprised to find me already in the kitchen wearing my sweats and my six-gun. I don't know what came over me but I kissed them both. Not like big romantic kisses, but more like a 'good morning, dear' kiss.

"We've got to get feed out to those horses," I said, pointing down to the lower pasture. The pregnant mares and our working stock were all up in the paddock where they had shelter and easy access to food and water. The rescues, farm stock, mules, and Harley were all down in the lower pasture. They had pretty good shelter and we had a bubbler in the stock tank, but we had to make sure there was adequate hay for them to keep grazing. We took a load down a couple times a week.

After breakfast, we got dressed for outdoor work. Poor Aubrey didn't come prepared to stay the week, so she got relegated to the kitchen helping get Thanksgiving dinner ready. Kyle and I bundled up in our parkas and Sorrels and loaded a dozen bales of hay on the wagon. He drove while I kept watch on the fender. I had my Remington 700 in the tractor scabbard and my 1911 on my hip. The kids rode on the hay wagon and they had their rifles with them. We just didn't go anyplace away from the house without arms these days. You could hear the wolves in the hills almost every day.

"Would you look at that?" Kyle said pointing.

There were twenty antelope mixed right in among the horses. It looked like even the wild things were huddling near the ranches. We discussed whether it was a good thing to have them up where we could protect them or whether having the deer around the ranch would entice the wolves down lower as well. One thing was for sure, we needed to start bringing each horse up to the barn once a week to curry come spring, so we could check for ticks. Mixing wild animals with domestic ones could have far-reaching consequences if any of the wilds bore Chronic Wasting Disease. We still didn't have a good handle on whether CWD could be spread to cattle, horses, or other livestock.

Old Blackfeather was sitting on the hay racks as the horses came running for the fresh food. Some of the antelope came right up with the horses to eat hay.

"I think we need another load of hay if we're feeding an extra twenty head," Kyle said, laughing.

"We'll go get it!" Caitlin yelled. She was in the tractor seat and had it started before Kyle and me could get around the hay rack.

"Yahoo!" Phile yelled. They had their guns in the scabbards and were putting toward the barn.

"It's all still a game to them," Kyle laughed.

"Not to me," I said. He turned toward me. "That's what I found out last night, Kyle. What we're doing? Going back in time? It's not a dream." I told him about marking my gun and then about seeing the mark last night. He clutched me in a big hug just as the raven called.

"I AM SO sorry to bring you this news, Miss Theresa," Jason said as he stood in front of us. "I was heading out to deliver dispatches and the lieutenant granted permission for me to find you. I felt it would be better coming from someone you know as a friend than in a telegram."

"Thank you, Corporal," Theresa said. "I need to walk a bit to take in this news. Katie, would you accompany me?" Theresa pulled on her muffler and coat. Katie followed her out, looking longingly behind her at Jason. "Oh, John Hamm, could we impose upon you to accompany us for safety? It is late." John looked at the two of us before he spun on his heel and followed the girls.

Suddenly I was alone with Jason.

The realization struck him as well.

"Miss Miranda, I apologize for this imposition on your hospitality," Jason sputtered. "I will take my departure and await the return of our companions." Miranda raised her hand to stop him.

"Jason, please do not rush to leave. I would feel more comforted in your presence," Miranda said.

"I do not wish to besmirch your reputation by entertaining a gentleman without a chaperone," he said, smiling.

"It is because you are a gentleman that I do not fear for my reputation," Miranda answered. "I am twenty years of age and in truth, I wish to speak to you of matters of the heart. Let us sit beside the fire." Jason held my chair to steady it while I sat and then sat in the other.

"Miranda, I have longed to speak with you—heart to heart."

"Do you think you could love a woman such as me? I have a raven lodged in my throat that caws his harsh cry when I speak. I am not a beauty. I have lived a hard life working with my hands and learning to use guns and knives. Is it in your heart to love such a woman as me?"

Jason slipped out of his chair and knelt before me. *Is he going to propose?* My heart skipped a beat.

"My dear Miranda, your hard life has proven you a woman of stature and beauty. I would sooner listen to your voice than that of a thousand babbling débutantes. Your words hold strength and command. And as such, I find my heart, my soul, and my body are yours to command." I could feel a trickle of tears on my cheeks. He was so beautiful. I stood and pulled him to his feet.

"Jason, there are many things to discuss before you next kneel before me. But know that my heart is yours. I… I wonder… Jason, I have never kissed a man. I must seem brazen, but…" He caught me in his arms and touched his lips tenderly to mine. I felt my heart flutter and my legs grow weak. I thought about pushing my tongue into his mouth, but restrained myself from taking over for Miranda. This was a different age than that in which I lived. We weren't going to tumble into bed tonight, no matter that I could feel Miranda's slickness in her privities.

Damn, I liked that kiss!

"Friend Ramie," Miranda said silently. "I love Jason. But I cannot deceive him. Help me. Help me tell him of you and… of Katie." With that, she gently slipped into the background leaving me hanging from his lips.

"Let us sit… by the fire… talk…" Jason stuttered. The kiss had affected him as well. I scooted our chairs closer together and we sat again.

"Do you always wear your gloves, Jason?" I asked.

"No, Miranda. It is merely a habit."

"Will you remove the glove on your left hand so that it is your flesh that I grip and not buckskin?" He was flustered, but hurriedly stripped off his glove and took my offered hand. We sat in silence watching the fire as I tried to decide what course to take. His face was red and I thought it was wonderful.

"Jason," I said at last, "I am Miranda's friend." I'd finally decided to take the bull by the horns and dive right in. Miranda cringed in the back of my mind. "I know you understand. I know your friend. Before you ask Miranda for her hand, are you willing to accept me as well?"

"Friend, I know not how to address you, but I believe that you are as real as he who visits me. Often he has gazed on Miranda's face with love as deep as my own. Sometimes he has provided words for my wooing. Is Miranda also willing to accept my friend?"

Yes!

"Yes, she understands. You are two unique people in all the world. It is a miracle that you have found each other. But there is more."

"More?"

"We must tread carefully. When we escaped our kidnappers, Katie and I made our way north together."

"Yes, Katie is…" Jason blushed in his enthusiasm.

"Ah. You *have* noticed her."

"She pales by comparison…"

"Hush, my brave soldier. Make no comparisons. Because we would have perished otherwise, I disguised myself as a man. Katie and I made our way to Omaha pretending to be husband and wife," I said. "She refers to me still as her husband. Before you bend your knee to Miranda, you must ask yourself if you can accept Katie in our family as well."

"So that you would have two husbands?" Oops. I was almost over Jason's head. He was confused.

"She has preferred to believe that she will be my mistress. And yours."

"She wishes to be with us both?"

"Do not judge her harshly, Jason. Nor me. Katie is a virgin. I am a virgin. We escaped a life that would have made us playthings for a penny. But think on this, Jason. We agreed to speak of the heart. In my heart, I know we both love you."

"I will think carefully on these things," Jason said. "But my dear Miranda, are these things also in your heart?" I yielded her body back to Miranda.

"I feel these things my friend has told you, Jason. When you decide if you can live with this, know that we both… all three of us love you."

We spent another half-hour sitting quietly by the fire, my hand held gently in his. Perhaps more was said in that silence than in the entire conversation that went before.

The door to our apartment opened and the three came in shaking snow from their hair and boots. December of 1869 was coming to an end. 1870 would find us in Laramie. I saw Blackfeather sitting on the railing outside and pouted as he called. I'd so hoped to make love with Katie.

THE RAVEN'S CAWS were still echoing as I realized Kyle was holding me. The kids were unloading the second wagon of hay, occasionally casting glances our direction. I squeezed Kyle.

"Do you love Miranda?" I whispered.

"Yes," he answered. "I don't know how it is possible to love Miranda and Katie and Aubrey and…" He stopped. I squeezed him and we ran to the tractor, fired it up, and hauled the kids hollering and screaming up to the house. I knew what he didn't say.

SENIORS. WE ALL three got our acceptance letters from the University of Wyoming. Our SATs were good enough and our grade point average just high enough to get automatic acceptance.

Folks started trailering in mares in estrus in March. Bolt and Harley were having a hell of a good time. We were banking stud fees every weekend. By April, the snow was all gone from Laramie except where they'd piled it high around the light posts in parking lots. It took a little longer to melt from the shaded part of the mountains, but we were warm and comfortable when last year's mares started foaling. Bells and Bows were the first to drop beautiful fillies. They had the distinctive pinto markings of their dams with the dun coloring of their sire. They were beautiful. By Kyle's birthday, we had six healthy foals on the ground.

Riders started coming out the first of May to start working their boarded horses. They were pleased to see each horse with a shiny and well-groomed coat. They were easy to handle since we handled them almost daily. Phile and Caitlin led horses in from the field each day and groomed them. Two years ago I'd never have believed what I was seeing today. I was really proud of those two kids.

As soon as the snow started melting, Aubrey started spending more and more time at the ranch. Before graduation, she was spending three nights a week with us on a regular basis. Sometimes she split the night between Kyle and me. Sometimes she stayed with him one night and me the next. Neither of us minded. I figured there was a limit to how much sex you could really enjoy. I just never figured out what Aubrey's limit was.

I knew Kyle was continuing to travel because I occasionally saw new information on the map. His dates were getting closer to mine. We talked generally about travel, but never specifically about our interactions. We agreed that some things had to be between Miranda and Jason as much as possible, and we tried not to influence them. It was their lives we were infringing on. What we could do was study and learn all we could about Laramie, if that was where our hosts were bound.

It was Kyle's Golden Birthday—he was 18 on the 18th. Mom Ash thought it was appropriate for him to have his own truck. He got the keys to a Ford F150 Lariat. It wasn't new, but it pretty much blew Kyle away. Mom Ash had carefully explained to me that it was because of his golden birthday and I could count on something at least as special for mine when I turned 22. It was okay with me anyway. This baby had a full towing package and a long bed with a crew cab. Kyle was going to be hauling a lot of horses in the future. The first thing he did was take Aubrey and me for a ride up behind the ski lodge. We parked out there looking up at the stars while we made out. Neither Kyle nor I got undressed, but Aubrey was practically naked between us. It was clear that while I was fingering her pussy and sucking a nipple, she was jacking Kyle off in his pants. When we got back to the ranch, she went with Kyle and I listened through the wall to half a dozen orgasms. I had a few, myself.

Six days after Kyle turned eighteen, we stood in the school auditorium as we waited to receive our diplomas.

179

I DON'T KNOW what inspired me that night. I'd kissed Aubrey until she couldn't catch her breath and then smacked her on the butt and sent her to Kyle. That was all I wanted that night.

I was a high school graduate.

I was excited about what the future would bring. We'd be starting something all new when we went to UWyo in the fall, but it didn't seem that different. Mom Ash was encouraging us to live on campus our freshman year, but we had a for-real business going now. We couldn't just leave and expect Phile and Caitlin to care for all the stock, especially since we picked up four mustangs in a government sale and another six old nags at auction. This summer we'd have to work on fences on the new leased land and make sure there were proper shelters and feed stations for next winter.

I wandered around the ranch outside in the moonlight. It was just past full and with the trees starting to leaf out, it was casting soft shadows over everything. I was standing by the corral in my sweats with just my 1911 on my hip. Pooky came trotting over to see if I had anything interesting and I decided to just slide onto his back. I clipped a lead rope to his halter and tied the other end. We walked out of the yard and down toward the river. The night was still and calm. I wasn't supposed to be out this far alone, but it was such a beautiful night.

I saw movement down by the water and regretted not having my 700 and backup. I didn't even have a saddle or proper riding clothes. I pulled out my Remington and jacked a shell into the chamber. I was wearing my boots, so I had my knife. I slid off Pooky and stood quietly beside him. I wasn't sure what I'd seen.

But there it was again. I was sure it was a wolf, though all I saw was the shadow moving across the ground. *Where is the damned thing?* I didn't dare turn my back on it to ride back to the house. I couldn't back up and lead Pooky because a horse always wants to face the same direction as the rider.

I saw the shadow again and it was closer. Much closer. I raised the gun, searching for my target.

Out of the shadow flew the raven.

Awkawkawkawk!

24
Laramie City

"**S**UNSET. WHAT an awful time to arrive in a frontier town. We have luggage and cargo. We cannot simply hide in the hotel."

I don't suppose you made a reservation.

"Demon Ramie! My friend. I am thankful for your company." We heard a gunshot from across what passed for a street and down a hundred yards.

"Don't let it startle you, ladies. Sometimes the boys get a little wound up at night when they get into town. Nothing like it used to be." We looked at the speaker and found a short man with a beard and slouched hat jammed down on his head. "How about if I take you to which ever bawdy house you are headed to. I would happily be your first customer."

"I beg your pardon. We will be going to no bawdy houses and will not require your assistance. We will take a room at a hotel," Theresa said. I looked up and down the street.

We'd better stay here at the station hotel. I don't think anything else is safe. What year is it?

"Twelfth May 1870. We are in Laramie City. We need to get off the street."

No kidding. Hustle the girls into the station. There's a hotel entrance from inside.

"Where is your husband then, girl?" the short man pressed on.

Knife? Gun?

"Boot and bag. You drive." I took control of Miranda's body and stepped between shorty and Theresa. My hand slipped into the bag and found the comforting grip of the Colt.

"If you wish to earn a nickel, I will pay you to carry our baggage into the station," I said in a growl. Miranda is a lot shorter than me, but she was still tall enough to look him in the eye.

181

"A nickel to carry the little satchels of the fine ladies?" he mocked, looking at the bags we carried.

"Not these. Those." I gestured behind us where a stevedore was still piling our dozen trunks on the platform. The man's eyes got round and he turned and stomped away. "Now inside, both of you," I commanded. "This is not a safe place." Katie jerked around and looked at me.

"Yes, Husband Ramie," she whispered. She took Theresa's hand and led her into the station and to the hotel desk. I let Theresa talk her way into a hotel room, fending off the initial response that this was not a whorehouse and there were no rentals except to travelers. Theresa simply talked over the clerk and told him we would need our dozen trunks and the three crates in the freight secured for the night so that we could move them to JB Mercantile in the morning.

"It's closed," the clerk said. "Good old Johnny got hisself shot tupping old man Arnold's missus. Soldiers boarded up the store."

"It will be open tomorrow," Theresa said. "I own it. Good old Johnny was my father and got exactly what he deserved. There will be no more arguments, boy. Give us our key and see to the luggage."

The desk clerk was so taken aback by Theresa's imperious tone that he immediately provided the key and called a porter to take care of the trunks, promising they would be placed under lock and key. I promised that I would inspect them after dinner. We went to our room on the other side of the building.

"The food smells good," Katie said as we passed through the dining area.

"We can come back for dinner once we have seen our room. I want to check on just how secure our freight is," I said. Theresa unlocked the door and we went in. As soon as the door closed behind us, Katie flung her arms around my neck and kissed me thoroughly. I could tell Miranda enjoyed the affection as much as I did.

"Do you two need your own room?" Theresa snapped. "If you bounce the bed all night I shall be cross."

"Sister, we will be quiet," I laughed. "I think." Katie did not release my hand.

"Why does everyone think we are whores?" Theresa complained.

"In this town, women are married, too young to marry, or working on their backs," I said. "We picked a fine time to arrive in this hell-hole. It won't be civilized for another five years."

"You know a lot about it all of a sudden."

"I've been studying, Theresa," I said. I removed my sister's shawl and petted her hair, "Let us not argue. We have journeyed far and are tired. And if Katie's stomach is any indication, we are hungry, as well." Katie's stomach was grumbling loudly. That broke the tension and we laughed. "Let us go back to the dining room and eat," I said. "Then I must check on our freight."

"Miranda, you are not going off on your own, are you?" Theresa asked. "I am sorry I have been snappish, but I am frightened. Please be careful."

"Thank you, dear sister. Food first, and then we will see what happens."

In 1870, the Thompson House hotel and train station was the only dependable dining room in Laramie. Certainly, food and drink were available in every establishment along Front Street, but ladies did not enter there unless they were working. We had a slice of roast, a potato, and drinking water. As we ate, I rummaged in Miranda's memories, soaking up all she'd done in the past six months and their correspondence with the circuit judge in Cheyenne and the captain at Fort Sanders, who had ordered the mercantile secured. Miranda had liquidated the entire homestead in a box stock in Omaha and packed everything that could be shipped with them to Laramie. Another shipment would arrive next week.

We saw only two other women in the dining hall, both with husbands and children. No wonder we stuck out like a sore thumb. I wished Jason had been able to meet us at the station. Our letters had been loving, but he was patrolling the tracks into Utah as workers erected telegraph lines and secured fuel and water stations.

When we had finished our dinner, the girls returned to our room and I approached the chief porter.

"I would like to inspect where you have stored our freight," I said. He nodded and got to his feet. I felt like every eye was on me as I left the safety of the station.

"Always got to store things when the night train arrives," he said. "Nobody wants to travel at night." We got to a rickety building at the end of the platform and he unlocked the padlock. I could see two of our trunks in the dim light through the door.

"And all our trunks and crates are in there?"

"Go in and check if you like," he said.

Right. Who wants to go in the spooky cellar first to see if there's anyone waiting for us? As if I hadn't seen any teen slasher movies.

"Lock it," I said. "If it is not all there when we collect it in the morning, I will know who to find." I was answered by a groan and turned to find the porter slumping to the ground as a black-gloved hand clamped down over my mouth. He wrapped an arm around me, trapping both my arms. I couldn't reach either my gun or my knife.

"Be silent and it will only hurt a little," the man growled at me. "Cry out and I will make it hurt for a long time." Miranda was screaming terror in my head and I tried to silence her so I could think. I could scarcely breathe in the corset she was wrapped in with his arms pulling me to him. He gave me a shove into the storehouse. I fell and turned to see him silhouetted against the opening of the door. I was scrambling to get to my gun when a shadow sprang from beside me, taking substance as I heard a wolf's growl. The stranger fell back as the wolf sank teeth into his throat. A total of only seconds passed from the opening of the lock to the dull thud as the dark man's body hit the dirt.

The porter groaned and I moved toward the open door. The wolf leapt the tracks and turned to look at me, gore dripping from his jowl. Then he was gone. Once I was certain the porter was coming around, I hurried back to the hotel.

A wolf had saved me. My throat burned.

"WAS THAT YOUR demon spirit form?" Miranda whispered in my mind.

That was a fucking wolf!

I'd abandoned control of Miranda's body a step from the door and she'd stumbled against it, adrenalin still coursing through our veins. I hated wolves. Why had this one come to my rescue? And it wasn't the first time. I remembered the wolf killing and leaving a deer the first time I hunted in Miranda's body. I'd seen it out the corner of my eye pacing our wagon. What did it want from me, and why was it apparently a friend of Miranda's and an enemy in my own time?

"Friend Ramie, please stay with me. I am as frightened as you."

I know, Miranda. I am worried that the body I left in my own time is still vulnerable. I thought I saw a wolf when the raven called me to you. I still function in my own time when I travel to you, but I am not as alert.

"You will do well, Ramie. I know you will. Now let us greet our sisters. Katie was so excited to see you. She knows when you arrive as well as I do. Will you not give her pleasure tonight?"

I do not wish to simply use your body for the pleasure it can offer me.

"But your pleasure is my pleasure. Truly, Ramie. Katie needs you."

MIRANDA AND I both needed Katie, as well, after our encounter with the wolf. Theresa slept on her side of the bed, or pretended to, while Katie and I ravished each other. I could not get enough of her juices on my tongue and actually passed out from her ministrations to my pussy. Poor Theresa.

"Husband Ramie, I love you," Katie whispered in my ear.

"As I love you, Katie. And do not think that it is only me."

"I know Miranda also loves me, but there is something special when you are here. Will it always be like that?"

"In my experience, people can seldom say with certainty what will always be. Will people always ride horses and drive wagons down the streets of Laramie? Will the streets always be made of mud? Will women always be looked upon as whores first? This very area is a center of change. Do you know that women here in Laramie vote and sit on juries?"

"The things you say are strange, but they sent a thrill up my spine."

"Where?" I whispered. "Here?" I licked her spine from her butt to her neck.

"Yes. Yes. I will believe you husband. I will love you and…"

"And Jason?" I asked.

"He looks upon me kindly and has touched my hand."

"I think there will come a day when he touches much more of you than that. Will you share faithfully with Miranda?"

"Always, my love."

THE STREET WAS lively when we ventured out in the morning. A crowd was on the platform and our porter was at the center of it.

"He hit me and knocked me out cold," the porter told the fascinated crowd. "Then the lady turned into a spirit and tore his throat out right before my eyes. And with the blood dripping from her maw, she turned her baleful gaze upon me."

"Oh dear," I said. "This is not good." I stepped into the crowd and looked squarely at the porter. He fell to his knees.

"There she is, returned to take my soul as well! Mercy!"

"Foolish man!" I snapped. "What drunkenness is this? If I find you did not safely keep my baggage last night I will demand your soul of the judge."

"I saw you! You changed your shape to a fierce dragon and ripped out his throat with your talons!"

"You old drunk! How could you see such a thing if you were knocked out cold? Whose throat was ripped out?"

"Simon Quince," one of the crowd said. "Old Tom here says he brought you out here and Simon attacked you. Then you turned into a beast and tore out his throat."

"I told this fool to relock the room and then returned to the hotel," I said. "But I confess that if I had been attacked I would have been more direct in defending myself." I pulled my revolver from my bag and held it steadily in my hand as I cocked it. Old Tom passed out. There was a fair amount of laughter. I almost felt sorry for the porter. Almost. "Nonetheless, if someone got his throat ripped out, we should mount a search for curs and half-wolves. If it attacked one man, it might attack any of us."

There was a noisy assent and someone mentioned seeing a coyote slinking along the tracks not a quarter of a mile from the station. There was an immediate movement to organize a search for strays and the crowd dispersed.

"Very well done," a voice said behind me. I still had the gun in my hand and turned to find a .45 pointing at my gut. "You can safety that and put it away now," the man said.

"And you are?" I asked.

"I am what passes for law in this territory. Nathaniel Boswell."

"Ah. Sheriff Boswell. Word of your *vigilance* precedes you." Late in 1868, Laramie had been so lawless that gangs roamed the streets taking whatever they desired. Boswell led a committee of vigilantes to drive out the scoundrels and then hung four of them. At that time, he was the top scoundrel left and was appointed sheriff of the newly formed Albany County.

"Something had to be done," he said obliquely.

"And exactly what did you do about the murder of my father, Jonathon Bell?" Theresa demanded, stepping to the fore.

"Miss Bell. Judge Jones sent me a message that you were imminently to arrive. Welcome to Laramie City," Boswell said. "As to your father's demise, there was little we could do to Jacob Arnold as he found the man buried to the hilt in his wife. Completely justifiable. There were many men unhappy with Jacob because he killed Annie Arnold as well. She was one of the few in town who did not charge for her favors."

"Well, we need transport of our goods to the store and a laborer to remove the boards," Theresa said. "Good riddance to my father. He was a foul man. But I want that store open by noon." The sheriff motioned to a couple of men and before long a buckboard had arrived to transport our goods to the store just three blocks away. Boswell turned to me again.

"Miss? Did you say you are Miss Bell's sister?"

"Stepsister, Sheriff. The other is our assistant, as close as a sister. I am Miranda Lewis."

"Miss Lewis, then. We are a rough-hewn city of nearly a thousand souls in the newly created Wyoming Territory. The law of might makes right is often the only law that is followed. You should know, though," he looked pointedly at my bag, "I have no qualms about hanging a woman, if she is found to be a murderer."

"Thank you for that enlightenment, Sheriff. Should I encounter such a woman, I will pass on your warning."

We slaved the rest of the morning, directing the men sent to help us in moving boxes and unboarding the windows. We chased them out with two bits each at noon and set about restoring order ourselves. The chimes on the door rang and we looked up to see Shorty, our first contact in Laramie, come through the door.

"Do you have tobacco?" he demanded as he came through the door. "Kuster says he has none for me."

"We are a dry-goods store, not a tobacconist," Theresa announced. Shorty looked up recognizing the three women in front of him for the first time.

"Well, damn. Begging your pardon ma'am." He pulled his hat off a greasy head. He looked around quickly. Most things were still in disarray, but his eyes fell at once on a harmonica. "How much for that mouth organ?" he asked. He looked at it almost hungrily.

"One nickel," Theresa said. "And it must have the shield of the United States of America on it. We do not accept Confederate coins, no matter what they are made of." Shorty dug in his pocket and pulled out an assortment of odd bits, finally coming up with a nickel. He squinted at it to make sure it had the shield then held it out to Theresa. She took the coin, looked at it and smiled.

"Would you like me to wrap it for you, sir?" she asked, reaching for the harmonica. He held out his hand and she gave it to him.

"No." He ran his lips over the harp and blew the notes. He grinned at Theresa. "I always wanted one of these."

"Well, I am glad you found it here. After all, it turns out you *were* our first customer." He shrugged his shoulders and blew into the mouthpiece again.

"Ladies," he said. "If I may be of service, please feel free to call upon me." He started blowing and sucking on the mouth organ as he left the shop. We looked at each other and burst out in giggles.

"We may have sealed our fate in Laramie if he inflicts that wretched noise on the city," Katie laughed.

WHY DID I never hear Theresa's last name before?

"I do not know. Is it important, Ramie?"

When she said 'Jonathon Bell' my mind short-circuited.

"What?"

I became very confused. It was as bad as a wolf protecting me.

"Why is this so important, Friend Ramie?"

Bell is my surname.

I lay in bed, holding Katie in my arms as Theresa hugged herself to us. I had been unable to make myself still enough in the midst of our labor and first customers, or during our lovemaking with Katie, to probe Miranda's mind. It was all there. Her mother, Dolly Lewis, married Jonathon Bell. His daughter was Theresa Ranae Bell. My great-great-great-great-grandmother. I was still battling within myself. My mind was overloaded and I could not think.

Perhaps this was why I was here—why Miranda was here. To protect my ancestor Theresa.

Miranda was quizzical but let me try to unscramble my thoughts. We heard a scratching at the windowsill and in silent consent, crawled from between the two younger girls and opened the sash. The raven hopped in and looked at us.

Keep yourself armed, Miranda. Laramie is a harsh place. If at all possible, get a small gun for Katie and Theresa that they can hide on their persons. I think I am going now. Please remember that I love you.

And I love you, Friend Ramie.

Awkawkawkawk!

25
Shacking Up

I WAS STILL holding my gun, cautiously scanning the riverbank Nothing. I holstered it and grabbed a fistful of Pooky's mane to swing onto his back.

"I'm tired now, Pooky," I whispered. "Let's go home." He turned and plodded back to the paddock where I removed the lead rope. He pushed his head into my armpit and nodded up and down, covering my left boob with his snot. "Nice one, buddy. Don't think I won't remember that!" I laughed and headed to my apartment and bed.

PA AGREED THAT we had too much to do with the horses this summer to be able to spend it up on the mountain. We needed to monitor our broodmares and foals, take care of our rescues, and tend to our boarders. We had fences to mend. We had trails to mark, veterinary visits, and farrier appointments. We had breeding records to maintain and accounting to do. And we'd been contacted by a group that was rescuing abused animals to see how many we could take.

They left me and Kyle at the ranch and took Caitlin and Phile to the upper range. They would turn fifteen this summer and Pa felt they needed the experience of working the herd. Their birthdays were so near together we practically considered them twins. Just different moms. That just left Kyle and me with twice the amount of work on the ranch. Maybe three times as much since Mom Mar decided that she was going to join them up on the range. After all, we were eighteen and could take care of ourselves.

And we had Aubrey. We presented her with an official contract to work on the ranch at L&K Stables. She moved in with me. And Kyle. It was difficult to tell which. We made the offer of her own room but she felt that would be a waste. I had room in my closet for her summer gear so that was her official lodging—especially when her parents came out for a visit. But neither of us ever knew whose bed she would be in when we retired for the night or if she'd stay there all night.

We didn't have sex every night. Not quite. Even Aubrey needed a break occasionally. But even on those nights when she slipped naked into my bed and just held me, I felt such a flood of joy and love that I wanted to cry. And I knew what I wanted.

Pa, Mom Mar, and Mom Ash came down for three days to celebrate Pa's birthday on July 4. I guess they wanted to check to make sure the ranch was still standing, too.

"You dared to leave those two up there without supervision?" Kyle laughed. "What is the world coming to?"

"Oh, they have supervision, all right. Neither of you got rode as hard as Rafe rides them. He doesn't even allow them to ride on the same shift. Laura and their little boy came up for the week so there'd be another woman up there with Caitlin. I don't think she'll let them get away with anything," Mom Ash said.

"Happy birthday, Pa!" Aubrey called as she walked into the room carrying a birthday cake with one candle on it. We all started singing. Pa blew out his candle and Aubrey set the cake down. "I didn't know how many candles it should have and didn't want to guess," Aubrey laughed.

"Come here, young lady," Pa said. Aubrey went to him and he pulled her down on his lap in his big leather chair. "You are so happy here that you want to be my daughter, do you?" Aubrey nodded. "Well, honey, hearing you call me Pa when you came in just did my heart good. You know we've been thinking of you like a daughter for a long time now. Welcome home." Aubrey hugged Pa and then got up to go hug both Moms.

"Uh, Pa?" I said. "I guess that would make this a good time to talk to you all about something."

"Something?" Pa asked.

"Well, yeah. I know Mom Ash felt pretty strongly about us living on campus this fall, but we just think that would make life harder all the way around. We've been increasing boarders and even though we lost a few for the summer, I expect we'll have twelve or fifteen by first snow. And you know what a time we had with the rescues last winter. And then there's six new foals and another six pregnant mares, and we need to be working with the young ones," I said.

"Yes? And what's that got to do with the price of bread?"

"Well, it just doesn't seem right for us to go off to school and saddle the kids with all the work on the ranch, even if they consider themselves hired hands. They still have school. We were thinking we should live out here and commute to school. I know there will be times when commuting will be tough, but with Kyle's new 4x4 we should be safer on the roads and we'll still be taking the kids to high school, too."

"So you want to stay in your apartments?" Mom Mar asked. Mom Ash snorted. *Here goes nothing.*

"Well, with Rafe and Laura having moved down to grandpa's where we're wintering the cattle, the two bedroom apartment is vacant. We sort of thought we could move into that apartment and out of the efficiencies. And then we could ask Aubrey to move in with us," I got out in a rush.

"I see. So you'd all be like roommates sharing an apartment. Well, that has some plusses. It would save on some expenses since we wouldn't have to pay for dormitory rooms. You and Aubrey were planning to room together anyway. We could put another twin bed in the second bedroom for you and Aubrey."

"Pa-ah!" He was going to make it as hard as possible on us. "Could we just get a big bed for that room? Aubrey and I don't mind sharing our bed, do we honey?"

"I don't mind! Really!" she practically shouted. "Ramie, could I really move in with you both?" Well, that put it in exactly the words I was trying to avoid saying to the parents but I found both Kyle and I were nodding our heads.

"You don't want to be roommates," Mom Mar said gently. "You want to live together. I understand, kids. We all do. If it's what you really want, I can't think of a reason why you shouldn't try it out. You're already sleeping with each other."

"I can think of a reason," Mom Ash sighed. We all looked at her. "You don't think we'll be able to keep Caitlin and Phile out of those efficiencies when they move out, do you?" We all laughed.

"Moms and Pa," Kyle said. "You mentioned we were sleeping with each other. I guess it's no secret that Ramie and I are both pretty much in love with Aubrey and she says she loves us, too. But Ramie and I don't sleep with each other. It's not like that." He was blushing so red I could feel the heat. "If it's okay, with Aubrey, Ramie and I will each have a bedroom and she can sleep in either one she wants to. Whenever she wants to."

"Oh, I didn't think you were fooling around with your sister," Mom Mar said. "But you've got a unique situation. You all need to be prepared to find out if it works or not. Maybe Aubrey needs one of the efficiencies so she has private space where she can go without sleeping with either of you."

"We'll work it out, Mom Mar," I said. "But could we go ahead and move this summer?"

The parents all burst out laughing.

"If I can actually get a piece of that cake before the ice cream is all melted, you can add moving to your chores for the summer," Pa said. "But Aubrey, you need to be straight with your parents, too. Don't pretend to them that you aren't sleeping with both these young coyotes."

AUBREY SPENT EVERY night since graduation sleeping with either Kyle or me—or sometimes both—so you'd think setting up housekeeping together would have been easy. Not so. We were *living* together. Kyle's room and my room had always been our private personal space. Now we had to share the housekeeping and make sure the common areas were picked up and cleaned up. We had a kitchen and had to figure out who was cooking and who was cleaning. The apartment had two bedrooms but only one bathroom. We had to take turns and "learn to put the fucking seat down on the toilet, Kyle!"

But the worst thing was sex.

I mean it was the best thing, too. But the shared bath and both closets were between our rooms. We no longer shared a common wall and that meant we could no longer hear each other.

"WHAT'S WRONG, HONEY?" Aubrey said as she sat beside me on our little living room sofa. "You look really sad. Didn't you get off last night?" I shook my head.

"Really? What happened?"

"I'm terrible," I whispered. The truth was I'd cried most of the night. "You were with Kyle all night and… I'm not jealous… I just felt… left out," I bawled. "I… we… just…" How could I put it in words? Strong arms surrounded me as I felt Kyle settle into the seat beside me.

"I know what you mean, Ramie. We all got used to being… What do they call them? …voyeurs," Kyle said. "When Aubrey was with you the night before I felt the same way. I wasn't jealous of you being with Aubrey. I just felt sort of left out. When it was just one wall between us, we were all included even if we were in different rooms." I nodded my head vigorously. God, we were a screwed up family!

"Oh!" Aubrey said. Of course, she'd never experienced it so this was something completely new to her. "We don't… Well, maybe we don't have to shut our doors. At least not all the way. I mean… I don't know how the two of you stand it anyway. I love you both like crazy, but I gotta tell you that if the two of you were doing it, I'd want to be right there watching." She started giggling and I started tickling her. Then Kyle started tickling and we turned around and got him, too. It ended up with me pulling Aubrey's shirt off over her head and Kyle and I each sucking on one of her nipples. Aubrey went off like a firecracker.

"You'd just like me to watch your tight little pussy getting filled by Kyle's cock, wouldn't you?" I whispered in her ear. "You want me to know how much he stretches you and how much you beg to have him pound into to your little twat." I snaked my hand down into Aubrey's shorts and found Kyle's hand right there with me. He grinned at me and did his own whispering in her ear. "You can't tell which of our hands is doing what can you? You're just leaning back with your titties exposed to both of us and waiting to see whose finger is going to slip into you or if we'll both get a finger in you. Does that make you hot, baby?" In fact, my brother's finger was right with mine and we both parted those slippery folds. Aubrey jerked forward and screamed.

"I want you! I want you both! I'm such a horny little bitch. One isn't enough. I want you both!"

"I love you, Aubrey," I whispered. "Maybe we could at least leave the doors open."

WE HAD THE big round-up and got the cattle down the last full week of August. Mom Mar rode down ahead of the crew and she and Aubrey went straight to work in the kitchen while Kyle and I rode to the herd. Aubrey did us proud and Mom Mar bragged about how the chili this year was all her doing. There were fresh tortillas, too, along with Mom Mar's cornbread. We all sat around the outdoor table eating once the cows were in the north pasture near the grandparents' ranch house. Gramma Bell and Gram and Grampa Alexander were all with us, too. We listened to the stories of this year's cattle drive.

"He was coming around the bush with his eye on that little calf and I drew a bead on him," Caitlin said.

"She'd have got him if she'd waited half a second before she fired," Phile said excitedly. All last year we'd never seen one of the wolves that attacked our cattle. We heard them. We saw the dead calves. But the last wolf we'd seen was the one that attacked me.

"Well, she got a little excited," Rafe said. "Can't say I blame her. Her horse isn't as steady as Spook or Shadow, though. It was the little side-step he made that probably saved that lobo's teeth."

"Well, I'm glad she missed," Pa said. "I couldn't afford to bail her out of jail. You kids forget that the rangers said we were guests on their land. They could have fined us for even firing."

"Damn wolves," Caitlin said. "Wish they'd go to hell."

"Where you think they came from, sister," Phile nudged her.

"Language, Caitlin," Mom Ash said. "You ain't too big to bend over my knee."

"Yes, Ma," they said together. I could see in their eyes, though, that Caitlin would fire again if she had an opportunity.

"CUB is this weekend!" Kyle said.

"CUB?" Aubrey asked.

"Centennial Uptown Breakdown," I explained. "Music!" That got everybody on a different subject and even the kids wanted to know if they could go in to hear the music.

"You can hear it clear out here at the ranch," Pa said.

"Cole, stop pretending to be an old fart," Mom Ash said. "What if your wives want to go dancing? Going to leave us to all those ranchers?"

"No reason we can't all go into town Saturday night." Mom Mar said. "The kids are fifteen and you know they'd sneak down there anyway. I'm sure Ramie, Kyle, and Aubrey will be going. School starts Monday."

All five of us groaned.

AUBREY GOT TO me and dressed me up. We didn't go out anyplace fun all that often and she said she wanted everybody to be jealous of her when they saw her girlfriend. She told Kyle to make sure he had clean jeans on. It was in the 80s and she was wearing the cutest little miniskirt and cropped peasant blouse that left her shoulders and her bellybutton bare. She put me in a little sundress with my short Lasso boots and an open-cut straw hat. We even put a little makeup on. With my hair pulled back in a ponytail, I figured I looked cute enough to be seen with the little hottie.

"Are you going to wear that with it?" she asked. *Mmm.* There were several 'thats' she could be referring to. I pointed to the bandana that I always wore to cover the scars on my throat. She shook her head. The wolf's teeth necklace? She shook her head. She poured me into this little dress so I pointed down at my boots. She pointed to the right one. *Oh.* It never even occurred to me to take off my ankle sheath and knife. It tucked down into my boot so it was hardly visible.

"I'm not wearing my gun," I said. She came to me and kissed me.

"I love you," she said. "I always feel safe with you. Wear it. It makes you comfortable."

"I love you," I said. I kissed her again and we spent a minute repairing our lipstick.

"Come on, Kyle!" Aubrey yelled. "Let's go. I been hearing music for the past two hours." Probably longer than that. They started playing around one and it was already past four. I planned to have a Bearclaw burger for dinner. Maybe one smothered in pork green chili. Kyle came out of his room settling his dress hat on his head. He polished his good boots on the back of his pants leg. He stopped at the door and stared at us.

"What's wrong?" I asked. *Shit! Did I smear my lipstick?*

"You. Both. I mean. Not wrong. Pretty." *Oh God! My brother was looking at me.*

"Close your mouth." I was turning red. "Don't we have the hottest girlfriend around?" I put my arm around Aubrey's bare waist. *Hell with the music. Maybe I'll just take her back to the bedroom.*

"We do," Kyle affirmed. "And she's got the hottest girlfriend she could find."

NOTHING EVER GOES quite the way you figure it ought to. We got attention, but it wasn't particularly good. We were just dancing. Some of the other girls from our graduating class were there and we did a lot of line dances while we caught up on what everyone was doing. Shelby was there with her new husband, another guy we graduated with. She barely got graduated and the knot tied before her baby bump was too big to hide. Even Caitlin and Phile joined in. Occasionally, a guy would come up and join us in a line dance or try to scoot a girl off on a slow dance to get his belt buckle polished. Kyle snatched up Aubrey for one and I lost track of where they were but we were all having fun.

This guy came up and started dancing with us and we let him in the line. I suppose he was pretty good looking in a kind of 'don't know what I'm doing' way. But he had to be at least thirty. *Yuck!* We girls were all in our teens and it wasn't like we were over near the entrance to the tavern. This guy kept making mistakes in the dance and stumbling into one of us—more and more often into me.

"What's your name, pretty lady?" he asked when he bumped me out of line the next time.

"Ramie," I answered automatically. Shouldn't have encouraged him.

"Well, I'm Joe, so we can be Joe Re Mi," he laughed. *Oh my god.* "Let's dance, Re Mi."

"We are dancing. Get back in line."

"Nah, dance with me. I got a few moves to show you." He pushed himself up against me and put his hands on my shoulders. I put my hands in the middle of his chest and pushed back, but he had me tight. He leaned in to kiss my neck and my reflexes kicked in.

My knife was in my hand and I drove at his gut. Luckily, Merv had been working with me on control and I punched him with my fist and not with the blade. He stumbled back and saw the knife in my hand.

He quickly looked to see if he was bleeding. I stalked toward him as he backed up. I pulled my bandana down.

"You see these marks, Joe Re Mi? I had no problem killing the four-legged wolf that left them. I would have no problem adding your teeth to my necklace," I growled. I was amazed at how much my voice sounded like Miranda's injured vocal cords.

"That bitch attacked me with a lethal weapon," Joe hollered.

"No she didn't," a voice said stepping up beside me. Harold Watson pointed at my knife. "Look at that blade. It's scarcely three inches long. She couldn't have hurt you with that. Unless you stepped toward her. We probably still could have gotten your gut sewed up before you died. If anybody cared." The guy spluttered but there were several locals who got up to join us. I slipped the knife back into my boot.

Next thing I knew there was a hand around my waist from either side and I was turned around and away from the bastard and Kyle, Aubrey, and I managed to two-step all together.

We saw the dude head for the parking lot and peel out in a red sports car. Right at the edge of town we saw the county sheriff's lights come on and he was pulled over at the top of the hill where we could all see. Talk about a way to spoil your weekend! As the sign said, he just blew ten grand.

I was so relieved that I kissed Aubrey hard and deep before I stood up on my tiptoes and kissed Kyle right on the lips. He was so surprised, he tripped over his own feet and landed on his back. Aubrey and I came down right on top of him. We rolled apart and sat on the ground laughing like we were drunk. He stood up and offered us each a hand. They were playing a real nice cover and we just went back to dancing. Kyle held both of us close to him and I could feel Aubrey's braless breasts pressed up against me. About every thirty seconds one of us would start giggling again.

"You kids have probably had enough excitement for one night," Pa said when the song finished. "Maybe you should go listen from a little more distance." Mom Mar and Mom Ash were plastered to his sides just like Kyle and I were to Aubrey. I watched and the three of them could two-step together just like we had.

We held hands as we walked over to where we parked the four-wheeler. Kyle was in a squirrelly mood after our little episode and decided to keep singing the last song over and over, grabbing hold of Aubrey and me and spinning us around. "Come a little closer, come a little closer…" I have to tell you, Kyle can't sing. I mean, usually it's forbidden.

"Oh Kyle, please stop!" Aubrey moaned. He looked at us.

"No actual music was harmed in the singing of this song," he deadpanned.

"Oh brother, you inherited every bit of your mother's complete inability to carry a tune," I laughed.

He pulled the four-wheeler up in front of our apartment. We sat there a second all looking at each other. That song kept echoing through my ears. "My eyes are the only thing I don't want to take off of you."

"Ramie, I…"

"I know, Kyle," I said cutting him off. I pointed toward the house. "We didn't get any food up there. I'm hungry, too." I jumped out of the four-wheeler and dragged Aubrey toward the house where I knew there was still left-over chili. Kyle followed.

AN HOUR LATER, I was nearly passed out and pushed at Aubrey's head between my thighs. She took another long lick of my slit.

"No more! No more!" I gasped. "I can't take any more."

"I'm not done with you, girlfriend!" Aubrey said. My little sundress was bunched up around my waist, the skirt raised and the top down. She was a wild woman. "I never saw you like that before, Ramie. I knew you were strong, but you doubled that hotshot up. And you were ready to gut him. You are so fucking hot!"

"Girl! Go fuck your boyfriend for a while and let me recover. You haven't even let me lick your pussy yet. Kyle! Come get your girlfriend. She's killing me!"

Kyle came busting into the room and grabbed Aubrey around the waist. *Shit! He didn't have anything on! Oh hell! Neither did I!* He looked. I looked, too. *Holy shit!* He picked Aubrey up and dragged her out of the room and in a minute I heard her start squealing. In a very good way. I staggered to the window trying to catch my breath and opened it wide. I stared right into the one good eye of old Blackfeather. *Oh fuck!*

Awkawkawkawk!

26
Demon Master

"PRAISE FATHER, Son, and Holy Ghost. Amen." The bellows in the pump organ wheezed as the congregation sat. Poor Miranda was silent throughout the singing while her sister and Katie joined in enthusiastically. I had a lot of sympathy for the way she was feeling. I was no opera singer, but I held my own in the school chorus. Unlike Kyle, who couldn't carry a tune in a bucket. Unlike Jason, whose rich baritone carried the harmony of the Doxology throughout the little church. So beautiful. Miranda gave me a mental squeeze to acknowledge my presence as we immersed ourselves in the warmth of his voice.

The new Methodist Episcopal Church was a sign of the civilizing of Laramie. A block away, the Catholics were erecting their church. The weather was cold, but the church was packed for the dedication this January morning. The service went on and on with some bishop or other having to preach after the preacher preached. We were packed onto the wooden bench so tightly that my elbow was securely tucked under Jason's and I was certain I could hear his heart beating. Katie was on his other side and Theresa was next to me. Poor John Hamm stood in a corner in the back of the church. The church was anxious to convert the savages, but it wasn't enthusiastic about worshipping with them. The fact that John could read and write better than most of the other members of the church did not help.

At long last, the service ended with the singing of "What a Friend" and we edged our way toward the door.

That was long.

"Yes, but for three hours we sat with our man touching us."

I wanted to take his hand.

"Ramie! Not in public. What would people say?"

Sorry, Miranda. I'll behave.

Still, I could feel her blush as she put her hand on his elbow. Katie took his other arm and Theresa followed behind next to John. Since there were five of us, no one was bothered with the fact that we were entertaining the gentlemen for Sunday dinner. We went to the rear of the store and mounted the stairs to the apartment above. While the menfolk built up the fire and sat in the chairs next to it, we women busied ourselves with the ham and sweet potato pie.

JASON SAT AT the head of our table. Katie and I sat on either side of him. Theresa sat more-or-less opposite Jason, but we had squeezed in another chair between her and Katie where John joined us. I was still fascinated with my comparably recent knowledge that Theresa was my ancestor. Pa had become his own ancestor when he rode in the body of Kyle Redtail and fell in love with my namesake. Here I was, just sitting at the dinner table with my four-times-great-grandmother who in this life was nearly three years younger than me.

She had just turned nineteen years old and was so beautiful it took my breath away. I wondered if my baby sister would turn out so lovely. Well, she had good genes.

"John Hamm does not sound like an Indian name," Theresa said, focusing our attention on John.

"My Cheyenne name would be difficult for you to pronounce, Miss Theresa. Our names are often descriptive of us or of our dreams. It would be like calling you Golden Hair. The English make it easy on themselves by calling me John Hamm."

"John is trying to help me build bridges between our people but it is a slow and painful process."

"Nonetheless, I would like to know the true name of this Cheyenne brave," Theresa said. "If that does not seem too forward of me, John," she hastened to add.

"*Vóhpo'háme,*" the Indian said. Theresa tried to say it and giggled.

"What does it mean?"

"White Horse."

"That is a much better name than John Hamm. With your permission, I shall call you White Horse. And you can call me Golden Hair forever." *Oh my.* Miranda dropped her fork as I struggled to keep the flood of new information from spilling over into her. *Our Family Bible. White Horse. I was looking at both my grandparents!*

"WHAT ARE YOU keeping from me?" Miranda demanded silently as we prepared for bed. Katie was brushing Miranda's hair and pausing to kiss the top of her head every few strokes.

I can't share this with you yet. I don't know what it means or why I'm even here.

"Is my sister in danger from that Indian?"

No! Nothing like that. He would do anything to keep her safe.

"That is it, isn't it? They are falling in love. How stupid and blind of me! This cannot continue. I will speak to her and ask Jason not to bring him back to our home."

Miranda, friend. Please don't do that. It would make no difference and would only drive a wedge between you. Please let it drop.

"HOW DARE YOU even suggest such a thing?" Theresa screamed at her sister. "He is as fine a man as Jason Wardlaw."

"He is a savage! How can you compare the two?" Of course, Miranda ignored my advice. I could have stepped in and made her say something else, but when I was gone she would just return to her ranting. Perhaps I could influence her gently.

"A savage? He went to Harvard College! He may be the best-educated man in Laramie. He has read more books than I have. More than you have."

"But he is not… like us," Miranda insisted.

"I will not discuss this further, *sister.* This is my home. My store. I will invite whomever *I* please to share *my* dinner table."

"I own…"

Miranda, let it drop for now. You are both speaking with your hearts, not your minds. Please, love. You are breaking my heart.

Miranda cut off what she was about to say and returned to the storeroom where she began unpacking a crate of China dishes. Dishes and glassware were a recent addition to the inventory of the newly renamed Sisters' Mercantile.

"Who does she think she is? Claiming ownership! She inherited a derelict property in a god-forsaken town. I provided all the stock that has come in. I am as much an owner as she is. We agreed to change the name. *Her* home. Indeed!"

I am not sure why I am here. You certainly do not need me for conversation. You're doing fine at talking to yourself.

"Demon Ramie, why can she not see what this will do to her. She would be forced out of town. They would never let him live here."

They? Dear Miranda, it seems you are the only one objecting.

"Am I indeed so primitive in your mind? Do people marry those of other races in your world?"

Didn't used to be common, but it is pretty much now. Not so much in Laramie because—well, Laramie just has never had a very interracial population. There are places in the United States in my time where you could marry Katie. In church!

"Both Katie and Jason? Oh, that it were!"

Well, we haven't gotten that far yet, but we might. Seems like some things go forward and some go back.

"Jason says that it is not unusual among the Mormonites for a man to have two wives or more."

Even that will change. Has he accepted that you and Katie come as a package deal?

"Package? You mean that he will have us both. I believe it has made him more excited. He holds both our hands when we sit by the fire. He kisses us both chastely when he leaves. Ramie, I am so much in love with him!"

Hold onto that feeling, Miranda. That is what will get us through everything we must face. We are in love.

"THE HARLOT IS among you!" screamed a voice in the street. There were always self-appointed evangelists in Laramie. One had gained a following and met with them in a tent beyond the city limits. The others had mysteriously vanished. My guess was this one would disappear, too. No one comes between Laramie City and its harlots.

"I do not mean the painted Jezebels from whom you take your pleasure. They are nothing in the eyes of God! They shall burn in the fire of perdition and none can save them. Among you is the mother of whores. She speaks with the tongues of demons and you believe her lies."

There was something familiar about that voice that nagged at me but I couldn't place it. Some long-ago tent meeting, perhaps? Still, this sounded like a boy's voice. Or perhaps a woman.

"Come hither. I will show you the judgment of the great whore that sitteth upon many waters: with whom the kings of earth have fornicated. She sits upon a scarlet beast with seven heads and ten horns. Upon her forehead are written the names Babylon, Mother of Harlots, Abomination of Demons. You welcome her here, though her arrival was heralded with gruesome murder. I have seen her tear the throats of helpless men. I have heard her summon her demons!"

Katie nearly knocked me over running into the storeroom. I had already moved to go see this evangelist.

"Husband Ramie," Katie whispered. "It is Harriet. The one who tried to kill you when you rescued us."

Oh fucking hell!

"I do not know how to handle this, Friend Ramie. I give you my body." I caught control as she collapsed against Katie.

I straightened myself and Katie kissed me.

"Be careful, Husband. I love you."

I walked into the shop and reached beneath the counter for my gunbelt. My knife was securely in my boot. I didn't know how this would work out, but I knew I had to stop the madwoman in the street. I saw Katie emerge with the Henry. I pulled the belt around my waist, thankful that we wore simple skirts when we worked in the store and not huge bustles.

"What is going on, Miranda?" Theresa asked. "Who is that person in the street? And why is she calling people's attention to our shop?"

"She tried to kill me once," I said. "It appears she wants another chance."

"Miranda!"

"Theresa, you are more precious to me than life itself. Forgive me for my cruel words. No matter how this turns out, know I love you, my dear sister." I walked out into the street. Twenty people at least were gathered, listening to Harriet as she pointed toward our shop.

"There she is!" Harriet yelled, turning everyone's attention toward me. "The demon's mistress has come to face her doom!"

"What do you want, Harriet?" I yelled at her. "Why are you parading in men's clothes and hiding your womanhood? Are you afraid people will see you for what you truly are?"

"Listen! Listen to her voice! It is the voice of Satan himself rasping from her lungs!"

"It is the voice you gave me when you tried to strangle me, you ungrateful wretch!" I called back. I kept my hands at my side. I could see she wore a gun, though I had no idea if she could really use it. She showed signs of having gone crazy when she tried to kill me. Now she was clearly off the deep end.

I felt a soft brushing against my left hand and an electric shock going through my body. I looked down to see the shoulders of the great gray wolf beneath my fingertips. I caught my breath.

"She called upon demons," Harriet continued. She was clearly working herself up and justifying anything she might do. She wanted the crowd in her hands and they tended toward her. "The demon rose from the excrement of her body in which she lay. He bit into the throat of one man and then another. She sapped the life from the woman who lay by her side as sacrifice to the demon. Look and see the demon that paces before her. This vessel of Satan must not live!"

I always thought gun-fights were fought on the length of a street, but we stood on opposite sides. Less than twenty-five yards. People cleared to either end of the block as the wolf paced slowly and deliberately toward Harriet.

"No! Don't rip out her throat!" I whispered. "They will burn me at the stake." A commotion on B Street drew our attention as eight uniformed riders swung toward us trotting in two columns. In the lead was Corporal Jason Wardlaw. The crowd parted as they approached and I saw him clearly. I looked directly into his eyes.

"Kyle!" He was there and would save me.

"Ramie!"

"He knows the demon by name!" Harriet screamed. "He is one of her minions!" With that, she swung her gun up and aimed, not at me, but at Kyle. The wolf brushed her hand as her gun went off. Mine was already held in both hands in front of me and before the smoke had cleared from before her, blood darkened her chest. The recoil of the Colt still stung my hand.

Jason… Kyle… was off his horse. I could not tell if he had been hit by her shot. There was no sign of the wolf. From above and to my right I heard the raven call.

27
Hard to Do

I WAS CURLED up in the middle of the bed with my knees against my nose crying when Aubrey found me. The raven called again. I felt the tug but stayed in Aubrey's arms. I buried my face between her breasts and continued to weep. Before I drifted off to sleep, I felt Kyle lie on my other side and hold both of us.

How could I ever explain this to my precious Aubrey? Four. I'd killed three men and a woman. It made no difference how Pa had tried to assure me that it was not me. I held the knife. I pulled the trigger. And I hadn't even been able to stay and defend Miranda. I might have gotten her hung! For the first time Kyle and I recognized each other at the same time. Then I was gone, leaving him to clean up my mess.

Why couldn't it just be a dream? Why couldn't I wake up?

KYLE WAS BEHIND Aubrey when I finally woke up Sunday morning. But he was reaching across her to hold me, as well. We were all three naked as babies. I got out of bed, pulled on a robe and went to take a shower. When I came out, Kyle was dressed and sitting on the sofa. Aubrey slipped behind me, still naked, and went in to shower. As soon as the door closed, Kyle motioned me to the sofa. I sat down and he pulled me to him with his arm around me.

"We were there," he whispered. "At the same time, or close enough to it. I think old Blackfeather might be synchronizing us at last."

"You saw me. You saw me kill her."

"Ramie, you saved my life. Jason's life. She hit him but just a scratch. He's fine and Miranda and Katie and Theresa are fine. Everyone in the street supported you and declared it was both self-defense and defense of a soldier," he said.

"How can it be both?" I laughed. It was a relief to know we were all okay.

"You know how people are. Some said she was shooting at you and missed. They swear the stray bullet hit Jason. Others say they were reaching for their guns to stop her firing on the cavalry but Miranda was faster. You know, by the way, that your stance is real twenty-first century."

"Can't help it," I answered. "Kurt taught me. It weighs almost exactly what my Remington 1911 weighs and it's comfortable to hold it that way."

"There was one other witness," Kyle said softly. "John says he saw a wolf guide the bullet. Of course, I'm the only one he's told that."

"Thank god. He's right, you know? That damned wolf has been stalking me for months and months. I met him first in Baltimore. He scares the bejeezus out of me, but he hasn't harmed me."

"I didn't see him. I guess he's somehow tied to you. Probably from this." Kyle stroked my neck. I was only wearing my robe so I hadn't tied on a bandana yet. I felt a chill go down my spine.

"You know about John and Theresa?"

"That they are in love? Got to be careful with that. They are really playing with fire."

"They're our grandparents, Kyle. Well, what's that come out to? Our four-times-great-grandparents. Theresa Ranae Bell and White Horse were Laramie Wyoming Bell's parents."

"Holy shit! I never connected that. It never even registered that her last name was Bell. That means that scoundrel who sold you into prostitution was our ancestor, too. Shit, shit, shit."

We sat there quietly for a few minutes until we heard the shower turn off.

"Thank you for comforting me last night, Kyle. You've always got my back." I got up and went to get ready for Sunday dinner.

I DIDN'T HAVE much time to think about what had happened in January of 1871. It was a good thing, I suppose. I'd have driven myself crazy. The first week of college classes pretty much set my schedule. We dropped the kids at the high school on our way to class. Kyle and I had several of the same classes, but Mom Ash had encouraged us to choose different specialties in our major so we could cover more territory.

We were both determined to major in Equine Science but decided to have complementary minors. Mine would be in Farm and Ranch Management and Kyle would minor in Agricultural Business. We were booked for a full load of 17 semester hours each. And they hit us hard starting on day one. We ended the week looking forward to Labor Day just so we could catch up on our reading.

Aubrey was majoring in Physiology and Kinesiology and we had no classes together at all. I wondered what good that degree would do on a ranch, but then I had to stop and think about it. Kyle and I hired Aubrey to do our books and accounting, but we hadn't talked to her about actually becoming a part of the ranch one day. I guess I just took it for granted that when she moved in with us it was going to be forever.

Well, maybe it would be, but we were only eighteen and I considered that too young to talk about forever. Still, we'd been invited to Shelby's wedding three weeks after we graduated and it was obvious she was pregnant. And she was happy about it. We hadn't been close since she and Forrest broke up, but I still considered her a friend. I'd have to talk to Aubrey about what she felt. It wasn't like we were fucking each other every night. In fact, I didn't think any of us had made love since school started.

By the last week of October, I started feeling like I'd about got the hang of college life. Then midterms hit and it was just as bad as the first week. We were up and studying in the living room until all hours of the early morning. Aubrey said she needed to meet with a study group over the weekend so she stayed at her parents' house. It was sad that we were in such different circles at school.

"Kyle." I threw my book on the floor. Our first exam in equine health was Monday morning and I was as ready as I was ever going to be. But if I didn't get my head on straight it wouldn't matter. I missed Aubrey. Kyle jumped and closed his book. He had the same exam and I know he knew everything as well as I did.

"What, Ramie?"

"We need to talk to Aubrey."

"She ain't here."

"That's the point." I could already feel my throat closing up and tears in my eyes. "I don't think she's happy here. I think we're losing her." Kyle scooted over on the couch and put an arm around me. I looked up at him and could see the truth in his eyes. He felt the same way I did. Since school started we'd hardly done anything fun and didn't even have sex much. Even this weekend when we were trying to study for mid-terms, we'd had to spend Saturday getting a new boarder squared away.

"What are we going to do, Ramie?" he asked. "I don't want to lose her. But we hardly see her except at night and then we aren't even studying the same subjects. I really love her."

"I do, too. We've got to talk to her."

"I know the answer to everything is 'talk about it'. Ramie, we've got exams this week. We're studying our fucking asses off. And that rescue organization is dropping six horses off on Wednesday. Right when we have our stupid English Lit exam."

"That's part of the problem. We have to cut back on new business. I'll talk to Pa about how to slow down. I never expected to have so many horses so soon," I said.

"What do we tell Aubrey?"

"I don't think we need to tell her anything. We need to ask her how we can make her happy. I can't stand not having her here. If we can't do it during the week, we have to do it next weekend. If she's still our girlfriend by then."

AUBREY SPENT ANOTHER night at her parents' house because she had a midterm at seven on Tuesday morning. But she came home with us Tuesday night. We all had English Lit exams on Wednesday, but at different times. It was one of those required classes all freshmen had to take but that had a dozen different sections.

We raced home to receive the six horses from the rescue organization. There was paperwork and we had to isolate them from the other horses while we got them acclimated to our ranch. That meant moving the boarders to the paddock and the new horses to our little pasture. We got hay out for them and then had to sign all the papers. The good part about working with this organization was that they were a non-profit and actually paid us a small stipend to take the horses they'd rescued. We'd spent two days with them this summer as they inspected our operation and had a vet come out to check the health of our other rescues. It was pretty intense, but they also didn't have places for the horses they rescued and we'd agreed that we could take a dozen this year.

"I have to go study," Aubrey announced as we were working with them.

"Okay, baby," I said. "We have to work with these guys but you don't."

"It just never stops! I'll put some spaghetti on for dinner." She caught Kyle and gave him a smooch and then headed for the apartment. I watched her go.

"Aubrey, we need to talk." We'd all gone out to a concert Friday night to celebrate finishing our exams. Aubrey had crashed with Kyle and by the sounds of it, they had their own little celebration. It gave me a warm feeling in my tummy. But Saturday was more of the same work, chores, and catching up. By evening, we were all ready to relax and unwind. I plopped down on the couch next to my girlfriend.

Aubrey looked up and saw Kyle approaching. He sat on her other side. She looked back at me and started crying.

"You're going to break up with me! I'm a terrible girlfriend and you hate me," she wailed. *Shit!* Kyle and I sandwiched her in a big hug.

"No we're not, honey," Kyle said. "We don't want to break up with you. Is that what you want?"

"No. Maybe. I'm not a good girlfriend. I love you so much!"

"It's been a really tough fall and we've all been a little crazy," I whispered as I kissed her ear. "Are you unhappy, honey? That's what we're really afraid of. We're afraid we're losing you." Aubrey's tears came out in a flood and I started crying, too.

"I love you. I don't want to lose you. But I'm not happy like we used to be."

"Tell us, baby."

"We worked hard this summer, but we had fun. We went out to the Cowboy Bar on teen night. We saw a few friends. We went to a movie. Now we're in college and there's all this stuff we could be doing! There's ballgames, and sororities, and clubs, and the Union. We don't do any of it. Last night was the first night we did something fun all fall," she moaned.

"I just didn't realize how much work college was going to be," Kyle sighed. "We've hardly even made love in the past two months."

"It's not just college," Aubrey sputtered. She took a deep breath. "We live way the fuck out here in the country. It takes us forty-five minutes to drive to class… make that fifty-five when we're dropping the kids off at the high school and have to find a parking place. We go to class and the library, meet up as soon as we're done, and drive home. As soon as we get here, there's all the chores to be done. And after dinner, there's studying. Last week I walked right through here without a stitch of clothing on and neither one of you even looked up from your books."

"I'm the bad girlfriend," I sighed. "I just ain't been paying attention."

"It sucks if you've got a boyfriend *and* a girlfriend and neither one of them pays attention to you," Kyle added. "I'm sorry, Aubs. I love you. I just been overwhelmed."

"That's… not all," she said, hanging her head. I could see *that* look.

"No. Aubrey, please don't say you met somebody and want…"

"Ramie! When would I have the fucking time to meet somebody?" she shouted. "Even if I had an interest in it. I could barely work out time to meet with a study group." She was angry now. I felt like I'd stepped in a fresh cow pie. "I'm sorry. I didn't mean to yell. The thing is that I always thought college was where I'd go and make a bunch of friends and figure out what I wanted to do with my life. Like, do I like kinesiology enough to become a Physical Therapist? But you two have your lives figured out already. You've got a business and it takes as much of your time as school does. You've got an apartment on a ranch where you figure you'll spend the rest of your lives. You already have your career and are just attending college to enhance what you already know. Life's set and we haven't even done anything yet!"

There was a lot of truth in what Aubrey was saying. If we'd only kept working the ranch as part of the family cattle business, we'd have taken off this fall and lived in a dormitory. We even used the business as an excuse to get the apartment and stay at the ranch. All I could do was shake my head.

"What about making new friends? What about traveling to new places and experiencing new things? What about wild parties, for Christ's sake? All the stuff we thought college would be when we were in high school?"

Kyle looked at me. We really screwed this up. We were older. Not that our ages were different. Aubrey's birthday was between Kyle's and mine. But Kyle and I had both lived extra months—years—in the bodies of other people. We'd tried to save President Lincoln. I'd been kidnapped. I'd killed four people. Kyle rode with the Dragoons and massacred helpless Indians. I'd lived off the land. In that other time, we'd been pretty much on our own from sixteen to twenty-one. That had been adventure enough for us. But not for Aubrey and if we were going to save our relationship, we needed to fix things big time.

"How can we make it better, Aubs?" I whispered. "I don't want to lose you. But I see where you're coming from. All we've done at college is go to classes. It's the same as high school."

"Can we just do something fun sometimes?" she asked.

"I think it's a good idea," Kyle said. "You know, I intended to try out for the rodeo team. Fall season's almost over. I could still make it for the spring season, though."

"I agree," I said. "College is supposed to be fun. We've got to figure out a way to have fun, even if we do have a ranch to run."

"Do you think we could make it work?" Aubrey whispered. "I don't want you to give up your dream. I just want a little part of it."

THE LITTLE PART of it she got that night was more orgasms than she could count. Kyle and I double-teamed her through three right there on the couch. We could pretty much ignore each other while we both focused on what our girlfriend needed. Kyle scooped her up and carried her to the bedroom and left the door open so I could hear every cry of joy while I cleaned up the mess we'd made of the couch. Then I stripped off my clothes and lay spread-eagle on my bed to wait my turn.

I wasn't expecting Kyle to deliver her to me. They were both stark naked as he carried her to my bed. I was so shocked I didn't even cover myself and Kyle just laid Aubrey down on top of me with her legs over my head and her face in my crotch.

"See if *you* can wear her out!" he laughed. I sort of watched his bare butt as he left the room, but Aubrey's tongue distracted me. Then her sweet honey. And then…

WE TALKED TO Moms and Pa. We talked to the kids. We talked to each other. Aubrey started spending a couple days a week at her folks' house in town so she could spend more time on campus and with people she met in her major. I stayed with her a couple nights and it was fun. Kyle even got to stay with her. Her parents sort of shrugged about it and said they knew we lived together anyway.

We spent weekends at the ranch, but we always did something special at least once each weekend. It was cold out, but so far not too much snow. We definitely decided not to go hunting over Thanksgiving. There wasn't much game and we could hear the wolves in the hills almost every night.

On my birthday, Tuesday before Thanksgiving, Aubrey kidnapped me. She borrowed her parents' car and drove me to Cheyenne where we checked into the Holiday Inn.

"What are we doing?" I asked. "I didn't know we were going any-place! I didn't pack anything."

"Don't you worry. I packed for both of us," Aubrey giggled. She led me to a really nice room—for a hotel. It had a big bed and a huge Jacuzzi tub that Aubrey started filling immediately. "Now let's get you out of those old ranch clothes," she said, stalking toward me. I'd never seen such a feral look in her eyes.

She tugged my boots and socks off my feet and worked her way up from there. She took my jeans and panties down at the same time and pushed me back to sit on the edge of the bed. She loved popping the snaps open on my shirt and then pulled my t-shirt off over my head. She hadn't really touched me yet and she kept pushing my hands away when I tried to get her clothes off her. Her last stop was to untie my neckerchief. When she got it off, she pushed me down on the bed and crawled on top of me. She lowered her lips toward me and I closed my eyes and raised my mouth for her kiss.

Instead of my lips, she kissed the scars on my throat—gently at first and then licking them. She nibbled all over my neck and I squirmed under her. Damn, she could make me feel good!

"Come on, now. Get in the tub. I want you nice and clean and relaxed when I start fucking you," she said. I sank into the tub, amazed at what my little girlfriend was doing to me. She stood beside me in the bathroom and slowly removed her own clothes one piece at a time. She tossed them out the bathroom door as she undressed. When she was naked, she slid into the tub behind me and began washing me as the bubbles from the jets worked all around us.

After our bath, Aubrey toweled me down and dried my hair. I'd been naked with Aubrey plenty of times, but when she made me just stand there and let her oil my body I somehow felt even more naked. And she oiled everything! Apparently she wasn't depending on me to produce enough lubrication for what she had in mind because she oiled right up inside me and then proceeded to make sure even my butthole was oiled.

She pulled back the covers on the bed and told me to lie down. That's when the serious kissing started. Finally, she let me touch her, too. I wanted to suck on her nips so bad I might have hurt her just a little when I latched on. Her fingers were tickling around my pussy lips and then I heard a buzz.

"Aubrey, what's that?"

"That's a little treat for my loving girlfriend," she said. She started running the vibrator around my breasts and then over my nipples. She was sucking on one and holding the vibrator on the other. Two such completely different feelings competing for my attention at the same time! When she moved down, she didn't push it straight against my clit. She ran it over my tummy, back and forth, driving me crazy. Even when she reached my mound, she didn't dive in. She vibrated right over the top, not quite low enough to touch my clit. It didn't make any difference. I came. Hard.

She slowed up, giving me a chance to catch my breath, but she wasn't done yet. This time she worked the vibrator down over my pubes and well-oiled lips. She was bringing me back to the edge again and I couldn't get my eyes to focus on anything. I kept squinching up my face and just knew I must look hideous, but I didn't care. All I could think about was my next come.

And then she pushed the damned thing inside of me!

There'd never been anything up there other than tampons and her fingers before. I suddenly realized how big—and how long—that vibrator was as it reached up inside me and hit places that had never been touched.

I could hear myself whining, but when I started screaming, Aubrey covered my mouth with her own and kept working the vibrator in and out of my sloppy hole. I couldn't see. I couldn't hear. I couldn't feel anything but the spasms clutching and releasing that hard thing inside me.

When I woke up, Aubrey was holding me in her arms, petting me and crooning how much she loved me. I hugged her tightly and buried my face between her tits and cried. I cried so long I fell asleep again and didn't wake up until she called me for dinner.

It was the best birthday ever!

28
Killers

AFTER THANKSGIVING, it was a two-week race toward finals. It felt like we were more in sync this time, though, and like we had our girlfriend back. We decided to move to campus for second semester. There were a few 'family' rooms in the student apartments and one came available. We'd done a fair amount of negotiating with Cait and Phile to take care of the bulk of the ranch chores during the week. Either Kyle or I would come back mid-week and we'd all come home most weekends. We were excited about school and about being together again.

Our parents finally relented and told Phile and Caitlin they could have the efficiencies. I offered to go in and clean the wall where Kyle and I had drawn our map, but Caitlin thought it was cool and she didn't have to worry about decorating so we left it.

WE WERE OUT of school with finals finished a week before Christmas and wouldn't return till the end of January. Aubrey promised to visit her parents for the week before Christmas and we'd come into town Christmas night, spend a night with her there and then all come up to the ranch for the next week. We were even thinking about spending a week someplace warm if we could find someplace that we could drive to. There just isn't much within reach of Laramie that's warm in the winter.

Kyle and I focused on our stock and our business. The kids had been doing a great job helping us and we loved watching the young colts and fillies romping around their mothers in the snow. It seemed like every chance they had, Caitlin and Phile would run out to check on the horses. *I thought I was horse-crazy!*

We still had antelope hanging around but they hadn't added much burden to the hay supplies. Mostly they kept to themselves, just in the same pasture as the horses. Of course, we had a couple boarders come out for a winter ride that week and they all wanted to take pictures of the crazy animals.

Christmas Eve I helped Moms make a big dinner. We just planned on a quiet family time that night. We shared little gifts with each other and all headed off to our rooms. It was fun to just be together.

"LET ME GO! I'll get my fucking gun and kill every fucking one of the fuckers!" Caitlin screamed.

"Pa! Ramie! Kyle! Moms!" Phile yelled as he stomped through the kitchen door. I turned to look at my brother and sister as he carried her into the house. She was beating against him and squirming all over everyplace.

"What is it? What's happened, honey?" I asked. Pa grabbed Caitlin out of Phile's arms and she turned to start beating on him.

"Wolves. Got Bows' foal," Phile sputtered out, still trying to hold on to Caitlin as she wailed. *Oh fuck!*

We all scrambled into our coats and boots. Moms wouldn't let Phile and Caitlin out of the house. Put a gun in that girl's hands at that moment and nothing would be safe. Phile wouldn't leave her side. She quit beating on him and just clung to her brother while she cried.

There was nothing we could do. The horses were all up under the shelter, nervous as hell. Harley kept pacing around the herd like he could protect them all. Bells and Bows stood with Bells' foal a little ways apart, looking off at the river. The antelope were all gone. The remains of the foal were a quarter mile away.

Arlen Logan got out there about midday and commiserated with us. Feds would compensate us $2,000 for the lost livestock. *Fuck that shit!* I held my little brother and sister as we cried over the carcass. *Little? Hell, they're as big as me now, but they're still my baby sister and baby brother.* Kyle held all three of us. Mom Mar and Mom Ash and Pa held all four of us.

"I'M SORRY, BABY," I said on the phone. "We've got an emergency. It's wolves. Kyle and I are going hunting. We've got to do this."

"But it's Christmas!" Aubrey cried.

"I don't know how I'll make it up to you, honey," Kyle said as we shared the phone. "I'll try, but I don't know how. We've got to stop this." It took us half an hour to calm Aubrey down and tell her we loved her. Then Kyle and I started scrambling. It was already getting dark and we weren't going to be leaving tonight, but we'd be on the trail at first light.

"You kids don't have to do this," Pa said as he inspected our gear. Mom Mar handed me the last of the trail rations and I stowed them in the panniers on the mule. Kyle packed plenty of ammunition for the guns we'd be carrying, including a shotgun in case we needed to hunt for food while we were gone. "I can have hired men out there within the week. Men who know how to stay clear of the law. You're both over eighteen and I can't keep you out of jail."

"Pa, did you just let other people fight for you in the range war? Or when six riders came to rape your wife and children? It's not just the stock, Pa. This is our land. Our home. We aren't safe to take a walk on the hillsides. The wolves have got to go," I declared.

"All God's critters got a place in the choir," Mom Mar sang softly. "Some sing low and some sing higher."

"Ma," I said through my tears, "they can sing in hell." She didn't warn me about my language.

"This GPS is set with the location of a special place up there," Pa said. "It's where Laramie made her home before they came down the mountain to homestead this ranch. It's a good place to set watch from. There's a tent platform and a strongbox for food. The wind can be pretty bad up there and you need to anchor your tent on the platform. I don't want to see you blowing across the valley."

"Thanks, Pa," Kyle said. "You've taught us well and had us camp in all kinds of weather. I think we're equipped."

"Just remember you've got your sister and your stock to protect," Mom Mar said. "Protect her first."

Caitlin and Phile stood beside us as we saddled in the morning. Then they hugged us something fierce.

"I want to go, too," Phile said. "But I understand. We've got to protect the herd."

"If you ain't back in twelve days, we're riding up with fresh supplies," Caitlin added. "I won't come back without killing wolves."

"When we see you, we'll welcome you," I said. Kyle and I mounted up and headed up toward the ridge. We rode slowly and quietly. On the way, we stopped to pay respects to our ancestors where they'd all been buried on the side of the mountain, neat little rows. Half an hour later, we saw the last glimpse of the house before we went over a low rise and lost sight of it.

We didn't talk other than to point something out here or there. We kept an eye on our surroundings. I was thankful this had been a mild winter so far. Even so, the horses broke through nearly a foot of snow by the time we got up to the base camp, just before dark. We staked out a pen for the horses and mule and got our saddles up off the ground and covered. I set up the tent while Kyle gathered firewood and cleared the well-used old firepit.

I made up a pot of coffee while I tended the fire and our dinner. "You reckon we should take turns standing watch?" Kyle asked. I thought about it.

"Nah. Then one or both of us would be out of it in the morning and not alert," I said. "I think we should get as much sleep as possible and depend on the livestock to alert us if there's any danger. You know they'd go crazy if there was a predator within a mile."

"Yeah. You're right. We should sleep in our clothes, though, and keep our guns and boots beside us. If they start raising a ruckus, we need to be out of here fast," he said. I agreed.

We crawled into our sleeping bags, checked our guns, and pressed our backs together.

"Kyle? Thank you, partner."

"I got your back, partner."

IT WAS ONLY a couple hours up over the ridge to where I reckoned we should find the spot Pa marked on the map. I checked the GPS and we corrected our course, then checked and corrected again.

"Seems this is about it," I said. It was beautiful. We were in a little clearing and a spring bubbled out of the ground nearby before the flow disappeared under the snow. I touched the water. "I think this is a thermal," I said. "The water is warm."

"You mean we don't have to melt snow? What a great place."

We settled the animals down and brushed the snow off the tent platform. After camp was set up, we began exploring farther and farther out. Then we worked our way back in. We had jerky and dried fruit for lunch, washed down with water from the spring. It tasted so fresh and sweet.

We planned to work our way out from base camp looking for signs of wolves. We'd seen some tracks on the way up but it didn't pay to just go running off after every track we saw. I brushed the snow off an old Douglas so I could lean against it and saw a blaze. More than a blaze; it was a carving on the trunk, scarred into the bark like a burn.

"Kyle. Look at this." He came over to see where I was pointing. It was old, but still clear. 'LK.' Our brand. "I think Pa's been here."

We scouted out some more and found a pretty flat outcropping where we could see over a good section of the surrounding territory. We figured that would be a good place to set up our scopes for trying to spot the pack in the morning.

"I hope Aubrey forgives us for missing Christmas," Kyle whispered as we settled into our bags for the night. I reached over and gave him a hug.

"She loves us," I said. "I just hope it's enough."

WE RODE OUT to various vantage points with our stock over the next couple days and scanned the surrounding area with spotting scopes. It was spooky. We knew they were out there. The horses were getting more nervous with each passing day. We never left them tied where we couldn't see them. The forest around us was quiet as if everything else had left. And if everything else had left, that meant we were the only prey around.

"Kyle, two o'clock." He swung his scope to match where mine was. We could look out over 180 degrees of valley from our perch. I'd seen movement on the slope opposite us. I focused more carefully and then I was sure.

"I see them," he said. I saw a long nose poke out of the underbrush followed by a mammoth body.

"Kyle? Them ain't ordinary wolves."

"Wait. There's a big grey on the left. A pair of them. But those others are different."

"They're big. But look at the shape of their heads. Shorter snout. Big ears. It's like they are some prehistoric granddaddy of wolves."

"Well, one thing for sure is they're headed this direction." Kyle pulled his rifle and put a scope on it. He was a good shot, but I wouldn't try from this distance. Those wolves were close to a mile away and across a gully from us.

Awk. I glanced up as I reached to put my hand on Kyle's arm. Our raven flitted down and landed on my shoulder.

"Now?" Kyle asked.

Awkawkawkawk.

I was gone.

29
Wolf

I WAS CRYING my eyes out. So many tears I couldn't even read the note in front of me.

Oh God, no! Please don't let it be Jason!

"Demon Ramie. It is too late to help." Miranda moaned.

Please tell me what it says. I can't see through your tears. Please, Miranda!

"Theresa. White Horse. The army sent him away. Told him he had to go to the reservation. They no longer need Indian scouts. He came in the middle of the night and Theresa simply packed a sack and went with him. She says she is going with the man she loves and will bear him many children."

I'm sorry, Miranda. It's all for the best. Theresa and White Horse love each other. She is safe.

"So you say."

Where is Katie?

"She went to open the store. I could not stop weeping."

She listlessly boiled water and made tea to ease the soreness in her throat caused by crying. As we drank the weak tea, she stood and retrieved a large book from above the mantel. She opened it and prepared a fresh pen and ink.

What is that?

"It is the Bell family Bible." Miranda opened the big book and I saw the words 'Jonathon Bell m. Clara Adams, 1852. Daughter Theresa Ranae Bell b. 1853.' Below was the date of Clara's death. On the next page was Theresa's name. Miranda wrote in neat script below her name, 'm. the Cheyenne brave White Horse, 20 June 1872.'

And suddenly I knew.

The Bell Family Bible I had seen in my father's hands. I'd read that script. This Bible had to go with Theresa Ranae.

We have to leave and catch her. Miranda it is urgent. We must take Theresa the family Bible.

"Why? She left hours ago. I do not even know which direction she went. She obviously doesn't care about a family Bible."

Miranda... What I hid from you... What I couldn't tell you was that Theresa and White Horse are my great-great-great-great-grandparents. That Bible has been handed down through the generations. She has to take it with her.

"You ask too much, Ramie. Even if we had a horse and wagon, we could never catch them."

We can. I know where they will go before they move to the reservation. It is a place that has always been special in our family. It holds the spirits of all our ancestors. But we must get a horse and go now.

"I do not know how."

Miranda! I have helped you whenever you've called on me. You've summoned me in times of distress. You left me in your body to find my way across Missouri. I have never asked one thing of you for my benefit. Please. I'm begging you now.

"My dear Friend Ramie. We must go tell Katie and then you must drive."

KATIE RECOGNIZED ME as soon as I walked into the store. Fortunately, there were no customers when she rushed to wrap her arms around me. After we had kissed, I explained what we had to do and promised that I would return to her. Katie closed the shop and ran to pack us food for our trip. I went to the livery stable located on the block behind our home.

Mr. Ingersoll at the livery was a wily character. He knew horseflesh and exactly how much he could get for a horse. But he had a reputation for good stock.

"I need a horse and saddle," I said when we walked into the stable.

"Good day to you, Miss Lewis. A horse, you say?" he was quickly contemplating how much he could earn from us. "Well now, I've a nice gentle nag that I could part with, I suppose. Let me see." I felt Miranda breathe a sigh of relief at the words 'gentle nag.'

"That won't do. I need a fast horse."

"Miss Lewis, a horse is not fast if you cannot ride it."

"Ah. You have one."

"Well, yes. But he is scarcely broke and certainly not gentled."

"Let me see."

"Certainly, Miss Lewis, but he is breeding stock and I will not sell him cheaply." He led me to the corral.

Unbelievable. Do animals have past lives? I swore I saw my own Pooky.

"He is a bit spirited. If you worked with him under my guidance for a few weeks he could be a good horse, but he is only three years old. I certainly cannot put a lady of your refinement on his back."

"Pooky!" I called. The black stallion lifted his head at my voice. After a moment's hesitation he began to amble toward me. "Fifty dollars and I want that old saddle and bridle with a clean blanket."

"Why that horse, if you could ride it, would be worth a hundred dollars."

"But you have already told me I cannot ride it, *n'est-ce pas?* Fifty dollars. Gold. Now." When he saw the five gold eagles in my hand, Mr. Ingersoll decided to sell me a horse. He pointed me at the saddle and said he would write up a bill of sale.

Miranda was atwitter in the back of my head, but she was still strong from a rigorous physical life. I tossed the blanket on Pooky's back as I continued to talk to him.

"I see they gave you your balls back, fellow," I said. He looked at me and snorted. "Of course, I'll see that you get a chance to use them. You are a fine, handsome man and deserve to sire many foals." I threw the saddle over his back. He side-stepped a little but I soothed him and pulled the cinch around his chest. "Now give us a blow there, boy," I said soothingly as I lifted a knee to his chest. He blew the air out of his lungs scattering snot everywhere. Mr. Ingersoll returned with the slip of paper saying we owned the horse.

"Glory be," he said looking over the job of cinching the saddle. I could tell he had planned to give me instructions on how to handle my horse. I took the paper and led Pooky out of the corral and across the plot between the livery and the back of Miranda's store. There I tied him to the doorpost.

"This would be easier in our buckskins," I told Katie as we came into the room.

Theresa wore them when she left. I will not wear trousers again.

"Yes, yes. I know. It would be much easier."

"Husband Ramie, I brought the Henry and your gunbelt from the store."

"You are a good wife, Katie," I said lovingly. I kissed her thoroughly and wished I could stay to love her like she wanted. I strapped the gun around my waist

People will stare!

"We will only be in town a few minutes. And they already know you can use it." I put the Henry in the scabbard and slung Katie's carefully packed saddlebags over Pooky. I tied the blanket Katie handed me and started to mount.

I nearly fell on my ass.

I will not spread my legs around that animal. Demon Ramie, you must consider my reputation. I hope to come back here and marry!

"Jesus Christ, Miranda!"

Do not take the name of the Lord in vain.

"Right, right. Sidesaddle? Really? I'm going to have such a sore ass. And it's your fault."

I will bear my sorrows for the Lord.

"No more religion, Miranda! Let's ride."

I had to use the steps to get mounted, sitting awkwardly across the hard saddle. It was barely a strip of leather fastened to the wooden frame. Pooky danced around a bit while I got settled. That finally shut Miranda up and I managed to get control of things.

"Katie, my love, if Jason returns before I do, please tell him I have gone to the Medicine Bow Ridge due west of here. I would welcome his company."

"Travel safely and swiftly, Husband Ramie," Katie said. "Return to me, my love."

Riding sidesaddle is not comfortable. And if you are doing it on a standard western saddle instead of one made to be ridden sidesaddle, it's like putting your shoe on sideways. I finally managed to convince Miranda that she could sit facing forward instead of facing the side with her left foot in the stirrup and her right knee hooked behind the horn. At least this way we had some control.

I just knew where White Horse and Theresa would go before they headed for the reservation and Black Kettle's Northern Cheyenne. I was headed to the same spot where the raven called me 150 years from now. It was where Theresa would one day bring Laramie back and she would meet Kyle Redtail.

Thirty miles, even on a strong horse like Pooky, is still a long day's ride and it was fully dark as we ascended the ridge. I kept scanning the surrounding area for signs of a fire. We were getting tired and I was nodding off as Pooky continued to climb. I jerked awake to a lovely sensation. Someone was playing with my sweet spot and I had a little fantasy of Aubrey and me. Then I realized I wasn't in control anymore and Miranda was diddling herself as we rode. And we were getting close. She had her eyes squeezed closed and I couldn't see where we were. I tried to get control, but stopping a woman in the middle of an orgasm isn't easy. Miranda cried out and I let the pleasure of her sensations wash over me.

Pooky sidestepped a little and Miranda lost her balance. Her eyes flew open and we were next to a rocky outcropping. Pooky had stepped aside to go around a huge boulder. I snatched at control of Miranda's body as she was flailing and tried to dismount but her long skirts got tangled up in the horn and the stirrup and one hand was still inside her skirt. I fell from that big horse and there was nothing I could do about it. We hit the ground hard and my left foot twisted under me. I cried out with the pain.

"I knew it was a bad idea to come out here. I don't even know where we are!" Miranda cried. "I can't move my foot."

Masturbating in the middle of the night while riding sidesaddle was the bad idea. Whatever possessed you?

"You went to sleep and were having such a lovely dream that I couldn't help myself."

So it's my fault. Actually I remembered snippets of that dream and it was a bit distracting.

I took back control and experimented with my left leg. There was no way I was going to stand up. My ass was sore from the long day in the saddle and it felt like I was bruised all across the inside of my right leg where I'd caught it on the horn and pommel. I managed to sit upright against the boulder. Pooky was a few yards away where he'd found a patch of grass to munch. I heard wolves howl off in the distance. They were on a hunt, but not a danger to us at the moment.

"I'm cold."

No kidding. Can you think of any way to get the bedroll off the saddle that is on a horse ten yards away and six feet tall?

"You're the western ranch girl. You should know these things."

At least we have your shawl on.

"It's ruined." She was quiet, but shaking with sobs. I was trying desperately to figure out how to call Pooky and climb up the saddle to grab the blanket. But I was so tired. "I can't feel my foot. I'm going to die out here and no one will even know."

I think we overshot where I was heading. There should be a spring near here.

There was no response from Miranda. She was going into shock. I had no idea if my mind could control a body that was in shock. I doubted it. No more than if I tried to force her to stand on her broken ankle. The pain would knock me out the same as it would her.

I looked at Pooky and tried to create a strategy for getting what I needed. I couldn't even light a fire. I was so sure we'd overtake Theresa and White Horse long before now that I hadn't stopped early enough to camp. I was stupid. Stupid. I looked up further. On the outcropping there was a shadow hopping back and forth. I wasn't sure at first, but in a minute it flitted down to the saddle and kept looking at us.

"No! Don't leave me! Don't leave me to die by myself. Ramie, please."

Don't worry. I'm not leaving you. Old Blackfeather can caw all he wants. I'm staying right here. You hear me, old crow?

I fingered the revolver still at my side. He sat on the saddle and nodded his head up and down as if he understood me.

Now we have to get our blanket and our rifle. This is going to hurt.

I firmly took control of Miranda and she watched in a daze.

"Pooky," I spoke softly. "Here, boy."

He looked at me but shuffled over. Then he nervously backed away. Wolves howled again. Closer. Glowing eyes in the darkness. No. Miranda was imagining things and I was letting her control me.

"Pooky. I won't mount. Come and let me loosen your cinch." I tried to send him calm thoughts in the midst of his nervousness with the wolves howling closer. He got close enough that I could reach up and touch the straps. This was going to hurt like hell, but we'd both be safer. I grabbed the cinch and pulled myself up on my right leg. Miranda cried out in pain. Or I did. It hurt.

I fumbled with the cinch strap trying to get it loose. It would be easier than untying everything from the saddle. When the straps let go, I tugged at the saddle.

Everything hurt. Tears were leaking out of my eyes as the saddle and all its gear slid toward me. I estimated my saddle and gear weighed well over 100 pounds and Miranda didn't weigh much if any more. I fell under the weight as the raven lifted from the sliding tack. This was going to hurt again, but just as I felt my head hitting the boulder, I heard the raven's call.

I EXPECTED TO find myself back in my own body on that ridge with Kyle looking at wolves a mile away. Instead I was just suspended there. I saw Miranda hit the rock and slump into unconsciousness with the saddle lying half on her. Pooky moved farther away and still looked nervous. Was she dead? *Raven, please don't let her be dead. She is… she's a part of me. I love her.*

I saw her bosom heave. She wasn't dead.

I heard the wolves again and this time I wasn't imagining glowing eyes through Miranda's subconscious. I was seeing through Blackfeather's one good eye.

I'm in the damned raven!

This wasn't possible. Even though I could still hear the baying of the wolf pack on their hunt, they were nowhere near us. Yet one gray wolf stood in the flickering moonlight as clouds began to clear and looked at us.

No! Don't make me watch him kill her. Stop it!

I didn't even try to control the bird body I was in or try to read the unintelligible thoughts that flitted through his mind. I watched as the scene kept shifting with the bird's bobbing head. The wolf came a step closer. Pooky edged farther away. The wolf wasn't looking at Miranda or the horse. He was fixed on the bird. It was like they were having some kind of silent communication I couldn't tap into.

The wolves that attacked me… The strange wolves Kyle and I spotted across the valley… They were pale imitations of the beast in front of me. He was of mythical proportions. I guessed he might stand three feet tall on all fours. Close to seven feet if he stood on his hinds. He was silver gray in the moonlight. We were four beings on the mountain who should never be together. A mythical wolf, a horse, an unconscious woman, and a bird who seemed to control it all. And me.

Wolf bowed his head and then looked back at Raven with what looked like a nod.

Raven cawed.

LONELY. ALONE FOR *so long.*

I was overwhelmed by the sense of aloneness. My heart broke. I realized I was seeing the world from the eyes of the wolf.

No pack mates for cycles of the seasons uncounted. Alone. Always alone.

The wolf was still gorged on the kill it ate before the sun rose. I was relieved that Pooky held no interest for him. The helpless female—My god! I'd never seen Miranda through the eyes of another being. She was so beautiful. To the wolf, she was not food. He knew she was female. No matter the species, females smell different. As he recognized my presence in his body, he shook his body from head to tail like shaking off water and wondered why Blackfeather called him here? Briefly he considered putting the injured out of her misery.

NO! I screamed in his mind. He shook again.

He approached Miranda's supine form and took in the strange smells all around her. He'd seen these creatures but avoided them. They were not food. They were dangerous. They did not know food from not food and killed indiscriminately. Like the hounds in the valley below. They had gorged but still hunted. The wolf's senses and condemnation of his own kind were flooding my consciousness.

I sniffed. I was beginning to get a feel for my host—separate my human senses from my wolf senses. I sniffed her feet encased in leather. I pushed my nose up under the folds that covered her and here caught strong scent of her heat. It was not unpleasant, even for the wolf. I caused my host to hesitate a moment and take another deep breath of her scent.

I licked her bare thigh where it was bruised from the saddle horn and she shifted as I withdrew. I continued my investigation of her body, poking under the saddle and pushing it aside. Combined scents of long dead food, the horse who nervously watched, and the female.

She was cold. She would heal as she slept. The wolf would see to that. He soothed her, rumbling deep in his throat, trying to tell her she had nothing to fear. There was a scent of blood near her ear. He licked it. Sweet, but not food. He sent healing energy into her skull. Her breathing evened out into calm sleep. He returned to her feet, covered in old leather. The boots made it difficult to touch... to lick... to heal. He sent healing into her leg. It would knit, though not so well as if he could have licked it.

She was cold. Wolf stretched out on her sharing the heat of his body and fur. In her dream, she nestled into his fur as if she were a pup. She slept.

I watched. I was overwhelmed by the primal instincts of Wolf. He had paced me for years. Ever since Baltimore, where he looked at me through the captive wolf's eyes. He had killed game for me. He had looked balefully at me when I dared think I could shoot him.

Wolf had a strange relationship with Raven—Grandsire Blackfeather. Raven had called him with the promise of a pack. Wolf had been alone for what should have been many generations. Raven had promised me to him.

It chilled my soul.

Miranda buried her hands in his coat, and I felt her grasping my fur.

MIRANDA AWOKE TO me/Wolf licking her face. The sun was coming up and Wolf was anxious to fade into the shadow. I was amused at Miranda's reaction to my presence. She was petting Wolf's fur when her eyes came open. He licked across her face and lips. She inhaled as if she would never exhale. In fact, she did not exhale until she passed out.

"Wolf," she squeaked when she woke again. "You are a wolf." I tried to send comforting vibes to her and felt her relax. "You did not eat me in the night. Will you spare me this morning as well?" She pushed herself up. Wolf rose and stepped away from her to mark a nearby bush. That was an interesting feeling. *Do human men feel that when they piss?* "That is an excellent idea," she said and stepped downhill a few paces to lift her skirts and squat. To Wolf, it seemed strange for an animal to waste all its urine in one spot. The horse, seeming to have gotten used to me, stretched forward and did the same thing. His urine ran down on the off side of the boulder.

Miranda, having finished her business, stood to assess her situation.

"I can stand and walk!" she suddenly exclaimed as though the realization had just burst into her consciousness. "Last night I was sure my ankle was broken. And my head." She felt through her thick tresses. "Ramie? Are you here? I can't feel you. I'm always so alone when you leave." She scowled at Blackfeather, who had returned to his post on the ledge. Wolf snuffled at her hand. She absently petted our fur.

"Wait? You? Are you there, Ramie?" I simply stood there. It felt good when she scratched behind my ears. I tried to send her warm thoughts but I wasn't certain I was getting through. "Who would ever believe I spent the night cuddled against the warm fur of a giant wolf, with a horse and a bird standing by?" Miranda mused. Wolf stepped away from her, looking back the way we'd come and growled low in his throat. Miranda stepped to his side and followed our gaze. Two Indian ponies were headed our way. I knew at once they must be White Horse and Theresa. Wolf turned and trotted toward the woods. Blackfeather swooped low, grabbing hold of his fur and cawed.

We were gone.

30
College

HERE'S SOMETHING that will scare the freakin' shit out of you. Go off time traveling in the body of an ancient wolf and when you get back home, realize that you're still in him and looking at yourself—only you're not home. I could feel my consciousness split. I was in Wolf. I was aware of myself.

My hand was on Kyle's arm to stop him from shooting. Blackfeather, still echoing his call, swooped in and sat on Kyle's rifle. Wolf sat on his haunches and began to snarl-bark.

Kyle turned and went pale.

"Ramie, let go of my arm. We've got wolf-company behind us. Get your gun, sister." My hand tightened on Kyle's arm. I didn't turn. "Ramie?" Wolf started snarl-barking again. I could feel my voice giving shape to Wolf's thoughts.

"I will thin my pack and teach my pups. We will abide in this land and share it for generations to come and generations past. We will avoid the man-lands and shepherd the prey."

Apparently, Blackfeather figured Kyle had seen enough. He called with his knocking voice and I could see Kyle change. He was time traveling. Blackfeather cawed again and I was in my own body. I turned to look at Wolf. He stood and shook himself. We heard the pack howling in the valley below. Wolf approached the overhang where Kyle and I were watching the pack. He sniffed Kyle up one side and down the other and then did the same to me. He licked the scars on my throat. They burned.

"Thank you for the ride," I said. "I think that's your new pack down there. You've got to lie low. They're being hunted. Even by me. I'll see you around."

The paw he placed on my chest nearly covered it. He didn't push me but just held the paw there, right over the necklace of wolves' teeth.

"We are one spirit." The words echoed in my head and I felt my senses heightened.

Wolf looked out over the valley to where we could still see the wolves moving south. He lifted his head and gave a howl that almost left me deaf. Wolf leapt over our shoulders and down toward the valley below.

Blackfeather, still perched on Kyle's gun, cawed and Kyle snapped back to himself. He jerked around to look for the wolf. I pointed down the hill. We could see him leap occasionally as he sprinted toward the pack.

"That wolf, Ramie. He was… he was talking to us."

"I don't think everybody in that pack is going to be happy to see him," I said. "Good luck, Wolf."

THE KIDS SAW us about the time we crested the last rise before the slope down to the ranch. They pushed the horses they were riding up the hill and met us half-way.

"Did you kill them?" Caitlin asked excitedly.

"Where's the teeth?" Phile added.

"You're back sooner than we expected," Caitlin continued, without giving us a chance to answer either question.

"We heard them howling two nights ago. Everyone was up all night and patrolling in pairs."

Pa and Moms were standing on the porch when we rode into the yard waiting for us. They stepped out to meet us and help us take the gear off the mule and horses, and make sure they were well-tended before we went in the house and sat down at the table. Smelling a kettle of Mom Mar's chili cooking set my stomach rumbling.

"That smells so good!" Kyle moaned. "Can we eat now?"

"I wasn't planning to starve you," Mom Mar said. "Sit down." She started ladling chili into bowls and put crackers on the table for us.

"That's so much better than trail rations," I sighed.

"And the wolves?" Mom Ash said, getting straight to the point. Kyle looked to me, and I took a deep breath and looked at Kyle. He looked down and shoveled another spoonful of chili in his mouth. Big help.

"The problem is over," I said with finality. "There are still wolves, but they won't be bothering us again."

"What do you mean they won't be bothering us again?" Caitlin demanded. "Are they dead? If I see a wolf near our horses, I'll shoot it, no matter what." Phile reached over and touched her arm.

Pa nodded and stood up. I knew we were headed to his office and I'd have to say more, but for now it was over.

"Don't forget they are Ramie and Kyle's horses. They've got a lot at stake here. If Ramie says they won't bother us, believe it. Don't go looking for trouble," he reprimanded Caitlin. "We'll talk in the office."

I HEDGED A lot, but Pa wasn't too demanding. When I told him Blackfeather had arranged a leader that would teach the pack, he and Moms just shrugged. They let us off. We headed out to call Aubrey.

We'd missed being with Aubrey on Christmas and on New Year's Eve, but we still had three weeks before classes started and we were determined to make the most of them. An hour after we'd called, the three of us were piled into the seat of Kyle's truck and headed for Roxie's Bistro for dinner. Aubrey was squirming between us. With Kyle focused on driving, she turned her lips to me and I got lost in her kiss.

"I'm so sorry we missed all the holiday with you," I whispered as I petted and kissed her.

"Hmmpff. Next time the two of you want to take off for a romantic getaway in the mountains for a week, give me a little advanced warning. I might have been able to arrange an affair while you were gone," she said.

"Aubrey! You wouldn't, would you, baby?" I pled.

"Aubs, we weren't having any romantic getaway," Kyle added. "No place either of us wanted to be as much as beside you."

"That's for sure. Freezing your ass off in a tent and eating trail rations three times a day is not what I call romantic," I added. "Aubrey, would you really have an affair?"

"Don't be silly," she whispered, as she kissed me again. "Kyle, get this thing parked so I can kiss you. I'm not even sure I want dinner before we make love."

Kyle obeyed pretty quickly and before we got out of the truck we'd all had another round of kissing. We got to Roxie's and all smashed in on one side of a booth.

"It's pretty bad when a girl has two lovers and still gets left alone," she sighed as we waited for our food. "You really weren't having a… romantic getaway together?" she asked.

"No, Aubs. Is that what you were really afraid of? Kyle and I both love you, but we're not into each other like that."

"We love each other, but we're brother and sister. You are our lover," Kyle added. He glanced at me for confirmation. Aubrey held one of our hands in each of hers and pulled them up to her lips.

"Sometimes I get worried," she said. "I don't know anybody who has a relationship like we do. I can't talk to anybody. I tried talking to my parents. They are supportive of my lifestyle as much as possible, but they don't really understand it and don't want to know the details. They just want to believe that Kyle is my boyfriend and Ramie is my best buddy. They have acknowledged that Kyle and I are living together and practicing to make them grandchildren. They really don't want to think about you getting your face between my legs, Ramie," she giggled.

"Damn. That talk always gets me hot," Kyle moaned. The back of my hand brushed his as we ran them up the inside of Aubrey's legs. We were going to get her out of those jeans as quick as possible when we got home.

"That's just it," Aubrey said. "You both get off when I'm with the other. You both really love me for me?" We kind of knocked heads as we both dove in to kiss her. I let Kyle go first but he yielded her lips to me and I kept them until our food arrived.

THERE WAS A LOT of squealing and a lot of coming in our apartment that night, and every night for the next two weeks. Kyle and I were both determined to knock our little dynamo's socks off. Whatever we could dish out, she could take and give back more. When I first got Kyle and Aubrey together, I never dreamed what a sexpot she was. She never wore clothes in the apartment and I kind of lost my inhibitions after I'd seen Kyle's bare butt enough times, when he was carrying her to me, or I was carrying her to him. Aubrey's nearly a foot shorter than Kyle and eight inches shorter than me. Either one of us can carry her around and she loves it.

The week before classes started, we got the keys to our new room on campus and started moving in. We still had responsibilities on the ranch and worked with the kids to get things split up so they wouldn't be over-burdened. Moving us into town meant they'd have to start riding the bus every day again. They weren't happy about that, but weren't old enough to drive yet. That's the problem with a summer birthday. Even as soph-omores in high school, they would never get to drive. Phile already had picked out the kind of truck he planned to get the day he turned sixteen.

Kyle and I got out of class early on Wednesdays, so we arranged that one of us would pick them up at the high school that night and go out to the ranch to help with chores and the big jobs. Then they could ride in Thursday morning with whichever of us was at the ranch. That meant that we each had the campus apartment alone with Aubrey every other week. It became our solo date night.

On the weekends, we all went out to the ranch unless one of us had an activity on campus. Lots of students go home on the weekend from UW unless there's a ballgame. We took care of our responsibilities on the ranch, loved on our horses, ate dinner with the family, studied, and made love. Monday morning, we'd all five pile into the truck and we'd drop Caitlin and Phile at school before we headed for class.

We started to realize what a mistake we'd made first semester by not living on campus. We were having fun in school. Our campus apartment was small, but no worse than our ranch apartment. We also shared a pretty normal bathroom, which was the same as we did at home, so it didn't bother us. We'd managed to train Kyle to put the seat down most of the time.

WE DIDN'T HEAR much about wolves for the rest of the winter. Whenever they were mentioned at home, Caitlin got a murderous look in her eyes. I tried to comfort her and talk to her, but the death of Bows' foal hit her harder than all the rest of us. Even Phile had trouble keeping her calm and he'd been the only one who could always soothe her.

We got through our final exams the second week of May and spent the entire weekend on campus partying. We didn't booze up, though there were plenty of opportunities. Aubrey pledged a sorority and I got dragged along to their year-end party. Some frat was there and it seemed like it was just a hook-up party. I was pretty uncomfortable, but Aubrey didn't want to make a big thing about us being together, so she flirted a lot and we got dragged out to dance. I caught myself reaching for my boot knife on one occasion when a guy made a pass at me. Another dude tapped him on the shoulder and reminded him that 'no means no.'

"You're Aubrey's girlfriend, right?" the newcomer said. "I'm Rick Miles. Aubrey and I are in the same study group."

"Um… thanks, Rick. I'm Ramie Bell."

"I have to tell you, Ramie; I'm a little envious of you. Aubrey made it clear to us last fall that she was in a serious relationship with her girlfriend. That was about the time I asked her out," Rick said. Aubrey never told me she'd been asked out. Or that she'd told her study group about me. Why me and not Kyle?

"We've been together for a while," I said. "Aubrey doesn't want to make a big deal about it here at the sorority, though. I don't blame her. It just isn't my scene. How did you know it was me?"

"I'm not much around horses and livestock, but a bunch of us who play football went to support our rodeo team. I spotted the two of you at one of the rodeos cheering up a storm. It was pretty obvious you were together," he laughed.

"My brother ropes on the team," I said. "We were having a good time cheering for him."

"Yeah. Bell. Kyle Bell, right? Couple of the brothers invited him to pledge our frat. He racked up some serious points in that last rodeo. Is he headed for Nationals?"

"No. Even though he did well in that last competition, he didn't compete in the fall season, so he doesn't have near enough points. Maybe next year."

"People think we're crazy to gear up and slam into each other while we try to move a football down field," Rick laughed. "But none of my opponents has horns or weighs 500 pounds! Those guys are crazy."

"Hey, you!" Aubrey said, coming up from behind me. She started poking Rick in the chest with her finger. "Are you putting the make on my girlfriend?" Her voice was just low enough so only we could hear her. I was worried she was angry with me.

"It's okay, Aubs. He kind of rescued me from a guy who was a little aggressive," I quickly explained. Aubrey giggled and I realized she was kidding with us and trying to make Rick blush. She was succeeding. He raised his hands like he was under arrest.

"Really, Aubrey. Just as your friend!"

"Yeah. Not that you're so much a friend that you wouldn't want to get these two hot girls alone together," she giggled. I wondered if she'd been drinking. She was really wound up tight.

"You know guys," Rick said innocently. "All we ever think about is having two hot girls to watch."

"I'll let you watch us kiss if you get us out of here," Aubrey whispered. She looked at me with her eyebrows raised. "I've really had enough."

"And me leaving with the two of you would help your image in the eyes of your sisters," Rick snorted. "Actually, it wouldn't do my reputation any harm either. Ramie?"

"I don't give a shit about my reputation, but if that's what it takes to get you out of here, honey, I'm all for it," I said to Aubrey.

"Let's go."

"I'd rather not show up at the frat house ten minutes after leaving a party with the two hottest girls there," Rick said. "How about we go to Shari's for a burger or something."

"Let's pick Kyle up on the way," Aubrey said. "He's just moping around the apartment waiting for us anyway."

"You all three live together?" Rick asked. We just nodded. I wasn't willing to give away any more of our relationship than necessary to a stranger.

"I guess you're kind of a fourth wheel tonight, Rick," Aubrey said. "Unless Ramie wants to do something. She's my girlfriend and Kyle's my boyfriend. You can back out now if you want."

"Look, if I'm interfering with something, I'll take off."

"We've got friends, Rick," I said. "We're just going out for a burger, right?"

We picked up Kyle and he recognized Rick. We all had a good time at the restaurant and when several other kids from school showed up we waved. Shari's is about the only place open in the middle of the night in Laramie. Aubrey was still at her best and flirted equally with all three of us. We finally left and Rick dropped us off at the dorm. He and Kyle shook hands and I gave him a kiss on the cheek to thank him for intervening at the party. Aubrey gave him a smooch right on the lips. She had to know Kyle and I both noticed.

31
Pack

WE HAD a regular roundup on Monday at the ranch. I needed all the rescues in the paddock for a visit from the vet. Phile, Caitlin, Kyle, and I mounted up. Aubrey used a four-wheeler to move from gate to gate as we drove the horses from one pasture to another and finally into the paddock. She proudly slammed the last gate closed and raised her fist in triumph. Kyle rode by and snatched her up in front of him on Dado. Aubrey screamed and started to hyperventilate, but Kyle kissed her and Dado didn't move a bit. She settled down.

"You want to ride with your girlfriend now?" Kyle laughed as she hugged him tightly.

"Really? How?" she asked. I rode up alongside and Kyle handed our little girlfriend over to me. I hugged her to me and she turned her face into my chest and bit my nipple. *Holy shit!* I laid a kiss on her that had us both near coming before we got off the horse.

"You are a bad girl!" I said. "Go to my room!" Aubrey giggled and went running to our apartment. I tossed my reins to Kyle. "You get to take care of the horses. I gotta go take care of a wildcat." Kyle laughed at me and led Pooky and Dado to the barn to get a well-deserved rub-down.

I FOLLOWED THE trail of clothes that Aubrey scattered across the apartment to my bedroom and heard the water running in the bathroom. I stripped off my jeans and shirt and went straight in. She was already in the shower. As soon as I stepped into the shower, she sank to her knees and looked up at me.

"Let me get you cleaned up, boss. There's another rodeo for you to ride in today." She plastered her mouth against my pussy and I sank back against the wall of the shower, letting the water beat down on my breasts and over my stomach onto her head. Occasionally, Aubrey lifted her head and shook the water out of her eyes, and then she went straight back to licking. My knees got so weak when I came that I sank down next to her and kissed her over and over.

EVERY DAY AFTER we got back to the ranch, Aubrey strutted around looking for trouble. In her book, that meant getting either Kyle or me in bed when we should have been working. I didn't really mind. It was going to be a long summer and we'd settle down once the high of being out of school tapered off. Right now, I just couldn't imagine anything better than what we had.

And she was pushing the limits. I walked into the apartment to find her stripped naked and kneeling in front of the couch with Kyle's cock in her mouth. I don't think he even knew where he was. His pants were around his ankles and his head was thrown back as if someone had knocked him out.

It's one thing to know they're doing all that stuff and to listen to them doing all that stuff. It's something else to *see* them doing it. Aubrey looked up at me while she licked him and sucked him into her mouth. I couldn't tear my eyes away from her. When he came, she let it dribble out her mouth and down her chin as she looked up at me. I was close to grabbing her right there and planting my pussy on her slimy face. When Kyle moaned and opened his eyes, I ran for the bedroom.

For the first time in my life, I wished I had a cock that she could suck the come out of.

I was coming in the shower when she stepped in.

She made a big show of rinsing her mouth, gargling, and spitting under the water before she turned and kissed me.

"What has come over you, girl?" I asked. "You're pushing all our boundaries."

"They don't seem to be too firm. You loved watching."

"I wanted to fuck you right there on the floor."

"I wish you had. Kyle wouldn't mind watching that," Aubrey said.

"What are you trying to get to? You want me to fuck my brother?"

"God, no!" she screeched. "I'm sorry, Ramie. I'm not trying to get you to do anything with him. I wouldn't *mind* if you did. But I just want you both with me. I want to wake up with you both in bed. An Aubrey sandwich. I suppose I'm some kind of pervert, but I just want you to both be with me."

"Oh, baby. Is it that important?"

"I have to leave one of you to be with the other. I shouldn't have to do that."

"I love you, Aubrey. If that's what you want and Kyle will agree, then let's do it tonight. Hell, it's his birthday. Might as well make it special."

OF COURSE, THERE was all the family celebration to get through. Kyle got gifts. We sang Happy Birthday and ate cake and ice cream. We hung around and chit-chatted politely with the family. Kyle kept looking at me like he'd just seen a ghost—all wide-eyed and pale. We finally excused ourselves and went back to the apartment. Caitlin and Phile went around to their apartments and I heard the door slam.

Only one.

Well, they were probably going to talk for a while before bed. After all, it was only ten o'clock.

Aubrey was naked before we were completely in the house and backed toward my room, crooking her finger at Kyle and me. My room had the biggest bed. I looked at Kyle as I was pulling off my boots.

"You love her, Kyle?" I said.

"Like my life, Ramie," he answered.

"Then let's give our girlfriend all the loving she wants."

We peeled ourselves down to our underwear and went to find our girl sprawled out on the bed waiting for us.

We just attacked her. Kyle started kissing her while I was sucking on a nipple and I just decided to keep going. I kissed over her soft round tummy and down into her pubes. I settled down to look up at her and Kyle had a hand lightly pinching her nipple like I knew she liked. I dipped my tongue into her hot wet pussy and started licking. I know Kyle glanced down at me a couple times and I was only a few inches from where his hard cock, still in his boxers, was rubbing up and down her leg. I figured I'd be kissing her while she rode him later.

Aubrey was getting exactly what she wanted. Her mouth was wide open as Kyle sucked on one nipple and thumbed the other while he watched me eating her. She was turning red and sucked in a big breath to scream out her orgasm.

A wolf's howl joined hers.

This was no distant howling up in the mountains. This sounded like it was practically in the same room. I rolled off Aubrey and ran for the door. I slammed my feet into my boots, not bothering to dress. Kyle was right behind me as we grabbed our rifles and ran outside. A dozen steps toward the house, I came face-to-face with Wolf. We were not more than a couple steps apart. I heard the other apartment door slam and the door to the house open.

"It's a wolf!" Caitlin screamed. "I'll kill it!"

"Caitlin, rest your gun," I commanded. "He won't hurt us."

"It's a wolf! They killed Bows' baby."

"Not this wolf, Caitlin. Put it up!" I turned to look back at my younger sibs. I had panties and a t-shirt on and was freezing to death in the thirty-degree weather. Neither of them had t-shirts. My baby sister was stacked. Like Mom Ash. Aubrey was shivering in a robe and slippers, and Kyle had his hand on her gun hand, holding it down.

"Here, baby," Pa said pulling his own shirt off. He handed it to Caitlin. "You're freezing your tits." Caitlin had to hand him her gun to put on the shirt. Pa didn't give it back.

"Come stand behind me, family," I said. As soon as I turned to Wolf there was a connection. I wasn't in him exactly. It was more like he was in me. He snarl-barked softly and I saw movement behind him. Caitlin whimpered behind me. Twenty wolves came out of the shadows behind him. He barked and they all laid down. Wolf took another step forward and I did the same, coming face to face. He reached out and licked the scars on my neck. They'd faded since the last time he'd done that. My heart was in my throat and I could feel Kyle tense up.

"He's taking his pack home," I said. I was in a trance. "They are going back to… to when they belong. They're leaving a new generation in the mountains. They haven't… bred with them. But they taught them. They will…" I stood up and stumbled back, grasping Kyle's hand. I could feel Wolf's thoughts become words in my throat and I spoke them for him. "This land is forever ours. Even our spirits will protect you, our pack, and our hunting. We will never rest. And we are deadly when we hunt."

The pack stood and I saw a shadow streaking out of the air toward the old, silver gray wolf.

Awkawkawkawk! Knock knock knock!

And we were gone.

32
That Which God Hath Joined

"**IN SICKNESS** and in health, to love and to cherish; until death do you part?"

"I do," I said. I turned to my right and looked at Jason Wardlaw. I could see my brother looking out of his eyes.

"Do you, Jason Wardlaw, take Miranda Lewis to be your lawfully wedded wife; to have and to hold from this day forward, for better or for worse, for richer, for poorer, in sickness and in health, to love and to cherish; until death do you part?"

"I do." It was Jason's voice but all I could still see was Kyle.

"Forasmuch as Miranda and Jason have consented together in holy matrimony, and have pledged their love and loyalty to each other, and have declared the same by the joining of hands and the giving of rings, by the power vested in me, and as witnessed by friends and family, I now pronounce you man and wife. That which God hath joined together, let no man rend asunder. You may kiss the bride," the preacher said.

Somewhere as I was lost in his lips, I heard the bellows of the pump organ puff and a joyous chorus rang out. Yet I felt a familiar presence and was aware of Katie's hand held in mine. We turned to face the few people who came to wish us well and walked down the aisle arm-in-arm. No one commented to us as Katie climbed the stairs to our apartment with us.

"**HUSBAND RAMIE,**" **KATIE** whispered. "Are you truly with us in our marriage?" I tried to answer but Miranda kept her voice.

"Katie, dear, Ramie is here and when you and I make love it will be as the three of us in holy matrimony. But before you and we have our moment of bliss, with which we are already familiar, we must discover how to please our husband," Miranda said. She kissed Katie softly and I felt the genuine love that had developed between the two women. It was not just me.

You will find Jason has ideas in that regard.

"Friend Ramie, how many weddings did we just have?" Miranda asked silently. "I fear our wedding bed will be crowded."

Miranda!

We giggled as Jason turned to look in my eyes and I was lost in his kiss once again. *How many of us, indeed?* I could still hear the echo of the preacher's voice declaring, "That which God hath joined…" My lips left Jason's and he turned his head only a fraction to capture Katie's mouth. I was so glad that we had joined together in courtship all the way back in Omaha. I had no discomfort seeing Jason kiss my wife.

"I do not know how to… what to do," Jason gasped. "My wives. My loving Miranda. My sweet, sweet Katie. Now that we are wed…" He was truly at a loss. Of course, the church would only recognize Jason and Miranda as husband and wife, but Katie was as married to us as we were. Even the people in church saw us sitting on either side of Jason every Sunday morning. But now that we were truly together, none of us had a good idea as to how to *do it*. And we were all just a little frightened.

"Do you wish me to leave you alone while you… consummate your marriage?" Katie asked quietly. I grabbed hold of my lover before she could back away and kissed her with ferocity.

"No, Katie. We have shared each other's love for four years. Do not abandon me. Let us find a way to share this time, as well," I said. "Perhaps we could make ourselves a bit more comfortable. Say, by removing our shoes so we do not scrape each other."

We worked on it. For once, corsets worked to our advantage. Neither Katie nor I could bend enough to remove our own shoes. Jason gallantly knelt before us as we sat in the fireside chairs and unlaced our shoes, as Katie and I giggled, and pulled our skirts up a little higher than strictly necessary. His touch, as he took our invitation to caress our calves and rub our feet, was electric.

"Stockings, too," I whispered. He looked up into my eyes as he rolled the silk stockings down and for the first time touched skin that was not my hand or face. Katie moaned as Jason stroked her skin. As quickly as we could manage it, the two of us set about removing Jason's boots.

And then we just kept going.

Bit by bit we revealed our lovers, laughing through the unlacing of corsets and unbuttoning of Jason's union suit. Jason bent to whisper in my ear as Katie and I reclined on the bed in our bloomers and chemises.

"My friend is encouraging me to remove all our clothing," he said. I could see the red flush in his cheeks. "Is that the proper way?"

"We are not whores. We are your wives. In the brothels, I am told, they simply pull up their skirts and plunder their sex. The privilege of a husband is to have all of us. And our privilege is to have all of you," Miranda said. "Please, my loving husband, help me to remove Katie's chemise. She has such wonderful, proud little breasts that I cannot help but worship them when I see them."

It made it easier for us to work two on one. With both Jason and I removing Katie's last articles of clothing it was a simple step to turn to my garments. We three finally lay on the bed, naked and gasping, as we kissed each other and let our hands explore for the first time.

I'd caught glimpses of Kyle's cock as he brought Aubrey to me or vice versa. But I'd never been confronted with a fully erect and ready penis. Certainly it was beyond Miranda's experience and our heart was attempting to escape our chest. I pulled Jason's hand to my privities and let him touch the wetness he found there. He did not need my guidance to locate the center of my pleasure. I had a feeling he was getting guidance from elsewhere.

"Jason. Husband. Cover me. Make me truly your wife. Please be gentle. But make me yours. I am ready."

Jason moved between my legs. Katie scooted closer to us and reached to hold Jason's cock at the entrance to my body.

"Yes!" Miranda hissed as he tore through the remnants of her maidenhead. I clutched him to me, holding him still while I adjusted to this new intrusion. I was full—stretched. In my other life, Aubrey had inserted a vibrator in me on occasion. That life was forgotten in the instant that Jason entered me. There had always been a kind of double-vision with both Miranda and my perceptions held separately. But in this instant, we were truly one person. We shared the joy. We shared the love. And as Jason moved through my slippery channel, we shared the orgasm that ripped through our body and the tears that fell from our eyes. "I love you.

I love you," I wept as I felt his seed flow into me. I looked into his eyes and saw the love, not only of Jason, but of Kyle. I came again.

It was not as awkward to shift the focus to Katie as I feared. As we basked in the afterglow, she covered our faces with kisses. Jason lifted himself from me and slipped to the other side of Katie so that she and I could embrace. I kept my fingers in her snatch to work her to a frenzy and as I kissed her lips, Jason covered her strong back with kisses. I pushed Katie to her back and grasped Jason's reawakened cock to pull him to her.

"Husbands. Lovers," Katie whispered as Jason entered her.

"Ramie? Are you there?" The whisper was so soft I thought it was Katie at first. I opened my eyes and looked at Jason. It was Kyle who looked back at me. "Ramie?"

"Yes, Kyle. It's me. You were such a wonderful lover to Miranda. No wonder Aubrey loves you so much."

"It was amazing. I love you Ramie."

"Kyle?"

"We made love, Ramie. I love you!"

"Kyle, Miranda and Jason made love. Not you and me." I caught my breath. I knew. I knew when I looked in his eyes that it was Kyle. I came as hard for him as for Jason. Was it possible? Was it possible that I was in love with my brother? A tear moistened Kyle's cheek. Even looking at Jason, suddenly all I could see was Kyle. "I love you, Kyle. In our world we are a brother and sister who love the same woman. In this world we are husband and wife with an extra wife tossed in."

"She is a spitfire. Ramie, I… we love her as much as Miranda. When we get back to our world, can we…?" He left it hanging and I could see the pleading in his eyes.

"No, Kyle. Here we can be together. Not there."

"I know. I didn't know how much I loved you until I spoke those vows in the church. Do you think they'd mind if we made love now?"

"That which God hath joined together," I whispered as I moved my hips. I felt Kyle harden and welcomed his loving with my whole body and my whole heart. It was long and slow and beautiful. I felt Miranda chuckle and then peacefully come along for the ride.

We kissed and stayed connected as we looked in each other's eyes, lying side-by-side. Kyle caressed my breasts and played with my nipples. He kissed my neck and throat and I threw back my head to give him better access, moaning as he loved me. I pushed him to his back and rolled on top of him as I increased the speed of our joining. He reached up and sucked my left nipple into his mouth and I pressed down on him, rotating my hips to rub my clit against his pubic bone. I pinched at his nipples and he almost came up off the bed. I felt the head of his cock flare inside me and it sent me near the edge. I moaned and, as if in stereo, I could hear Miranda echoing me in the back of my mind.

"Fill me. Let me feel you deep inside. I love you. I'm gonna . . ." I couldn't hold back the spasms as my pussy clenched around his cock and milked it and I came in a gusher that soaked the bed beneath us. He pulsed and I felt every hot jet of his sperm splash within my vagina. "I love you."

I felt Katie's embrace as she whispered, "I love you, Husband Ramie."

Once was not enough.

We did not go to church on the Sabbath. Jason worshipped Miranda's body and joined her in driving Katie to yet another climax. In an act of sublime submission, Miranda let me drive as I sucked Jason until he came in my mouth. It choked me a little and brought tears to my eyes. The look of rapture on Jason's face made it worthwhile, though. And once Katie saw it, she had to try it as often as she could, sometimes switching back and forth between eating my pussy and sucking Jason's cock.

It was so strange for me to be able to look at Jason and see Kyle. They weren't that much alike. Kyle was much taller and Jason was even fairer, though always red from the sun. He must be of some Scandinavian stock somewhere along the line. Of course, I wasn't much like me, either. Miranda barely topped five-foot in her stocking feet. I felt downright dainty in Miranda's body. Even though she had bigger tits.

Still, we seemed to have all five accepted each other. And we loved what we shared. Katie had an uncanny ability to recognize when either

Kyle or I was driving and even, on occasion, demanded that Kyle make love to her. Miranda and I could speak aloud, one after the other, and she could follow which was which without hesitation.

And that had changed as well. Miranda's damaged voice had softened. It was not quite the sweet musicality that it had once been, but it was no longer harsh and raspy. Her throat no longer burned with the remembered injury.

What happened to your voice?

"The night of the wolf."

Just 'Wolf.' Not 'the wolf.'

"You did not leave, after all. I sensed your presence as it calmed me. I was in the middle of the wilderness with a horse, a crow, and a wolf. But you calmed me. Just before you departed, Wolf licked me. I knew in my heart that he had healed my head and my ankle. I silently asked him for my voice. He licked my throat and then you were gone."

He had to come to my time to collect his pack—his family. Then he returned to his own time. It happened just when we joined you for the wedding.

"When is his time? Has he come back here? I mean now?"

I believe his time is before what we know as time. I was inside his head, Miranda. It was amazing. He is Wolf. The first of his name. Just as that old crow you mentioned is Raven. Not a raven, but the first of his kind. The Raven of Indian legends.

"Why did you choose such an ignorant host for your travel, Friend Ramie? You know so much more about everything than I do."

Not so. I have learned from you more about love and labor than I ever could in my time. You are quick and clever. I have done little more than awaken you to the possibilities.

"And I will never close my mind to them again."

"Husband Ramie," Katie whispered as she kissed my lips. I still loved the taste of her—whichever lips I kissed.

"What is it, Katie dear?"

"Will you and Husband Kyle make love to me? I feel that we shall lose you soon. I will love and cherish Miranda and Jason. But once more, will the two of you make love to me?"

"I'm here, beloved," Kyle whispered behind her. "You are a treasure, Katie, and we love you."

I kissed her deeply, touching her nipples. Kyle's fingers joined mine as we loved her. My hand drifted to her sex to find it moist and open. I reached through to guide Kyle's cock into her. Katie's fingers began searching the folds of my pussy and soon found my clit, ready for her attentions.

It was so beautiful—so loving. In all the time since our first coupling, I had not thought of Kyle as my brother, but as one of the five of us bound together in marriage. This was no different. In my mind, I felt Miranda cuddle against me, almost as if she and I were lovers. I wondered if Kyle felt the same relationship with Jason.

I lifted my lips to kiss Kyle over the top of Katie as Katie nibbled my ear and neck, sending chills up and down my spine. Kyle's tongue gently probed into my mouth. I met it with a feeling of complete love and sensuality as all three of us rose to our climax. Katie had managed to latch onto my nipple and I stroked both Kyle's balls and her clit as we all three came together.

And Raven called.

33
Deception

I IGNORED HIM. Damned old bird could just wait. I was coming and I couldn't let go of either Katie's pussy or Kyle's lips. I hugged them to me and desperately held her to my breast as I kissed and kissed. My climax wouldn't stop. Her fingers pumped into me in rhythm with Kyle's cock pumping into her. I could feel her pulses on my fingers and knew she was coming as hard as I was.

I'd never come so hard. Tears ran from my eyes as I opened them and looked into Kyle's eyes.

And saw his face.

Our eyes went wide as we pulled away from each other and looked down into Aubrey's eyes between us.

I jumped out of bed. We were all naked. I ran for the bathroom and locked the door behind me. I turned on the water and got in the shower. I sank down on the floor and cried as the water pelted down on me. What had I done? I was kissing Kyle instead of Aubrey. Granted, he wasn't making love to me. But I felt every pulse of his cock as he shot into her. I knew that in our other time I had been making love to Kyle every bit as much as to Katie and we loved it.

But that was then. I couldn't let that affect how I felt or behaved now.

BREAKFAST WAS EERILY quiet. The kids were leaving the house as we walked in and Caitlin gave me an angry look. I think she was still mad that she hadn't killed a wolf last night. I hadn't been able to look either Kyle or Aubrey in the eye all morning. They'd been dressed and waiting for me when I came out of the shower and I hurried myself up to go in for breakfast.

Moms and Pa looked at us strangely. Everybody seemed to look at me like I was some mentally fragile inmate on the verge of suicide.

Maybe I was.

I caught Kyle's eye for a second and he blushed out to his ears and put his head back down toward his plate.

Pa filled his coffee cup and pointed at me. He turned and went to his office. I followed. He closed the door behind us. He almost never closed the office door.

"Wolves," Pa said as he sat in his leather chair. At least he hadn't gone to his desk. I sat at the edge of the couch.

"They're gone," I said. I struggled to regain the crystal clarity I'd had when I explained it to Miranda. Wolf and Raven? The icons of Indian legends. In the harsh light of day, in my own body, it seemed far-fetched to me.

"And you and Kyle?" he asked.

"We went traveling at the same time, but not with the wolves. We were gone a long time. Maybe a couple months. It was the first time we'd actually traveled together at the same time."

"And now Aubrey knows," Pa said. I shook my head. He let out a big puff of air like he was suddenly deflating or something. "She knows something. I warned you some time ago. If she's important to you, you have to talk to her—tell her."

"I don't know how."

"I don't think she's going to give you an option. You get your brother and go tell her. Kids will take care of the horses today."

I got up and left. Kyle and Aubrey had already gone back to our apartment.

I FOUND THEM sitting on opposite ends of the couch. Both had their arms folded. Kyle was looking down at his knees. Aubrey was staring at me as I walked in.

"All right. You're both here. Now tell me," she demanded. "I want to know what the fuck is going on. It was all I could do last night to get you to consider both making love to me and letting me wake up between you. Before we could even do anything, we get attacked by a pack of wolves in the yard and you look like you're talking to them. Then they all just fade away and we come back to the bedroom. I couldn't get you to do anything. We just cuddled up in bed and went to sleep." She was getting more wound up as she talked. Her chest was heaving as she took deeper breaths and kept steaming on. "This morning I wake up and we're all naked. Kyle's cock is pumping into me from behind and you've got your fingers in my pussy while I licked your nipples and fingered your clit. But I look up and the two of you are kissing. Not little kisses like you've always done. You were kissing as if he was pumping into you. You were making love with me in the middle. How long have you been lovers? How long have you been hiding this from me?" Her eyes sparkled with tears. I sighed.

"It's not like that, honey. Not really. I owe you both an apology. I got carried away. I didn't mean to use you like that, Aubrey. Please believe me," I whispered.

"We both got carried away. We weren't expecting to be here. There. Like that," Kyle added.

"There's always been something. I always suspected it was that you were in love with each other and couldn't admit it. But I'm not buying what you're selling. There's more than that and I want to know it all. I want to know what really happened." Aubrey was determined and Pa had just told me I had to tell her. I took a deep breath. She was going to look at me the same way Kyle and I looked at Pa when he told us.

"We're time travelers," I said. "When the wolves left last night, so did we. Our minds. Or a part of us. We got plunked down in our hosts just as they were saying their wedding vows. We were in their heads as they were making love. We didn't realize we were back."

"Time travelers? What do you think I am?"

We got her calmed down enough to start from the beginning. Told her that Pa was a time traveler and our response when he told us was the same as hers. It took us all day. We went into Caitlin's room that used to be mine and showed her the map and where we'd been. I'd written on the map in black Sharpie. Kyle had used a blue one. There were more marks on the map in red, but they didn't make any sense to me. I figured the kids must have decided to play games on it.

I confessed.

I cried while I told her about killing three men and a woman. I told her about meeting with Wolf and finally pointed to my throat where he'd licked me last night. She looked at my neck. My scars were so faint as to be unnoticeable. Aubrey kind of glazed over when she flopped back on the sofa and listened as Kyle and I filled her in on the rest of our story. Miranda, Jason, and Katie. How the five of us had married together and ultimately come to the threesome that had ended in our bed this morning.

THE ONLY SOUND in the room was the three of us sniffling. Kyle at one end of the sofa and Aubrey at the other. I sat in our only soft chair. It wasn't that comfortable and I wanted to hold my girlfriend in my arms. She wouldn't look at me or Kyle.

She finally stood up. I opened my arms to her but she turned away.

"I need to go now. I'll bring the truck back to you tomorrow."

"Aubrey, honey, please don't go."

"You lied to me!" she shouted. "Even when I told you I could accept a relationship with both of you on any terms, you still are lying to me. You still have to make up some fantastic bullshit instead of saying right out that you want your brother. You used me as a placeholder. I thought you loved me."

"We love you!" Kyle burst out. "Everything we've told you was the truth."

"Then that's worse!" Aubrey was leaning against the wall next to the door and sank down against it as she cried. I started toward her but she waved me away, scrunching into a little ball like I'd hurt her.

"If what you say is true, you just wanted to fuck me so you could time travel. I didn't expect a fairy tale love affair. I didn't expect it to be forever. We were only sixteen. But you let me fall in love with you both. And for three fucking years you hid what was really going on. You had a whole secret life. You lived five more years in that time than I did. No fucking wonder you always act so mature. I thought it was just because of the way you were raised on the ranch to be self-sufficient. But you were pioneering out in the wilderness. You were riding with the U.S. Cavalry. You were killing kidnappers. You were fighting Indians. You had another lover. You had another whole fucking family! You could have told me. You could have taken me with you. You didn't need to deceive me. You didn't need to lie." She pushed herself up, grabbed the keys to Kyle's truck off the peg by the door, and walked out.

"Don't!" I cried out. "Don't leave me!"

Kyle had me wrapped in his arms and carried me to my bedroom as we heard the truck start and drive away. The sheets were still mussed from where we'd all made love this morning. He held me until we'd both settled down, our tears washing each other's faces. He started to stand up but I wouldn't let go of him. He finally lay down beside me and we held each other through the night.

IT WAS THE start of the longest and coldest summer of my life. Kyle and I got in from driving the horse herd out to a new thousand-acre leased parcel on the south edge of our property. His truck was at the apartment but Aubrey wasn't. Her closet was empty.

"She's gone," I whimpered. "She's gone."

Kyle and I had our arms wrapped around each other when we came in for dinner. Even though I had no appetite, we were expected to join the family if we were at home. Aubrey's chair and place-setting were there and it broke my heart. Mom Mar looked at us and picked up the extra place setting. Pa moved Aubrey's chair out to the dining room. We paused to consider the land before food was passed around the kitchen table.

Even Phile and Caitlin hugged us after we left the table.

"Sorry," Caitlin said. "And sorry I've been such a bitch. We've got mares coming in to stand stud Monday. Let us know what all you need us to do."

Work. That was the solution. The four of us got a five mile trail marked out in the new acreage and gave our boarders maps so they could try it out. They loved it and sometimes they brought friends along to ride our trails. We didn't charge for day use if riders were with one of our boarders. Nor did we charge our neighbors who wanted to see what we'd done. We got a lot of praise and showed the USGS maps that we'd hung in the barn to map out our new network of pleasure trails. The rules were constant. Don't bother the cattle and don't bother the retired horses. That was it.

We set about painting the stables. Painting a structure as big as our barn is a major undertaking. Kyle and I checked the shingles and repaired a couple damaged places on the roof. Wind will do that. Then we scraped the old rust-colored paint and primed the boards with new rubberized primer. Just getting the scaffolding rented and erected took us two days and we figured another two days each time we had to move it. We bought paint in fifty-five gallon drums and hooked the compressor to two spray guns to get it done.

At sunset, we'd clean up and go in for dinner. Mom Mar was used to summer feeding hours as Pa was often out checking on cattle or improving the facilities himself. L&K Stables actually stood to make a profit this year. We'd collected nearly $15,000 in stud fees and were boarding eight pregnant mares in addition to our own eight. Bells and Bows had caught again and it pleased the kids no end.

Somewhere around late-June, Kyle and I stopped wearing our jeans to bed. We hadn't spent a night apart since Aubrey left. I couldn't stand to be alone and I think Kyle thought the same. We were on our own the first week in July. Moms and Pa decided to spend a week camped up with the cattle, even though there had been no sign of predators this year. Even the Forest Service was confused as to where all the wolves were. Every so often we'd see one of their yellow helicopters fly over. There was only one small pack and they were keeping to the wilderness. Order was being restored.

Kyle gave the kids the keys to the truck and they took off to go to the rodeo and watch the fireworks in Laramie. Kyle and I watched the sun go down and sat on the front porch swing. I reached over and took his hand.

"Right out there," I whispered. "When Pa told me he'd killed five men right there, I could see it all happening, Kyle. Now it's so peaceful. Do you suppose we'll ever go back?"

"I hope so, Ramie," Kyle said, squeezing my hand. "I hope so, because I still love you."

Seems like that must have been the cue. I heard the flutter of wings and old Blackfeather landed on my shoulder. He turned his one good eye to look at me. It still put my heart in my throat to see that big beak so close to my face. Then he turned to look at Kyle. He had to turn all the way around on my shoulder to get his good eye in line with Kyle's. It was like he was assessing whether or not we were worthy. Off in the distance I could hear an owl hoo-hooting and Blackfeather bobbed his head up and down.

Then, right between our ears, he screamed out his call.

34
Life and Death

"**I** WILL NOT put on the blues again," Jason said firmly.

"We can make… accommodations," the officer facing him said. Miranda watched as the two argued at the kitchen table. She didn't like him. He'd been the one to twice deny them permission to marry until Jason was discharged. Now he wanted him back. She poured coffee. Her aching back and protruding belly complained at the effort. "You will not be an official part of the army. You can even wear buckskins like your *Indian* friends." There was a note of scorn in the captain's voice that grated on my ears.

"What is this all about?"

"Red Cloud signed a treaty after the devil massacred Fetterman's unit. He fashioned himself chief of all the Sioux and visited President Grant himself in Washington, D.C. Now he has his tribe at Red Cloud Agency east of Fort Laramie. We ceded the land near there and abandoned Fort Phil Kearny. But that damned Crazy Horse has refused to recognize the treaty. He prances all up and down the Dakota and Wyoming Territories harassing anyone who even ventures across the plains. Then there is Black Kettle, who just sits up north and waits for an opportunity. Nobody knows who is chief of what. The only Indians you can tell apart are the dead ones."

"Sounds like you have it all figured out already," Jason said bitterly.

"Red Cloud is sending his niece, Nellie Larrabee, to Crazy Horse as a bride to encourage him to become part of the family. You are to be part of the escort. There will be an official army representative to try to parlay with Crazy Horse, but you know and understand those savages. We need to know what that renegade is planning and how many people are in his camp," the captain said.

"Nellie Larrabee does not sound like a Lakota name to me," Jason responded.

"She is a half-breed. And do not get too close to her. She is a sneaky little savage whose loyalties are as divided as her breeding. She is supposed to get Crazy Horse to sign the treaty."

"He won't," I heard Jason's voice but recognized Kyle.

"Then she will probably kill him. Be fine by me. Never trust her or anything she says," the captain said.

"Why would I be with that kind of party? Crazy Horse is no fool. He would know me no matter what I wore," Jason said. He kept shaking his head and I knew that he was fighting against every word the captain said. Miranda held her peace, sitting in the chair by the fire, but her mind was in turmoil. She was near her time and the thought of Jason leaving was terrifying.

"You have that Indian friend, John Hamm. He and his white bride—your sister-in-law, I believe—are living somewhere up there either with Crazy Horse or Black Kettle. Your reason for being with this party is to find your old friend and tell your sister-in-law of your wife's condition. Invite her back with you to tend your wife and child," the captain said.

"Jason, don't go," Miranda moaned. "I'm near my time. I need you." I'd have just demanded my husband stay put, but this was a different age.

"A husband is needed only for the sowing, not the reaping. Your women would chase him out of the house while you give birth regardless. Corporal Wardlaw will return within a few months."

"I am not a corporal, Captain. I left the army behind and took a wife. I keep a shop."

"The United States of America has need of your service, *Mister* Wardlaw. I would not expect a man who served under me for six years to have turned a coward in ten months. The unit with which you will travel will depart Fort Sanders at dawn. Good day. Missus Wardlaw, congratulations on your impending motherhood." The captain stood and made his own way to the door. Jason did not stand to see him out. He nearly knocked Katie back down the stairs as she came up.

MIRANDA HAD BEGUN to cry, but I took control and stood to face Jason.

"Husband Ramie!" Katie shouted as soon as she saw me. She rushed to me and kissed me, softly petting my distended belly. She turned to look at Jason. "Husband Kyle!" She gave Jason the same treatment.

I swear that Katie knows I've arrived before you do, Miranda.

"Jason, you must not leave me," Miranda commanded.

"Leave?" Katie asked. "Why ever would he leave us? You are near term and little Katie-Lynn will be here to greet her brother just five months later."

"Of course he's not leaving," I asserted. "Kyle, tell him. My god! What year is it?"

"Mid-June of '73," Katie supplied.

"What year, Kyle? I can't remember. What year was the Little Big Horn?" I screamed. We could not let Jason go to Crazy Horse. His long yellow hair would make him an easy target.

"I don't know," Kyle said. "I don't think it's yet, but it is soon."

"Has Custer taken charge of the 7th Cavalry, Jason?"

"He has been around the 7th since '68 when he led the Battle of Washita down south. I have not heard of him lately. Why?"

"Custer led his troops into an ambush at Little Bighorn led by Crazy Horse. The entire cavalry was wiped out."

"Wiped out?" Katie asked.

"No survivors," Kyle said. I saw Jason pale and knew that Kyle must be sharing as much of the history as we knew.

"I do not believe that is what we are facing," Jason said. There has been no word of that kind of uprising."

"But you are not going!" I shouted. "Kyle, make him see reason!"

"My loves," Jason said after visibly struggling. "I have no choice. Captain Riggs has the power to conscript me if he chooses. If I go willingly, at least I am not under his command. I have freedom to go where I choose within the commission," Jason said. "My darling Miranda, I do not wish to leave you. I will rush back to your side as quickly as I can."

THE BATTLE WASN'T over but it was clear that we'd lost the war. As we talked into the night, we became convinced that it was too early for the Battle of Little Bighorn. But it still wasn't safe.

"I'll send a message and warn Custer," Jason said. "I can't let my fellow soldiers march into their death without warning them."

"Didn't you learn anything from trying to save Lincoln?" I shot back. "To you, it is a dreadful thing that will happen sometime in the future. To us it is history. Nothing you say or do will change the outcome."

"But don't I have to try?"

I knew that Kyle was having the same argument inside Jason's head as I was having outside. And I knew Kyle was just as conflicted. Just because we could not change history didn't mean we shouldn't try, did it? I just wanted them safe.

"Husband Ramie," Katie said abruptly. "Husband Kyle, Husband Jason, and Wife Miranda are ignoring my needs. Will you not take your pleasure with me? I ache to feel you touch me. I would have Jason and Kyle with me as well, but they are determined to spend the night arguing."

I could see what Katie was doing as soon as I felt Jason reach across me to pet our wife's side. We needed to be together. All five of us.

"Katie dear, I cannot lie comfortably to kiss your privities. I will lie on my back for a while and if you can get them to my mouth, I will kiss them with ardor." Katie scrambled to get us in a position that was comfortable. I scooted down on the bed so she could get her legs on either side of my head and I tasted her sweet nectar against my tongue. So wonderful. So intense. Her slight baby-bump—four months?—pressed against my breasts. She could not reach my pussy with her mouth. It was simply too far across my baby belly to reach it. Then I felt a tongue and knew Jason had edged down the bed and buried his face in my pussy.

Oh my! He's never done that before!

I smiled and then gasped. Perhaps Jason did not know how to lick a pussy, but Kyle did.

Even after Katie and I had climaxed, I held her there as Jason climbed over me and entered our lover above my face. In this position I could kiss and lick both of them—all three?—and Miranda cherished the loving. At last we were together.

"KYLE? ARE YOU there?"

Jason's eyes opened and Kyle looked back at me.

"I'm here, love. I don't like this."

"What's really going on?" I asked. "I can't believe Jason could be con-scripted back into the army after already serving six years."

"It's like being in the reserves. He can be called up at any time if he is near a conflict."

"I'm worried, Kyle."

"Me, too. I'll do my best to protect him. At least one of us will always be awake."

"Make love to me, Kyle. Gently. Don't squash our baby."

MIRANDA AND KATIE rose early, fed Jason well, and packed his panniers. He wore frontier buckskins Katie had made for him, but they covered his cavalry boots, not moccasins. We wept on his shoulder until he had to go round up Shadow and leave for Fort Sanders. He kissed us tenderly, kissed Katie, and hugged us to him. I shared their tears as I watched our men leave.

We've shared so much these years. Now you are alone. Perhaps I'm just here to keep you company.

"Will he be safe?"

Kyle will do his best to keep them safe.

"But you know things. You are from the future. Does he come home safely?"

I only know what history has recorded. And not even all of that. The rest is what my Pa called a box that contains the unknown. Inside the box, all futures are possible. It stays that way until we open the box and then only one emerges. Believe me, I went to the library and researched everything I could find about this time. I can't find a mention of you or Jason or even the name of this store.

"Please, dear God, bring our husband home safely. Amen."

It was the first time I ever felt I had prayed.

ONE DAY AFTER school a few years ago, there was a prayer rally. It was held in the gymnasium because there just isn't as big a deal about keeping church and school separate in Wyoming. God help the atheist who tries to protest a prayer meeting. If you are some other religion, go someplace else. School buses left an hour late that day and the gym was packed with community people. At the center of the rally were the wives, parents, and children of three soldiers who had been killed overseas. The prayers were for their support and comfort. But I heard a woman not far from me pray almost those exact words. *Please bring my husband home safely.* She was very pregnant. I wondered if God had answered her prayer.

KATIE KEPT THE store open, though we operated on less than business hours. I waddled in to help behind the counter as long as I could sit in one place. I was strangely comforted by the sight of my Colt under the counter. In the afternoon, when we closed the store, I took the gun with me to our apartment. Katie and I held each other through the night, kissing softly and whispering words of encouragement.

Jason had left on a Monday morning and it was Wednesday night, two weeks later, when Miranda's water broke and labor began.

I thought I would die!

I was in no way prepared for the pains of delivering a baby. Miranda was scarcely better prepared. Thursday morning, Katie prepared to open the store as we labored in bed.

"Damn the store!" Miranda said. "My husband has left me. Do not also leave me." Katie sat by our side, wiping sweat from our brow with a damp cloth.

"I know nothing of delivering babies, my love," Katie said. "Rest while I run to get the midwife." Miranda finally agreed and Katie ran off.

"This is much worse than I expected," Miranda said between contractions. I'd delivered foals and calves before, but I had no experience with human labor. I certainly never expected I'd be experiencing it.

I'm here, Miranda. I'm sharing every contraction with you. We'll see it through, you and me.

"You are a comfort, but I wish I was riding and you were driving," she laughed weakly.

I'll do my best, but from what I'm feeling, it might not give you much of a rest.

For the next few hours we traded back and forth. We each got a little rest while the other endured the direct pain. But just like with sex, we both had the experience. We could drive the body we shared a little harder, but our body was weakening. *And where is Katie?*

I lost track of time. I heard voices so I knew someone had been there, but it did nothing to relieve the pain.

"There now, love; it seems like forever, but you will triumph. Women have been giving birth since God cursed Eve in the Garden. Seeing you gives me courage for when Katie-Lynn is born."

"Katie?"

"Yes, darling. I am here."

"Where is the midwife?" Miranda asked.

"She's drunk. Doctor Finrock stopped and gave instructions for seeing you through your labor. He had to leave for surgery and promised he would be back to congratulate you tomorrow morning," Katie said.

I moaned through another contraction and time dissolved again.

"I SEE HIM!" Katie screamed. "There's a little foot here." It was light out. Morning again, I supposed. But at least we were having a baby. It had been at least thirty hours of agony.

Wait! A foot? Oh God, no! That's wrong. There should be a head.

I grabbed Katie's hair from where she was staring up between my legs and dragged her to my face. I was delirious.

"Ow! Husband Ramie, you are hurting me!"

"Katie, listen to me," I gasped. I loosened my grip so I wasn't pulling her hair. "That's the wrong way for the baby to come. He's breeched. I can't deliver him that way."

"But I can see it."

"Katie, babies come head first. You have to turn him around."

"But how?" I'd watched the vet turn a breech calf once. This was going to hurt.

"You have to… have to reach in and push the foot back up and pull the head down. Here. I can feel his head right here. He wants to get turned around but his foot is stuck. Push it… Push it back into my womb so his head can get into the opening." I was crying. I hurt so much. I fought not to push when the next contraction hit.

Miranda was hysterical. We would be damaged for life. But with one foot presenting and the head at the cervix, we'd both die.

"But…"

"Do it, Katie. Or else we will die!"

I felt her hand. Thank God she had small hands. And I felt the baby reverse direction.

"There's blood!"

"Finish it, Katie!"

"The foot is in but where is the head?" I put my hand on my abdomen and more from hope than knowledge pushed my baby's head down.

"I see… I see hair," she screamed. I rallied all the strength Miranda had left in her body and pushed. "He's coming. One more time." I knew she'd keep saying one more time forever. It was always just one more time.

We're birthing, Miranda. Don't leave me now. Our son is being born.

"Are we alive?"

There couldn't be this much pain if we were dead. Push! Push with me, Miranda. Help!

Together we united ourselves. Together we silently swore we would cut our husband's cock off. Together we pushed again. And again.

"It's a baby boy!" Katie screamed. There was a cry from the child and I reached to pull him to my breast. He was slimy and crying and when he grabbed for my teat his hands clenched so tightly I cried out again. I was sure there was no milk there yet but he started sucking vigorously. I could scarcely see him through my tears. I could hear Katie with a pan of water and felt its warmth as she began to sponge him off.

"The after birth," I croaked as another cramp hit me.

"Oh Miranda. Husband Ramie. Is there supposed to be so much blood?" *Blood? It's always messy, I guess.*

"It's okay. The cord has stopped pulsing. Tie some of that silk thread on the night stand around it near the baby. Then use my sewing shears and cut the cord."

I was so tired. Miranda had kept our eyes on our baby's blond head since he found her breast. She was delirious. I was conscious, but Miranda faded in and out. Katie cleaned away the afterbirth and placed a towel against my vagina.

"I wish the doctor would hurry and get here. It's still bleeding," the worried girl said.

I shouldn't still be bleeding, should I? I was slipping into another world—afraid Raven would call and I would not be here with my baby. But Raven was busy. I could see him swooping down on a man in buckskins and an Indian as they rode side-by-side. The man looked up. A pack of wolves bore down on him. No! Not wolves. Renegades dressed in wolfskins. Jason pulled his rifle and swung to shoot, as did his companion. He hesitated and pulled the rifle up.

Two arrows struck his chest. His gun fired into the air. The Indian companion fell from his horse.

"Kyle!" I screamed. I heard Miranda echo Jason's name in my head.

"Don't you worry, Husband Ramie. I'll take care of little Kyle for you. You rest now. I hear the doctor on the stairs."

The door opened and Doctor Finrock spoke.

"So we have a baby?" Footsteps. I no longer felt my body. "What is this? She's hemorrhaged! Girl why didn't you…" I felt their presence but could no longer hear them. I no longer felt my baby at my breast. All I could feel was the last gasp of breath that Jason/Kyle took. Only it was mine.

Awkawkawkawk!

And I was no longer in Miranda's body.

Ramie! Don't leave me!

35
Not My Brother

I HAD AWARENESS, but no sensations. I clutched imaginary hands trying to hold onto Miranda. I couldn't see, hear, touch, smell, or taste anything. Yet I was aware of my surroundings and what was happening. I floated alone, yearning toward my baby. I caught glimpses of other people's thoughts.

"Poor woman." "Poor baby." "Never should have been left." "Wait until her husband hears." "Burial." "Baby." "Baby boy." "Kyle."

Death in 1873 was common. Death in childbirth was not uncommon. Life was hard, even in the better strata of society. People mourned and moved on. I moved. With my baby. They didn't know. Wouldn't know for weeks that his father was not returning. Poor Katie took care of little Kyle as she tried to tend the store and get ready for her own impending delivery. I tried to comfort her—to tell her I was here. My poor Katie. *I am here. I love you.* I heard her sigh my name in her sleep. I willed her child to be healthy and held her in my imaginary arms as she gave birth to her little Katie Lynn.

When word finally arrived that Jason was dead she wept. I wanted so much to hold her. To whisper that I loved her.

I love you. I'm here. I love you.

A fire—all to common among the wooden structures of early Laramie—broke out on our street and the store and apartment were burned to the ground. Katie escaped with the babies, a few coins, and my six-shooter.

The last I felt from her, she was handling my Colt in the back room of a dingy whorehouse. "I love you, Husband Ramie." The babies cried.

I don't think she heard Raven call me.

I WAS CHOKING. Coughing. Retching. My body was wracked with spasms. I threw myself to the side and heaved. Nothing. I heaved again and again. Cold compresses against my head, wiping my mouth.

"It's all right. You're safe. You are here with us." Caitlin! I was alive.

"Kyle's coming around. Get ready," Phile said, nearby.

"It's okay. You're safe." My family. Kyle was alive.

"I radioed up and Moms and Pa are on their way down," Phile said. "When we got home, you were just sitting in the porch swing like zombies. We couldn't wake you up. Pa told us to carry you to bed."

"I hear the horses," Caitlin said. "They must have ridden all night. It's almost dawn."

I reached out and clutched at Kyle's hand. I could hear him crying.

"Okay, kids," Pa said. "How are our invalids? Caitlin, go get us some tea made. Phile, take care of our horses, please." The kids left and it was just our parents. I couldn't hold it any longer.

"Momma!" I wailed. "They're dead!"

Kyle's hand gripped mine and we rolled toward each other, clutching and crying.

Moms and Pa tried to talk to us, but they couldn't pry us apart, and I wasn't going to stop holding my Kyle. They just had to wait. We were all we had now.

"It will be all right, babies," our moms crooned. "It will be all right."

"When you are ready, you can tell us about it. Let's get you up and get some breakfast. You might need to sleep more after that," Pa said. "I don't think I was worth shit for a week after."

WE SPENT AN hour after breakfast with the parents. They didn't judge anything. They just held us while we cried for our dead hosts. Our friends. We could only lay out the facts. It was as much for each other as it was for them. Kyle told about riding out from Crazy Horse's camp and meeting up with White Horse. Pa smiled when he heard that Jason and White Horse were friends.

"The renegades hit us by surprise. I barely got my gun up before I was hit by arrows," Kyle said. "I got Jason killed because I distracted him. We could have shot them."

"What distracted you, son?" Pa asked.

"Stupid things. It wasn't just me. Jason didn't want to shoot anybody. Me? I thought I recognized the horses and they were friends."

"I don't think there was anything you could have done to stop it. Was White Horse killed, too?"

"I don't know for sure. I know he was off his horse, but they might have left him. I don't know," Kyle said.

Then the moms were on me about what I'd experienced. When I told about having to turn the baby, Mom Ash left and we heard her throw up in the bathroom across the hall.

"You're right," Mom Mar said. "You had to do that or you'd both have died. Your baby survived?"

"Yeah. Little Kyle." *Oh my god!* "Pa, when you traveled, your host was Kyle Redtail. Did he have another name?"

"Of course, sweetie. Redtail was the name Laramie gave him. It was because my totem was the redtail hawk, like yours is the raven. His given name was Kyle Wardlaw. As far as he knew, his mother was a prostitute and he was raised in the brothels after she died."

"The fuckers!" I screamed. My baby. My baby. I buried my head against Kyle's shoulder. It was all too fresh. It hurt. I turned back to our parents with tears in my eyes.

"I think... me and Kyle... I think..."

Kyle took a noisy breath in and hissed between his teeth as he let it out.

"I'm your father, Cole," he said in his best Darth Vader voice. It wasn't very good but it got the point across. I blessed his heart for making me laugh but I hit him anyway.

"You're Kyle Wardlaw's parents?" Pa asked. Our family was so fucked up!

"When I felt him dying, I screamed out Kyle's name. Katie—my sweet, sweet Katie—heard me yell 'Kyle' and immediately thought I'd just named my son. She said they'd take care of little Kyle for me while I got better. Only I didn't get better. I died. I died, Papa. Just this morning back in 1873 and my baby never had a mother or father."

"And so he was raised in the brothel," Pa said.

"She lost the store and apartment in a fire. Poor Katie took Kyle and little Katie-Lynn and had to live in that whorehouse. My poor Katie. I didn't save her after all.

"Katie-Lynn?" Pa said. He looked like I felt. He was all pasty white. "Laramie," he whispered to me, "what was Katie's last name?" I thought a minute.

"Forster. Katie Forster. She could always tell when I was there, Pa. She knew almost before Miranda did. With Kyle, too. She called me her Husband Ramie."

"My sister," Pa moaned. "She was my sister and I never even knew." His eyes were dripping tears and Mom Ash went to hold him. "I know you kids have been through a lot," Pa said. "But we need to make a trip into town. Now."

THE KIDS BEGGED off and stayed at the ranch. We piled into the Explorer and drove down to Laramie. Mom Mar sat up front with Pa and Mom Ash just kept hugging us in the back seat. Whatever was so urgent didn't keep Pa from stopping at Safeway and telling us to wait. He was back out a few minutes later with a couple flowers and we turned down Harney Street to 15th. Pa pulled in at Green Hill Cemetery and parked.

"Your Pa comes out here at least once a month," Mom Ash whispered to us. "It must be important to come now."

We followed Pa out into the Potter's Field section of the cemetery, in the far Northwest corner. There aren't many stones there. A few are broken and a few are just flat slabs that lay in the ground with grass growing all around them. Pa walked straight to a section where you could barely see a flat stone. He knelt there and wiped the grass off the stone and set up one of those little flower planters. He put two carnations in it. Then he called us to look at the stone. The inscription was faint. I had to shade it in order to see the relief. Caitlin Forster, 1890. My sister's name. Caitlin. Katie-Lynn.

"I never knew she was my sister. She died… aborting our baby. I just came back from one of my trips expecting to see her and she was gone. She was Kyle's first love. He never knew she was his sister." Pa wept over her grave. It had been a long time ago. Pa hadn't traveled since I was born and still he came to her grave every month and left flowers. I already knew the answer, but I had to ask the question.

"Pa? Why… two flowers?"

"Geneive," he whispered. "My high school girlfriend and my lover. She was a time traveler, too, and I never realized it the whole time we were together. Caitlin was her host."

I wept. I held Pa, and my brother held us both, as we wept. My precious Katie. Miranda's son and Katie's daughter, raised in the whorehouses of Laramie. Both Kyle's… Jason's children. What's fair about that? Why did Blackfeather ever send us traveling? *I hate you old crow!*

KYLE AND I had to get on with our lives. Ranches don't leave time for mourning unless you find a way to express it. We expressed it by painting the trim of the barn and then whitewashing all the fence posts. We decided a stable should have a three-rail horse fence at least around the paddock. The kids worked quietly beside us all the rest of the summer to make L&K Stables shine. By the end of summer, we had five of our first crop of foals working with us in the paddock. Phile and Caitlin were naturals with them and it didn't take long before they were gentled, and we could handle them. I loved brushing the two-year-olds and just running my hands along their sleek strong muscles.

The whole summer, Kyle was never more than a few steps from me. Sometimes we'd start to speak and say the same thing. We'd been through more together than any siblings we could imagine. But by mid-August, I realized that I was in love with my brother. No one else could possibly share what we had shared. No one could understand. My head couldn't come to grips with where my heart was, and I begged off a week in August to go help with the cattle drive. Kyle was ready to ride.

"I hate to put this on you, Kyle," I said, "but we've got fall boarders showing up this week and I need you to be here. This ride I'm taking is something I've got to do." I kissed him softly on the cheek and mounted Pooky.

IT WAS ONLY a few days, but I had to get my head on straight. I could not be in love with my brother. My head rebelled so thoroughly that I couldn't even fathom it. *I've smelled his farts.* That thought brought a tear to my eye. It's what I'd told Aubrey when she was with us. *Why did she have to go?*

As our horse operation had gotten bigger, Pa had reduced his cattle operation. There were only 400 head on the upper range and half of them were yearlings and calves. That meant only a hundred head would go to market this year. I wondered if Pa was okay with that, but the folks had thoroughly embraced the concept of ranch-raised, grass-fed cattle. That meant they weren't buying calves at auction to fatten and sell later. Anything sold these days had been bred and born on the ranch. It takes two years from birth to market.

Before we turned the herd for home, I spent a couple nights by the thermal spring by myself. Then I joined the drive down the mountain. By the time we got the cattle wrangled into Pa's cattle pens, I'd made up my mind. It was going to hurt. But it had to be.

I saw Kyle's face light up when I rode Pooky to the stable and he ran out to meet me. He reached for me and I held him off.

"We gotta talk, Kyle," I said. "Saddle up. This can't wait." I could see his face fall and it about broke my heart. We rode out to the family plot and let the horses graze as we looked at the stones. They meant so much more to us now. I'd slept in the bed with Theresa Ranae Bell and watched her as she courted with White Horse. Her baby, my namesake, Laramie Wyoming Bell was Miranda's niece. The stone marking Kyle Redtail Wardlaw's grave… My pa's host when he traveled. Kyle's and my son when we traveled. We cried a little. The wounds were still too fresh. I motioned Kyle to sit by me as I looked out over our beautiful little ranch.

"Kyle," I said softly. He turned toward me. "I need you to stop…" He was shaking his head violently and held up his hand to stop me speaking.

"Laramie Wyoming Bell, you can't tell me to stop loving you. I do. I thought it was just me in Jason loving Miranda, but I fell in love with you, Ramie. You. And I took my vows in front of the preacher. It might have been a century and a half ago, but that which God hath joined together, let no man rend asunder. It might be wrong. You might not be able to accept my love. If I need to, I'll go away. But I can't stop loving you, Ramie. I can't." I just wanted to pull him into my arms and love him. Instead I shifted away slightly.

"You've had your say. Now let me have mine," I said. "Kyle, I love you to the depth of my soul. But you have to stop being my brother. I can't reconcile loving you, the man I fell in love with in two different centuries, with loving my brother. I don't know how you do it. But you can't just walk across the hall into my bedroom as my brother. I don't mean legal things. I don't mean you can't have the same parents. But I have to stop being your sister in order to be your lover. If you can't... if *we* can't do that, then we can't ever be together."

"How?"

"I don't know, Kyle. I just know it has to happen."

CLASSES STARTED WEDNESDAY of all the stupid things. Three days and then Labor Day weekend. It was hardly worth driving in for. We didn't move back to campus. There didn't seem to be a point to it. We drove the kids to high school for their junior year and we went on to our classes.

Kyle met me after my equine bloodlines class on Friday. It was one that we didn't both have together. He was standing there with his hat in his hands looking gawky as a freshman.

"Miss Laramie Wyoming," he said as I approached. He pulled a ragged batch of flowers out from behind his hat. "There is a dance tonight in the Union. I know it is short notice, but may I buy you dinner and enjoy your company at the dance?"

My god! Kyle was asking me out on a date! I couldn't even say anything. I just nodded my head. We got in the truck and picked up Caitlin and Phile. Everyone was quiet on the way home. I kept lifting the flowers to my nose. When we got to the apartment, Kyle opened the door for me. He grinned.

"I'll pick you up at six." Then he walked into his bedroom and closed the door.

I grabbed a pickle jar and put water in it to hold the flowers. I started to leave them on the kitchen counter but took them into my bedroom instead. I tried them several different places and settled them on the bedside table. It was only four o'clock. *What am I going to do for two hours?* I ran up to the house where Mom Mar was cooking.

"Ma, I've got a date tonight. I won't be here for dinner," I said. I was so out of breath I could hardly get the words out. It isn't that much of a run to the house!

"Oh," she said. "I won't set your plate. What are you wearing?" *Oh no! What am I wearing?*

"I don't know. I'm going to a dance, but it will be casual. I gotta go figure out what to wear!"

"Okay, dear. Let me know if you need help with your hair or anything. I've never fixed you up for a date," she said. I kissed her on the cheek. "Thanks, Ma." I ran back to my room, stripped, and put my robe on to shower. Only two hours? How am I ever going to get ready in time?

I finished my shower and dried my hair, looking at the disgusting haystack in the mirror. I finally decided to just let it stick out any way it felt like. I put a foundation on and powdered my ruddy complexion. I didn't look too bad. The rest I could do in my room. I put on panties and a bra. I couldn't even remember the last time I wore a bra. I guess it still fit. I pulled it off and threw it in the trash. I had a camisole that would do better. Aubrey gave it to me. I felt a tear coming and pushed it back.

I had half my closet tossed onto the bed which amounted to three outfits. Everything else was jeans. There was one just stood out. I started to put it on and stopped to call Mom Mar. She was out to my room in two jerks and started buttoning my blouse for me. I'd picked it up at Martingale's Store on Grand. It just called out to me, even though I couldn't think of a place I could wear it. Maybe it was a little dressy for a school dance, but I was going with it anyway. Problem was it had about twenty buttons up the front and came right up under my chin. The skirt was three-quarter length and Ma helped get my boots on. She looked up at me and held out her hand. I thought about it for a minute and handed her my boot knife. She strapped it on and stood me up.

"What about your hair, girl?"

"Nothin' I can do about it. Do I look okay?"

"Laramie, my daughter, you have no idea how beautiful you are."

"I'm nervous. Wait with me until he picks me up?" I said. She sat beside me on the edge of the bed. "I haven't been on a date with a boy since that disaster with Forrest in tenth grade," I laughed. "I hope I don't mess this one up." There was a knock on my door.

"I don't think you *could* mess this one up, sweetie," Mom Mar said. I opened the door and Kyle stood there with his dress boots on, pressed jeans, a nice shirt I'd never seen before, and even wearing a bolo.

"You… you look really pretty," he stammered. He was as nervous as I was.

It was a great evening. We ate at Roxie's and then went to the dance. We just listened to the music for a while and eventually I pulled him out onto the floor and we started two-stepping. The thing about two-stepping is that you can do it to just about any music. I didn't care what was playing. We stayed on the dance floor until the band stopped playing and everyone was headed out.

He offered me his hand and I took it as we walked to his truck. He opened the door for me and lifted me up by the waist so I didn't have to pull my skirts up to get in. When we got back to the apartment, he stopped at my bedroom door.

"I had a great time," I said.

"I hope that means you'll go out with me again," he said. "I have family obligations Monday afternoon, but I'd love to go out to eat with you again in the evening if you would like."

"I'd like that. I'd like it very much." He leaned toward me. I licked my lips and leaned in. The kiss he gave me was pretty reserved and not pushy. He didn't try to grab hold of me or push his tongue in my mouth. It was just so sweet and gentle that I nearly cried. He grinned at me.

"Good night, Laramie. Until Monday, then."

He went to his room, glanced at me, and then closed his door. I nearly swooned.

Kyle is courting me.

36
Reconciliation

I'D HAD a sandwich, but mostly I was studying. I just liked to be out in the Student Union. When I sat in the food court it felt like I was more a part of college life. Even though we were living out at the ranch, we really tried to be more involved with campus activities this year. Most days, I went to watch Kyle at rodeo practice, but I was concerned about my ranch management class and needed to study today.

"May I join you?" a soft voice said. I looked up and my heart did a flip-flop. I know my mouth worked because I could feel it moving up and down. But no sound was coming out. "If it's not okay, I understand," Aubrey said. She started to back away.

"Aubrey! Please! Sit with me. Damn, it's good to see you."

"It's good to see you, too. I've missed you, Ramie."

"What have you been doing? I saw you once but you looked like you were... busy." She looked puzzled. "With... um... Rick Miles."

"Oh," she sighed and looked relieved. "I couldn't figure out who you could have seen me with. Rick's been nice. We study together. When he's not lecturing me."

"What would he lecture you about?" I asked.

"How stupid I was to lose you and Kyle." Aubrey had a tear threatening to leak from her eye. It didn't quite break free. "So, are you seeing anyone?" she said brightly.

"Um... yeah, I sort of am. But..."

"I'm happy for you. I..." she broke off when she saw I wasn't paying attention. I smiled as Kyle came across the cafeteria to our table. I'd let him go a little further Saturday night than I'd intended and I was still tingly from feeling his hand against my bare skin.

"Laramie," he said as he bent to kiss me. I almost let him make a scene before I remembered Aubrey was there.

"Kyle," I whispered. "Sit with Aubrey and me."

"Aubrey?" He turned so fast toward her that he lost his balance and landed on the floor. At least that got us over the awkward part as we all started laughing and I helped him up off the floor.

"Wouldn't you rather sit on a chair?" I asked.

"Yeah. Sure. Aubrey. How are you?" He was as thrown as I was and I could see in his eyes that he loved her as much as I did.

"You… uh… You are seeing each other now?" she squeaked. I suppose I had the stupidest grin on my face in the world when I nodded.

"We're dating. He's kind of hard to resist."

"I always thought… I'm happy for you. I'll see you." She pushed her chair back and I looked at Kyle. He looked as panicked as I felt. We both reached out to catch her hands.

"Aubrey…"

"Would you like to go out with us this week?" Kyle finished.

"We could go to the Cowboy Bar and Grill Wednesday night. That's when they allow underaged kids in until ten," I added.

"We could pick you up early and go to dinner first."

"Or we could go to the arcade if you'd prefer."

"Or just go get coffee," Kyle finished. We were both holding her hands and she squeezed them.

"You don't think I'd just be a third wheel?" she asked.

"Nothing's more stable than a tricycle," Kyle answered. Aubrey nodded.

"WE NEED TO talk," Kyle said as we walked into the apartment after dinner. I was pretty well caught up on my homework and I nodded.

"Let's sit in the living room," I suggested. It was already cold out and I was hoping we weren't headed for another hard winter.

"I can tell you still love Aubrey," he said. I nodded. "And so do I. But Laramie, I'm in love with you, too, and I won't do anything to hurt what we have together." Ever since he'd stopped 'being my brother,' he'd been using my full name instead of the family nickname. I liked it. It was special between us.

"Kyle, I won't trade what we have for anything in the world. But I miss her and so do you."

"Do you think she'd come back to us? The new us?" he asked.

"We can't know until we ask her. She was never upset about us. It was all the other stuff. And that we deceived her. I won't do that again," I said.

"I agree. I won't deceive her but I won't let anything come between us, either," Kyle said. He reached out and took my hand. I pulled him toward me.

"Do you have a lot of homework tonight?" I asked.

"I got most all the reading done while I was waiting at the arena," he said, leaning toward me.

"Could we make out a while, then?"

I guess that kiss was a yes.

WE ENDED UP just going out for dinner Wednesday night. We had a lot to talk about and the other venues weren't for talking.

"I love that you are together," Aubrey said as she sat across from us. We'd had burgers and were drinking coffee. It was beginning to look like we'd be drinking a lot of coffee tonight. "You look so good together. Are you still… um… traveling?"

I knew the subject would come up again. There was no way we could get back together without talking about it. And it sure looked like Aubrey was interested in getting back together. But it hurt so damned much to talk about. I could feel my face squinch up and tears in my eyes. Poor Miranda. Poor Jason. Poor Katie. I loved them all so much. Aubrey reached out and took our hands and brought them together so she was holding Kyle and me between her hands.

"I promise I won't freak out. I'm so sorry that I ran away from you before. I'm so sorry."

"It's not that, honey," I said. "They're dead." I saw her try to comprehend what I was saying as she creased her eyebrows together.

"You mean like they lived a couple centuries ago, right? But you still go back?" she asked. I shook my head.

"We were there, Aubrey. I know it's hard for you to believe," Kyle said. "It's why we never told you or anyone. We thought it was just a dream for a while. When I killed all those helpless women and children and old men, I prayed that it was a dream and I'd wake up from it. But we were there when they died, Aubrey. We can't change it. We can't go back and make them alive. No matter how much we want to."

I just knew this was going to end up in a river of tears.

"And that's the end?"

"So far as we know," I said. "Pa says he traveled a few times after his host died but it was because he was anchored to his wife. When she died, he stopped traveling. Our hosts—who were married to each other—both died. I so want to go back and see my baby. And my Katie."

We just held hands. Aubrey had a lot to take in.

"See? We're still crazy," Kyle said. He tried to laugh it off like Pa did when we told him we thought he was crazy.

"No. I don't believe that," Aubrey said.

"What changed for you, honey?" I asked.

"Rick. I've been hanging around campus ever since football practice started the first of August. He was nice to me and I thought we were dating but we weren't. He was just being a friend. Whenever we got together all I did was talk about the two of you. I… I sort of told him… everything. Please don't be mad at me for that. I had to. One day he took me by the hand and we walked out to Green Hill Cemetery. It's really big. There's a whole section where they just buried babies. He walked me up and down every avenue in the cemetery pointing out different stones and how long the people lived. He's a history major and he kept telling me what was happening in Laramie or in the U.S. or in the world when that person lived. Then he'd say things like, 'You think that person ever imagined there'd be airplanes?' Finally, he looked at me and said, 'You can't imagine what the future will bring. But you can't imagine the lives these people lived, either. Who is to say that no one ever bridged the gap?' And that's when I… It was like I heard a voice from somewhere out in that cemetery telling me I could be the bridge. I had to come and find you."

"But time travel wasn't really the issue," I said. "We deceived you. I'm so sorry, Aubrey. There is nothing I can do to make up for that. I can only promise I'll never lie to you again… no matter how unbelievable the truth is." Kyle nodded his head.

"Can we go on another date and… um… do something fun?"

WE WERE ALL taking it slow. Well, sort of. I was having more and more trouble keeping my panties on. One night we were parked and Kyle and Aubrey both got their hands down there and I screamed into Kyle's mouth as I came. Then I just kept kissing him until Aubrey pushed his face away and claimed my mouth for her own. We hadn't gone all the way yet, but my boyfriend and my girlfriend were ready. When I stopped to think about it, so was I.

It was my twentieth birthday and I was nervous. There were no classes because the next day was Thanksgiving. Aubrey came home with us Tuesday night and very circumspectly spent the night on the sofa. Before we went to bed, the three of us had a hot make-out session on that couch that included Aubrey and me stroking Kyle to a huge come. *Wow! Just wow!* No one was going all the way this time, though, until we all did it together.

Today—tonight—sometime—I was going to lose my virginity. Again.

That thought gave me pause. I was going to be the first girl in history to lose her virginity twice. I'd already lost it once riding inside Miranda's head the first time Jason pierced her maidenhead. Of course, my maidenhead was long gone—probably before I had my first period. I guess I understood Miranda's objection to riding astride a horse. I don't think any of the girls who rode on a regular basis kept that tiny little membrane intact for long. But to Miranda it had been important.

Dear, sweet Miranda. How I wish you here with me now.

The three of us walked up to the house for my birthday breakfast and all of a sudden Raven was sitting on my shoulder. He gave Aubrey quite a start and she squealed. He looked at her. I held my breath.

"What do you want, Blackfeather?" I asked. "There isn't any place for you to take me anymore. They're dead. Why'd you have to let them die?" I broke down. I hadn't seen the old bird since Kyle and I got back in July. I thought he was done with us. Seeing him again just opened all the wounds as if they were fresh. But he didn't caw. He just looked me in my teary eye. "Kyle?" I whispered. "Go get a piece of bacon, would you? Raw." Kyle left and was back in a minute with a two-inch chunk of bacon. I took it in my fingers and held it up. The whole time, the bird never stopped staring at me. He bobbed his head a couple times and plucked the bacon out of my fingers. Then he hopped off to the porch railing and started pecking at his prize. We went on in to breakfast.

Of course, Mom Mar saw Kyle take bacon and saw the tears in my eyes when I walked in to sit down. Kyle and Aubrey sat on either side of me and hugged me. Ma set plates of food in front of us. Phile and Caitlin were already out riding bareback on Bells and Bows. The pregnant mares didn't seem to mind.

"That's really the bird?" Aubrey finally whispered. "He's so… awesome. Is he taking you back again, Ramie? Kyle? Can you take me with you? Will you still be here? With me?"

"Sweetheart, there's nothing for him to take us back to," Kyle said. He ran a finger along her cheek and lifted her chin. I was between the two of them, so I kissed her.

"It was like he was searching my soul for something," I said. "I knew he wanted some meat and that's why I sent Kyle for bacon. But he wanted something more. I've ridden in that bird's head. Even then, I couldn't understand what he was thinking."

Mom Mar set two cups of coffee in front of me.

"Take them with you and go visit Pa in his office," Mom Mar said. "You come with me, Aubrey. Ashley will be along for you in a minute, Kyle." Aubrey and I got up to do as we were told. Ashley passed me coming out of Pa's office. I handed Pa a cup of coffee and he patted the footstool in front of his chair for me to sit on.

"Happy birthday, baby girl," Pa said. He didn't usually call me 'baby girl' these days. That was sort of reserved for Caitlin.

"Thanks, Pa." Maybe he was going to give me my birthday present privately. I wondered what he got me.

"Laramie, have you thought through what you are doing? Your moms and I try not to interfere. You're an adult. But you are walking on dangerous ground," he said. There was only one thing he could be referring to. It had been pretty obvious all fall that Kyle and I were doing more than carpooling to classes. Especially once Aubrey joined us again.

"I only know my heart, Pa."

"You've loved your brother for years, but I… Well, I'm worried about both of you. This isn't a trifling thing."

"Pa, Phile is my brother. I know you have another son, but I only have one brother. Kyle is my boyfriend. He's been courting me and I love him. We've been courting Aubrey and she's in love with us both. We aren't sneaking around, Pa. We learned our lessons. But we've got to follow our hearts." I was amazed at how calm and sure of myself I felt. I was in love with Kyle. I truly didn't think about him as a brother any longer. He was my mate.

Pa was staring into his coffee cup and tears were running down his cheeks. I put a hand on his and he set the cup aside, opening his arms to me. I jumped into his lap as quickly as I could. He hugged me. It was only the second time I'd ever seen my father so overwhelmed with emotion.

"I've only ever wanted what was best for my children," he whispered. "You know Caitlin and Phile are nowhere near as clever as they think they are. I don't think Phile's slept in his own bed since they moved out to the efficiencies. Maybe not since they were eleven or twelve years old. But they are special. I don't think they see a distinction like you do. I don't think in all their lives that they've ever considered any other possibility than being together. And I doubt they will have much to do with the outside world—as long as you and Kyle protect them. I hope to get them through high school, but even that is touch and go." Pa sighed. I suspected all along that Caitlin and Phile were 'special.'

"We'll protect them, Pa," I said. "We knew they were going to depend on us when they first asked to be our hired hands. Maybe when they first laid eyes on those rescues. Something changed."

"It did. But that is different from you and Kyle. You know you won't be able to bear him a child. A child would be… admissible evidence. You can't marry him. No matter how you've managed to separate your lives, the State is the law," Pa said. "Are you okay with that?"

"I guess if it ever comes down to wanting a child—and based on my experience in the 1800s, I'm not sure I ever want to go through that again—I'll find a sperm donor. We're going to marry Aubrey if she'll have us. I know only Kyle and Aubrey can legally marry, but only you and Ashley could legally marry, too. If we decide to have children, Aubrey will bear them," I said.

"When the wedding day comes, I'll write the three of your names on the eighth page of the Bible."

37
The Bridge

WHEN I walked into the kitchen, Mom Mar was cleaning up and starting lunch already. She pointed out the front door, and I found Aubrey sitting on the steps feeding Blackfeather scraps of our breakfast. They seemed to have become good buddies all of a sudden. Raven was taking each offered scrap politely from her fingers and stepping aside to eat it. When he was finished, he would sidestep toward her and wait for her to feed him another piece.

"I'm glad my breakfast isn't going to waste," I laughed. Kyle came around the corner of the house and walked up to where Aubrey was sitting.

"Blackfeather and I have been having a very nice chat, Husband Ramie," Aubrey said dreamily.

Awk!

THE NEXT THING I knew I was being given sips of water as Kyle held my head and Aubrey held the glass. Mom Mar was hovering over me. Mom Ash and Pa were kneeling on the other side. I hadn't traveled. I hadn't been anywhere. I just passed out when Aubrey called me…

"Why did you say that, Aubrey?" I demanded. "Why did you call me 'Husband Ramie'? Why would you do that?"

"He said it would be okay," she gasped. "No. He didn't say anything. He just… I just felt it in my head. That's not right, either," she struggled. "Ever since that time Rick lectured me in the cemetery, I've had this feeling of deep peace and love. It was like love transcends all ages and times. If I opened myself up, I could feel love for everyone, but especially for you two and… And for everyone you've loved. I was looking at Blackfeather as he picked at that crust and just knew that I was sitting here with my Husband Kyle and my Husband Ramie. Why would he call you 'Husband'? Wouldn't you be my wife if we all got married?"

I could see that Aubrey was confused with what she had said and how she thought Raven had influenced her. I sat up and held her to me. But I wondered. If Blackfeather was at work, then maybe there was hope.

"It's what my sweet, sweet Katie called me," I said. "She started when I was disguised as a man and she was traveling as my wife. Aubrey… Katie, are you here?" I said, looking desperately into her eyes.

"Oh! Do you think she might be time traveling from the past and be here?" Aubrey said, pointing at her head.

"Nobody travels from the past to the present," Pa said firmly.

"Not true, Pa," I said. "The rules you had when you traveled haven't all applied to us. When I was fevered with the wolf-bite, just before you called Merv, Miranda spent a few minutes in my body. It scared her half to death. Kyle and Aubrey were watching a movie on the laptop and she thought they'd captured people's souls and had them trapped in a box," I laughed and looked desperately into Aubrey's eyes. *Oh, please tell me my sweet darling Katie has come to live in Aubrey! That something survived.*

11She got a scrunched up look on her face and I held my breath. Then she shook her head. "I don't think so. I'm just here and I love you. I had this wonderful sense of complete love come over me and the sure knowledge that I was going to…" She caught her breath and her eyes popped wide open. She looked like she was starting to panic. But no Katie looked out her eyes. *Oh my!* I knew what she was going to say. I looked at Kyle and we looked over at Blackfeather. He was bobbing his head up and down. Of course, he might have just been looking for another crumb. I got to my feet and came around by Kyle. We both knew. We knelt in front of Aubrey.

"Aubrey Diaz," I started.

"Will you marry us," Kyle and I finished. The smile broke out on her face like sunshine.

"Yes!" She hugged us both to her. "I think we should wait a while before we start having babies, though," she whispered. We laughed. Then Aubrey pulled me to the step beside her and turned to kneel next to Kyle.

"Laramie Wyoming," Kyle started.

"Will you marry us?" he and Aubrey finished. They proposed to me! I couldn't find my voice. I just kept nodding my head and kissing them. I pulled Kyle to the step and knelt beside Aubrey.

"Kyle Redtail," she said.

"Will you marry us?"

Moms and Pa clapped their hands behind us. Moms both grabbed hold of Pa and dragged him into the house.

I hate to admit it, but I've read a few romance novels. Mom Mar is a sucker for them and I used to sneak them out of her room and read them at night. It's almost impossible for two people to unbutton each other's shirts at the same time. Add a third person and it gets even more complicated. Clothes don't just 'fall off' as if they were leaves on trees. They get hooked on your earrings and tangled in your hair. Then there's that moment when you start to pull your man's shirt off and discover you didn't unbutton the cuffs and he's hogtied. Aubrey got to giggling so hard that we almost couldn't get his hands free.

Romance novels don't talk about that—laughing over your own clumsiness. Being embarrassed when you get your shirt off, even though your lovers have seen you in less before. Getting caught up in a kiss and forgetting to keep undressing. Being in awe of the unbelievably beautiful lovers who are holding you. They don't talk about how many times you stop and just hold each other and kiss with your hearts beating so hard you think you'll die. I don't remember one romance novel mentioning that when you were stripped down to your panties and cami and your lovers were about to expose parts of you you've never—well, almost never—shown them before, that you'd say, "Let's brush our teeth, honeys."

"Now?" Kyle said as he kissed my shoulders and pulled at the straps of my camisole. "Why now?"

"I want you minty fresh the first time you lick my clit." Kyle choked and Aubrey howled. We followed him into the bathroom and all three stared at each other while we brushed our teeth.

We stopped a couple feet from the bed, looking at it. It seemed like a big important place tonight. I kissed each of my lovers again, savoring the differences in their touch and taste as they kissed each other. Aubrey played with the straps of my cami and I pulled it off. Kyle got her bra unfastened like he'd done it a thousand times before. Well, I suppose he'd done it a lot. So had I. I tugged at his t-shirt and got it over his head. As I pulled it up, Aubrey leaned forward and licked his nipples. He yelped a little and she dragged his shorts down.

I was still a little shy and let Aubrey lead. She'd been with each of us before. She pushed Kyle down on the bed and let him watch as she nibbled and sucked on my nipples next to the bed. I almost collapsed—not just from the sensations she was creating, but from looking into Kyle's eyes. And then she dragged my panties off and pushed me into bed next to Kyle.

We both lay there on our backs next to each other.

I was trembling. I held out my hand to Aubrey. She slipped out of her panties and crawled in next to me.

"I plan to make love to both of you. A lot," she whispered. "But this first time belongs to the two of you. You've wanted it for so long. I'll be here next to you, loving the two of you loving each other."

I rolled toward Kyle just as he was rolling toward me and we met with our lips in the middle. I clutched at him and he held me tight. Our naked bodies were pressed against each other. I was on fire.

"I love you. I love you," I said, hearing Kyle and Aubrey echoing my words. He kissed around my face and down my throat. She kissed my back all the way from my neck to my butt. When Kyle licked my right nipple and sucked on it just a little, a million volts of electricity went through my body and I could feel my moisture gathering, waiting for him. Waiting for my lover.

"Kyle, come to me. Make me yours." He rose from the feast of my bosom to my lips and I spread my legs beneath him to welcome him home. Aubrey guided him to my wet folds and he sank into to me. My world stopped.

And Raven called.

NOTHING HAPPENED. KYLE and I froze, looking into each other's eyes.

"Did you…?" he started. I shook my head. We looked at Aubrey.

"What?"

"Every time that bird caws, I expect a miracle," I whispered, kissing her. It was still Aubrey.

Raven's sudden interruption relaxed us a little, too. I giggled under Kyle and enjoyed the way it made his cock jump inside me.

"I don't think I'm a virgin any longer," I laughed. "Again. Kyle, make love to me. I love you so much, my husband."

He did. What Kyle couldn't reach, Aubrey was paying attention to. Her hand stroked down my back and across my butt. I rose steadily and knew that it would be earth-shattering. I could feel how Kyle tightened up. I knew he was ready, and when his dam burst and started flooding my pussy, I gasped and then screamed. I started my orgasm and it wouldn't stop. Every one of his pulses sent a new wave crashing over my head, threatening to drown me in the pleasure. I could hear myself coming and hoped we'd remembered to close the window.

And then everything was quiet and blissful and I was just floating in space in the arms of my lovers.

38
Demons

RAMIE? *PLEASE don't leave me, Ramie. I'm frightened. Where are you? Don't leave me here alone!*

I was dreaming. Had to be dreaming. Miranda was dead.

Please, please, take me with you, Ramie? I'm so frightened. Please.

She was begging me and sounded so much like my Miranda. I wanted to take her into my arms and hold her. I wanted desperately to believe I was back in her body. That she was alive and we could watch our baby grow up. We would change history!

"Miranda? How...? Was it a dream?"

Where are we? I remember my baby, and pain, and Raven calling. I tried to hold fast to you, but I lost your hand. I remember... Blessed Lord save me! I remember dying, Ramie. Where are we? Did you die with me? I was pulled and sucked in a torrent like being caught in a tornado. And then I felt you and I had hope. Are we in hell, Demon Ramie? Where are we, Ramie?

"I don't know where we are. I was just... Oh! I think it feels too good to be hell."

Are you playing with my privities?

"I was making love for the first time with my... with Kyle. I must have passed out. I'm dreaming about you. I miss you so much. We died, Miranda. You died. I came back to my body," I thought to my hallucination.

I am not a dream. I can still feel Jason pulsing within me.

"No. It can only be Kyle."

Perhaps we should open our eyes and find out.

I struggled against the weights that seemed to be holding my eyes closed and looked up into Kyle's loving face.

"Jason!" Miranda shouted through my voice. "Jason, I thought I'd lost you."

289

Kyle looked wide-eyed and his mouth made grimaces but no sound came out as he nodded up and down.

"Husband Jason," Aubrey purred, lifting her lips to kiss Kyle. "My dear wife, Miranda," she repeated kissing me. "Welcome to our world, my loves."

"Katie?" Miranda said. I was still too stunned to get control of my voice. Aubrey shook her head. "No. I know you. Many times I have relived Ramie loving you. You are Aubrey. And already, I love you."

"Miranda," Jason said, finally capturing Kyle's voice. "I thought we were lost to each other forever." I wasn't expecting Miranda to swing at Kyle and slap him across the face so hard it stung my hand.

"Don't you ever leave us again!" we cried together. "Raven called me. I had to watch… watch while you died! Don't ever leave us again."

"I knew the moment your spirit left your body, darling Miranda. I stayed my hand from defending myself. There was no reason left for me to live," Jason said. "Wife Ramie, Friend Kyle. Aubrey. Are we truly here with you in a different time?"

"Unless we walk outside and hell has frozen over, welcome to the twenty-first century," Aubrey smiled. She kissed us both again. "I thought this was going to be my first time making love to two lovers at once," she sighed. "It seems that it will be a fivesome, instead!"

"Aubrey, how can you tell the difference?" I asked.

"I don't know, Ramie. I just knew who was here as soon as Miranda spoke. Just like I knew you'd just taken over and asked me that question. I can see Miranda. I can see Jason. And in spite of the fact that I've never met them, I love them both," Aubrey said. "But, I'm getting a little impatient. You were supposed to start on me, next."

We laughed. Jason and Miranda retreated just enough that Kyle and I could make love to Aubrey. We did the best we could. I licked her to an orgasm while Kyle feasted on her lips and nipples and then we traded places and I fingered her clit as Kyle plunged into our lover and filled her as he'd filled me. And we kissed. We kissed, and each time Miranda would switch with me or Jason with Kyle, Aubrey would moan.

"You are such a dreamy kisser, Miranda. Jason, stay in me just a moment longer. I want to feel you. Oh, Ramie, I love you. Kyle! Yes! You're hard again!" Our girlfriend was delirious, but I think she knew it was Jason that came in her the second time, while Miranda kissed her.

Such a wonderful dream. I would remember having Jason and Miranda with us for as long as Kyle and I lived. The second time Kyle filled me, we drifted off to sleep again.

Ramie, it is not a dream.

"Who are you?" My hand rose of its own accord and my fingers pinched my left nipple.

Don't you ignore me, you evil girl!

"Demon Miranda! Are you really here? Or do I only want you so desperately that I imagine you?"

I am not a demon!

"That sounds familiar. I have been possessed by a demon. I shall go to a priest and have her exorcised," I thought sleepily at her. She was truly terrified.

Friend Ramie. Dear, sweet Friend Ramie. I am not a demon. Truly. Please, do not send me away.

"So now that it is *my* body being inhabited, I am *Friend* Ramie instead of Demon Ramie. Now how fair is that, Demon Miranda?" I tried to let my sense of humor seep through my thoughts. It took her a while to catch on.

Oh, Ramie. I am so sorry. Through all our time together, you were my friend. I am sorry I fought you. I am sorry I called you... Oh!

"You'll have to get used to my sense of humor if you are going to share my body and my time with me," I laughed in my mind. I think I shook the bed a little. Aubrey reached up to touch my nipple. I sighed.

I will try not to be a burden.

"Miranda, I love you. You will never be a burden to me."

I have remembered things. You saw our baby. You saw sweet Katie give birth.

"Yes. Well, not really saw. Sensed. Knew they were healthy. Oh, Miranda, I'm so sorry. I'm so sorry for our baby. For Katie. And for our short lives."

But we are alive! I can feel. I can feel your hot tears on your cheeks and I can smell your body in bed. I can feel Kyle lying next to us. I can hear him breathing. And Aubrey next to you. Your memories tell me that we did not take care of Katie and she suffered.

"I don't know for sure. Kyle and Katie-Lynn were raised in the whorehouse. I'm afraid Katie may have embraced her destiny and have spread her legs for many men. We went to Caitlin's grave, but I don't know where Katie lies. Perhaps nearby. Maybe that's what Aubrey sensed in the cemetery."

Our poor, dear Katie.

TELLING OUR PARENTS was going to be a challenge. And we wanted to set a wedding date. Now! The three of us—five of us?—walked up to the house on Thanksgiving morning and there was a non-stop commentary in my head on everything Miranda was seeing for the first time. She immediately pointed at the cars and four-wheelers and demanded to know what they were. I managed to convince her that they were trains that ran without tracks.

She'd balked at wearing jeans and I'd finally acquiesced to wearing a skirt. She'd been scandalized, though, when I'd refused to wear 'bloomers.'

"My privities are a little sore," I said. I spoke aloud so that Kyle and Aubrey could hear me talking to Miranda. "I am not going to shove cotton panties up my crotch. Besides, our husband or our wife might want access to take their pleasure from us," I giggled, using Katie's phrasing. Aubrey and I laughed and Miranda took the opportunity to commandeer my voice.

"Jason! This wicked girl refuses to let me put on underwear!"

"Oh, now, I find that hard to believe," Jason drawled. He'd heard the entire conversation and either he was getting coached or he was adapting very quickly. "I will have to verify this information." He firmly bent me over the back of the couch in our apartment living room and began pulling up my skirt. I yelped, but Aubrey sealed my mouth with hers as Jason felt around my butt and between my legs. *Sore be damned. I want him to fuck me.* I broke from Aubrey's lips long enough for Miranda to whimper.

"Are you able to tell, husband? Or will you need to… probe deeper?" she gasped. *Well, hell! If that wasn't an invitation.* I went back to Aubrey's lips as Jason pushed his cock into me. Jason! Even I could tell the difference when it was Jason instead of Kyle. Oh, god! A new man was plundering my pussy. Miranda was soaking it up and I was coming!

I panted. I really needed to focus on not passing out every time I got fucked. Aubrey kissed me lightly and tweaked my nipples as Jason withdrew.

"Now, can we put on drawers? Or shall we let this drip down our legs when we go to meet your parents?" Miranda smirked.

I put on panties.

I STOOD AT the kitchen counter, absently making pie crust and chatting with Moms. Aubrey was making sopapillas. I greased and lined two pie pans, trimmed the crust, filled them, and handed them to Mom Mar. She put them in the oven and turned me to face her. She looked me up and down. I was wearing a skirt that came just below my knees.

Scandalous!

"Just wait till we go swimming," I thought to Miranda, flashing her an image of the bikini Aubrey bought for me last year. Miranda was shocked silent.

Mom Ash turned me around and looked at the other side. I'd chosen a nice western shirt that even had darts in the front.

"I just felt like dressing like a girl today," I explained lamely. Moms looked at each other and nodded.

"Are you going to introduce us?" Mom Mar asked. Aubrey laughed so hard she choked, and after a little backslapping and a glass of water, we sat at the table with cups of coffee.

"Moms," Aubrey said. "Please allow me to do the honors. May I introduce you to Laramie Wyoming Bell and her great-great-great-great-grandmother, Miranda Lewis Wardlaw."

"Oh my god," Ashley moaned. "Does your father know?"

"I believe Jason and Kyle are talking to him," Miranda said. "I am so pleased to meet you face-to-face instead of just through Ramie's memories." Moms hugged us.

"You know, this just throws another whole batch of Pa's theories out the window," Mom Mar said. "Uh… is Ramie still there, too?"

"I'm here, Ma. But I have Miranda with me. Isn't it wonderful?" I was gushing. "How did you know?"

"Your cooking skills tend toward burning beans on a campfire," Mom Mar said. "But here you just threw together a flawless pie crust and didn't even stop to measure anything. Let's get those trimmings in the oven with a sprinkle of cinnamon and sugar to have with our coffee."

"And let's make sure there's an ambulance standing by to restart our men's hearts after they eat that pie!" Ashley said. "Lard? I didn't even know we had lard in the house." She looked at Mom Mar, who blushed.

"I use it sometimes," she whispered.

Just then we heard the guitar strumming in the office and a beautiful baritone voice singing 'What a Friend.'

"Mercy! Who's here?" asked Mom Mar. Mom Ash just shrugged. She could hear music, she just couldn't sing it. Like Kyle! I looked at Aubrey and we rushed to the office with Moms behind us. Jason was sitting across from Pa's big chair strumming the guitar and singing. I rushed to him and kissed him.

"That, more than anything, convinces me that we are really here," Miranda said. "And makes me so pleased to meet my son," she said, embracing Pa.

"I'm not really Kyle Wardlaw," Pa said. "He was my host. I'm sorry about what happened to him… and to Caitlin. But I am so glad to meet my great-great-great grandparents."

Well, it was complicated. Pa, of course, had a million questions for Miranda and Jason, but we also knew we couldn't really talk about anything in front of the kids. We'd just have to go one day at a time. When they came in for dinner from being out with the horses, they were in jeans and work shirts, with bandanas around their heads to keep their hair out of their eyes.

"You kids could have showered before you came to the holiday table," Mom Ash lectured them. They looked around and shrugged.

"It's just us. Aubrey's part of the family," Phile said. Then his eyes came to rest upon Kyle, and I saw his expression change. It was unreadable. He whispered to Caitlin and she held Kyle's eyes for a few minutes. Pa had us sit and bow our heads to consider the land and then we ate. Neither Kyle nor the kids said anything, so I guessed it was all okay.

WE WERE MARRIED at Christmas. Justice Samuels came out to our house. Aubrey's parents were there and her oldest sister. Gramma Bell and Gram and Grampa Alexander were there and commented over and over about how much it was like Cole and Ashley's wedding. Moms fussed over Aubrey and me, playing with our hair, brushing imaginary lint off our dresses, and holding up different ribbons for our flowers.

Rick Miles had become a pretty good friend over the past couple years. He was the only one outside our family who knew the whole story. If that guy got tired of teaching history one day, maybe he'd become a shaman. He stood beside Kyle as best man.

I held Aubrey's hand as Kyle slipped the simple gold band on it. She was so beautiful! Her dress was strapless with a brightly embroidered bodice that hugged her curves and fell in white ruffles all the way to the floor. I just wanted to eat her up. While the three of us held hands, Kyle slipped a second ring on my finger. Justice Samuels pretended not to notice. My dress was more conservative. I wore a long blue skirt with a plain white blouse and a knit shawl over my shoulders. There was no way to confuse me with the bride.

We had quite a celebration after we'd all looked into each other's eyes and whispered, 'I do.'

"I BELIEVE THESE words will be the ones you want remembered," Pa said as he turned the Bible so we could read what he had written. Our three names and today's date.

They have loved each other over time we cannot fathom. The circle is complete. That which God hath joined, let no man rend asunder.

All five of us rejoiced.

"THIS IS SO unbelievable. I have someone living in my head with me. How can that be?" Our lovers were asleep on our wedding night, and we all held each other tightly. Kyle was sandwiched between Aubrey and me. We had made love in every combination before we started to drift off. Now, though, as I drifted near sleep, I reached out to touch Miranda in my mind.

You are a fine one to ask such a question! It is a question I asked of myself for seven years.

"And now you are Demon Miranda. How will you handle that?"

Oh, Ramie. Sweet, loving, kind, Friend Ramie. I am no demon. I promise, I will not torment you.

"It must have been so difficult for you, love. I have missed you so much. Please stay with me. Please be my friend."

Ramie, I know that I am dead. Blackfeather showed me a path but I wanted to stay with you. May I? Please, Ramie. I will be quiet. Please let me live on in you.

"Don't ever go away from me, Miranda. I hope… I want you to stay with me forever. And love us. I know you love Aubrey."

After what she did to our privities tonight, how could I not?

"I love you, Miranda. You made me strong. You made me a better woman."

I love you, Ramie. I love you like my own soul. Rest, sweetheart. Rest and know that I am with you.

39
Golden Birthday

I LOVED HAVING Miranda in my head and in my body. The longer she was with me, the less I could tell the difference between us. We no longer even thought about who had control. We just did things. Kyle and Jason got along just as well. Aubrey adored Miranda and thought Jason's cock was bigger than Kyle's. I don't know how she figured that since they share the same body. But she always knew who was in control at any time. There were a few times when *I* got confused. Over the next two years and even though there were a few little spats, we managed to work things out.

I had to pay a $500 fine and nearly lost my driver's license the first time I let Miranda drive my Wrangler. We fought viciously the first time I threw my leg over the saddle on Pooky. I found myself wearing more skirts and dresses when we weren't working and she complained less about wearing jeans when we were. Life was good.

I AWOKE ONE morning to find myself standing in front of the bathroom mirror. I had no clothes on and Miranda was examining my body. I was still a little sleepy, so I just let her conduct her examination while I drifted in and out of my conscious mind. Mirrors are a funny thing. In Miranda's little home, she had a tiny mirror that Jason used for shaving. Other than the times we looked at our reflection in the window of the train and the brief time I saw her through Wolf's eyes, I'd never really had the chance to look at her like she was looking at me now. I regretted that and I wasn't about to interrupt her now.

She pulled my hair away from my head and let it slip through her fingers. It wasn't as light as Kyle's and nowhere near as blond as Jason's had been, but it was still fine and silky. Kyle and Aubrey had taken time in the shower the night before to wash my hair and put conditioner in it as we stood beneath the spray of hot water. Both Jason and Miranda loved the shower and wanted to spend every moment they could there.

Miranda seemed fascinated by my little breasts and drew circles around my nipples with my finger. That just always drove me crazy and she was enjoying the feeling. She was equally intrigued by my armpits. Ever since Kyle and I started dating, I'd been careful to keep my pits and my legs shaved. I didn't see any reason to shave the sparse hair of my pussy. It was only slightly thicker than the hair on my head and never seemed to be in the way of anything. Aubrey trimmed her thick black pussy hair but neither of us minded burying our faces in the other's crotch. Or Kyle's.

My pussy was the next place Miranda was headed. I blushed as she played with my hair and then spread my lips to look at me. It was different than Aubrey's and certainly different from the wild tangle and thick, puffy lips I remembered of Katie's. Miranda probed a little and touched my clit. I shivered.

If we're going to do that, wouldn't it be more comfortable in bed with our lovers?

"Ramie! You were so quiet in the back of my mind I thought you were asleep."

I was, but having my nipples and clit played with gave me a wonderful dream of sexual congress.

She didn't take her fingers away. I could feel my lubrication flowing with the stimulation. Well, I'd certainly played with her pussy enough times back in the nineteenth century.

"I never knew back then. It seems like just a day ago. A century and a half. I never knew if I was a comely woman. My voice was so ugly until Wolf healed my throat. And though they are scarcely visible now, you still feel the scars on your throat. It is so smooth and lovely now. Was that also the work of Wolf?" I nodded, lost in the sensations of her touch. She looked into my eyes. I could see her looking out of them. "We're beautiful, Ramie. I love you."

She continued to strum my clit with my fingers and when I came I had to grab hold of the sink to keep from dropping to the floor. I saw something I'd never seen before. I'd never watched myself in a mirror while I had an orgasm but she'd held my eyes through the entire experience. I realized in that moment that it was not only Kyle, Aubrey, and Jason who were my lovers. Miranda and I had long since become lovers, too. It was a little confusing to have a lover sharing the same body with me. As I reached my peak, I moaned, "I love you."

IT HAD BEEN difficult last summer with Caitlin and Phile. We'd been working on a section of fence and all stopped for a water break. Kyle was looking at Bells and Bows with his head nodding a little. Of course, paying attention to those two horses is the same as paying attention to Caitlin and Phile. The three of them started talking quietly. Aubrey and I looked over and they were locked in each other's gaze.

When Kyle turned to get back to work, there were tears in his eyes. The kids jumped on Bells and Bows bareback and took off. They never rode with saddles and most of the time without reins, either. Of course, there was always a rifle scabbard on a horse we were riding and we still carried our handguns anywhere on the ranch. I watched them head up the mountain and turned to look at Kyle. He just shook his head.

The kids were gone for six weeks. When they came back, they looked just the same as when they left. They weren't starving or ragged or dirty. They just said they had to take a break now that they'd graduated, and they knew how to live off the land. Kyle never said what they talked about.

TODAY IS MY golden birthday. I am twenty-two on November 22. Nearly all my senior classes are advanced practicums and my professors frequently bring students out to the ranch for practical equine management classes. I only have to go in to campus twice a week. Kyle, Aubrey, and I will graduate the day before Kyle's 22nd birthday.

The family gathered together in the evening and Mom Mar brought out a birthday cake. On Kyle's golden birthday, he got a truck. I bought my own Wrangler at the end of sophomore year. I figured at this age, I didn't need any more presents than the hands that were held in mine.

I still got a couple surprises, though.

"What do you get the girl who has everything?" Mom Ash sighed. "You need to come to the barn for this." If there is one thing that a

horsewoman loves, it's the thought of getting a new horse. I was right
behind Mom Ash, dragging Kyle and Aubrey with me. Caitlin and Phile
were laughing in the barn as we walked in. Standing between them was
a beautiful black stallion. I approached him slowly so he could see me
coming. Caitlin handed me the lead rope.

"The name, Midnight, isn't all that original," Ashley said. "But we
registered him as Laramie's Midnight Ride. He's the last colt that Spook
and Shadow's sire threw. We got him from the same breeder and he's
a full sibling of your geldings. It's not quite the same as being able to
breed the geldings, but it's close. He's six years old. He can be ridden,
but that's not his major purpose. We figured L&K Stables needed a
trademark stud."

I handed the lead back to Caitlin and went to hug Mom Ash and
then Mom Mar and Pa. This day couldn't get much better.

LATER ON, THE three of us—or five of us—were sitting on the sofa in our
little apartment just hugging each other. We hadn't gotten ready for bed
yet. We just wanted to sit and make out for a while. I got up to answer
the knock on our door and let Caitlin and Phile in.

"Happy birthday," Caitlin said.

"Happy birthday," Phile added. I hugged the kids.

"We didn't give you your birthday present." She handed me a beautiful polished wooden box.

"You two! This is beautiful!" It looked like a high grade silverware
box that you'd find in an antique store and weighed enough to be full.
"It's locked."

"Did Pa ever tell you about Schrödinger's cat?" Phile asked. I glanced
at Kyle and nodded.

"Yes. That all outcomes are possible until you open the box. Then the
cat is either dead or alive."

"Well, this has got a cat in it," Caitlin said. "It's both dead and alive
until you open the box."

"The thing is that you have to decide when you are ready to accept the
outcome," Phile continued. "When is it that your curiosity is so strong
that you are willing to accept a dead cat over not knowing for sure?"

"When you make that decision, then you can open the box," Caitlin said. She held out the key. All of a sudden I didn't even want to touch it. "You're right. It's not good to keep them together. I'll keep the box safe. You take the key."

"You know what?" I laughed. "You two are still brats."

"Yeah," Phile admitted, "but thank you for letting us be who we are." He put his arm around his sister and hugged her close, as they kissed. "Goodnight." They left.

"I've always kind of figured that," Kyle said. "They just never show it."

"They're special. Different than us," I said.

"You aren't brother and sister," Aubrey said. She'd long since accepted that in our heads, Kyle and I were no longer related, except as husband and wife. "And they just don't care."

"Is it that uncommon for siblings to wed?" Miranda asked. "In our time, it was not usual but was largely accepted, especially on the frontier. There often weren't that many alternatives for women."

"It's illegal these days," Kyle said. "The law assumes that all forms of incest are abusive. They use all kinds of garbage to support it that doesn't make sense. There are genetic risks, but we live in the age of birth control. They can't really use that to justify the law. It's just that everybody seems to want to tell everybody else what marriage is or isn't, or can or can't be. Just understand that if anybody comes onto this ranch to take them away, there will be more dead bodies lying in the lawn." Kyle was fierce and I thought I saw a glimpse of Jason speaking through him—like they were in unison. Aubrey kissed him.

I tied the key to my wolf's teeth necklace. Someday I might open the box. Right now, though, I'm too happy to face the possibility of a dead cat.

As soon as the kids were gone, Aubrey started removing her clothes. When we started to join her, she pushed us back down on the couch and 'made us' watch her.

"Well, what do you think?" she asked, as she stood naked in front of us. Kyle let out a low whistle.

"I think you are the most beautiful wife in the world," I said. "The most beautiful woman."

"I think the same thing every time I see you naked," Kyle laughed. "Is it bedtime?"

"May I say that I hope you think kindly of my tongue and my privities tonight?" Miranda asked. Aubrey giggled.

"Well? Jason?"

"Aubrey, wife, when Miranda and Katie first broached the idea of both marrying me, I was overwhelmed. I was still reeling from thinking about Ramie and Kyle in our heads," Jason said. "I loved Katie completely. I will always miss her. But you have found that hollow emptiness inside me and filled it with your love and passion. I see you standing before me naked and can only think how I would like to fill your hollow emptiness as well."

"Wow! That was a pretty speech, Jason," I said. "I hope you'll consider filling me, too!"

"You don't think I'm fat?" Aubrey said, prancing in front of us, but just out of reach.

"Honey! How could you even imagine that?" I cried. I caught hold of her and pulled her into my arms and Kyle stretched out to pillow his head on her thigh. "You have never been fat, Aubrey. Whatever gave you such an idea?"

"Well… I've never been pregnant before."

 The End